VANISHED

VANISHED

CIRCLE OF THE RED LILY

BOOK TWO

ANNA J. STEWART

CAEZIK
ROMANCE
ARC MANOR
ROCKVILLE, MARYLAND

SHAHID MAHMUD
PUBLISHER

www.CaezikRomance.com

Cover Designer: Authors on a Dime

ISBN: 978-1-64710-080-3

First Edition, First Printing, November 2023
1 2 3 4 5 6 7 8 9 10

An imprint of Arc Manor LLC

www.CaezikRomance.com

For Victoria Fliess and Kristin Wong

Childhood friends gone far too soon.

You will be missed.

CHAPTER ONE

"YOU were a lot more fun before I died."

Mabel's minivan tires ground into the gravel, the sound a crisp, distinct crunch as she eased to the side of the road. She clenched her chilled hands around the steering wheel. Moonlight streamed through the windshield, a spotlight in the darkness of the thickening fog.

She could drive these winding Hollywood Hills roads blindfolded by now. She knew when to ease off the gas and when to expect potholes. She knew the dog in the backyard of the house at the bottom of the hill would bark when she drove past. And she knew to be careful rounding one particular corner, so as not to run over a family of opossums crossing the street.

And Mabel knew with absolute, terrifying certainty that no matter which turn her dream took, she'd find herself in the one place she never wanted to see again—the only place that held any hope of answers.

"The least you could have done is bring Barksy along for the ride." Sylvie heaved a theatrical sigh that nearly brought a smile to Mabel's lips. "I would have liked to have seen my dog again. Honestly, Mabel. I know this is your subconscious and all, but couldn't you take us

1

someplace a bit more exciting?" She shifted in her seat and turned to look behind them before facing forward, staring into the fog ahead. "A club, maybe? Or a party. How about the movies? I really miss going to the movies."

The longing Mabel heard in her sister's voice pinged painful and deep in her heart. Words stuck in her throat.

"Remember when we used to sneak into the theater at the mall back in Wisconsin for the Sunday afternoon shows?" Sylvie gushed. "Let's go do that."

Mabel squeezed her eyes shut before focusing back on the road. She wanted nothing more than to feel her sister's hand actually grab hold when Sylvie reached for her. Instead, Mabel shivered at the icy chill racing up her arm.

Outside, the fog swirled, mingling with the shadows in her mind as the wind began to howl.

"Mabel," Sylvie whispered. "Why do you keep coming back here?"

"You know why. Because *you're* here. At least, part of you is." Mabel kept her gaze pinned to the top of the hill, willing herself not to look into the passenger seat. As long as she didn't look, Sylvie would stay where she was, beside her. But the second she turned her head …

"You're here because *you're* stuck," Sylvie accused, then her voice gentled. "It's been eight years. Eight years of your life, Mabe. It's time you moved on."

"I know how long it's been." She knew because she'd counted every single day she'd spent without her sister—her twin. There had been endless days where she'd counted each second of each hour. It was impossible not to when half your heart and just as much of your soul was missing. "I miss you, Syl." Some days, so much it physically hurt. "I can't move on. Not until …" Not until she knew the truth.

"Well, I'm bored," Sylvie teased. "The view never changes."

"You're always bored."

"Yeah? Well, you don't know how hard it is to be bored when you're dead," Sylvie said.

"Stop it," Mabel whispered and squeezed her eyes shut.

As close as they were, Mabel often wondered if two twins had ever been more different. Practical, level-headed, logic-minded Mabel and stars in her eyes, flit-about Sylvie, whose mind had been filled with dreams of performing and stardom from the second she'd taken her first breath. In high school, Mabel had been part of the chess club, the debate team, and the band. Sylvie had devoted herself to drama class, starred in every school production, and was named most likely to see her name in lights.

Instead, Sylvie Reynolds's name had been destined to appear in headlines.

"I'm just saying—" Sylvie tried again.

"Don't say it. Not again." Mabel refused to wake. Even as she willed the dream to shift, for Sylvie to go silent, she also wished it would never end. This was where Sylvie belonged: here, with Mabel. Instead … "Maybe you're not dead," Mabel told herself. "And you're not here, in this *place*. Maybe I'm the one haunting this place because I miss you, and it's the only lead I've got. You could still be alive." It was a futile hope, perhaps. But it was still hope. "They've spent the last two months searching every inch of this property, and not one body has been found." Her photograph had been, though. Along with the others. So … many others.

"Not one body," Sylvie agreed quietly.

Angry tears scorched Mabel's throat. "Stop trying to make a point. You aren't really here. This is just a dream." *Why* wasn't she here?! The not knowing, the idea that her sister was completely lost to all of them was the worst type of torture she could imagine.

"No, I'm not here, Mabel," Sylvie murmured. "I'm here." Mabel shivered at the chill against her temple. "And here." The coldness against her heart felt like a kind of jump-start to a dead battery. "I'm where you need me to be. Where you can't let me go."

Mabel shoved herself out of the car, shaking her head as if she could dislodge the spinning miasma of disconnected thoughts that refused to coalesce when she was awake. The night closed in around her, the darkness pressing down. She looked at the flashlight in her hand. *Where did that—?*

"Remember when Dad gave us those automotive repair kits for Christmas when we first got our cars?" Sylvie's voice echoed behind her now, her presence casting an illuminating glow bright enough to counter the flashlight's beam. "You gave him such a hard time because they were pink."

"An argument I lost when you added rhinestones to yours," Mabel muttered.

Keep your eyes ahead. Keep moving forward. Keep her with you. Maybe then ...

"Man, it's cold out here." Sylvie's teeth chattered. "Next time, put some jackets in the minivan, would you? Which reminds me: a minivan? Really?" The disdain in Sylvie's voice would have had Mabel laughing under different circumstances. "Remember the grief we gave Mom and Dad when they bought theirs? It's just *embarrassing.*"

"It's practical and carries all of Keeley's stuff, and she has a ton of stuff." Mabel smirked. "Reminds me of another eight-year-old I used to know."

"Heaven help me from practicality." Sylvie laughed. "She's a hoot, that niece of mine. I'm really sorry I'm not around to see her grow up."

"Yeah." Mabel's lungs burned as her steps slowed. "Me, too."

Instead of getting closer, the top of the hill seemed farther away. Every step she took felt as if her feet were trapped in quick-drying cement.

"Let's go back to the car, Mabe," Sylvie pleaded. "There's nothing for you up there. Nothing you need to see."

Mabel shook her head. "There has to be something." She crouched forward, gripped the fingers of her free hand into the ground that turned to sludge beneath her touch, and tried to haul herself forward. "I'm not going to stop, Sylvie. I'm not stopping until I get you home!"

The flashlight flickered to life.

The hill vanished.

The road ahead of her flattened.

She felt a strange, disorienting sensation and turned in a slow-motion circle, looking out into the blinking lights of Los Angeles; the city Sylvie had set all her dreams upon lay behind her now. The barely there twinkles of sky-skimming buildings broke through the ever-thickening fog that left her with only one path to walk. Around her, an odd whining, a keening, echoed in her ears.

Yellow crime scene tape snapped in the midnight wind as it surrendered its hold across the black iron gates beyond which the Tenado estate stood.

"There's nothing up here. There's nothing in *there*." Sylvie's voice trailed off.

Panicked, Mabel faced her sister, worried she was going to lose her. She found a warning in her ghostly eyes.

"Go home, Mabel. Please. I don't want you here."

"I'm not leaving you in there!" Mabel dived forward.

Her sister's form burst apart in the fog, dissipating. Mabel fell forward, catching her footing before she dropped face-first into the ground and grabbed hold of the chilled metal pickets of the gates. At least she didn't wake up this time. Maybe she could find her sister again.

The loneliness struck as it always did, with the ferocity and finality of a world completely changed in an instant. A loneliness that, at times, didn't allow her to breathe.

Mabel shook the bars so hard her teeth rattled. Beyond the chain and lock, the Tenado Estate stood eerily silent and empty. The stark white paint a complete misnomer to the horrors it held within its expansive walls. Even now, standing outside the perimeter of the property, Mabel could only imagine the screams.

The whining grew louder, the stabbing cold at her back harsher as she got up and pried the gates open enough to squeeze through. Her boots crunched in the loose gravel of the path, circling up to the front porch and door. Around her, the fog thickened, coating her skin like a slick film.

She angled the beam of her flashlight up until she captured the red lily etched into the stained-glass window above the front door in its beam. She crept closer and stepped onto the porch, her footfalls dull against the painted wood.

Mabel pressed her palm flat against the wood, closed her eyes, and whispered, "Sylvie."

A scream ripped through the night, erupting from inside the house with such force that the door vibrated beneath her hand. Something wet plopped onto her cheek. She swiped at it, drew away fingers covered in thick, red blood. Mabel stepped back, shined the flashlight up on the window again as the flower turned to liquid and drained, spattering on the ground in front of her.

Mabel. I'm here, Mabel. I'm here!

What was left of Mabel's pounding heart leapt to life. She'd heard her! This was the first time she'd gotten far enough in the dream to hear her sister *in* this house of horrors!

"Sylvie!"

She'd been right; her twin bond had told her she'd been here! That she returned here in her dreams, night after night, because her sister's spirit was stuck here in some kind of purgatory.

Slipping in the slick blood, Mabel dived back to the door, shoved it open, and raced inside.

"I'm coming!" she yelled into the echoing shadows of the house. Her voice tumbled back toward her, multiplying and ricocheting off the walls as if bouncing off fun-house mirrors.

The hallways twisted and turned in front of her, disappeared behind her. Rooms swam around her, moving in and out, drawing her in and pushing her away as she twisted and spun her way to the only doorway that mattered.

Don't stop. Don't wake up. Not yet. Don't stop. You have to find her—

Mabel threw herself forward, grabbed the black iron knob of the thick wooden door the police investigative team had walked her through two months ago. Her flashlight clattered to the ground and dimmed. Mabel picked it up, shook the handle, twisting and turning, but it slipped in her hand.

"Sylvie!" She rattled the door harder. "Sylvie, I'm here. I'm coming, I promise. I hear … you."

A skittering erupted behind her. Mabel turned, pressed her back flat against the door even as she continued to cling to the handle. Someone else was here. In the house.

She wasn't alone.

The darkness moved in, suffocating, blinding. The hiss of the flashlight bulb sounded before the last thread-like beam popped and died.

"Let me in," she pleaded, twisting her hand and arm in every way to open the door. "She needs me. She can't be in there alone."

Her entire body went numb, and her chest grew tight as grief twisted into that familiar knot of anger and rage she'd been carrying around for weeks. Months. Years.

That cold sensation against her back intensified, and she inexplicably felt a tugging at her clothes, even though her back was against the door. A low growl overtook the tap, tap, tapping, moving closer. Shadows loomed and threatened to suffocate her.

Mabel pushed harder into the door, her hand cramping as she gave the knob one final twist. "Let. Me. In!"

The door flew open right as the shadows pounced. There was no stopping the momentum. No preventing herself from falling backward into the dank, musty stairwell that should have been there but wasn't. She dropped straight down into a black and red swirling darkness, arms and legs flailing, soft blood-red flower petals cascading around her. She tried to catch hold of something, anything …

She was tumbling away from the doorway, and then it was as if time stopped—she froze mid-fall as her mind fractured. The doorway was filled with a familiar face. A face dripping with water and blood, a blood-red lily tucked behind one ear. Sylvie's eyes were as vacant as the house Mabel had stepped into.

"Sylvie!" Mabel held out her hands, flexed her fingers. Hope caught uselessly in her chest as she continued to reach …

The cold prodding against her spine intensified—an incessant poking and nudging. The whining became even more persistent until it shifted into a low, throaty growl. Mabel sucked in a breath as the dream shattered, the shards hurling her back into consciousness.

Mabel shot up in bed.

Air came in giant gasps and gulps. Terror lodged in her throat. Mabel swept her hair out of her eyes and nearly yelped at the furry head that forced its way under her arm. A cold, wet nose nudged against her chest before climbing into her lap and burrowing his snout against her neck.

"Barksy."

Mabel didn't hesitate to wrap her arm around the eight-year-old gray Australian cattle dog. The instant sense of peace the animal brought came with its own spear of grief and sadness.

She kicked free of the sheet and blanket, shifted to more fully embrace the animal that had originally belonged to Sylvie.

Returning the abject comfort, Mabel buried her face in his fur, wiping her tears away even as the vestiges of terror remained.

"Even in my dreams, you're protecting me." She lifted her head, caught his snout between her hands, and looked down into the black eyes filled with concern and understanding. "After all these years, you're still looking for her, too, aren't you, boy?"

But she'd seen her this time. For a blink of a moment, she'd seen Sylvie before she'd faded into mist. Mabel had *seen* her sister— felt her.

"Mom?"

The soft knock on the doorframe pulled Mabel the rest of the way out of the nightmare. The sight of her daughter standing in the doorway, much the way Sylvie had been standing in her dream, clogged Mabel's throat with tears.

"Are you okay?"

The concern in Keeley's voice broke Mabel's heart in a completely different way. This was why she tried so hard to stay strong. She didn't want Keeley thinking for one second that she needed to take care of her mother.

"Hey, baby." Mabel sniffed and tried to swipe away the tears covering her cheeks. She reached back to click on the bedside lamp. Seeing the small, framed photo of Sylvie the instant she did nearly pushed her over the edge. "Yeah, I'm fine. Bad dream is all. Barksy helped pull me out of it." Those cold nudges had been the only real thing about the dream. She hesitated, thinking of Sylvie's face. *Almost* the only real thing. "I'm sorry if I woke you up."

She patted the mattress, and eight-year-old Keeley bolted to the bed. It was a sight that lightened Mabel's heavy heart as Keeley was fast moving into the age beyond little girl snuggles and giggles, never mind late-night post-nightmare cuddles. Of course, she had yet to outgrow her Mickey Mouse pajamas, but that probably wouldn't ever happen given Mabel owned a few pairs herself.

"Wasn't asleep yet." Keeley reached across Mabel to scrub Barksy's chin. "Good boy, Barksy."

8

"He's a very good boy." Mabel kissed his snout and earned an approving whimper in return. "What time is it?" She glanced around for her phone.

"It's not even midnight yet." Keeley attempted to straighten the blankets.

"And you weren't asleep?" Mabel frowned. "What happened to our deal?"

Keeley rolled her eyes. "It's Friday night, Mom. The deal was I could stay up as late as I wanted if I was reading."

She grinned up at Mabel. and for an instant, Mabel saw a young Sylvie in her own daughter's face. Dark green, almost hazel eyes. Streaky blonde hair. Chipmunk cheeks that appeared whenever she smiled. And she smiled a lot, thank goodness. The sight nearly tore Mabel in two.

"Your iPad is supposed to be in the charging station in the kitchen by eight," Mabel reminded her.

"I wasn't on my iPad. I was reading a book. Aunt Riley said I could raid her and Moxie's bookshelves whenever I wanted."

Mabel pursed her lips. Knowing her best friend Riley Temple's reading preferences, Mabel wasn't entirely sure she wanted to know what Keeley had acquired. As far as what Riley's great aunt Moxie read for pleasure …

Mabel's face flushed at the thought.

Not that she had ever restricted Keeley's book selections. One of the most important parenting lessons she'd learned from her own mother was to never say no to a book. Any book. Even books that might make her cringe.

"It's like having a library just downstairs," Keeley went on as Mabel shoved back against the headboard and drew both her dog and daughter with her. "Especially now that detective man has moved in with them." Keeley drew up the blankets and tucked them in, resting her head on Mabel's shoulder. "He has a whole collection of Stephen King books. Some of them are even signed! How cool is that?"

"Stephen …" Mabel drew in a deep breath. Leave it to Keeley to test her own boundaries. "Is that what you picked to read?"

"Uh-huh. I figured it was okay since I've already seen the movie."

"What movie?"

"*Carrie.*" Keeley looked up at her. "I watched it with Aunt Laurel on Halloween. It's okay, isn't it?"

That one of Mabel's other best friends had introduced her child to classic horror movies? Or that said introduction had now led Keeley to Detective Quinn Burton's horror novel collection? Where to begin?

"You don't think you're a little young to be reading books like that?"

"Mom." Keeley rolled her eyes. "I'm going to be *nine* in a few weeks."

"Right." Mabel tightened her hold. "Nine. Silly of me to have forgotten." Inspiration struck like a lightning bolt. "You have any questions about any of those books, you feel free to take them to Quinn, okay?"

Oh, yeah. If she was going to have to suffer the slings and arrows of her daughter's new horror fascination, so was the man who made them possible.

Keeley had always been dangerously curious about, well, everything. Forbidding her to do or read anything would only result in secretive, deceitful behavior, and that was something Mabel was not about to put up with or inadvertently encourage. Even if some people considered certain works inappropriate for youngsters, as far as Mabel was concerned, the conversations that resulted kept the lines of communication open, something that would only become more important as Keeley got older. There was too much of her twin in the girl …. Her heart constricted.

Keeley fidgeted with the fraying hem of the blanket. "I was going to tell you about the books. You know, 'cause we don't have secrets. Right, Mom?"

"Right." She smoothed Keeley's hair back, rested her cheek on the top of her head. "Something else you need to tell me?"

"No." She hesitated. "Something I want to ask."

Mabel frowned. "You can ask me anything. You know that."

"You've always told me I should do what I love to do. When I grow up. You know, like with college and stuff."

"Are you about to tell me you want to run off and join the circus?"

Keeley tilted her chin up. Her face scrunched. "Is that really a thing?"

"It's—never mind. What's your question?"

"I dunno. I guess I just wanted to …" She heaved a sigh so similar to the one Sylvie had in the dream, Mabel almost fell right back into it. "Do you like your job, Mom?"

"Sure." Mabel shrugged. "Being a record keeper gives me the chance to work with a lot of interesting people and help their businesses." It also fed her desire for order and rationality. Numbers didn't lie or deceive or threaten. They just *were*. "Plus, it lets me work from home. Where I can keep an eye on you." She tickled her fingers against Keeley's stomach, and her heart soared when Keeley giggled. "Although, I must not be doing a very good job if you're bringing Stephen King books into the house."

"*Mo-ooom*." Keeley rolled her eyes again. "You know the rules. You never say no to a book."

"Right. Sorry. Did I answer your question?"

"No," Keeley said. "That wasn't the job I was talking about."

"Oh." Because there was no way to hide her own uncertain expression, she tucked Keeley back into her arms and squeezed. "You mean the volunteer work I do with Soteria."

The charitable organization was named for the Greek Goddess of safety and salvation. They'd opened their doors as a safe haven for abuse and rape victims years before Mabel had moved to Los Angeles. They provided rooms and shelter, both short- and long-term, to aid in recovery. Mabel had begun working as a rape victim advocate shortly after Sylvie's disappearance. At the time, it seemed the only way Mabel could process losing her sister to the unknown.

"I don't know whether 'like' enters into that work, Kee." Mabel struggled to find the right words. "It's important. For the people I work with and for me. It makes me feel useful. As if I'm helping them through what, for a lot of them, is the most horrible thing that will ever happen in their lives. Do you understand that?"

"I do." Keeley was back to plucking at the blanket but stopped when Barksy splayed across Mabel's legs and pushed his nose under Keeley's hand. "And I know what happens is really, really bad."

"Yes, it is." There were times Mabel was shocked she could be surprised by the cruelty people were capable of inflicting on one another, and yet ... she was. Constantly.

"It's just ..." Keeley hedged. "You're always so sad when you come home. Like tonight."

"I'm sorry I missed pizza night, kiddo."

"It's okay." Keeley shrugged. "I like Sutton's homemade pizza better than take-out, anyway."

Mabel squeezed her eyes closed, giving silent thanks yet again for the tight circle of friends she'd made when she'd moved into Temple House—one of whom, Sutton O'Hara, had two kids the same age as Keeley. They'd found a family here. A family who always provided Mabel somewhere to turn, a family whose doors were always open to both Mabel and her daughter—especially given Mabel's sometimes erratic and unpredictable schedule.

"Yes, well." Mabel cleared her throat. "Sutton's pizza is in a class of its own."

"I don't like it when you're sad, Mama," Keeley whispered. "Is that what you were dreaming about? The woman you had to help tonight?"

"No." Keeley was right. They didn't lie to one another. About anything. But that didn't mean Mabel didn't censor herself. "No, baby, I wasn't dreaming about her."

She didn't want to think about nineteen-year-old Eva Hudson, who had been beaten, raped, and thrown out of a car near the Hollywood Reservoir hiking trail sometime after midnight last night, a woman who had yet to regain consciousness. But Mabel had gone to the hospital and remained by Eva's side for hours. Just in case.

She didn't want to sit here, in the home she'd made for herself and her child, and dwell on the fact that the young woman had to have her jaw wired shut because it had been fractured. Or that Mabel had spent the time rehearsing how she'd attempt to convince the young woman to allow for a Sexual Assault exam, even though it could be too late to find any prosecutorial evidence. Beyond that, the only thing she could do when Eva awoke was convince her she was safe.

Safe.

12

What did that word even mean?

Mabel swallowed hard.

How could anyone ever convince Eva she was safe from anyone when the police, as far as Mabel had been told, had little to go on other than Eva's blood soaking into the dry ground of a trail few people traversed this time of year? She'd been thrown out on the side of the road. As if she'd been nothing more than a bag of garbage. Sadly, it wasn't an uncommon occurrence. Here or anywhere.

"You always tell me I should talk about my bad dreams," Keeley said. "But you never talk about yours."

"That's because I'm the mom, and you're the kid." Mabel held on tighter. "Kids aren't supposed to worry about their parents."

"But you worry about Grammy and Gramps." Keeley's narrowed eyes were filled with confusion. "I've heard you talking to Aunt Riley and Aunt Cass. You even had Cass send them special video systems so you could check in on them easier. Why is that different?"

Mabel should have been more disturbed by how easily Dr. Cassia Davis had set her parents up with an in-home video system from halfway across the country. Then again, Cass's reputation as one of the country's best criminalists and computer specialists had been well earned. There was very little the woman didn't know how to do despite not having stepped foot outside Temple House for the past three-plus years.

"Well," Mabel said. "I'm an adult, and I get to make different decisions."

"You mean I can't worry about you until I'm all grown up?" Keeley frowned. "That doesn't make sense. Age doesn't dictate my emotions."

Mabel couldn't have hidden her smile if she'd tried. Oh, how she loved her daughter's erudite vocabulary. "You're right. It doesn't." She just wanted, more than anything, for Keeley to have as normal of a life as possible. She didn't want her child to go through her days haunted. She wouldn't wish that on anyone, especially someone she loved. "If it'll make you feel better, I will tell you I was dreaming about your Aunt Sylvie."

"Oh." Keeley's eyes widened. "She makes you sad, too, though, doesn't she?"

"She doesn't make me sad, baby."

13

"You were crying just now."

"Yes. Because …" Her breath caught in her chest. "Because whenever I wake up from one of those dreams, there's this moment when I forget she's really gone. And then I remember." Tears burned her throat. "And it hurts all over again. I'm sorry." She pulled Keeley closer. "I'm so sorry you're worried about me. I'll do better, so you don't have to, okay?"

"I don't think Aunt Sylvie would want you to be sad all the time." Keeley pointed to one of the framed photos on the tall, art-deco-inspired dresser against the closet wall.

A picture of Mabel and Sylvie together at their high school grad-uation in their caps and gowns sat in a thick silver frame. Sylvie, with her sights already set on Hollywood, and Mabel, exhausted from trying to talk her sister out of her pipe dreams. The apartment was filled with images of Sylvie, as if Mabel was afraid she'd forget what she looked like. But the pictures stopped at age twenty-four. When both of their adult lives were only just getting started.

"Grammy says Sylvie was always very happy," Keeley said. "She calls her shinny."

"Shinny." Mabel nodded, laughing a little. "That's as perfect a description as I can ever imagine." Her sister had sparkled from the second she'd been born. And Mabel had been more than happy to let her. "I miss her every single day."

"I wish we knew what happened to her."

"So do I, kiddo," Mabel admitted, wishing she wasn't having this conversation, especially with her almost nine-year-old daughter. "I don't like not knowing. And back to your question, Kee, that's why I do the work I do. Because the women I try to help, they deserve to have someone who will fight for them. Stand for them."

She'd failed her sister in so many ways. But she wasn't going to fail Sylvie again. She'd spent the last eight years waiting for a knock on the door, for someone, *anyone*, to tell her what had be-come of her sister.

Two months ago, just before Christmas, she'd gotten at least part of an answer when Sylvie's image had been found on a wall filled with photographs in that horrid basement of that mansion, where it was suspected dozens of women had been held. But since then ….

Since then, there had been nothing. Nothing other than a growing anger, frustration, and a sadness that had seeped into Keeley's life. That needed to stop. And the only way to stop it once and for all was to find out exactly what had happened to Sylvie.

"You know what?" Mabel took a deep breath and let it out, looking at a picture of Sylvie in less morbid, happier times. "I think you were very brave to tell me you're worried about me. I'm going to do better, okay? I'll try harder not to be so sad."

"You can be sad, Mama." Keeley decided with a firm nod. "Maybe what you need is someone to be sad with. You know, like Riley and Quinn."

"I don't know what that means."

"Riley's a lot happier now that she's with Quinn. They're fun together. *He's* fun. Maybe you need someone like him. Someone who will make you laugh."

"You make me laugh, and that's all I need."

Mabel did not need someone like Quinn—or *any* man for that matter. Quinn was great—for Riley. And he'd pretty much appointed himself as the unofficial big brother Mabel had never wanted. He was a good addition, peripherally. But the idea that her daughter believed a man could resolve all the supposed problems Mabel was tackling? That was just ridiculous.

The only thing that was going to turn Mabel's life around was to get answers about Sylvie. It was all she wanted. It was all she needed. End of story.

She was tired of the lip services. Frustrated by the non-answers. Furious at having her questions and demands brushed aside. She'd made some enemies over the years, even more in recent weeks. She'd earned herself a reputation as a troublemaker as far as the District Attorney was concerned, but hey …. No one ever got anywhere by being silent.

"Mom?" Keeley looked back up at her, her eyes drooping sleepily. "Are you sure you're okay? You're squeezing me really hard."

"I'm fine, baby." But she didn't release her hold on her daughter. Not yet. Probably not ever. She knew better than most how easily people could slip away and simply … vanish. "Go to sleep, okay?"

"Only if you do." Keeley snuggled into her side.

"You just want to sleep in this bed because it's bigger than yours."

"I'm a big girl now, Mom. Twin beds are for babies."

"You're *my* baby." Mabel pressed her lips to Keeley's forehead and reached back for the light. As the darkness returned and Mabel pulled the blankets up and over the both of them, Barksy let out a bit of a whine, walked around them both, and wedged himself against Keeley's back, resting his muzzle on her hip. "Someday, Sylvie will rest, too," Mabel whispered, rubbing the dog's scruffy ears. "If nothing else, she deserves that, right boy?"

Barksy whined and let out another sigh that, for an instant, sounded exactly like the one Sylvie had issued in the dream. Even as the sound tugged at Mabel's heart, she let the idea of it push her gently back into sleep.

CHAPTER TWO

WHEN Paul Flynn was fifteen years old, he promised himself three things.

Promise number one cemented his determination to make certain the Flynn family line—and all its contaminated DNA—ended with him.

Promise two declared his intention to get the hell out of Los Angeles, break the family curse of being nothing more than drunken, violent, toxic bastards, and do something significant and meaningful with his life.

And promise three? Well, he'd written "promise three" in boldface lettering on a napkin stained with his own blood: Once you're out of LA, don't ever, EVER, come back.

Funny that the one promise he'd actually written down was the one he'd ended up breaking.

Every once in a while, when Paul felt particularly edgy, he could feel that napkin pulse from where he kept it folded in his wallet, like a portable telltale heart. Since he'd hit LA a few days ago after his cross-country drive out from New York, that pulsing had grown loud enough for him to hear it in his sleep.

He didn't relish the idea of spending the next few weeks silently shouting at it to keep quiet, but if that's what he had to do …

In law school, he'd learned to tolerate and eventually embrace late nights spent pouring over textbooks and written opinions that would guide him on his way to fulfilling promise number two. Occasionally, he'd ditch the schoolwork and head out with his roommates or frat brothers, drinking their way to sunrise.

But while most of his fellow students dreaded that cornea-blinding daily event, he thrived on it.

Early mornings offered the most promise of the day. Not because of the clichéd fresh start, but because it was just as the sun peeked up that the world dropped into the silence that made everything, even the impossible, seem possible.

He'd learned to command the minutes, and he did that now, as the light streamed across the Hollywood Hills.

Light that could, in the best of times, remove the shadows and darkness that dwelled here.

And the darkness did dwell. So very, very deep.

Standing on the other side of eight-foot-tall black wrought iron gates, welded in place decades before Paul had even been born, he could feel that darkness hovering above the Tenado estate.

It wasn't the same kind of sensation one got while visiting, say … the haunted property of Netherworld in Georgia or the 13th Gate House in Louisiana. Those places left you with the screaming willies for weeks after. That said, Paul had no doubt that in the years to come, this property could reach Amityville House status.

It was, after all, located in the most make-believe capital of the world.

He'd made the drive—he wanted the extra time to read up on the case and gird his soul against the ghosts he'd be facing in this town—in relatively good time and discovered his fair share of decent motels along the way. He'd arrived a few days earlier than the DA expected, but one thing Paul had learned was that doing the unexpected often provided more information and opportunity than predictable behavior. Keeping people off guard had always served him well.

Paul dug out the key he'd picked up from the security desk in the lobby, where his temporarily assigned office was in the Los Angeles District Attorney's building. The fact that the key itself had rust spots dotting the thin metal was yet another reminder of how far removed this estate was from reality. He could only imagine the number of hands it had passed through over the decades since it had first been built.

The padlock gave an odd, dull click when he twisted the key. He unwrapped the triple-linked chain. The right-side gate uttered a loud whining protest as he shoved it open just enough to walk through. The thick foliage of the surrounding properties had grown up in a kind of curtain, separating this estate from the myriad of neighboring properties that continued up the winding roads, higher into the silent hills overlooking the smog-blanketed city.

People who lived up here liked their privacy. They liked being shuttered away, far back from the roads like this one was, with its winding gravel drive dotted with determined, dying weeds stretching for an all too cruel sun. Secrets dwelled best in areas like this, where reputation and image outweighed reality.

Paul's loafers crunched as he walked, the sound striking his ears like a rattling drumbeat. He'd left the files back at the office, his cell phone in the car, and set his watch alarm so he wouldn't be late for his breakfast meeting.

He'd wanted—no, *needed*—this time. These quiet minutes on a Monday morning to push himself past the dread and disgust he felt at taking a job that broke one of the three promises he'd all but sworn to keep by blood oath. He was determined to compartmentalize and keep the case separate from the past that had driven him out of Los Angeles in the first place.

This was the kind of case he'd built his reputation on. That said, this was also a case that, even in his wildest dreams, he'd never anticipated leading.

True house-of-horrors cases were unicorn rare. The cases that had cropped up over time had been relegated to history, urban legend, or the memories of crazy old caretakers haunted by whatever they imagined had taken place. But this one.

Paul stopped at the base of the porch, hands on his hips, and stared up at the stained-glass window situated perfectly over the hand-carved, heavy wooden door.

Oh, this one was all too real.

The multi-petaled lily was displayed against a stark, cloudy white background. If he looked closely enough, he could imagine droplets of red splashing down to the planked boards below. His imagination was already kicking into overdrive as he envisioned the cruel, heinous acts that had taken place on the other side of the door. On the other side of the window.

He used the second key in his pocket to unlock the door.

When he stepped inside, he could smell dust, stale air, and the faint hint of chemicals left behind by the countless crime scene techs who had swept through the house over the past two months.

They'd spent weeks inside, examining every single inch. A house that was a maze of hallways, rooms, and windows that twisted upon themselves. Hallways that seemed to circle inside and out the back door to the property line a hundred yards on the other side of the parched and cracked swimming pool.

Paul had memorized the internal diagram the investigating detectives had sketched out and included in the files he'd been sent. The eight-bedroom, six-bath house felt equal parts egocentric obscenity and exemplified accomplishment.

Its style wasn't particularly anything special, with its arched doorways and expensive tiled floors. Originally built in the nineteen forties, it had undergone multiple upgrades, a number of which didn't come close to unifying the design flow. Since he had no interest in anything on this level, he made his way past the dining room, turned a corner, and found the thick wooden door with the iron fixtures waiting for him.

The silence of the dwelling was exacerbated by the lack of electrical hum. They'd killed the power in this place weeks ago so as not to tempt any curious lookie-loos inside. The bare minimum of security features remained in place, but as far as Paul knew, he was the first person in weeks to walk through the gates.

Paul clicked on the small flashlight he'd brought with him, pulled open the door, and angled the beam straight down the dark, musty, curving staircase.

20

It was impossible for the past not to creep alongside him. This estate had acted as host not only to numerous owners over the years but also to hundreds of celebrities, actors, actresses, directors, producers, and even studio bigwigs at various events. Even now, he could hear the ghostly clink of martini glasses and undertones of mumblings and conversations that had faded with time.

He'd been in plenty of structures that carried energy left behind by former occupants. Early in his career as a prosecutor, he'd made it a point to always walk the scene of the crime. The sensations, that residual force that continued to pulse through walls and windows and doors, guided him on his journey toward resolution.

The Tenado estate would be no different.

He stepped onto the firmly packed dirt floor coated thick with the smell of mold, mildew, and stale, stagnant water.

He flashed the light down the right-hand corridor where the supposed sacrificial pool lay beyond broken doors. The pool where Riley Temple, a Los Angeles photographer and paparazzi, had nearly lost her life before Christmas. But the pool wasn't what he needed to see.

Paul turned, kept the light waist high, and walked the curving passage. The echoes of clinking martini glasses and polite laughter shifted into ghostly cries and sobs. He could all but see the wafting, dusty, bare footprints of the women who had been brought here. Not countless women. They had a specific number. A horrific, sobering number that equated to the responsibility placed on his shoulders.

The voices, the faces that belonged to those voices, all remained here. In the darkness. In the stillness.

His skin prickled, and he shivered.

The door at the dead end of the corridor had his heart rate picking up once more. He'd imagined standing here so many times since he'd gotten the call asking him to come out to lead the special investigation. An investigation he knew local officials wanted closed as quickly and quietly as possible. They wanted all questions shut down and the opportunity to move on.

Paul simply wanted answers. But he wanted one other thing more.

He wanted to find the women.

Most investigation teams consisted of ... well, a team. So far, Paul was a one-man show. Still, he was prepared to give it his all, fight for the women who'd walked the same hall he was now in, once he got his footing and a plan of action in place. That said, more people working with him meant speeding up the process, which would get him the second thing he wanted most: returning home to New York.

"Plenty of ghosts around here," Paul chided himself and cringed as his voice echoed against the thick stone walls. "No need to bring your own along for the ride."

He reached out, pushed open the door, and stepped inside the enormous, circular, stone room.

It was empty now. The furniture—the enormous red-velvet-covered brass bed, the triple mirrored vanity displaying makeup, perfume bottles, and dishes holding various jewelry pieces were all stored in evidence now. Locked away until the case was brought to trial.

"*If* it's brought to trial." For the life of him, Paul could barely conceive of a solitary individual being held responsible for the crimes that had taken place here. As of now, only one name, Anthony Tenado, Hollywood agent and party-thrower extraordinaire, was associated with this place. But Anthony Tenado had been dead for years. In theory, at least in the DA's eyes, that made the case even more open and shut.

It would be easy to lay blame to whatever atrocities had occurred down there at the feet of a dead man. Except that didn't explain Riley Temple's attempted murder on these very grounds by a man who seemingly had intimate knowledge that this was the venue of previous kidnappings, presumed murders ...

"The atrocities didn't stop with you, did they, Anthony? Did you have a partner?" He arced the light around the room. "Or did some-one pick up where you left off?"

It wasn't a theory he'd come up with. It was a theory pretty much implied in the files for anyone who chose to see it. One he suspected Simone Chapman, Zinnia Danvers, and Tabitha Harris would agree with. All three women—wannabe starlets in their early to late twenties, whose photos had been on display with the many others in this very room—had disappeared *after* Tenado was in the ground. That wasn't public knowledge, of course, and it wouldn't become public unless …

Paul's jaw tensed.

Unless he wasn't given a choice.

He'd play nice with the bigwigs wanting this wrapped up in a tight little bow for as long as he could—but nothing was going to stop him from doing his job and getting answers for the victims and their families.

The raised platform in the center of the room was made of sturdy, polished wood. He walked up the two stairs and shone his beam high into the air where, more than three stories above, a skylight offered bare hints of sun.

The pictures had all been here, nailed into the stone—black-and-white photographs of the women's faces. Most of the women had been alive in the images. Some had been unconscious. Others were clearly dead. All were now officially listed as "missing" in his reports.

The noir-inspired pictures had been taken in the same fashion as movie studio portraits in the 30s and 40s. He clicked off the flashlight, stood still as stone as the vibrations of the room washed over him through the wisps of light coming down through the skylight.

Dozens of women were captured on film before they were tossed aside … somewhere.

"Where are you?" Paul whispered into the darkness.

The whispers that answered slipped through his mind, not his ears. His mind had been working tirelessly ever since he'd taken on the case, even though he knew the chances of finding actual answers—of locating all the women—were so far out of his reach he could barely grasp a thread of hope.

But there was one. A feeling he hadn't been able to shake. A feeling that continued to beat around him even now.

They were *here*. Not in this house. Not on this property. Both had been forensically examined from top to bottom and even beneath. But they were somewhere in this city; he was sure of it.

"I feel you," he said to the ghosts. "I will find you. I'm not going anywhere." An odd, cool breeze brushed across his cheek and made him shiver. "I promise I'm going to bring you all home."

He left the basement without turning his light back on. Instead of dragging the door closed behind him, he left it open and walked back out into the sunlight.

"I'll trade you." Lounging against the doorframe of apartment 3A, only one floor down from her own two-bedroom apartment in Temple House, Mabel held out the manila envelope she'd only just finished stuffing this morning. "Your finished taxes for a gallon of coffee."

Riley Temple, looking irritatingly coherent and smug for so early on a Monday morning, stepped back and waved her in. The living room television was tuned to the local morning news but with its volume on mute.

"You forget your key?" Riley asked.

"Right now, I don't think I could spell key," Mabel confessed as Riley shut the door behind her. "Let alone find where I left it."

"Coffee's hot and brewed." Riley followed close at her heels as they headed for the kitchen. "Rough weekend?"

"Mildly." She set the envelope on the counter, replaying her initial and very brief conversation yesterday with a still-sedated Eva Hudson who had barely been able to open her eyes. "Why do you ask?" Mabel didn't look up again until she'd taken a good two throat-scalding glugs of coffee. "Ahhh," she sighed. "And the world rights itself once more. You were saying?"

"Well, I was going to say you look like crap," Riley said cautiously, "but I'm having second thoughts."

"Good idea," Mabel agreed. "Although, you're still irritating me. How do you wake up so … alert?"

Riley grinned, retrieved her own half-filled mug from the side counter, and took a seat at the breakfast bar. She wore her typical jeans and worn Princess Leia rebel T-shirt, her damp, dark hair tied back in a neat ponytail. Gone were the tension lines that came with a love-hate relationship with her previous career as a paparazzo as well as the residual effects of having been targeted by a pair of twin homicidal, fanatical maniacs. For the most part, at least.

Keeley was right. Riley did look … happier.

"I have a special Monday-morning weapon," Riley bragged. "Clears out all the cobwebs. Revs up the engine for the week."

"Let me guess …" Mabel rolled her eyes. "Said weapon is about six feet tall, tends to display that same goofy grin you've got on your face right now, and wears a badge?"

Riley waggled her brows. "Sometimes, that's all he wears."

"Oh, gah." Mabel pretended to gag. "Rub it in, why don't you?"

"Actually—"

"Stop!" Mabel held up her hand, shook her head, and found her sour mood lifting. She could have easily left the envelope outside Mabel's door. This was why she'd knocked instead. No one was better at distracting her and making her feel better than a happy and satisfied Riley Temple. Mabel was determined, for Keeley's sake at least, to make an effort at finding some joy in life. "Where is Detective Sexy Pants, anyway?"

"DSP is in the shower." Riley sipped her coffee. "What's going on? Bad dreams again?"

Mabel hesitated. The last thing she wanted to do was burden her friends—her *best* friends—with how badly she was handling things, but as she'd learned frequently since moving into Temple House a little over seven years ago, that's what they were there for. "I saw her this time."

Riley cupped both hands around her mug. "Sylvie?"

"Yeah." Mabel sighed. "It was for like a fraction of a second, but for the first time, I reached her …" She frowned, lifted a hand to the half-heart pendant that had been severed permanently when Sylvie went missing. "She called me boring." She didn't know what irritated her more, that her subconscious was clearly playing games with her or that her sister's teasing was what had stuck with her the most.

Riley's lips twitched.

"Keep laughing," Mabel warned. "I can take those taxes back, you know? Move a couple of decimal places around and sic the IRS on you."

"Sorry." Riley laughed softly, shaking her head. "Putting on my supportive face right now." She laughed a bit more. "Nope—I'll need a few extra seconds here. I just hear things like that and realize how much I would have loved your sister." She glanced over her shoulder as a side door opened.

"Morning, Moxie," Mabel said with forced cheer as Riley's great aunt joined them. "Coffee?"

"Does the Wicked Witch lust after Dorothy's red slippers?" Clad in a pair of bright yellow silk pajamas—right down to her matching pom-pom slippers—Moxie Temple, one time star of the silver screen and octogenarian extraordinaire, shuffled her way out of her bedroom, her hand-painted sleep mask shoved crookedly on top of her mussed red hair.

"Hope we didn't wake you up," Mabel said as she poured coffee and retrieved the creamer out of the fridge.

"You're fine." Moxie waved her concern away. "Had a late dinner with my agent last night." She eyed Riley with caution. "He told me Granger Powell reached out again. Made me another offer to be in that Sally Tate remake his studio's heading up."

"Did he?" Mabel asked, grateful for the shift of subject.

"He upped my salary offer significantly," Moxie informed them. "Which I guess he can do, given he's the head of the studio. He suggested I might even get a producing credit."

"People who can't take no for an answer irritate the crap out of me," Riley muttered.

Mabel wasn't surprised the mention of Powell Films' studio head was enough to wipe away Riley's good mood.

"What did Edgar tell him this time?" Riley asked.

"Nothing yet," Moxie admitted with a sheepish look at her great-niece. "Other than to remind Mr. Powell that Temple House is not for sale at any price, no matter how flattering a film offer he sends my way to tempt me."

"Damn right it's not," Riley agreed.

There were four things in this world Riley would guard with her life: her friends, her family, her camera collection, and Temple House—not necessarily in that order. The building had been in Riley's family for decades and housed not only numerous tenants and families but also almost as much silver screen history as Hollywood itself. A history both Riley and Moxie showed off with pride. They considered it a personal responsibility to shine a light on the days that had brought Hollywood to its current status. Like almost every-thing else, Hollywood was nothing without its history.

"If Granger Powell's not careful," Riley continued. "I'm going to sic Laurel on him, this time in person."

"You could sell tickets to that meeting." Mabel pressed her lips together. "Fund your own Sally Tate feature." Laurel Fontaine was the kind of lawyer—hell, she was the kind of woman—no one with functioning brain cells wanted to go up against.

Mabel had no trouble admitting Laurel was smarter than pretty much everyone else she'd ever met or that the attorney knew just about everyone in Los Angeles and Hollywood. Or that she was considered far more verbally lethal than the killer stilettos she was known for wearing. She was one of the best friends a person could have but also the kind of enemy that kept people awake at night.

"Sounds like Powell might deserve some attention from Laurel," Mabel suggested cheekily.

Moxie didn't look convinced. "They're doing a rewrite of the script, expanding the role they want me for." She hesitated. "They've asked me to read it."

It would have been impossible for Mabel to miss the spark of hope in Moxie's eyes. The older woman's portrayal of Sally Tate—a Rosie the Riveter-type character who, while working in a factory during WWII, solved murders in her spare time—was iconic and beloved. It had been more than six decades since Moxie had played a starring role in anything, but she continued to make frequent guest appearances on television and the late-night talk circuit. No doubt the very idea of a return to the limelight held incredible appeal for her.

"Don't you worry, Riley." Moxie reached across the counter and patted her great-niece's hand before she picked up her cell phone and began doom scrolling. "I'm just stringing him along. But it can't hurt to read it, can it?"

"Not so sure about that," Riley mumbled as Mabel drew her away and out of earshot. "What?"

Mabel frowned. "Have you talked to her at all?"

"About what?" Riley's far-too-innocent tone told Mabel that Ri-ley knew precisely what Mabel referred to.

"You know what."

It wasn't often she used her 'walk with caution tone' with one of her friends. Neither of them had forgotten Moxie's concerning behavior over the holidays, behavior that, as a rape and violence survivor advocate, Mabel recognized immediately.

Something had happened to Moxie in the past, something disturbing and violent that had triggered, on a couple of occasions, a kind of panic attack that had left all of them shaking. Moxie had a mark, a branding of sorts, on the back of her neck. One she kept covered by her hair. One Riley had seen herself on the back of one of Moxie's contemporaries currently residing in an elder-care home.

Mabel was convinced that mark was connected to their search efforts for answers regarding Sylvie and the other missing women. But as determined as Mabel was to broach the subject with Moxie, albeit it in a compassionate, caring way, Riley was equally protective and had ruled it out of the question.

"Riley, we need to ask her about that mark on her neck. It might give us a lead." It wasn't the first time Mabel had pushed, but each time she did, she knew she risked alienating her friend.

"No." Riley's voice lowered and quivered. "*You* need to ask her about it. I'm not going to re-subject her to whatever horror she might have lived through. She's in her eighties, Mabel. I think she's earned the right to a calm, safe, and trauma-free remaining years."

"But …"

"Don't ask me again." The order came out whip-fast, and as intense as the words felt, Mabel also saw regret and a plea in Riley's eyes. "Leave it alone, Mabel. *Please*."

It felt like walking away from a winning hand. That lily mark had made an appearance in multiple avenues of their under-the-table "investigation." They still didn't have solid information on what the mark actually represented. They had the perfect opportunity to find out, and yet …

"All right," Mabel acquiesced. She would stop asking—for now. But the day was coming when Riley wasn't going to be able to say no. "Okay, we'll try to find answers another way first." But Riley knew as well as Mabel that, so far, there was no other way.

"Ah—an email from Edgar," Moxie announced and flipped her phone around. "I was right. They've sent a revamped treatment for the script. I'm going to go read it right now."

"I don't understand why Powell's still pushing you on this, Moxie," Riley said. "He only offered you the role to sweeten his offer to buy Temple House."

Mabel cleared her throat when Moxie's eyes sparked. "I don't think that's the *only* reason he's interested in Moxie, Riley." Mabel jerked her head toward the elderly aunt and shot a warning look at Riley. "The man is running a film studio that's been around since Buster Keaton was hanging off fire engine ladders. Movies are in young Granger's blood, and he knows a good bet when he sees it. Plus, his grandfather was responsible for the original series of films. They know a lot of people would love to see Moxie back on the big screen. We live in the era of reboots and remakes. Moxie being involved would be guaranteed bang for the box-office buck," Mabel added.

"Thank you, Mabel. What she said." Moxie poked a finger at Mabel and glared at her niece. "I'm *viable*. In fact, Edgar suggested I start my own TikTok channel." She straightened her shoulders. "Not sure what the heck that is exactly, but I aim to find out. Course, all of this about the movie is moot. I'm sure not going to do anything that's going straight to one of those steamy services."

"*Streaming*," Riley corrected. "Streaming services."

"I've seen what they have on those channels," Moxie countered. "I stand by steamy. Maybe that's what I'll ask for. A love scene. You think that George Clooney might be up for a geriatric challenge?"

Laughing, Mabel walked around the counter and hugged Moxie tight. "I adore you, Moxie Temple. And George would, too, if it ever comes to that."

"You bet your grape stompers." Moxie nodded and slipped an arm around her waist. "Your girl gone for school already?"

"She jackrabbited out of the apartment after her bowl of Lucky Charms." Mabel beamed at Riley. "I'm so winning at this parenting thing. Sugar loaded and downstairs ten minutes early. With her homework done, I might add." Despite having to be harangued about finishing her math assignment.

29

"Helps that Sutton has her early morning baking deliveries on Mondays, so adding Keeley to her carpool run is a breeze," Riley added. "Just saying!" She shrugged at Mabel's arched brow. "Driving three kids to school is just as easy as driving her two." Then she grinned. "Speaking of Sutton: She reminded me we haven't started our Saturday morning mimosas yet this year."

"When the sun decides to turn its heat back on in the morning, call me," Mabel said easily.

"Cass suggested we are due for a meeting. You know"—Riley angled her head at Moxie, who was busy digging through the refrigerator, muttering about kombucha—"about our investigation." She grimaced. "She thinks we should share any new information any of us might have come across."

Mabel pursed her lips. The investigation Riley was referring to was enough to trigger another kind of nightmare for Mabel. Sometimes, she couldn't quite believe they were researching the existence of a secret society dwelling in the underbelly of Los Angeles. That they could find information that might lead to solving the disappearance of her twin.

Excitement replaced her apprehension.

"Does anyone have new information?"

"Given who the suggestion came from, I'm guessing yes. It's been a while since we all touched base on the …" Riley cast a nervous glance at her great-aunt. "Well, on all the stuff we've been working on. What's your schedule like this week? You free?"

"Outrageously expensive, actually," Mabel teased while she took the time to compose herself, reminding herself not to hope too much. "Yeah, the calendar's clear as far as I know."

Especially if any information discussed led to more answers. Led to *Sylvie*.

Her heart skipped a beat.

"Leftovers are likely included," Riley teased.

Mabel groaned. She and Keeley could get by for days on Sutton's leftovers. She could also do with quality time with her friends. She'd already given Theresa at Soteria a call and taken herself off emergency standby notice for any potential new rape cases. She was emotionally wiped out, having dealt with Eva Hudson's case the past few days; taking on another person might just push her over the edge. "You think Cass is doing better?"

"Must be, if she's talking about hosting a get-together. Sutton's talking with her about it." Riley flinched. "I know Cass is still suffering some of those aftereffects from our December visitor downstairs in the basement. Nox almost convinced her to come down to get the mail the other day, but it turned into a no-go. She hasn't stepped foot out of that apartment in months."

"Definitely a setback," Mabel agreed. As good as she was with victims of abuse and violence, she had yet to connect to Cass on a level to deal with whatever event had turned her friend into a complete recluse.

"December visitor?" Moxie demanded of Riley. "Is that what you're calling that little creep who finagled his way into this building and tried to kill you?"

" 'December visitor' is more polite than what *I* call him."

Mabel and the other two women turned at the deep voice belonging to Detective Quinn Burton, who strode down the hall from Riley's (and now his) bedroom. Mabel had to admit, the man was easy on the eyes. With his roguish, dark brown hair, Hollywood mega-star good looks, and unabashed devotion to her best friend, the sexy didn't stop at that quirk of amusement on his lips or the autographed baseball collection that now sat beside one of Riley's prized cameras in a corner glass cabinet.

He'd foregone his usual tan slacks and blazer for crisp navy pants, a bright white shirt, and a matching tie. A pressed jacket was draped over one shoulder.

Mabel wondered if either Riley or Quinn realized how much envy they triggered when people saw the two of them together. Not because they made a spectacularly attractive couple but because they were so easy with one another. They fit, as if they'd each been waiting for the other to simply slip into the other's life and continue moving on. Together.

Maybe that's what Keeley had picked up on. Not that Mabel *needed* a man in her life, but she could see where the idea of being as happy as Riley and Quinn appeared would appeal to her daughter.

Of course, it was harder for Mabel to see things that positively, given her track record. She was coming off a thirty-one-year run of zero successes in the romance department. At least her last partner had left her with the jackpot win of Keeley. Hard to be completely resentful of a man who had given her the best part of her life.

"Wearing a big-boy suit today, huh?" Riley slid off her stool and approached Quinn. She took the jacket and set it over the back of her vacated chair and quickly buttoned the cuff, giving him trouble before she rested her palm against his heart and tilted her face up for a quick kiss. "Something important going on downtown?"

"Hell if I know. Word got around we should be ready for a special meeting." He flashed a smile at Mabel, then at Moxie. "Morning, ladies. Please tell me there's some coffee left."

"Maybe." Mabel took a step back, planted herself between Quinn and the coffee machine, and folded her arms over her chest. "Keeley stayed up late reading the last three nights."

"That's great." Quinn grinned and tried to get around her. She blocked him, and he frowned. "Isn't it? I mean, it's better than video gaming. Right?"

"It is. She's very excited at the new selection of books available to her on those shelves over there." Mabel pointed to the bookcase lining the long hallway to the door. "She came home with an armload of them."

"Ah." Quinn grimaced. "Right. I might have had a beer or two before she stopped by after school on Friday."

"So, you're saying your judgment might have been a bit impaired?" Mabel fluttered her lashes at him.

"I wasn't home Friday afternoon," Riley explained as she moved forward. "What did he do?" She narrowed her eyes at Quinn. "What did you do?"

"Nothing he won't be paying for dearly for in the foreseeable future." Mabel's smile widened. "If I have to suffer through her reading the entirety of the Stephen King library, so do you, Detective. She started with *Carrie*, just so you know."

Quinn cringed. "Bad Detective."

"Very bad detective." Riley smacked him on the back of the head. "Isn't that the book that starts with—"

"The main character getting her first period at school?" Mabel said easily and basked in the discomfort of Detective Burton. "Yes, it is. Don't worry. I told Keeley to come to you with any questions she might have, Quinn. About *anything*." Her grin widened at Quinn's pained expression. Moxie chuckled before heading back into her room. "That look right there?" Mabel pointed at Quinn. "Totally worth my child starting to read horror novels. Better do your research, Detective. In case you've forgotten, Keeley knows how to ask questions."

"I can't have the rest of this conversation without coffee," he muttered. "Or Scotch. Yeah, might need both."

Mabel moved out of his way and winked at Riley, letting her know she wasn't that upset about it. She picked her coffee back up, glanced toward the television.

"I'm going to make a special trip to the bookstore today," Riley announced. "See if I can't find a fully informative and perhaps illustrated manual about the female reproductive—"

Mabel's eyes went wide as the image of the Tenado estate appeared on the television. It wasn't the image that caught her attention as much as the *Breaking News* crawl scrolling across the bottom of the screen.

"Something's happening."

Heart hammering in her throat, Mabel shot around the kitchen island, all but dived for the remote, and clicked the volume button.

She could feel Riley and Quinn move in behind her. Riley rested a gentle hand on her arm, squeezed as Mabel tried to remember to breathe as she scanned the screen.

"Reporting again on the announcement the Los Angeles District Attorney released only a few moments ago." Mabel could barely hear the female newscaster's voice above the roaring in her ears. "New York attorney Paul Flynn, perhaps best known for his special investigation handling of the Clarissa Conrad case in New York last year, has been brought in to oversee the investigation into the Lily Girls case. In mid-December of last year, the long-abandoned Tenado estate in the Hollywood Hills was exposed as a possible house-of-horrors type setting that could, if the unofficial word holds true, shed light on the suspected disappearances of dozens of women, dating back decades."

"Suspected disappearances," Mabel muttered in disgust. "They make it sound like a rash of alien abductions."

"Hush," Riley urged and rubbed her arm.

"While we've confirmed Mr. Flynn arrived in Los Angeles over the weekend," the woman continued, "we've been told the DA has tentative plans to introduce him at a press conference later this week. The DA will be returning shortly from an extended trip to Sacramento, where she and other high-level state officials have been discussing judicial appointments and legislation. In a statement released this morning, DA Eichorn says, 'The appointment of Paul Flynn hopefully illustrates my office's determination to get to the truth of what happened. The fact he's already hard at work is evidence of that. His reputation when it comes to dealing with complicated cases in difficult atmospheres is one that I hope will serve the county of Los Angeles well. I can assure you: Mr. Flynn has my utmost faith as he works to bring his investigation to a rightful and quick conclusion.' We'll update you more on this case as the story develops," the newscaster said as the camera switched back to her. "Back to you, at the desk."

"Thanks, Sharon," the anchor said as Mabel clicked the TV off.

"Think this is what your suit is about today?" Riley asked Quinn as she and Mabel faced him.

"Possibly." He shook his head. "Even if it's not, at least naming Flynn is progress." He glanced at Mabel. "That's what you've been pushing for, isn't it? A special investigator?"

Mabel bit her tongue. She'd have thought he'd be pushing, too. Quinn hadn't been standing on the sidelines last year when Riley found herself threatened after trying to discover who had attacked one friend and killed another. Hell, he'd been the one who had dragged her out of the sacrificial pool in that mansion of horrors.

Riley had been the one targeted after the photographs she'd exposed led her to being stalked by a pair of psychopathic killers. Killers who, from what Mabel had subsequently learned, couldn't have been acting alone.

Not that there had been any signs of this so-called Circle cult in recent weeks. It was almost as if the group had scurried back under their rocks like seasonal cockroaches.

"They're really going to keep calling this case by that ridiculous name?" Mabel asked. The Lily Girls. The press made it sound more like a Lifetime Original movie rather than a case involving dozens of actual missing women.

"I imagine the Tenado family lawyers tried to prevent *any* collective name for the victims that implies a serial killer was using their client's property," Quinn said. "Especially now that there will be an official investigation. I know the lawyers would have ensured the missing cases wouldn't be named using their family name, even if the potential killer is dead, as it could irrevocably sully their name with a possible mass murder site. And no," he added quickly as he walked back into the kitchen to retrieve his jacket. "That isn't me being dismissive about the situation. It's me reminding you both that cases run at different bureaucratic levels and progress speeds."

"If you can call glacial a speed," Mabel muttered. "What do you know about him?"

"Paul Flynn?" Quinn shrugged into his jacket. "Not much."

Mabel glanced at Riley, who looked as skeptical as Mabel felt. "But you know something."

"I know *of* him," Quinn said. "Generally."

"That doesn't sound hinky at all," Riley said. "Spill."

"I've never met the man, Riley. Which means I haven't worked with him."

"Maybe Google will be more forthcoming." Mabel pried open her oversized black leather hobo bag and dug in for her phone.

"Wikipedia isn't going to give you the feel for the man, Mabel," Quinn warned. "Only time and patience will do that."

"I'm sorry, have you two met before?" Riley said before Mabel could. "She's been waiting for answers for over eight years, Quinn. How much longer is she expected to be patient?"

Mabel only half-listened as her fingers flew on the digital keyboard. Her eyes scanned text the second it appeared on screen. "Paul Flynn is thirty-eight. Member of the bar in New York, California, and Nevada. Well, he's smart at least." Way easy on the eyes. With that dark curly hair and piercing light blue eyes, he was going to fit in perfectly in this town. Even his candid, unprepared pictures looked as if they'd been professionally edited. As she stared at him, she attempted to convince herself that the heat in her cheeks was temper. "Stanford educated. Honor roll. Edited the Yale newspaper for a couple of semesters." She snorted. "Huh. This is interesting. He's originally from Los Angeles. He grew up here," she added at Riley's arched brow. "He's worked for various prosecutor offices in New York and Connecticut. He was lead prosecutor for the Southern District of New York where his investigation into the drowning death of Clarissa Conrad led to the arrest of an up-and-coming congressman who subsequently … oh." She stood up straighter, her heart twisting into a knot. "Well, that's tragic." She touched a hand to her unsettled stomach.

"Ross McFiltry," Riley said as if trying to recall the name. "Freshman congressman accused of killing his mistress? Didn't even get to trial, did it?"

"No." Quinn returned his attention to his already buttoned cuff. "McFiltry killed himself after getting released on bail. Bail that was posted by his mother, a former New York senator."

"There's more, isn't there?" Riley stepped in front of him, touched her hands to his face. "What did you leave out?"

"There's a lot more, mostly rumors." Quinn seemed to find comfort in Riley's touch. "One is Flynn lost his nerve after McFiltry's death and took himself out of play on the big cases. Moved behind the scenes, so to speak. Another says he was targeted by McFiltry's mother, that she blamed him for her son's death and used whatever power she had to blackball Flynn and shove him into professional obscurity."

"I hate to say it, but that sounds more likely," Riley said.

"Today's the first I've heard of him in a while," Quinn said. "Before the McFiltry case, Flynn was considered a fixer. The kind of lawyer you bring in when you're expecting blowback and roadblocks. Fearless. Seriously smart. Tenacious. In a way, he's a good choice for this, Mabel. He's great with the press and even better with witnesses and victims' families. Doesn't take orders well, from what I understand. Doesn't really care who he offends or ticks off."

"But in other ways?" Mabel hedged.

"Like I said, I haven't met the man," Quinn stated firmly. "And I'm not about to judge him based on what I've read in the press or online." He jerked his chin toward Mabel's cell phone. "I suggest you do the same."

"You know what?" Mabel clicked her phone off, shoved it back into her bag. "You're absolutely right." She hauled her bag over her shoulder and headed for the door. "Best way to get a feel for the man is to meet him face-to-face."

"Mabel!" Riley dived for her, barely grabbed hold of her arm, and spun her around. "You aren't going down there."

"To the DA's office? You bet I am."

"You can't. *Mabel.*" Riley's warning tone barely registered as she leaped around Mabel and blocked the door. "You've been banned from the building. You show up there, guns blazing—"

"I don't own a gun," Mabel said calmly.

"You know what I mean."

"Riley's right," Quinn said as he came up behind her.

Rather than feeling trapped, Mabel's determination and energy zinged into the stratosphere.

"You go down there with an attitude," Quinn went on, "you'll be lucky if they just escort you out of the building. Worst case, they'll arrest you for trespassing. Do you really want to pay Laurel an arm-and-a-leg to get you out on bail?"

"I'm on her pro-bono plan," Mabel argued.

"You go down there, you need to be smart about it," Quinn continued. "Don't go burning whatever bridges you've got left when you're getting closer to the answers you want. Alienating Paul Flynn before he even gets his footing with the case isn't going to get you anywhere except in trouble."

"I just need to talk to this man." Temper thudded in her chest. "I need to look him in the eye. Not for my sake, but for Sylvie's. I need to know what kind of man is going to be looking for my sister and the other missing women." Better yet, she needed to know if he had any intention of looking for anyone or if this was some big show being put on by the DA. "I just need to meet him."

"All right." Quinn stepped back, nodded. "All right. I can understand that."

"You—?" Riley balked. "Quinn, she can't go down there on her own—"

"We can't stop her," Quinn said. "I have to get to work, and Merle is expecting you to help get Buried Treasures ready to reopen now that reconstruction is finished. Besides," his brow arched in a way that told Mabel he'd made up his mind, "it might actually work in your favor, Mabel. To come face-to-face with him without any warning but from the perspective of calling a truce with the DA's office. Maybe catch him before he's had time to make up his mind about you."

He had a point. Mabel had certainly caused some upheaval at the DA's office with her very public demands that they open a special investigation into the missing women. Women that included her sister. If this Paul Flynn's been here even a few minutes, he'd no doubt gotten an earful from either the DA herself or her employees.

Mabel wasn't about to apologize for being vocal. These women needed a voice, and as a result, Paul Flynn was now here.

"You're right." Mabel's anger faded beneath reignited resolve and reason. "It wouldn't make any sense to alienate him. Right away, anyway." Her attempt at humor didn't even earn her a flicker of a smile. "I'll ease up on the hostility and go in with a mask of optimism."

"Maybe someone should come with you." Riley scowled. "I can call, and—"

"No." Mabel reached out, grabbed her friend's hand, and squeezed. "Merle needs you. He's still not a hundred percent since getting released from the hospital, and you don't want him overdoing it. You being there is good for him, and besides, who better to redo his antique camera display than 'renowned photographer' Riley Temple?"

Riley snorted. "As if he'll let me touch any of those cameras."

"You'll find a way. I'll be careful," Mabel assured them. "I'll be polite and respectful." And if that didn't get her anywhere ... "And you'll both keep your phone on just in case I need a phone call."

"You won't," Quinn said firmly. "Because you know what's at stake."

Mabel pinched her lips together. He really did have all this locked down, didn't he?

"The head security officer's name is Charlie Prentiss," Quinn continued. "He was on the job for twenty-five years before he retired for health reasons. He has an affinity for chocolate cupcakes and a pretty smile. Just sayin'," he added at Mabel's dubious look. "His daughter's about your age, about the age Sylvie would be, and he's good enough at his job that he'll know who you are. More importantly, he'll know *why* you're there." Riley stepped aside, and Quinn pulled open the door. Mabel stepped into the hall and Quinn paused in the doorway. "Just do me a favor, will you? Please, *please* don't make me have to come down to arrest you. Stephen King's menstrual plot lines are one thing, but I have no idea how I'd ever explain you being a felon to Keeley."

She would never risk Sylvie's case, despite her impulsive, hot-headed response earlier. But, because she couldn't let him have the last word, she shrugged even as he smiled. "I'll do my best."

CHAPTER THREE

PAUL bypassed the line of customers outside The Original Pantry Café and ducked inside. Being a couple minutes late didn't prevent him from pausing to take in the long-forgotten sights and sounds of what had, once upon a time, served as his go-to eatery. Inhaling the familiar and intoxicating aroma of coffee, oil-slick overheated griddles, and fresh-baked biscuits set his stomach to growling. He found an odd comfort in the clanging dishes and yelled orders echoing from the kitchen and order window.

Ignoring the irritated glances from people waiting for tables, he headed down the partitioned isle to one of the tables in the far back corner.

"Just like old times, meeting you here," Paul said as his breakfast companion got to his feet. The other man stretched out his hand and kept his blue suit jacket in place over the slight paunch of his stomach. "Good to see you, Jeff."

"Definitely like old times." Jeff Chambers chuckled as he motioned for Paul to take a seat in one of the low-back, maroon cushioned chairs. "You're late."

"I forgot just how bad LA traffic is. And that's coming from a New Yorker." The second he sat down, he was treated to the view of a server balancing a myriad of plates piled high with delectable staples like pancakes, fried eggs, and crispy cooked hash brown potatoes. One of her younger, female counterparts nipped at her heels, a pot of coffee in each hand, paused at their table, and lifted one of the pots in silent question. "Please." Paul flipped one of the white mugs over and nudged it toward the young woman. "Thanks."

"My pleasure." The smile she offered was quick before she moved off.

"I swear to God, it's like we really are back in high school." Jeff shook his head, which was covered in a haystack of dark blond hair with hints of gray shimmering at the temples. He'd trimmed down some since the last time they'd seen one another two years ago in New York, but Jeff continued to carry that hint of roundness Paul himself avoided by a strict workout routine and an even stricter avoidance of sugar. "Serves me right, bringing you back to LA," Jeff continued. "Forgot how completely invisible I become being anywhere near you."

"No one's falling anywhere over me these days." Unless you counted the media hoard back in New York. A hoard that thankfully had begun to drop off after four months of incessant, irritating attention. Leave it to Paul to dive headfirst into an entirely different type of attention-grabbing cesspool.

"For the record, Jeff," Paul continued, "you made yourself invisible the second you met Lindsay in our sophomore year of high school … Speaking of Lindsay—" He leaned back as another server, this one a middle-aged man with thick wire-rim glasses, set two plates on their table. One look at Jeff's carb-loaded order had Paul's lips twitching. "Your better half is out of town, isn't she?"

"You know it." But Jeff grinned even as he picked up a fork. "The second she's out the door, it's no carb left behind."

"Can I get you anything to eat?" the server asked Paul.

"Yeah, thanks. Steel-cut oatmeal and …. What's the fresh fruit this morning?"

"Dude." Jeff shook his head and chuckled.

"Oh, right." Paul grimaced. Diners weren't exactly on the fresh fruit delivery route. "Just the oatmeal, thank you. You could do with some more fruit in your life." Paul turned the teasing table on his friend. "Carbs and fat make your mind sluggish."

"As the head of the Special Investigations Unit at the DA's office and the man who convinced the DA to give you a very high-profile—not to mention a career-saving—job, I take offense to that comment." Jeff shoveled up a good forkful of shredded potatoes dripping with runny egg yolk and pinned Paul with a look. "How are you settling in?"

"Managing." His ears were still ringing with the emotional re-entry. He hated this town with the passion of a thousand suns, and so far, that loathing hadn't abated one iota.

"How are you finding things now that you're back?" Jeff asked.

"Exactly where I left them." Paul hoped his tone shut down any further personal questions Jeff might be poised to ask.

For a lawyer, especially a prosecutor, Jeff was strangely and annoyingly optimistic. Because of that, his friend couldn't conceive of anyone having a less than stellar relationship with their family and loved ones.

Paul hesitated. "I know I said this on the phone, but thank you for the job." It wasn't his most gracious statements of appreciation. He could only imagine it had taken either a lot of guts or a complete abandonment of intelligence to even bring up his name in the discussion with his bosses.

"Might want to hold off on thanking me." Jeff's quick and dismissive smile didn't do anything to ease his mind. "These cases are a mess, and honestly? The list of people who fit for this kind of thing was very short." He paused as Jeff's breakfast was served. "I also have a confession to make."

That unsettled Paul, but he didn't let it show. "Okay."

"I have ulterior motives for wanting you here," Jeff told him.

Paul didn't blink. "This is my shocked face." Even over the phone, he'd known something was off. Now that they were face-to-face, seeing the lines of worry around his friend's eyes, the perpetual frown of concern marring his brow—not to mention the way he seemed to be keeping his voice down and his eyes on constant scanning mode—only added to Paul's concern. "And here I thought you were just looking for someone to shove the Tenado estate case onto."

"Thanks for not calling it the Lily Girls case," Jeff muttered.

"Yeah, I won't." Disgust surged through him. Leave it to certain wings of the media to reduce missing women to a punchy headline. Paul stabbed his spoon into the thick oatmeal and earned a grimace of sympathy from Jeff. "What? What's wrong?"

"You're just going to …" Jeff pointed to the soup-bowl-sized portion. "No sugar or milk or anything? Stuff looks like wallpaper paste."

To prove he planned to do exactly that, Paul took a huge bite. "Since this case is probably going to wreak havoc with my blood pressure, I may as well pay attention to my cholesterol." Still, the oats could use a little … oomph. He reached over and snatched a crispy piece of bacon off Jeff's plate, crumbled it up, and mixed it in. He nodded after another spoonful. "Yep. Much better."

"Man, I've missed you." Jeff laughed and shook his head. "Lindsay's already talking about having you over for dinner once she and Max are back from her folks. You get tired of the city footing your hotel bill, we've got the room at the house."

Paul smirked. "A, I'm footing my own bill, thank you very much, and B, I still can't believe some little human calls you Dad." His change of subject was abrupt yet effective. "How old is Max now? Three? Four?"

"Six." Jeff's clarification proved just how fast time did indeed pass. The sublime affection on his face sent an unexpected and surprising pang of envy chiming through Paul. "He has his heart set on a dog for his birthday."

"What six-year-old boy doesn't," Paul countered as old memories surged. He'd wanted one, once upon a time. But not for long. Bringing a dog into the house he'd grown up in would have only resulted in tragedy. For Paul *and* the animal.

His family had, for decades, been wildly successful in the act of procreation, but there was a disturbing attention to a lack of follow-up where parenting was concerned. Whatever gene most people possessed in that department, in the Flynn family, it had been replaced with vitriol and an abject loathing of their offspring, if not a complete disinterest in nurturing or responsibility.

Paul hadn't been on this earth long before he'd been violently introduced to that reality—hence, his early life decision to put an end to the generational suffering and eradicate his tainted DNA from the gene pool.

Friends were a risky enough venture, but a wife? Kids? Yeah, there wasn't a force on this planet that could make him take that chance in life. Besides, emotional investment required one very important thing he'd always been accused of not possessing: a heart.

"So." Before the trip down memory lane led to a dangerous part of town he wasn't anxious to traverse, Paul covered his mouth and cleared his throat. "These ulterior motives of yours …"

"You read the files I sent you?" Jeff slathered a piece of sourdough toast with blackberry jam out of one of those tiny plastic packets.

"I've been bored out of my mind for months. What do you think?" Being shoved into a proverbial closet of an office and forgotten by his superiors tended to stall whatever brain power Paul still possessed. "I burned out two printers getting up to speed. Is the DA still determined to keep the Tenado case separate from the investigation into the Dean Samuels's conviction?"

"More than ever," Jeff confirmed. "I've only started digging into the Samuels conviction, but before we get into that, regarding what I sent you, did anything stand out? Anything, I don't know … sinister?"

Sinister? "On the page? Not much." *But in the subtext?* Yeah, the cold calculation and determination to close the case in a way benefiting the DA's office. Sure. Sinister fit. "If you're worried I don't know what I'm walking in to, don't be."

"What do you think you're walking in to?"

"A political quagmire of secrets and ass covering." He shoved his spoon into the thick porridge. "On the one hand, you've got dozens of women who have gone missing over decades, an abandoned estate owned by a man who, in hindsight, should have been considered at least a person of interest in the Melanie Dennings's murder, and a law firm doing its best to keep every detail about their aforementioned now-deceased client under wraps." He took another bite. "Then there's the LAPD, past and present members, who could be considered by some as clueless, negligent, or, at worst, complicit in the wrongful conviction of Dean Samuels. Personally, I'm leaning toward all three which is a whole other kettle of worms."

"Fish," Jeff corrected. "Kettle of fish."

Paul grinned. "And then there's District Attorney Johanna Eichorn, who was appointed only a few months ago by her predecessor and whose large circle of friends include—wait for it—Anthony Tenado, the estate owner who suspiciously drowned in his swimming pool three years ago and has yet to be removed as the owner of record of a potential torture and mass murder site." He arched his own brow now. "Did I miss anything?"

Jeff shook his head. "And still you came out here. I can't decide if that makes you stupid or desperate."

"Probably a little of both." He hadn't waited a day after Jeff's offer before he'd packed up a handful of suits, the printed-out files in a trio of office boxes, a suitcase of essentials, his laptop, and, most importantly, his coffee machine into his Mercedes and hit the road, stopping only long enough on his drive west to sleep, read, and eat. At his friend's now dubious expression, Paul sighed. "I'm a big boy, Jeff. I can take care of myself."

"That's what I'm counting on." Jeff finished his toast and sat back, shoved his empty plate away. "You know better than most how any high-profile case these days qualifies as slippery and potentially explosive, but this one." He shook his head. "I can't believe I'm saying this, but these cases actually have me scared. I'd honestly give just about anything to close the book on them and walk away."

Jeff had Paul's attention. Jeff was one of the most justice-minded people he knew. He wasn't a man to let even the hint of impropriety or miscarriage of justice pass. Paul shoved his breakfast aside and leaned his arms on the table. "Explain."

Jeff shook his head.

"Break it down for me, Jeff," Paul pushed. "What's bothering you?"

"What *isn't*?" Jeff's almost desperate whisper sent chills down Paul's spine. "The Tenado discovery is bad enough, but looking into a wrongful conviction? That's a level too deep to be comfortable with. That said, everything I've found out so far regarding the Dennings investigation and conviction was tied up with a neat little bow."

"Too neat?" Paul prodded.

Jeff shrugged in the affirmative. "Everyone I've spoken to who worked on the case originally said they were just relieved it was over. All of them were shocked Samuels changed his plea at the last second. At the time, they expected it to raise all kinds of alarms. And yet it didn't."

"Unless the alarms were ignored by the authorities involved. Like the lead investigators." If Paul's memory served, and his memory always served, that lead investigator had been … "Chief Alexander Burton. Burton." He frowned and considered the current Chief of Police. "Why do I know that name?"

"Because his son is Detective Quinn Burton," Jeff said.

"The Detective Burton responsible for reopening the Melanie Dennings case." Paul let out a low whistle. The detective who, along with photographer Riley Temple, had discovered the horrific scene at the Tenado estate and set everything in motion? "Well, hell. You think the detective is covering for his dad?" Although, he was not sure how that was likely, since he was the one who officially re-opened the case.

"No." Jeff's answer was instant and firm. "No, Quinn Burton is a stand-up guy. The kind of cop we didn't think existed anymore. And his father's the same. Their reputation is solid."

"So, you don't think Chief Burton is responsible for the cover-up?"

"No, I don't." He hesitated, inclined his head. "I do, however, think he's responsible for the evidence leak that reopened the case." Jeff flinched. "I haven't shared that suspicion with anyone until now."

Whatever pride Paul might have felt at the confidence was drowned out by the tremor in his friend's voice. Accusing the current chief of police of leaking sensitive information wasn't something that was done. Not if you planned to have a career on the other side of things. "Who are you looking at, then?"

"Everyone," Jeff admitted. "Believe me, no one is happy about it. Including me." Jeff appeared to sag in his chair, as if he were suddenly exhausted. "Maybe it's all my imagination on overdrive and I'm spinning, but I swear, every time I walk into a meeting at the DA's office, I feel like I'm interrupting something. There are whispers. Secrets. And these looks, like they're wondering how much I've heard or what I know." He tapped his index finger three times on the table. "Sounds paranoid, doesn't it?"

"A little." Paul hesitated. "Doesn't mean you're wrong. What else is there?"

46

"What do you mean, what else?"

Paul jutted his chin toward Jeff's hand. "That's your tell. You always do that when you're holding something back, so let's have it."

Jeff shook his head. "I shouldn't—"

"Who am I going to tell?" Paul countered. "I'm working alone on my part of the case. You're my only friend in town, so there's no one else for me to talk to. Which reminds me, since I'm not inclined to make friends, I'd like to make the argument to the DA myself about establishing an official task force."

"Feel free," Jeff scoffed. "She'll say no. Bringing you in was a hard sell."

"It won't hurt for me to ask," Paul countered. But if she wouldn't give him a task force, maybe he could talk her into giving him something else he needed. "What is it you don't think you should tell me?"

Jeff glanced around again, then leaned forward. "No one can locate Dean Samuels."

"What do you mean 'can't locate' him?" Paul scoffed, even as something inside of him tightened. "He's in prison." Paul paused. "Isn't he?"

"Not the prison he was sent to," Jeff countered. "And not in all the ones we've had searched since. He's vanished."

"That's not possible." Paul couldn't help but frown. "Even in the highest profile of cases, someone always knows where prisoners are. What about his family? He had a wife, didn't he? Two kids?"

"They're in witness protection. Part of the deal Samuels made when he pled guilty," Jeff said. "Total identity change, and the Marshalls aren't interested in sharing information. If I keep getting blocked, I'm going to have to take this to the DOJ."

"At which point, nothing will be kept quiet," Paul observed. "I've still got a few friends in federal law enforcement. Let me throw some lines in the water and see what bites."

"Thanks." The relief on Jeff's face made Paul feel a little better. "Now that we've discussed the details of *my* case, I do feel better."

Paul snort-laughed and pushed his mug to the edge of the table. "I wondered if you'd drop a bomb on me once I got here." He smiled at the server who refilled his coffee. "I told you, I read everything you sent me."

"What about the video links?" Jeff's eyes narrowed. "Did you watch those?"

"Most of them."

"How about the one with Mabel Reynolds? At the DA's press conference a couple of weeks ago?"

"That one I watched." He'd been transfixed by her calm despite the raging fire of grief in her eyes. A grief he'd seen in a lot of eyes belonging to victims' families. "Her sister is one of the missing women. Sylvia. No..." Paul searched his memory. "No, her name's Sylvie." Whatever pride he felt in remembering was doused immediately by another thought. Most of the women had little to no information in their missing person's files, but Sylvie was an exception, which was probably why the details had stuck with him. "Sylvie was Mabel's sister. Her twin sister. Damn." Losing a sibling was hard enough. But losing a twin?

"Mabel's been leading the charge to keep Sylvie's case front and center for years," Jeff continued. "She only became more determined after the Tenado house was found late last year. Local news interviews, national channels, newspapers, blogs—you name it, she's done it. She'd finally run out of places to speak out, so she crashed the DA's press conference and demanded attention be paid to her sister's case."

"She made a public spectacle," Paul mused. That explained why the DA caved and assigned a special investigator. "From what I saw, Mabel Reynolds doesn't pull any punches." Not even when it took two security officers to remove her from the building.

"No, she does not," Jeff agreed. "And she hasn't won many fans in law enforcement. She speaks, all anyone hears are accusations of misconduct, incompetence, and cover-ups."

"The trifecta of the justice system these days," Paul agreed.

"Yeah, well, you name it, she's done it—and it's only upped her profile as a victim's advocate. You ever heard of Eden on Ice?"

"Sure," Paul nodded. "Cold-case crime blogger out of Sacramento, isn't she? Didn't she have a hand in capturing a serial killer a few years back? She recently started a podcast. I listened to a few episodes on the drive out from New York. She's good."

"She's also earned a reputation for getting law enforcement off its collective asses where some cases are concerned. Eden's interview with Mabel last December got over a hundred thousand downloads in the first twenty-four hours."

"Everyone loves a good conspiracy theory," Paul muttered. "Throw in a serial killer, and of course it'll go viral."

"Theory or not, listeners flooded the DA's office with phone calls. Slammed the email system, demanding action. The deluge went on for days," Jeff added. "Then the press conference happened, Mabel was filmed being removed, and—"

"I get a phone call." Ah, politics, Paul thought. The games just never stopped. "You aren't saying Ms. Reynolds is already being critical about how the investigation is being handled, are you? I haven't even gotten started yet."

"Critical is a word," Jeff confirmed. "Persistent doesn't come close to describing her, Paul. She reminds me of you, actually. She has that pit-bull attitude when it comes to things she cares about."

"You sound as if you think I should be worried about her." Paul couldn't keep the amusement out of his voice.

"I'm saying you should be aware of her." Jeff shrugged. "And okay, maybe a little worried."

"No reason to be." Paul shrugged his concern off. "I can handle a grieving sister. I've dealt with plenty of people like her in the past. It's the lack of answers that's driving her; she doesn't do well with being ignored. One healthy, semi-informative conversation should satisfy her and back her off. In fact, I'll make you a bet that says I can get her to quiet down and fade into the shadows by the end of the week."

"Good to know you didn't forget to pack your ego," Jeff said.

"I never leave home without it. On the bright side, getting her off the DA's back should earn me some goodwill with my new boss."

"You really have to dig deep for silver linings, don't you?" Jeff didn't look convinced. "I should have remembered sooner you tend to see some cases as a kind of game."

"Some cases, sure." Paul shook his head. "I won't deny that. There's nothing fun about this one, Jeff. I've been up there. To the Tenado estate. I'm not laughing."

"Impressions?"

"Too many. Not enough. It's hard to make sixty-seven women vanish without a trace. They aren't there. They've just, well … like Dean Samuels. They've vanished."

"So, what are you thinking?" Jeff prodded. "Trafficking?"

"No," Paul admitted darkly. "I'm not thinking trafficking. And neither are you."

"No," Jeff agreed without hesitation. "I'm not."

"Someone connected with that property knows something." Paul's job was to find a starting point and hope it led to actual answers and, more importantly, evidence. "I'll find them. And, since you won't suggest it, I'll say flat out that I'm happy to step into the line of fire for you with our boss and the press. That's the ulterior motive you were talking about, isn't it?"

"No, actually." Jeff shook his head. "No. I need someone around here I can trust."

"You've got it."

"I need you to rethink the task force idea."

"Why?"

"Because a task force means more eyes on the case and too many mouths that can leak back to people that might be involved in this— people in power who'd want to bury this case."

Paul considered Jeff's concern. "How about I use my task force request as leverage to get something else that I need?"

"Like what?"

"I want full access to any and all information connected to Anthony Tenado."

"You mean you want Tenado's lawyers to cooperate."

"Yes. I'll give in on the task force, for now at least," he told Jeff. "But I need that information, Jeff. What can we get out of them?"

"Other than a lawsuit?" Jeff asked. "Not much. What are you looking for?"

"I won't be sure until I see it." It was one of those he'd know it when he found it. "Dead or not, Tenado was at least peripherally involved with what happened to those women. He lived in that house for more than twenty years. He surely had to have known what was going on in his own basement. I'd want details about his business deals, client lists. Cell phone records."

"It's too late for those." Jeff shook his head. "Tenado's been dead too long."

"Then I'll settle for financials. Bank and investment records. If I spun it as a way for me to find out who else caused the disappearances, to rule Tenado out as the ringleader, maybe the lawyer will help." Nine times out of ten, the money always told the story.

"When are you scheduled to meet with the DA?"

"I'm supposed to talk to her sometime this week. I'll hit her with both requests: the task force and the attorney records. Then back off the former to get the latter."

"Look at you, playing the game." Jeff's lips twitched. "Fair warning. Be prepared for some epic stonewalling. She's a master at it. That said, if we can get her to make the request of the attorneys, it might actually go somewhere."

Paul glanced up at their server as their bill was set on the edge of the table. "No, I've got this." Paul waved Jeff's hand away when he reached for the check. "I owe you for like twenty years' worth of missed meals." He reached into his back pocket for his wallet. "Anything else you want to fill me in on before I step fully into the lion's den?"

Paul shrugged.

"I'm just glad to have someone in this town that I can trust. And as happy as I am to have you back in Los Angeles, I'll be really glad when these cases are put to bed."

"Yeah," Paul agreed. "Me, too."

"Be careful in the office," Jeff warned. "Everyone there walks around with a dagger they're just waiting to plunge into someone's back. We both know this city either breaks you or turns you into something you never imagined yourself capable of becoming. Don't ever assume you know where anyone's loyalties lie." His eyes narrowed. "You're immune to both temptations, Paul. You already fought yourself free of this place, and you know what people will do to scratch their way to the top. No one can throw anything at you that you can't deflect or defend against. That's why I called you."

Paul grimaced, sad to agree. "I won't let you down."

"I know you won't."

Paul's phone buzzed in his pocket. He pulled it free, glanced at the screen. "Huh."

"DA Eichorn?" Jeff asked.

"No." He avoided his friend's gaze. "It's security from the DA's office. Seems Mabel Reynolds is waiting in the lobby and is requesting to meet at my earliest convenience." He clicked the screen off, unable to stop the smile from forming. "I guess I won't have to go looking for her, after all."

"You never could resist playing with fire." Jeff's amusement almost had Paul's face flushing. "How I wish I could go with you, but I wouldn't worry about it. Or Mabel." Jeff's grin widened as they got to their feet. "Like you said, I'm sure you can handle her just fine."

CHAPTER FOUR

"NO." Perched on the edge of her metal folding chair in the lobby of the District Attorney's building, cell phone tucked between her ear and shoulder, she kept her datebook open and balanced on her knees. "No, please just tell Alicia I called, and if she could let me know when Eva is back in her room, I'd be grate—"

"Ms. Reynolds?"

Mabel glanced up and stared into a pair of the most crystal-blue eyes she'd ever seen in her life. It took her a moment to see the rest of the face. Those eyes had a kind of gravitational pull that made looking anywhere else impossible. She sat up a bit straighter, murmured a goodbye to the nurse on the other end of her call, and quickly tapped off.

"Mr. Flynn." She was up in a shot, her datebook dropping to the floor with a bit of a thud. They both bent, both reached out, finger-tips grazing over one another as their heads nearly knocked together. Mabel jumped back, her face going hot. "Sorry. You, ah—you startled me."

She prided herself on always being aware of her surroundings. Always. How had the man appeared out of nowhere? Had technology secretly come so far that he'd beamed himself in on some kind of stealth transporter beam?

"Then I'm the one who should apologize to you. Paul Flynn, ma'am." He inclined his head.

His voice sounded like the smoothest bourbon—a little smoky, well-aged, and temptingly tantalizing.

Temptingly?

What on earth was the matter with her?

They stood, Mabel juggling her datebook and phone as she quickly shoved both into her oversized, worn shoulder tote. Not looking directly at him didn't seem to re-center her equilibrium. Her heart was ka-thudding all over the place, as if it had forgotten where it was supposed to be housed.

Paul Flynn was a man who commanded attention. Not only in stature and appearance but in attitude. She'd dealt with confident men before. Confident, egotistical, overbearing even. But this man displayed his self-assuredness on an entirely different and charming level. Her tingling toes signified that.

Mabel frowned. She didn't tingle. She certainly never had before. Okay, once—maybe twice—but she also prided herself on being an excellent judge of character from the instant she met someone. It was nerves, she reminded herself. There was a lot riding on this meeting, so …. Yes, it was just nerves.

"Nice cupcakes."

"I beg your pardon?" Mabel blinked, trying to connect what he'd said to reality. He lifted one hand to show her the Matterhorn frosting-topped cupcake he held. "Oh. Right." She pinched her toes inside her boots, slung her bag over her shoulder, and wished she could turn down the flush in her cheeks to simmer. She glanced at the older security guard standing next to the metal detector near the entrance. "Charlie gave you one, huh?"

"He's an ex-cop," He shifted a thick, leather-strapped bag behind him and offered his other hand in greeting. "I have a feeling he was spreading the potential bribery evidence around."

She accepted without thinking, the instant thrill of his touch shooting through her system and resetting her brain. "I don't think bribery is the right—"

"You must be here to talk about Sylvie's case." His hold was firm, gentle, and without any hint of sweaty nerves. He wasn't just cool as a cucumber; he could qualify as a subterranean deep freeze.

"I—" she almost lost her breath. Not *the* case. Not the *Tenado* case or, God forbid, the Lily Girls. *Sylvie's* case. Something inside of her unexpectedly broke open even as she reminded herself he was well-versed at playing games. "Yes, I am. I would like to. Please."

Way to sound non-pathetic, Mabel.

Whatever control and determination she'd built up the past eight years seemed to be crumbling at this man's imported leather-encased feet.

"How about we go upstairs to my office?" That smile of his came far too easily. "It's a bit of a mess right now. Haven't had a lot of time to unpack, but it'll be more private than standing down here in the lobby." He inclined his head and urged her to follow him. "Unless you're adverse to chaos."

"I have an eight-year-old. Chaos and I are old friends."

"I'll bet." Was it her imagination, or had his attitude shifted? "Shall we?"

As they approached security, she glanced up at one of the security cameras in the corner of the lobby. Part of her wondered if this was a trick, a setup of some kind to get her to violate the restrictions his boss had placed on her.

"Would you like some coffee?" He motioned her ahead of him and quickly followed. "I haven't gotten my brewer unpacked yet, but we could—" He indicated the coffee stand in the far corner of the lobby.

"No. No coffee, thanks." She couldn't seem to get a foothold on their conversation. Then she realized her uncertainty was probably what he wanted. Charm disarmed, especially when it was unexpected. Given that almost smirk of a smile on his full lips, things were going precisely as he'd planned for them to. "Would you mind if we took the stairs?" She hung back as he approached the bank of elevators nearby. "I missed my workout this morning." Nothing like starting their professional relationship with a lie. The only workout Mabel tended to get was pulling open the fridge.

"The stairs it is."

So easy, so congenial. So …. Mabel blew out a frustrated breath. This was not going at all the way she'd intended. Or expected. She was going to have to wrestle control back if she was going to find her footing.

The special investigator wore his tailored suit far more easily than most, as if he'd somehow been born in it. There was a relaxed presence about him that certainly didn't scream lawyer or even prosecutor. The wavy hair she'd seen in her online search had been combed back and certainly spoke of the professionalism she knew him to possess. He was clearly someone who knew how to present himself.

She was not the kind of woman to have her head turned easily by a handsome man or her goals derailed by a charming smile. Keeley's father had cured her of those trivialities. That said, Paul Flynn struck her as the kind of man who could change her mind.

About a lot of things. Her flat-heeled boots clacked against the steps.

Okay, this is your chance. Maybe your last chance. Keep it short. Keep it succinct. Keep it friendly. Be nice. Find out information. Above all, don't get arrested.

"Must be nice to be back here. In Los Angeles," she added when he glanced back at her over his shoulder.

"It's not New York." The light in his eyes dimmed a bit. "For future reference, I like caramel."

"Caramel?"

"My favorite cupcake. For the next time you visit."

"You sound pretty sure there's going to be a next time."

"Wishful thinking."

"I think it's pure luck I'm being let up here at all," she countered. "I have a pretty good idea my picture is up in security's office as one of LA's most wanted."

"You're not quite at that level." He turned on a smile so bright it could have powered one of a dozen power stations in the city. "Not yet, anyway."

The second-floor landing led to a long, wide hall lined with open doors and people milling about. "It's just down here." He reached into his pocket, pulled out a set of keys as they approached a door that, unlike the others around them, didn't display a name or title.

"I'm used to an office with a view. I'm not entirely sure what I have qualifies." The door swung open before he could slide the key into the lock.

The young man with dark, short hair pushed his glasses up with one finger, a surprisingly confident smile on his face. "Mr. Flynn. Kent Clark." He stuck out his hand for an eager shake. "I've been assigned as your paralegal and office assistant."

"Kent … Clark?"

Try as she might, Mabel couldn't help but duck her head to hide her smile.

After shaking Kent's hand, Paul stepped into the reception area of his office. "Your dad a comic fan, Kent?"

Tan walls, Mabel noted. Tan carpet. Wood paneling. Completely nondescript, expected, and … boring. She glanced at Paul. All that described the office perfectly. Paul Flynn, on the other hand? Not so much.

"No, sir," Clark stated. "My mom. DC, though. Dad's the Marvel …" Kent eyed Mabel with more than a hint of suspicion. "When she's trying to irritate him, she tells him she only married him for his name."

"Family dynamics never fail to surprise me," Paul told Mabel. "Kent, this is Mabel Reynolds."

"Yes, sir." Again with the less-than-approving look. "Everyone in this building is familiar with who she is."

Mabel didn't miss the way *she* sounded like a curse word.

"Ms. Reynolds and I are going to chat for a while. Get yourself settled in, Kent," Paul told him, gesturing to the young man's collection of boxes. "You and I can talk once Ms. Reynolds leaves."

"Ah, yes, sir." Kent hovered behind Mabel as she followed Paul through the wooden door to his office. "Ah, sir? DA Eichorn called. Your meeting with her has been shifted—"

"We can discuss my schedule later, Kent. Thanks." His flash of a smile had Kent stepping back as Paul closed the door in his face. He turned and smiled at Mabel. "Please, have a seat."

"I wouldn't be surprised if Kent's out there looking for a pitchfork," Mabel said as Paul set the cupcake down in front of his computer monitor, set his case on his desk, and headed for the stack of three boxes piled in the back corner of the office. Beyond them was a small wet-bar area where he washed his hands before he dived into one of the boxes. Other than two padded chairs on the other side of the desk, a too-short, worn sofa across the room beneath a framed photograph of the Griffin Observatory, and some law texts lining bookshelves, the space was bare.

"Either a pitchfork or a torch," he agreed. "I understand your reputation is well earned."

"Good." Mabel, still standing, crossed her arms over her chest. "Reputations are difficult to ignore. I like to think I'm equally so."

"Can't imagine anyone ignoring you."

Mabel frowned. It was a line. Had to be. An effective one, given the way her heart jolted, but it was still a line. Rather than responding, she shoved her hands into the back pocket of her jeans and wandered over to look out the window.

Across the street sat the East Los Angeles Farmer's Market where stands offered a variety of fresh fruit and veggies along with homemade goods. Just beyond the tents one could see Belvedere Park Lake, with its spacious expanses of grass offering sunny snack sites in the warmer seasons. In February, though? Not so much. "I can see why this view might be disappointing compared to New York, but it's not bad." Quintessential Los Angeles with its slightly hazy morning fog, with the promise of sunshine poking through the clouds.

"Actually, my New York office overlooks a deli and Indian restaurant." Paul shifted one of the boxes to the counter, flipped open the top. "Best chole masala I've ever had. Just need to find that … aha. Here we go." He reached in with both hands and lifted out the rather elaborate coffee machine. "Never leave home without it."

"I think you need to rethink your definition of chaos," she said as she glanced around the rather spartan office. Even with the boxes, it was far from cluttered. She set her bag down in one of the two empty chairs across from his. "You travel pretty light if that's all you brought."

"Lighter than you think." He glanced over his shoulder before refocusing his attention on setting the coffee machine near the outlet and plugging it in. After removing a handful of mugs from the box, he made quick work to set the small metal pot to brewing before he retrieved his attaché and removed his jacket. "Most of those boxes are printed-out files and documents I was sent regarding the case."

"For the record, this is the neatest move-in I've ever seen." Mabel turned away, not ready to face the sight of the man in well-fitted white shirtsleeves and a surprisingly sexy tie. Clearing her throat, she scrambled for something else to say. "Your office doesn't even register on the chaos meter."

"No?"

She snuck a glance to see he was grinning, then looked away again. "Chaos is stepping on Legos in the middle of the night on your way to the bathroom or finding Barbie's clothes in the laundry."

"I imagine even Barbie needs to use the washing machine from time to time. The question is: Does Barbie do her own ironing?"

She turned back to him in time to catch him unbuttoning his cuffs and rolling up his sleeves. Her cheeks went warm at the sight of taut, toned forearms. Arm porn, Cass called Mabel's affection for those particular appendages. That description wasn't the least bit wrong.

Mabel fought back a smile even as she steeled herself. She'd been right about the charm. He had it in spades. Clearly, she needed to focus on building up an immunity to it. "Mr. Flynn—"

"Paul, please. May I call you Mabel?"

"Sure." She crossed her arms over her chest again; then, realizing that made her come off as insecure, she shifted and dropped her arms to her sides. "Paul, I wanted to—"

"Sit, please." He motioned to the chair while he shifted the stack of folders into more manageable piles along the counter behind his desk. Before he faced her again, he did a quick flip-through and pulled one free. "You sure I can't get you some coffee? I know a caffeine addict when I see one."

"Stop. Please." Perched on the edge of the cushioned chair, she took a calming breath. She was here for Sylvie. To give her sister a voice. That was all that mattered. There wasn't a force in the universe that could puncture the balloon of determination that had inflated eight years ago. "I've been through this polite get-me-to-drop-my-guard routine before with your boss. And with at least three of her underlings—and, to be honest, I'm tired of it. I came here today to get an assurance from you that you're taking these disappearances seriously. Not to just charm me into a false sense of security before you usher me out again with no more answers than I walked in with."

"I *am* taking the disappearances seriously." His smile was quick but more somber this time. "I hope that doesn't mean our meeting is over already."

She simply stared, waiting, her pulse thudding in her throat.

"Underlings, huh?" Paul's eyes sparked with dull amusement. "Please tell me you called them that to their faces, and where can I see a video of that interaction?"

Mabel's mouth twisted. She might have called them that and worse, but only *after* they'd given her the runaround and she'd threatened a sit-in. Not that she was going to admit it to Paul. "How about we cut through all the bullshit?"

His eyes cooled. "I wasn't aware—"

"Seriously." Exhaustion she hadn't expected to surge threatened to drain the energy completely out of her. She didn't want to piss Paul off and close off the only remaining avenue in the DA's office to get answers, but she needed him to know she meant business. "I'm running on sugar, adrenaline, and about ten hours sleep over the past three nights. I've got an eight-year-old with a sudden Stephen King obsession, tax season is about to land on me like a two-ton boulder on my shoulders, and you're sitting there with a smile that looks like you just walked off the pages of *Vanity Fair*'s Hollywood issue."

His brows shot up.

"So, please," she said, finishing on a wave of anxiety she hadn't realized she'd been riding. "Don't continue with the affectations and devil-may-care attitude. I can assure you: This devil does care. A lot."

He looked at her, a good amount of the humor falling away from his face as he nodded. He sat back, rested an elbow on the arm of his chair, and brought his hand to his mouth. "I was up there this morning."

"Up. Where?" She couldn't for the life of her …

"The Tenado estate. You mentioning the devil reminded me. I parked outside just as the sun went up." He leaned back, reached into his pants pocket, and pulled out two keys that he set on the desk.

"Place is creepy as hell to say the least, but you know that already. Because you've been there."

"Yes." She cleared her throat—almost every night in her dreams. "Before they took all the evidence away. Riley and Quinn brought me out there so I could see—"

"Sylvie's picture." His nod of understanding was the first time she'd believed anything she'd been told in this building. "I don't sleep much," he said. "And I like to make the most of my time, so I got a good, quiet look at the place. It was as if I could hear them. The women." His eyes glossed over as if he were hearing the ghosts of that house now. "So, yes, I can assure you that I am taking this case seriously. I'll even go one step further and make you a promise: I'm going to find them. Find her."

She knew he meant her—Sylvie. She didn't dare let herself believe. "Are you really?"

He nodded. Once. Assertive. "I am."

She didn't know why she didn't pick up on the aroma of bullshit, but there wasn't any hint of it. She cocked her head, considered him. "Are you in the habit of keeping your promises?"

"I don't make them unless I intend on keeping them." His lips quirked. "The DA might think I'm a showpiece or scapegoat, Mabel. I can assure you that I'm not. When I take on a job, I work it until it's done and it's reached a satisfactory conclusion that suits me. No one else but me. End of story."

"I'm sorry." Mabel swallowed hard. "I'm used to being placated by a bunch of promises and platitudes and empty smiles. I find it a little difficult to believe you intend to follow up your promises with actual action. I'm willing to keep an open mind and discourse if you are."

"I am." Then his gaze flickered, his expression unreadable. "Is that all you've faced in this office? Empty platitudes?"

"This office. With the police. With the press." She liked the spark of irritation she saw in his eyes. "You aren't surprised."

"Not even a little."

"For going on two months, it's been one big runaround." Ever since she'd first seen those photos on the wall in the basement. Ever since she'd first seen that picture of Sylvie …. She almost couldn't breathe. "And that was after eight years of silence. I've all but memorized the entirety of the District Attorney employee roster."

"That's better than I've done," he said. "Guess I'm going to have to tell Jeff he was right."

"Jeff Chandler?" Mabel demanded. "Tell him you were right about what?"

"Nothing," he seemed to mutter to himself. "Okay, Mabel. Where do you want to start? What do you want to know? Throw everything you have at me." He made a bring-it-on gesture with both hands. "I'm listening."

"I—" Her mind went blank. Damn the man; he'd done it again. Her jaw ached from clenching. "You're good." She shook her head, actually laughed as she pinched the bridge of her nose. It was no use. There was no stopping the headache that was brewing. "No wonder they brought you all the way out here. You're really good."

"Yes," he said without hesitation, "I am. But I actually wasn't trying to disarm you … this time. And maybe that's where we start, with us laying all our cards onto the table. A woman like you, coming to this office this morning as you did, when you'd been told to stay away—I'm going to assume you've done your homework. Without going into the details of the last few months for me, you know I have a superior success rate when it comes to closing difficult investigations and cases."

"I couldn't care less about your conviction rate. Samuels was *wrongly* convicted. I'm more interested in how you feel about uncovering the *truth*."

"I'm a fan."

She narrowed her eyes. "You know what I mean."

"I do." He sighed. "I do know what you mean, and I also understand your need to ask me that particular question. Answers haven't exactly been forthcoming, have they?"

"No."

"Would you believe me if I told you the DA feels the same way? That she wants answers about what was found at the Tenado estate as much as you do?"

"I believe she wants this case closed as quickly and quietly as possible," Mabel countered. "And I don't think she's the only one."

His gaze flickered from hers. In the silence, the sound of the coffee machine gurgling and brewing filled the air, even as the warm steam wafted past her nose, tempting her almost as much as the man sitting across from her.

"I've been looking for my sister for eight years, Mr. Flynn. Ever since she came out here from Wisconsin, following her dreams of becoming an actress." Mabel purposely stopped using his first name. She didn't want to use it. It felt too … familiar. Too intimate. Despite the monstrous desk sitting between them, the room felt entirely too small. "You know what's happened in those eight years other than no progress on her case? I've only gotten more determined. I *need* answers. I *need* to know what happened to my sister. My parents need to know what happened to their daughter—and I can assure you as certain as I am sitting in this chair, nothing you say or do is going to get me to back down." She stopped herself from blowing out a relieved breath. Now was not the time to show weakness of any kind.

He made to talk but she held up her hand. "I'll believe you for now," she continued before she lost her nerve. "Whether you were brought here to actually work this case or simply to placate the media with your sparkly smile and charming attitude, I wanted to meet you. I wanted to look into your eyes so I could determine what kind of man you are."

"You've had a bit of time," he said quietly as a blanket of detachment draped over his face. "What kind of man am I?"

"Too early to be certain." She wasn't going to lie to herself when she expected the truth from him. She wanted—oh, how desperately she wanted—to believe he was going to do exactly what he promised. "How about you just tell me so we can push through the verbal foreplay portion of the conversation?"

"Pity. I happen to enjoy foreplay." His lips did that twitching thing again, and he lowered his hand, those gold-flecked eyes of his all but dancing.

Her cheeks went wildfire hot. Damn it if her toes weren't tingling again.

"I apologize." He cleared his throat and sat up straight, folding his hands on the top of his desk. He appeared to have shocked himself. "That was completely inappropriate, especially given the situation."

"Apology accepted." Knowing the attraction she felt was mutual did not ease her nerves.

"To be honest, I'm not entirely sure where that came from. But let's move on." His frown appeared genuine, as if he was confused by his inadvertent flirt. "I am more than happy to address your question head on, but first, I really am interested in your take—your gut reaction. Right now. You're afraid I'm a puppet and mouthpiece for the DA." He lifted his hands, tilted his head. "Funny. I don't see any strings."

"Not all strings are visible," she countered.

This time, his smile carried no hint of humor. But it was intense. So intense she could feel a wave of heat rising from her overactive toes.

"I may be a lot of things, Mabel, but I'm no one's puppet. Whatever the DA does or does not expect, she hired me, and I go where the evidence takes me. More importantly"—he held up a finger when she opened her mouth to respond— "I go where my instinct tells me to go. Most of the time, it's bang-on right. There's something important I need for you to understand, however."

"What?"

"This isn't going to be an easy or remotely fast resolution. It's going to take months, if I'm lucky, to get to the bottom of what's happened here. I don't believe in sugarcoating anything. Don't expect me to have answers for you in days or even weeks. That's just not going to happen."

Mabel swallowed hard. "Right." She knew that, of course, but hearing it spoken out loud felt like another setback of sorts. It shouldn't have surprised her, though. She'd given up believing in miracles years ago.

"I know it's easy for me to sit here and say all this," Paul continued. "But truth is one thing that has always mattered to me." He stood up, walked around to stand in front of her, and leaned back, bracing his hands on the edge of the desk. "However inconvenient it might be. I don't tell you that to be discouraged but so we're on the same page moving forward."

It was all she could do not to sink back in her chair, but once again, she couldn't help but think that was what he expected and wanted her to do. He was a man used to being …. Well, he was used to being on top.

That made two of them.

"Whatever you think about the other people in this office," he continued, "let me assure you, Mabel—all jokes and platitudes aside—I want to find out what happened to these women." His voice lowered and softened. "I want to find out what happened to Sylvie. Not as much as you do. No one else other than family could. Believe me or don't—that's your choice. Won't change anything of what I plan to do."

Without thinking, she reached up to clasp the half-heart pendant at her throat. Something inside of her broke open. Or maybe it woke up. She couldn't be certain. All she did know was that her world shifted with his words, and she couldn't find her balance right away.

This was too good to be true. *He* was too good to be true. He was saying everything she wanted to hear. In a way she wanted to hear it. With kindness and understanding and empathy.

Three things she couldn't let herself count on for one second.

She wanted to believe him, but faith was more fragile than the thinnest spun glass. Nevertheless, she let herself, just for the moment, believe.

"You're the only one in this office who has ever said her name rather than 'your sister.'" Not once, but three times now. That had to count for something, didn't it?

"Then, on behalf of everyone in this office, I'm sorry. Truly, I am" He considered her for a long beat, intent on choosing his words carefully. "Sylvie deserves better than vanishing without a trace. She deserves better than to be relegated to a few pieces of paper stuck in a folder that went forgotten or maybe even ignored all these years." He straightened up. "I can't do anything to change the past, Mabel. But I'd appreciate the benefit of the doubt moving forward. Especially since I'm likely going to need your help by the time this investigation concludes."

Relief, gratitude—or maybe it was exhaustion—nearly had her surrendering and sagging in the chair. "I must be more tired than I realized. I think I might actually believe you." She narrowed her gaze on his face, searching his handsome features for a hint of deception. "Are you that good a lawyer, that good an investigator, or that good a liar?"

"A lot of people would say I'm all three." He hesitated. "I'm a good judge of people, Mabel. I understand them. The good ones and the bad ones. I know how people think, and I know that the better angels of our nature rarely win. I'm also—and this might not come as a complete surprise—not a nice man when I'm arrowing in on the truth. I make enemies far easier than I make friends, and the friends I do have aren't all that plentiful in number. Call it a character flaw or a severe fault; no one stands in the way of me doing my job. Even when someone probably should."

The opportunity was there to ask about what had really happened in New York that sent him all the way across the country to find another job. The details remained, for want of a better term, nebulous. But for right now? Right now, she was willing to pretend that everything he'd told her was true. If only to get a good night's sleep for once.

"Sixty-six." The words slipped out of her lips before she could stop them. "As important as Sylvie is to me, there are sixty-six other women that we know of who will never come home to their families. Are you willing to stand for them, too? Or are you saying you'll stand for Sylvie because I'm sitting right here?"

"They all matter, Mabel," he said quietly. "One case might have brought me out here, but it's one case with dozens of faces. And before you lump everyone in this office into the same negligent bunch of ass-covering kiss-ups, I can assure you, there are others here who feel the same way I do."

She shook her head.

"You don't believe me."

"No. You lost me on that one. Eight years of runaround make it hard to believe." She stood, pushed the chair back, and held out her head. "It's taken almost two months to get you here, so yes, I'm a skeptic. But like you said, feel free to prove me wrong." Her phone rang, and she jumped.

Paul raised an inquiring eyebrow. "Is that the theme for the Red Wedding?"

"Yeah." She leaned down, picked up her purse, and grabbed her phone.

"Wouldn't have pegged you as a Game of Thrones fan."

She flashed a tight smile. "That episode struck a chord."

"Sums up your ideas about marriage?" he challenged.

"More about men in general. And betrayal. Excuse me." She stood, frowning. "I need to take this."

"Sure. I'll just—" he pointed to the side counter where his coffee machine sat.

She answered the number from St. Marcus Hospital. "Mabel Reynolds."

"Mabel, hey—it's Alicia Florendo over at St. Marcus Hospital. I heard you called about an update on Eva Hudson."

"I did, yes," Mabel assured the senior floor nurse. "Is she ready to make an official statement?" She glanced over her shoulder. Either Paul Flynn was really good at surreptitiously eavesdropping, or he wasn't even attempting to listen in.

"She's ready to talk. To you, at least," Alicia confirmed. "The detective who caught her case stopped by earlier, but that didn't go well. On either side. He opened a file at least, so it's a start."

"She remembers me?" That was good yet unexpected news.

"She does," Alicia said. "She's sleeping right now, but—"

Mabel turned her back on Paul, stepped further into the corner, and lowered her voice. She checked her watch. "I've got a couple of stops to make first, but I can be there in a couple of hours?"

"I'll let her know," Alicia lowered her voice. "She's still shaky, but I think she's showing some spark. I'm hoping seeing you will help."

"I hope so, too." Mabel ducked her head, felt a headache pinging against her temple. "Thanks for calling me back."

"No problem." Alicia seemed to breathe a sigh of relief. "Don't know what we'd do without you, Mabel. You're a soul saver."

Mabel didn't know about that. How could she be a soul saver when she'd lost the one soul that had mattered to her the most? "See you soon." She turned around, reached for her bag that she'd set on the floor. "I'm sorry. I need to go."

"I heard. Here." He retrieved a card from his desk, scribbled on the back of it before he handed it over. "My number, including my cell for off-hours. You want to talk to me about the case or any-thing—the phone's never off."

She stared at the card, then up at him. Back to the card. How was she supposed to feel about this? Other than confused—and oddly thrilled, which was completely inappropriate, wasn't it?

"Do you mind me asking?" He didn't strike her as the kind of man often at a loss for words, but he paused, nonetheless. "What is it you do exactly?"

Mabel shoved her phone and his card into her bag. "By pro-fession, I'm a small-business record keeper and tax preparer. But if you're asking in regards to that call, I also volunteer as a rape and abuse advocate on behalf of Soteria."

"The women's shelter."

"You know it?" She didn't want to be impressed, but she was. He'd only just returned to the city.

"I do, yes." The flash in his eyes raised questions in her own mind. "I can't imagine doing what you do," Paul said as she gathered her purse and slung it over her shoulder.

"My best advice? Don't try to." She focused her gaze and intensi-ty directly on him. "I'm not going away. I mean, I *am* going now, but this"—she waved a hand between the two of them— "this conver-sation, this advance truce you're attempting to establish .... I do ap-preciate the effort, but don't for a second think you have placated me one iota. And just to make things clear," she said as she stepped close to him while he straightened to his full height, "if I think for *one* second you're dropping the ball or turning a blind eye to anything involved with this case, I won't just stalk you." She took one step closer. The heat of his body radiated against hers. "I will haunt you."

Just like my sister haunts me.

Those light blue eyes of his darkened as if storm clouds had de-scended. He leaned down toward her, and one corner of his mouth twitched as if resisting a smile. "I don't think that's the threat you intended." He lifted a hand to her face, trailed a solitary finger down her cheek until he seemed to realize what he'd done. He drew his hand away, clenched his fist.

Before she had time to process that, he shook his head a bit, as if attempting to clear his thoughts. "I want to make this right, Mabel. I intend to make this right."

"There's only one way you can do that." She resisted the urge to shiver beneath his touch. "Find out what happened to my sister."

CHAPTER FIVE

PAUL wasn't a man often taken off guard. He definitely wasn't the kind of man who spoke without thinking. He aired on the side of caution, especially with words, if only because he understood the damage the wrong words could do.

Being prepared for anything was how he'd reached the age of thirty-eight. He spent an inordinate amount of time making sure he was always, *always* ready for whatever the universe threw in front of him: education opportunities, job offers, tricky defense lawyers. His father's fists.

Being un-surpriseable (was that even a word?) had, on more than one occasion, saved, if not his life, certainly his sanity.

But all that was before Mabel Reynolds.

He had completely underestimated the power of one determined, angry, gorgeous woman. Not just any woman. The twin sister of one of his assigned victims.

A beautiful sister of one of his victims.

And it wasn't just anger he picked up on but a deep-seated thirst for vengeance he'd bet had no bottom.

He'd felt the fury wafting off her in waves big enough to shut down the Santa Monica Pier. It was the kind of sensation that left him feeling both sympathetic and determined to help her rid herself of it. He wanted to attempt to heal her emotional wounds. Or at the very least, start to stitch them back together.

He flexed his hands, as if he could dislodge the sparks he'd felt the instant he'd touched her. The last time he'd felt this shaken, his professional life had begun to fall apart. No—no, no, no. This was *not* going to happen. He'd already broken one of his personal promises.

He had no intention of breaking another.

Paul walked back around his desk and took a seat, his gaze caught by the solitary cupcake sitting in front of his computer screen. He reached out, dipped his finger into the creamy frosting, and took a taste. His tastebuds grabbed hold of the sugar almost immediately as the earthy chocolate danced on his tongue.

He could almost hear Mabel's laughter—a sound he had to imagine as he hadn't quite been able to make her laugh. He suspected he'd prefer that sound to the howling cries that had followed him out of the Tenado estate.

The very idea of her laughter instantly brought to mind her face: those wildly determined eyes and a smile that almost made him forget anything other than Mabel Reynolds existed.

"Okay, that just won't do at all," he muttered to himself before calling for his assistant. "Kent!"

His assistant appeared in the doorway almost instantly. "Sir?"

This feeling of being off-kilter, that one woman had the power to shove him off balance to the point he couldn't quite decide which way to go, was not something he intended to get used to. "Two things."

"Yes, sir." Kent practically shot to attention.

"Make that three," Paul said. "First, relax. This isn't a military academy, and I'm not your superior officer."

Kent tilted his head. "Well, actually, sir—"

"Second." Paul stood back up and stepped around his desk, unable to ignore the floral scent left by Mabel's perfume. He blew out a breath. This might end up being more difficult than he thought. "I'd like you to build a file for me on Mabel Reynolds. Everything you can find. Nothing is too small to note."

"Yes, sir." Kent nodded. "And third?"

And third.

71

Paul rested his hands on his hips, looked at her now vacant chair. "Anytime Ms. Reynolds calls, I want you to put her through. Open-door policy from here on."

"But—"

"If she comes to the building, I want her to be cleared to come up."

"Ah, sir, the District Attorney—"

"Doesn't want to deal with her. And she won't have to," Paul said. "I will. This is my case now. Mabel Reynolds is my problem. Understood?"

"Yes, sir." Kent didn't look entirely convinced.

"Do *you* have a problem, Kent?"

"No, sir. I'll call Charlie down in security right now. And I'll get that report going."

"Great. Thanks. Oh, and you can put that call through to the DA," he said after Kent turned to leave.

"Yes, sir. I'll get her on the phone right now." Kent closed the door behind him.

Paul sighed. They were going to have work on this *sir* thing. He knew it was the professional thing to do, but every time he heard it ….

His head was beginning to feel like an old-fashioned Etch-a-sketch with the number of thoughts he kept trying to erase from his mind. Didn't matter how much he tried, however. All his thoughts—both impressive and inappropriate—about Mabel weren't going anywhere.

And neither, it seemed, he reminded himself as he grabbed a stack of file folders and set them on his desk, was she.

"This is what you get for being late."

Mabel circled up and around the next floor of the public parking lot, irritated she'd let the afternoon get away from her. Normally, the lot located only a block away from St. Marcus Hospital was relatively empty, but with the storm that moved in the second she'd left the DA's office, clearly, people had abandoned street parking and instead made her afternoon more frustrating by taking every single space on the first three floors.

"Here's hoping level four is ... ah, finally!" She swung the mini-van into the first empty space she found.

A glance at her watch had her pulse kicking up. She'd seriously underestimated the stops she had to make on the way. Or rather, she'd somehow forgotten just how crappy downtown LA's traffic could be, especially when attempting to make your way across the city.

She climbed out of the car and popped open the back door to retrieve her bag from where it hung against the back of her seat. She could smell the rain, the damp cement, and the wafting aroma of cigarette smoke mingling in the gasoline-tainted air. Car keychain in hand, she quickly locked up and tugged the collar of her jacket close as she headed to the metal staircase near the bank of elevators across the way.

She'd managed to complete three out of the five tax meetings she'd scheduled for the day with her small-business clients. If she was lucky, she could squeeze in the other two before heading home. "Shoot. Need to stop at the grocery store." On Mondays, she and Keeley cooked dinner together, or rather *attempted* to as Mabel spent most of the time praying whatever they fixed was edible.

Pasta, she told herself. Pasta made the most sense at it was fairly impossible to screw up. Most of the time.

She grabbed hold of the stair railing before she thought about it, making a mental note to dig for her hand sanitizer once she hit the ground floor. Above her, footsteps sounded on the metal treads. She rounded the landing, heading down, whipping around the corners.

The footsteps above her got faster. She looked behind her, glanced up and nearly tripped on the next step as her head spun. Damned vertigo. Most people only had a problem when they looked down from heights, but not Mabel. Oh, no. She was just special enough to have issues looking up at anything more than a couple stories high.

The footsteps stopped.

"Hello?" Mabel's hand tightened around the railing, and she squeezed her eyes shut.

The stairwell was silent.

Telling herself not to panic, that she was just tired and imagining things, Mabel increased her speed, the soles of her boots slipping and twisting as her jacket snapped behind her. She yanked open the door, hurried out, and raced toward the exit to the sidewalk straight ahead.

Chin up, hand clutching her jacket closed at her throat, she didn't breathe easy until raindrops spattered her face.

A hand landed on her shoulder and spun her around.

Mabel yelped, keys still in hand. She brought her arm up and down, dislodging his hold as she shoved the neon plastic cylinder containing pepper spray into his face. "Back off!"

The man stepped back, held up both hands, shoved his hood off his head. He was taller than her, had a paler complexion, and was quite a bit younger. "I need your help. You're Mabel Reynolds, aren't you?"

Like she was going to confirm anything this guy asked. "Who are you?"

"I'm a friend of Eva's." There was a defiance in his voice, a tone she couldn't quite reconcile with helplessness.

"Eva who?"

"Please." His eyes glittered with desperation. "I know you're working with her. I just want to see her. They won't let me up."

She didn't respond. What was there to say? She wasn't about to acknowledge even knowing Eva, and she certainly wasn't going to give a perfect stranger any information. For all she knew, he could be the person responsible for her injuries. "What makes you think I—"

"I heard a couple of the nurses talking while they were on a coffee break. They mentioned your name and where you work." The rain cascaded down, drenching them both, making him hard to hear as he spoke. "I looked you up online, and I've been waiting to talk to you. You need to help me." Desperation that fierce rarely revealed anything positive. His eyes were wide, his breathing erratic, and he was jumpier than a flea at a dog show. "Please. They're going to—" He glanced behind him as a car sped past.

"What's your name?" Mabel demanded.

He hesitated, as if her question caught him off guard. "Leo."

"Leo what?"

"Leo Capallini. I—"

"How do you know Eva?" There was only one thing on her mind, and that was protecting her charge.

"I—" His gaze hardened. He inclined his head. "You aren't going to help me, are you?"

"No." Mabel's fingers were going numb from the cold. She lowered her arm, kept her finger on the trigger just to be safe. "I'm not."

He shifted, and for an instant, she expected him to lunge at her, but instead, he pulled his arms in around his waist, his legs snapping together like a turtle withdrawing into his shell. "Will you tell her I was here?"

Oh, *that* she'd do. If only to confirm Leo here was responsible for Eva being in the hospital in the first place. Eva's reaction to his name would do that.

"Will you?" he yelled as the rain fell harder. "Just … tell her. Please." Grief clouded his eyes. "Tell her I'm sorry. I didn't know. I … I didn't know what they were going to …"

"Didn't know … what?" she yelled after him as he turned and raced away, looking cautiously before he crossed the street and hurried away. She stared after him as he disappeared into the gray gloom of the afternoon.

A couple wrapped around each other passed by when she turned around. In the distance, she could see the bright lights of the hospital entrance. Not that it gave her much comfort. The adrenaline coursing through her system abated, leaving behind the familiar nausea rolling in her stomach. Mabel shoved her hands into her jacket pockets, ducked her head, and resumed her path, her sopping boots slopping through ankle-deep puddles.

She didn't breathe easy until she was inside. Water plumed off her jacket as she stepped to the side of the entry, ran a hand through her drenched hair, and resisted the urge to shake herself like Barksy when he emerged from a summer ocean dip. Her chilly feet squished in her boots as she made her way down the wide tiled hallway toward the bank of elevators and emergency staircase. She took the climb at a quick pace and by the time she reached the third floor was reminded that the Saturday morning yoga classes weren't cutting it in the physical fitness department.

Her heart was racing when she stopped at the landing door and finally released the death grip she had on her pepper spray.

Once she breathed easier, she opened the door, righted herself, and plastered on the mask of control she'd found herself donning more difficultly these days.

By the time she reached the nurses' station, whatever shaking she was doing could easily be attributed to the cold rain.

"I'm Mabel Reynolds from Soteria," she said to the unfamiliar redhead behind the desk. "Is Alicia around? I'm here to visit Eva Hudson."

"Oh, Mabel, yes—hi! It's good to meet you." The young woman's badge identified her as Erin, student nurse, which meant she had yet to pass her licensing exam, so she was shiny new off the training-room floor. "I'll let Alicia know—" Her phone rang, and she heaved out an I-don't-know-if-I-can-handle-this sigh. "I'm so sorry. I need to—"

"Of course," Mabel assured her and set her bag down to shrug out of her jacket.

This was the third time in as many days as she'd been here. She'd be surprised if there was any new information since her last visit; although, she was keeping the name Leo Capallini in the forefront of her thoughts.

She knew what the responding patrol officers knew. That Eva Hudson had been at a party; she hadn't said where or with whom. The last thing the young woman remembered was an older man who had bought her a drink and …. From there, the nightmare had begun. "Is Eva still in room two eleven?" she asked Erin when she hung up.

"Yes, that's right," Erin confirmed. "I'll page Alicia."

"Thanks." Mabel flashed an appreciative smile before dodging her way among nurses, orderlies, and tech and medicine carts. Echoes of beeping and monitors chiming added a familiarity Mabel had gotten used to years before.

St. Marcus was one of the smaller hospitals out of the nearly eighty facilities in the city, and with its beige, water-stained walls, somewhat threadbare blue curtains, and yellowed tiled floors, it was showing its age. It needed a good dose of the TLC its staff provided without hesitation.

With the greater Los Angeles area boasting more than ten million residents, resources, especially medical ones, were stretched to the limits. But what St. Marcus lacked in aesthetics with its drab décor and smaller-than-normal patient bays, it surpassed some of the more state-of-the-art hospitals with its dedicated staff of doctors and nurses.

While a lot of Mabel's calls came through Soteria's sexual assault line, she remained on call for notifications and requests coming in personally from ER nurses and attendants she'd become friendly with over the years. Whenever her name went up in the nurse's break room as a point of contact, Mabel considered it a badge of honor. And a step in the right direction as far as dealing with, for want of a better word, survivors.

"Oh, I'm sorry, Doctor." Distracted, Mabel didn't see him until she'd all but bashed into the turquoise scrub-clad man. He wore a dark blue cap pulled down low on his forehead, and a disposable mask covered the bottom half of his face. There was no obscuring his stony expression when he looked at Mabel.

"I'm Mabel Reynolds." She held out her hand, which he stared at before accepting it. Her nose twitched. There was something odd, something spicy and fragrant in the air rising above the disinfectant. "I'm a counselor and advocate with Soteria. How is she? Eva," she clarified at his blank look.

"She'll be fine. Won't you, Eva?" He turned, his heavy shoes squeaking against the polished floor. Only then did Mabel notice Eva's deer-in-the-headlight's stare from her bed. Her heart monitor beeped at a concerning, frenetic rate, the small-framed, frail-appearing woman all but swallowed whole by the pile of blankets on top of her.

"How are you doing, Eva?" Mabel stepped around the doctor, walked slowly to the young woman lying shaking in the high-railed bed. The terror in her eyes was as stark and gutting as it had been the last time she'd visited. Eva looked from Mabel to the doctor who, when Mabel glanced back, was no longer there.

Mabel shivered, the hair on the back of her neck prickling even as she kept her voice calm and soothing. "Alicia let me know you wanted to talk to me. Sorry I'm late." She set her bag down on the floor beside the chair and carefully plied herself out of her jacket, which she hung on one of the hooks by the window. "The rain took me a little by surprise."

"Where's your umbrella?" Eva's slow-motion question came out from between gritted teeth that had been wired together during the reconstructive surgery for her jaw.

Mabel chuckled. "I'm umbrella challenged," she admitted. "Seriously, I've gone through dozens of them. Finally gave up and decided getting wet wasn't so bad."

Eva looked as if she wanted to smile, but that might have been Mabel's optimism shining through the dreary day. She scrubbed her palms on her damp jeans, wishing there was a faster way to warm her numb fingers.

"You look a little better than the last time I saw you." It was a lie, one Mabel had uttered so often it had become routine now. In the few days since Eva had been admitted, the bruises had taken form, the abrasions had intensified, and the new normal of Eva's life had settled in. "I'm glad you remembered me. I wasn't sure you would."

"I remember." Her long blonde hair wasn't streaked and matted with blood any longer, but the bandages covering nearly half her swollen and bruised face spoke of the surgery she'd undergone. Eva winced as if Mabel's words physically hurt.

The slightly dazed fog in her blue eye—the only one that showed—seemed clearer than before now that the drugs she'd been given by her attacker had worn off. Now she was just flying on the painkillers dripping out of the bag hanging off the pole at the head of the bed. Even with the brutal, physical injuries that escaped the stalwart attempts at treatment, Mabel knew they paled in comparison to the yet-to-be-determined damage done to Eva's soul.

The damage was there, reflected in the dimmed blue eye that continually scanned the room. The monitors' beeping slowed enough to be noticed, but the numbers had, at least, finally, dropped into the safe range.

Right now, there was no use in attempting, even in a small way, to convince Eva that while she'd been beaten and violated, she hadn't been defeated. It didn't feel like it now, but she was alive, even if it was by a miracle thread.

Mabel pulled the cushioned chair over beside the bed and sat down. "I met your friend Leo a little while ago." Eva's gaze flitted back to the door, but she didn't react. While there wasn't excitement or anticipation on her face, there was no fear, either. Mabel breathed a bit easier. He hadn't put her in here. "He wanted to come up and see you, but I told him you couldn't have visitors yet."

Eva's brow furrowed, but that was the only response she gave, which told Mabel Leo wasn't anyone she was particularly afraid of. "So, what would you like to talk about?"

"I—" Eva blinked, shook her head, and curled up on her side, facing away from Mabel. "I changed my mind." Her voice came out a broken whisper. "I don't want to talk anymore."

"Anything you have to say is important," Mabel assured her as alarm bells rang in her mind. "If you're worried about your privacy, everything you tell me will remain between us. I'm your advocate, Eva. I don't work for anyone other than you. You understand that, right?"

No response. The mothering instinct Mabel possessed had to be set aside. Her desire to reach out, to touch, to soothe, to reassure— that was all an attempt to ease her own inner turmoil and discomfort, not Eva's. The last thing Eva wanted right now was to be touched.

"I can't. I don't want to talk," Eva whispered again.

"All right." Disappointment crashed through her but not surprise. Every person she dealt with had to take things in their own time. "I'm glad you agreed to the sexual assault exam."

Eva shrugged. "Doesn't change anything."

"No," Mabel agreed, stunned she still had enough of a heart left to break. "It won't change what happened to you, Eva. Nothing can. But it can change everything that happens from here."

Eva stared at the wall.

"I'm not here to talk you into doing anything you don't want to do." Mabel's primary intention was to be a source of calm for Eva. Calm, reassurance, and, most importantly, safety. "What I can tell you is having this test and exam done can only be to your benefit. That's all I'm going to say on the matter. What I am going to do, if you want me to, is help you navigate everything that happens from here on. Do you remember being told about the organization I work for? Soteria?"

Eva nodded.

"Is that someplace you think you might want to go?"

"I don't know." Eva hesitated, the uncertainty in her eyes all too familiar. "Does it mean I have to talk—?"

"It doesn't mean anything other than it will be someplace safe for you to go. No requirements. You can stay there as long as you need and figure out what comes next."

"Nothing comes next."

"I imagine it feels that way." Needing to broach another subject, Mabel sat back in her chair. "I understand you're from Idaho. Is your family back there? Would you like to call someone, maybe? Or a friend or sibling?" She looked down at Eva's hand clutching her blanket. No ring. No sign she'd worn one. Chances were, she wasn't married. "How about a boyfriend?"

"I don't have a boyfriend. I never—" A tear trickled down her bruised cheek as the panic returned. She struggled to sit up, turned over, and flailed against the IV line and monitor cord. Her vitals skyrocketed, and alarms went off. "I don't want anyone to know. Don't call my parents, please." She grabbed Mabel's arm when Mabel attempted to settle her back. "Please, I can't—"

"Shhh." Now Mabel surrendered to that urge to soothe by covering her hand with hers. "I told you I won't do anything you don't want. One step at a time, yeah?"

Eva turned her hand over, slipped her fingers through Mabel's, and hung on. "Is Soteria safe?"

"Yes." Mabel felt the tension in her chest ease. "They have private security, and no one can get in without approval. I can call over and make sure they set up a room for you. What about your things? Can I get them for you?"

"I—I don't know." Eva hesitated. "I don't know what to do." Despite the anger and the fear, she turned a pleading expression on Mabel that had her reaching for a chair. "It wasn't supposed to be this way. He told me …"

He who, Mabel wondered. *He told you what?*

Mabel wanted to ask, but it was evident by the suddenly stony expression on her face that she didn't want to complete the thought.

"Okay," Mabel assured her. "How about we talk about what makes you feel safe. Do you feel safe where you live?"

Eva nodded but also shrugged. "It's just a rented room. But my landlady's nice. She's older. Makes me hot chocolate at night." Tears pooled again. Every word she uttered sounded as if it took effort. "I don't know if I can go back there. All the questions. I don't think I—"

"It's okay." Mabel squeezed her hand. "You don't have to."

"What about my job?" She hiccupped and lifted a hand to her face. "I can't work like this."

"I can talk to your boss," Mabel offered, recalling Eva had been working as a cocktail waitress in a Los Angeles club.

"No." Eva shook her head and whimpered as she forced herself to lie still. "No. You can't. I can't go back. I don't want to."

"Then you don't have to." Every alarm bell in Mabel's head was blaring.

"I want to go home." Her lips trembled. "I want my mom and dad. But they can't see me like this. Not yet. I don't want them to know what happened." Every breath she took seemed to be forced. "How do I go home and not tell them?"

Mabel hoped that would change—that Eva would one day feel strong enough to tell the people who loved her most what had happened. "That's not something you need to worry about right now, Eva. How does this sound? They're going to keep you here for at least another few days. When you're discharged, you can go straight to Soteria. I'll make sure your things are waiting for you. You'll have your own room, and you can stay as long as you like or need."

"Y-you'd do that?" The doubt in her voice was almost as stark as the fear on her face. "You'd get my things?"

"Of course." Mabel offered her other hand and felt a bit of triumph when Eva grabbed hold. "It's what I'm here for. To make things easier for you when I can."

"My bag …" Eva gave Mabel her address, pointed at the small, sequined, fabric purse slumped on the top of the nightstand. "My key's in there. My landlady is going to be worried about me." She added after adding a phone number that Mabel scribbled in her day planner. "Would you tell her I'm okay? But—"

"I won't tell her what happened." Mabel reached over for the bag, pried open the strings, and dug inside for the key. The only thing inside was a water-logged Idaho driver's license. "No phone?"

"Must have lost it," Eva whispered brokenly.

"Okay." Internally, she cursed. The police could have tracked her cell's location throughout the night she was attacked. They could request the information from the cell company, but that could take weeks, if not months, to obtain legally. "Okay, is there anything in particular you'd like with you now? Pictures, maybe?"

"There's a stuffed rabbit," Eva whispered. "On my bed. I've had him since I was little. Would you mind bringing him the next time you come? I know it sounds stupid—"

"It's not stupid at all," Mabel said firmly and squeezed her hand. "Does he have a name? Your rabbit?" Mabel lightened her voice. "My daughter has this purple octopus she won at a school fair a couple of years ago. It goes almost everywhere with her. She named him Lord Squidly."

Eva actually smiled, giving Mabel the first indication of how she'd been pre-attack. "Benedict Cumberbunny." Horror rose in her face again and she started to curl up. "I'm so stupid."

"Eva, stop." Mabel's already bruised heart ached. "You're not—"

"I never should have gotten involved," she sobbed. "This is all my fault."

"You are not stupid." Mabel leaned down, looked at the young woman directly. "None of this—absolutely none of it—is your fault. The only person responsible for what happened to you is the person who attacked you. Them. Not you."

"They were so nice to me before," Eva whispered. "They had me going to these amazing parties, and they gave me these beautiful dresses."

"Is that where you met Leo? At these parties?"

Lana's eye drooped as if she was getting sleepy. "He said they'd take my picture. Introduce me to agents," Eva whispered brokenly before the sobs began, and any impulse Mabel had to push evaporated. "I was going to be a star. It was all lies. He hurt me. He hurt me so bad."

He.

It was all Mabel could do not to pounce on her confession, to ask who *he was*, but now wasn't the time. Was it possible Eva had been targeted by the Circle? Then she shook her head—not every case had to do with the Circle. She was projecting her sister's case onto Eva's.

She didn't say a word. She simply sat there, holding Eva's hand, as she cried out her anguish and pain, pinning her tear-filled gaze to the beeping monitors.

"Everything okay here?" Mabel glanced and found floor nurse Alicia Florendo standing in the doorway. Her straight black hair was cropped close to her round face, her dark eyes accentuated by the smattering of freckles across her nose—a showcase of her Filipino and Irish heritage.

Alicia was the kind of nurse who always went *beyond* the extra mile, right down to her becoming conversant in Spanish in order to better serve the patients in her community. She turned her compassionate gaze on her patient. "Eva?"

"I'm fine." Eva lifted her gaze to Mabel, the plea crystal clear to Mabel's broken heart.

She squeezed Eva's hand once more. "You get some rest. I'll see you soon, okay?"

"Yeah."

She was asleep before Mabel could gather her things. Regret pinged against anger and more than a little fear. Cases like this were excruciating for so many reasons, but inevitably, when Mabel walked away, she couldn't help but wonder what Sylvie had gone through. If she'd been hurt or beaten or raped or …

She'd been alone.

Mabel touched a finger to her pendant.

Sylvie had been alone.

It was that certainty, that knowledge, more than anything, that had Mabel picking up the phone each and every time it rang. Every one of them was potentially another Sylvie.

"Eva's lab results came in," Alicia said as Mabel joined her in the hall. "I can't give you specifics, but she was drugged. Heavily. Weird combination of narcotics—one of the reasons we're going to keep her longer. Her heart rate is still irregular." She closed the door to Eva's room and motioned for Mabel to follow her down the hall to the break room. "Looking at the levels, I'd bet they didn't expect her to wake up."

Out of the corner of her eye, Mabel spotted an anemic, silver tinsel garland hanging in the corner above the coffee station. Mabel had never related more to sagging, overstretched décor in her life.

It was hard to believe they were two months into the new year. This was meant to be a time of hope and promise and new beginnings, and yet …

"Any update on her case from the police?" Mabel asked.

"Not yet, no," Alicia said. "But I'm sure we'll hear something soon."

"Right, sure." Mabel nodded even though she wouldn't believe it until she saw actual evidence. Her smile was quick, almost cursory, and not close to genuine. "Sorry I'm cranky. It's been a weird day." And it was still weird. The only thing unnerving her more than her encounter with Leo Capallini was the afterburn of her meeting with Paul Flynn.

What in the world was that man still doing in her head?

It made total sense she'd still be thinking about their conversation, but the idea that the man himself had left her completely knocked off-kilter wasn't sitting well. She shouldn't be thinking about that smile of his or the way he'd spoken of Sylvie as if Mabel's sister actually mattered to him. She wanted to believe him. More than she'd wanted anything in a very long time.

Almost as much as she wanted …

"I know that look." Alicia's grin tugged a smile out of Mabel. "That's a man-on-my-mind smile."

Oh. God. "It most definitely is *not*. It's a …" Mabel's mind raced, "counting-my-blessings smile." Something she frequently did whenever she thought about her friends at Temple House.

She'd hit the jackpot when she'd moved, not only because of a fabulous living space for her and Keeley but due to the family she'd found. Family that often stepped in when Mabel came up emotionally short where her daughter was concerned. Riley, Sutton, Cass, and Laurel had picked up the slack, spoiling her little girl as if she was their own, showering her with the most important things any child needed: time, affection, and attention.

And so, so, *so* much sugar.

"You look like you could use a pick-me-up," Alicia said. "How about some coffee?" She knocked her knuckles on the top of one of the tables as she passed and motioned for Mabel to sit.

"Sure."

At this point, caffeine couldn't do much damage. Mabel couldn't recall the last day she hadn't had a headache, but that was probably due to her constant teeth grinding and jaw clenching. She just felt so exhausted, and at times, the effort it took to smile was overwhelming. Depression wasn't new, but its ups and downs certainly felt harsher of late, but that could easily be the result of the holiday season, which was always difficult for Mabel.

After murmured greetings and nods to other nurses heading back on shift, Mabel lowered herself into one of the empty chairs at the chipped Formica table. Resting her chin in her hand, she frowned. "What is it with these coffee machines that look like you need an engineering degree from CalTech to make it work?"

Dammit! There he was again. Paul Flynn in full technicolor, blasting through her thoughts again.

She closed her eyes but only managed to make her toes tingle again even as an odd sliver of hope slipped through the darkness, squeezing her heart.

Alicia popped off the top, worked some kind of magic, and soon had it brewing and bubbling productively.

"I don't suppose whoever called 9-1-1 about Eva hung around to give a statement?" Mabel asked.

Alicia's "oh please" expression only added to Mabel's mood. She frowned, watching Alicia grab a step stool and climb it to reach into one of the top shelves of the weathered blue cabinet overhead. "What on earth—?"

Alicia pulled out a rectangular metal container, held it over her head as if showing off a first-place trophy. "The last of my mother's fudge. Saving it for a special occasion." She climbed back down, pried off the lid, and set it on the table with a clang. "Grab a piece fast. My fellow nurses have been known to come to blows over the last piece. And they can smell it from the desk."

Stomach growling, Mabel plucked up a square of triple-layered sugary goodness and bit in. The flavors of chocolate, caramel and—if she wasn't mistaken—a generous hit of bourbon hit her tongue.

"I think this might be eighty-proof," Mabel joked and reached for a second piece. Sipping on the coffee that appeared in front of her moments later had bits of her settling even as the sugar zinged through her system. "Thanks. I needed this. You going anywhere special for your time off?"

Mabel couldn't recall the last time she'd had anything close to a vacation. All the more reason to live vicariously through her friend.

"We're renting a house in Santa Barbara. Just far enough away to clear our heads," Alicia said with an anticipatory smile that told Mabel she was already halfway out of town. "Close enough for family to join us."

"Well, before you leave, is there anything else can you tell me?" Mabel attempted to keep Alicia's focus off of her own personal life. "About Eva? On the night she was brought in?" She'd spent most of her time at the hospital with Eva in her room, which meant asking for details wasn't appropriate or possible. Now, having the chance to speak privately with Alicia, who had been working a fill-in shift in the ER the night Eva had been brought in, offered her the opportunity she'd been waiting for.

"Nothing I haven't told you already." Alicia said as she took a seat across from Mabel after their coffee brewed.

"How extensive are her injuries?"

"Mabel." Alicia shook her head. "You don't want—"

"She won't talk to anyone else. Someone should know exactly what she's going through."

"Why does that someone always have to be you?" Alicia challenged in a gentle but disapproving tone. "You've seen her multiple times now, Mabel. You know what her injuries are. You don't need them spelled out."

"Did you get pictures? Of all the bruises and abrasions?"

"We did," Alicia assured her. "And we'll take some more again before she's discharged. I asked the detective to send over copies to include in her medical file, but—"

"I can't access that information without her permission." Mabel knew the routine and the restrictions due to HIPAA, the medical privacy and protection law. "At least the doctor I ran into earlier said she'd be fine." Mabel murmured. "That was good to hear."

"Dr. Chen was by?" Alicia asked with a frown. "I thought she was in surgery for the rest of the day."

"She?" The fudge caught in Mabel's throat. "No, this doctor was a man. I didn't get his name." Come to think of it, she hadn't seen him wearing a badge, either. "It's funny. I remember thinking his shoes were odd." Heavy hiking boots, not the soft-soled footwear medical professionals typically wore.

Alicia frowned then shrugged. "Maybe the wires got crossed and Dr. Chen requested a consult. I'll check her chart and see what notations he made. Needless to say, Eva's got a long road ahead of her." Alicia shook her head. "She agreed to move into Soteria?"

"Yeah." Mabel checked her watch, making a mental note to have time to get to Eva's landlady's house. "What about the EMTs? Did they say anything beyond how chaotic the scene was?"

"Like what exactly?"

"I don't know." She wasn't an investigator. She didn't have Riley's bottomless curiosity and open mind when it came to mysteries or Quinn's training on how to investigate anything. She didn't see crimes in the analytical way Cassia did or the straightforward way Laurel, an attorney, did.

She could only piece together the emotional bits and pieces she'd come across, like where Eva had been found, in a remote area near the Hollywood reservoir hiking trail. "Was anyone around when they got there? The police should look into traffic cameras in the area. Did—"

"Mabel." Alicia reached across the table and grabbed her flailing hand. "Honey, the police know what to do. What's going on? You're all over the place tonight. You never ask these kinds of questions. Where's your head?"

She tried to laugh off her friend's concern even as she felt herself turn a corner she'd been avoiding for months. "Sorry. You're right. I don't need to know any of that. It's Eva I need to focus on."

"Or yourself." Alicia let her go, but the concern in her eyes didn't fade. "How's Keeley doing?"

"She's good." Better than Mabel was, anyway. And just the mention of her daughter took the sharp edges off her spiraling thoughts. "She took first place in the science fair, so now she's all excited about getting into this special STEM program at the Academy this summer." Pride seeped in and overtook the despair. All Mabel had to do was come up with the money to pay for it. Which meant she needed to get her butt in gear and meet with the rest of her tax clients. "The other day, she was showing me these fancy dresses she likes. Fancy dresses? She's too young!"

"She'll be nine next month," Alicia reminded her.

"Nine, not nineteen." At some point, time was going to slow down, right? It had to, but Mabel couldn't help but think Keeley's birthdays were circling around faster every year. "I thought I'd have at least another three, maybe four years before I'd need to start worrying about fancy dresses." She could only hope it stopped there for a bit. She wasn't nearly ready to go shopping for kitten heels and make-up kits.

"At least she hasn't broken her arm jumping off the roof because she thought she was Iron Man," Alicia teased, her face lighting up at the mere thought of her two sons. "Or lost a tooth after falling down while chasing down our chickens. Believe me, the Tooth Fairy was not happy about that pick-up. Trust me when I say no stain remover can attack chicken poop effectively."

Mabel laughed, but even to hear own ears, it sounded hollow. The sugar from the fudge didn't do much to charge her system, which gave her the excuse to eat another piece and slug down half her coffee.

"She has a stuffed rabbit." The comment slipped out before she could think it through. "Eva. The rabbit's name is Benedict Cumberbunny." Tears burned the back of Mabel's throat. "Jesus, Alicia. She has a stuffed bunny on her bed."

The grief twisted hard inside of her, around anger and helplessness and a hopelessness she'd never wanted to feel.

"Hey." Alicia grabbed both her hands and squeezed. "Mabel. I think maybe you need to stop."

"I know." She sniffled, forced a laugh. "No crying in public, right?"

"That's not what I mean." Alicia waited for Mabel to look at her before she continued. "You need to start thinking about not working cases like this anymore. You've been showing up in ERs around the city for almost a decade. Day or night, no matter what, you take every call, you work with every victim. I'm really starting to worry about you."

"I have to do it," Mabel insisted. "I need to." There were too many victims and most of them without anyone to stand for them. Without anyone to stand beside them. Like Sylvie would have been had things gone differently.

"I'm just saying, maybe it's time you think about stepping back," Alicia offered. "There's other work you can do, other work that doesn't break your heart every time you walk out the door. You don't have to be boots-on-the-ground your entire life."

Except she did. Every time she took a call, it was as if she was being given a chance she'd missed with Sylvie. She could be of help, even just an ear to listen. How did she just walk away when there were people out there who needed her?

But she still nodded. Alicia was right, too. But not doing this work meant that out there, some woman or man or child could very well break. Or be lost forever. "I'll think about it."

"No, you won't." Alicia sighed and sat back. "But I said my piece. It's in your head now, so you won't have any choice but to think about it."

Mabel pulled out her phone. "I need to call Theresa and have her get a room ready for Eva for after she's discharged. Any idea when that might be?"

"Later this week. Thursday, probably Friday. Good to know she's accepting placement at Soteria. That'll make things easier," Alicia agreed, leaning over to read the notation in Mabel's day planner. "Mrs. Lancaster?"

"Eva's landlady. I'm going to go by and pick up her things, settle any rent issues."

"Mabel." Alicia's warning tone had Mabel flinching.

"It's something I can do to help," she said. "And yes, I know that's not in my job description. But it gets me the one thing Eva actually asked me for. Her bunny."

"If you say so," Alicia said, her voice clearly dismissive and disbelieving. "But forgive me if I say I hope it stops there."

CHAPTER SIX

"**YES,** Madam District Attorney." Paul pinched the bridge of his nose and rested his elbow on his desk. "I completely understand. Of course, Holland Young is a busy man." Any lawyer in Los Angeles would be. "I appreciate you considering requesting—"

"Young & Fairbanks is one of the most well-respected law firms not only in Los Angeles but in the entire country." DA Johanna Eichorn's voice carried the all-too-familiar combination of irritation and condescension. "I can't just call them up and ask for confidential information on one of their clients."

"One of their *deceased* clients," Paul argued. "Given your personal connection with Mr. Young, having the request come from you might carry significantly more weight." Sometimes he had to suck up so hard he felt like a freaking Roomba. "I was also trying to save some time—you're right. I'll file a report with the court and have a judge sign off and endorse the request. Since that's the case, I'd like to readdress my request for a dedicated investigative task force."

The silence that resulted told him he'd hit just the right buttons. Right now, the DA was weighing her options. If she asked the lawyer herself, she'd be stepping into the case she was desperately trying to remain detached from. But if she didn't and Paul did take his request to a judge, whether it was approved or not, word would leak that he was looking directly into Anthony Tenado, and that wouldn't win her any points with Mr. Young. Or his partner, Ms. Fairbanks.

"When I spoke with Jeff earlier this afternoon," DA Eichorn said slowly, "he intimated you had hit the ground running and had a plan of action already in mind. I take it this information you're requesting is part of that plan?"

"I have to start somewhere. If you have a better idea—"

"If I had a better idea, you'd still be in New York," the DA said. "The Tenado family is anxious to put this entire ordeal behind them. His children have been tormented with the press coverage and speculation. His mother is quite elderly and not doing well, and his children have been unable to get on with their lives. They shouldn't be going through this."

The children, a son and daughter ages thirty and twenty-six respectively, weren't exactly avoiding the spotlight. Word had it Tony Tenado Jr. was shopping the idea of a screenplay based on his father's suspected activities, while Gina Tenado had jumped on her brother's coattails in an effort to win a starring role. He really hated this town.

"The sooner we answer questions about their father," Paul said carefully, "the sooner all of us can move on."

It burned not to remind his new boss that there were sixty-seven other families, Mabel's included, who had been tormented for far longer than the Tenado offspring.

"Is there anything else Young & Fairbanks can do to facilitate the investigation?"

"I have no doubt I'll have questions for them in the future." Paul tried not to let his excitement get the better of him. "Just knowing their door is open and they're willing to cooperate would be enough at this time. In addition to the requested files on Anthony Tenado, of course."

"All right." DA Eichhorn sighed. "I'm having breakfast at the club tomorrow morning, and I usually see Holland there. I'll let you know how things go. Good night, Mr. Flynn."

"Good night, ma'am."

The second his phone hit the cradle, he felt the need for a decontamination shower. He'd kept himself out of the direct line of fire so far, at least where Tenado's lawyers were concerned. There'd be time enough for him to personally tick them off down the road.

An unfamiliar pressure weighed him down as he ran a finger over the edge of the folder Kent had set on his desk before Paul had put in a call to the DA. The file on Mabel felt like a distraction and a necessity. He'd been replaying portions of their conversation in his head all afternoon.

What was it Mabel had said? He might have been distracted by the few strands of blonde hair that had escaped the tight control of her ponytail. Or the way her hands fisted in frustration in a way that said she wasn't aware of it. *"There are sixty-six other women that we know of who will never come home to their families."*

That we know of. Odd phrasing, wasn't it? Not *I* know but *we*.

He double tapped his pencil.

Who exactly was this *we*?

Outside, the sun began its daily dip toward the horizon, casting both the city and Paul's office into shadows. The remnants of his deli sandwich sat half-eaten in the biodegradable take-out container on the corner of his desk. His long-gone cold coffee held no more appeal. Once four o'clock rolled around, he was ready for the one thing his office was not yet equipped with: Scotch.

Yeah. He scrubbed his hands down his face. He needed a drink.

"I can kill two birds with one stone on that one."

Paul logged into the LAPD employee and police directory. It didn't take him long to find the link to the Hollywood division. He picked his cell off his desk and dialed, leaning back in his chair as the other end rang.

"Burton, Homicide."

"Detective Burton." Paul swung his chair around and looked out the window into the darkening sky. "Paul Flynn. I've been brought in by the DA to work—"

"The Tenado estate case," Burton cut him off. "My partner and I bet on how long it would take you to call."

"Yeah?" He liked the man already. "You win?"

"Depends. Are you calling because you want to talk about the case, or is this about something else?"

"A little bit of both." First Mabel, now Burton. For a town filled with liars and pretenders, he'd somehow managed to find the rarest of things in LA: at least two people who had no trouble speaking truth. "You are on the top of my list to discuss the case, so I was wondering—"

"You want me to make an appointment?"

"No, actually." Paul glanced at the clock. "I was wondering if I could buy you a drink?"

"Not going to say no to that. You know the Formosa?"

"On Santa Monica? Sure." One of those places he'd always ridden past as a kid but had never had the courage—or bank account—to venture into. "How's six tonight?"

"Six thirty's better," Burton suggested. "Working on a report that's going to take a little extra mulling. I'll meet you in the bar."

Paul smiled. He hung up, and instantly, his attention was right back on Mabel Reynolds's file. Surrendering to temptation, he flipped open the cover and found her staring back at him. Even in her DMV photo, she had a bit of a haughty look about her, but having spoken to her, he suspected it was more of an "I've had it with bullshit" expression. She wasn't a woman who gave in easily or walked away from anything she felt was important. An admirable and appealing quality.

She struck him as practical, which he appreciated. He'd dated enough within the upper echelons of New York society to have at least a passing grasp of fashion forwardness. He knew designer labels. Valentino. Balenciaga. Jimmy Choo. La Perla. Hell, he had a closet back home filled with Tom Ford, Canali, and Brioni suits. He'd even packed his Armani tux because who didn't travel to Los Angeles without one?

He would bet all of those suits—and more—that the only designer anything Mabel Reynolds owned was that oversized Coach hobo bag that looked as if it had been through half a dozen fashion wars. If he had to guess, she spent more time perusing the local bookstore than the designer rack at Nordstrom or Saks Fifth Avenue. But she'd do both with a sexy little quirk of lips that, had he given into temptation and completely forgotten where they were, he'd come very close to kissing.

It unnerved him how completely unprofessional he'd been. He was a man who prided himself on planning every word he uttered, and yet he'd said something completely inappropriate almost from the start. It didn't make any sense. She wasn't remotely close to his type, and yet …

Mabel intrigued him. On every single level.

In an attempt to convince himself he wasn't entirely smitten, he skimmed the information Kent had collected. Mabel Constance Reynolds. Age thirty-two. Marital status: single.

His lips twitched.

He hadn't seen a ring—and he had looked—but good to know. Current residence, Temple House Apartments, a name that rang the bell of a distant, different life memory. Offspring, one daughter: Keeley Raye Reynolds, age eight. Interesting. The girl had Mabel's name, not her father's, who was clearly named on the birth certificate. Keeley was an honor roll student—they had honor rolls for eight-year-olds?—at Summercrest Academy, a small private school with a stellar reputation for its students. Extensive with its after-school programs and activities. And expensive. Not obscenely so, but it left his healthy bank account wincing in sympathy.

Paul frowned, ran his finger down the details. Keeley had been born only months before Mabel's sister was reported missing. Something twisted around his heart.

Anniversaries were tough, especially when entwined with celebratory events. Keeley's birthday was only a few weeks away, which meant another year will have gone by without giving Mabel answers about Sylvie. Nine years.

But instead of sinking into the grief, she continued to battle against it. One sunrise at a time.

The rest of the Mabel details paled by comparison, reiterating what he already knew about her work, both professional and volunteer. Her work with Soteria, particularly focusing on rape and assault victims, explained the thick skin and steely determination he'd picked up on. She'd no doubt seen things he couldn't conceive of, let alone face down.

He flipped to the next page, skimmed, and frowned harder before calling for Kent.

"Sir." Kent opened the door and stepped inside.

"I told you before, call me Paul."

"Yes, sir. Paul," Kent corrected himself. "I'm working on it. I'm compiling that list of detectives who worked any of the missing women's cases."

"Good idea. I'm going to need you to set that aside for a while, though."

"But—"

"I've used one goodwill request with the DA right out of the gate," Paul explained. "She won't sign off on a task force anytime soon." But she would. He'd already planted the seed. "Keep that list on the back burner for now. About these notes in the back of Mabel Reynolds's file …" Paul held up the last page. "Where did this information come from?"

"Ah, the notes. Right." Kent's smile flashed faster than a short-circuiting sparkplug. "My, um …. Sandra Chissim's a …. Well, she's a friend. And I knew she's been working in DA Eichorn's office as of late, so I gave her a call. I thought—"

"You thought gossip regarding Mabel's interactions with the DA might prove useful to me."

"Yes?" It was obvious by the doubt on his assistant's face Kent was having second thoughts about that now.

Paul focused on keeping his temper out of the situation. He was new to the office. He had no standing to lay claim to any behavior guidelines. Not yet, at least. It was something he might have included in a report himself if he saw the need. That said, he couldn't explain why this initiative rubbed him the wrong way, but it did.

"I consider gossip, for the most part, to be petty and typically useless. Not to mention that it has the propensity to include personal feelings that have nothing to do with actual information." He kept his tone measured and level. "For instance, I don't think the phrase 'overbearing, obnoxious, and bombastic' is particularly helpful."

He also considered it a trio of misnomers when put into the context of Mabel's experience and frustration. It certainly had no relation to the sudden shield of protection he felt inclined to establish around her. A shield he had no doubt she'd take every exception to.

"I'll keep that in mind for next time, sir. Paul," he added with a frustrated eye roll. "I'm working on it."

"You don't like her, do you?" Paul asked. "Mabel Reynolds."

Kent shrugged. "It's not my place—"

"You made it your place with these comments," Paul cut him off. "You know her sister is one of the suspected victims up at the Tenado house?"

"Yes, sir."

"Do you have a sister, Kent?" Paul already knew the answer. Kent had two. But he wanted to make a point.

"Yes, sir. Diana and Barbara."

"Imagine something for me. Imagine one of them was one of the pictures on that wall."

Kent visibly swallowed.

"Do you think," Paul asked, "in defense of one or maybe both of your sisters you could see how you might be labeled overbearing, obnoxious, or bombastic? When all you were trying to do was find out answers?"

"Yes." The uncertain light in his eyes dimmed. "I see your point."

"Good. I think we have the potential to be a good team, you and I," Paul said. "But in order for that to happen, I need to trust you. I need to know you understand that there's a time and place for gossip. You want to work for me, what happens in this office, stays in this office. Does that sound doable?"

"Yes, s—Paul." He nodded and instead of stiffening appeared to make an effort to relax and slouch. "I'd like to keep working with you. On this case."

"Okay then." Paul indicated the clock. "I won't be leaving for a while, but you can take off. Go home, get your bearings—back here first thing in the morning, yeah? I'll show you how to use the coffee machine."

Now that put a spark back in his eyes. "Sounds like a plan. Thanks."

"See you tomorrow."

"I'm sorry, Keeley. I know, I'm late." From where she'd parked in front of the two weathered two-story houses in East LA, Mabel climbed out of her minivan and grabbed her purse out of the back seat, juggling her phone in her other hand so she could still hear her daughter. She shielded her eyes against the headlights coming toward her as the streetlamps clicked on.

At least the rain had stopped.

Once again, it had taken her longer than expected to meet with the last of her tax clients, and she was still a good half hour away from heading home.

At least she didn't have to transport Benedict Cumberbunny to the hospital until visiting hours tomorrow. A drive back to the hospital might just be the last straw. "Set your math homework aside for now, and we'll tackle it after dinner, okay?"

"You were supposed to be home by now." Keeley sounded as if she has somehow become the parent during this conversation. "Tonight is cooking night, remember? We *always* cook together on Monday nights."

Mabel curtailed a sigh. Times like this she'd almost take whining over stoic acceptance. Wasn't she lamenting earlier today she didn't like her little girl growing up so fast? "We'll just change it to tomorrow night and have tacos. How about that?"

"You hate tacos," Keeley accused, and Mabel smiled down at the phone.

"I don't hate them," she informed her daughter. She just preferred them with a blender full of margaritas. "But you love them, and I love you." Slinging her bag over her shoulder, she grabbed the empty box she'd dragged out of a kitchen closet at Soteria when she'd stopped in to talk to Theresa about a room for Eva. That talk had resulted in a consultation with a handful of new volunteers followed by an unexpected meeting with some former clients …

Mabel hurried down the short path to the small metal gate leading to the house where Eva had been renting an upstairs room for the past six months. "I promise: tacos tomorrow, kiddo. Homework when I get home. I've already called Sutton. She has plenty of food for—"

97

"I'll just have cereal," Keeley said. "I'll be fine."

Sugar for breakfast, now sugar for dinner. Mabel was headed straight for the parental nutritionist circle of hell in the afterlife at this point. "Baby, I'm sorry. I'll make this up to you, I promise." At her daughter's non-response, Mabel suddenly felt like she'd been caught in a perfectly laid trap. "Kee?"

"If you really want to make it up to me …"

Uh-oh. Here it comes.

"I know it's probably too big a thing and that you're super busy, but I was thinking—"

"Thinking what?" Best to just get it all out in the open.

"It's probably super late, and maybe no one can come," Keeley hedged. "But can I have a birthday party? A real one at home with a cake and karaoke and stuff?"

"A party?" Mabel almost sank into the ground. Karaoke? "Honey, the apartment is a mess, and it's not really set up for—"

"We could have it on the patio of Temple House. I already asked Riley, and she and Moxie said it's totally cool with them if you okay it—so will you, please? Please, please, *please,* Mom? Sutton said she'd take care of the food, and Moxie wants to decorate, and I haven't ever had a real party before. Not one that didn't include a creepy clown and crappy pizza."

"Hey, language."

"Sorry. Terrible, horrible, *disgusting* pizza," Keeley said instead. "Is that better?"

No, it wasn't, but her daughter excelled at making a good argument. Creepy clown aside, the pizza really had been crap, which never made for a stellar birthday.

"You wouldn't have to do anything other than show up," Keeley said as if that was a deciding factor. "I promise it won't interfere with your schedule. I'll keep it totally calm and low-key."

Mabel stopped at the bottom step, guilt washing over her with the force of a hurricane. Birthdays should be all about crazy, happy, fun times that completely destroyed schedules. No child should have to promise to keep her birthday party low-key and calm. "All right. I want to talk to Sutton and Riley about this, though. I don't want them—"

Keeley squealed, and Mabel could hear her feet hitting the floor as she jumped up and down. "Thank you, thank you, thank you!!"

Mabel didn't want her friends footing the bill for whatever they were in store for. But that was a conversation she could have with them herself.

"I'm going to go to Sutton's right now so we can talk about food," Keeley announced. "Don't worry, Mom. No tacos, I promise. Wait 'til I tell Addie and Lucas! The karaoke was their idea! How cool is that going to be?"

"Completely cool," Mabel said, absently wondering where on earth she was going to come up with one of those machines. There had to be an app for that, didn't there? "Do me a favor, and eat some real dinner when you're at Sutton's, please. And don't forget to walk and feed—" she stared at her dead phone. "Barksy. There it is. The final proof I need another me."

She instantly thought of her twin, sadness washing over her, before she pushed it aside. Now was not the time.

She shoved her phone in the back pocket of her jeans, stashed her keys in her purse, and climbed the trio of stairs leading to the screened-in front door. No sooner had she rang the bell than it was pulled open, and the porch light clicked on.

"Mrs. Lancaster?"

The older woman, silver-gray hair pulled back tight in a knot, a four-footed cane clutched in one hand, stood stooped over in the doorway. She was a bit hunched, clearly a bit sight challenged—those glasses were thick enough to stop a bullet—and wore a smile of welcome that eased Mabel's tension from the jump.

"I'm Mabel Reynolds. I called earlier about picking up Eva's things?" She stood back so she could be easily seen and identified under the porch light. "I'm so sorry I'm late."

"Oh, of course, come in. No problem at all." Mrs. Lancaster nodded her bobbing head and motioned Mabel inside. The smell of hot tea and overcooked vegetables filled her nose. "I'm just watching my programs."

"I don't want to intrude." Mabel glanced into the living room and the large screen television currently running the opening credits to the *Real Housewives of* ... something. Riley would know. Mabel glanced up the narrow staircase. "I'll be as quick as I can." She needed to get home before Keeley somehow managed to hire a look-alike K-Pop band for her party.

"Oh, it's no bother, dear," Mrs. Lancaster assured her. "I record them all, just to be safe." A sad smile tilted her lips down. "Eva used to watch them with me sometimes. We'd have ourselves a giggle fest over those women's antics." She tugged at the tight collar button of her blue-flowered housedress as she closed the door. "I'm sorry to hear Eva's been hurt and that she's moving on. She's all right, isn't she?"

"She will be." Mabel hoped out loud. "She'll be out of the hospital pretty soon." Mabel pointed to the second floor. "Just up there, isn't it?"

"Yes, yes, it is," Mrs. Lancaster cackled and patted her arm. "I'm going to fix myself an Irish coffee before I settle in to watch. I take it you have Eva's key?"

"I do. I'll leave it on the table here before I go." Mabel rifled in her purse until she came up with it. "I'm sure she'd have preferred to return it in person."

"Such a shame. She's a good girl. This town isn't for everyone. Still, she's reliable. Quiet. None of that partying business so many young people partake in." She shook her head. "It was so thoughtful of her to recommend a new tenant for me. Now I won't have to worry about advertising for one."

"I'm sorry?" Mabel stopped two steps up and looked down. "Eva recommended a new tenant? When was this?"

"Oh, I've no idea." Mrs. Lancaster waved off the question. "He seemed a nice enough man when he stopped by just a little while ago."

"Was his name Leo, by any chance?" Mabel asked. "Tall. Dark hair. Gray hooded sweatshirt?" *Penchant for stalking women in parking lots?*

"Well, he was tall, but that's about all. He said his name was …. Now, what was it?" She poked a finger against her forehead as if accessing a particular circuit. "Claude Shride. I've got his number around here somewhere. Said he and Eva had been dating for a couple of weeks, and he likes the neighborhood."

"This Claude person said he was her boyfriend?"

"Well, I don't know what young people call each other these days, but that's certainly the impression he gave. Such a gentleman. And, oh, he's saving me a bundle of bother, I can tell you." Mrs. Lancaster tapped her cane on the floor. "Do you have any idea how long it takes to put together an ad—"

"I'm sorry, Mrs. Lancaster." Mabel gripped the stair rail. Eva hadn't had a cell phone with her; she hadn't had much of anything, and given that Mabel had been with her for most of the day, she didn't recall Eva making any phone call. "This new tenant? Did you, by any chance, let him into Eva's room?"

"Heavens, no." Obviously, the suggestion offended her. "Oh, he wanted to see the room for himself, of course, but I told him, until her things were picked up, that room is Eva's. Of course, by then you'd called to say you'd be dropping by, so I said he could come back tomorrow and have a looksie once you'd been here." She glanced at the clock. "Although, I'm a bit cross. I went to get him some water, and when I came back, he was gone." She tsked. "Not sure I care for his manners after that, but something must have come up. Something always comes up in this town." She beamed up at Mabel in a way that took ten years off her face. "Do you know, I was a Hollywood extra back in the day? Tony Curtis even flirted with me once. Oh, it was nothing, of course—but my Abel, he was positively livid." She cackled, shook her head. "That was the last movie I ever worked on. Too bad. It was a real stinker when it came out. Would have been nice to go out on a high note."

Mabel's mind was still racing, so she could only smile and nod.

"I'd best let you get on with things," Mrs. Lancaster said. "Last door on the left, upstairs. Front of the house. Just say goodbye before you leave, please. I don't want to forget to lock up after you."

"Of course."

Mabel flashed a smile and headed up the stairs, glancing at the collection of framed photos lining the wall. A number of them featured a much younger Mrs. Lancaster, along with a handsome, suited man standing in front of various Los Angeles landmarks. Abel, no doubt. Mabel always liked seeing older photos of places like the observatory, the Chinese theater, and the Santa Monica pier. And there they were, along with an older actress receiving her star on the walk of fame. Most of the pictures were candid shots, but those, at least in Mabel's opinion, were the best kind of images to display.

Not that she'd ever say so in Riley's presence. The woman composed pictures the way most four-star chefs composed a plate of food. Which reminded Mabel: She'd have to ask Riley if she'd be willing to take pictures at Keeley's birthday party. It had been a while since they'd had some photos taken of the two of them together.

Mabel hugged the box against her front as she made her way down the narrow second-floor hallway. She pushed the key into the scratched-up tumbler and unlocked the door, reaching inside to turn on the light. A small ceiling light burst to life, along with a curved glass lamp on the dresser, both just bright enough to erase the shadows.

The bedroom was a comfortable size, with a large square window overlooking the front yard and the massive oak tree that no doubt provided an impressive amount of shade. Mabel closed the door, set the box on the twin bed covered by a dated crocheted pink comforter, and glanced outside. A beige sedan even older than Mabel's minivan slowly drove past before pulling into the driveway of a home down the street.

When the headlights snapped off, she turned to the light-pink, tall dresser beside the closet. She could smell the faintest hint of clove cigarettes—spicy, sweet, with a trace of vanilla. The aroma made her slightly sick to her stomach.

She made quick work of Eva's few mementos lining the high-top dresser. Next came the collection of photos tucked into the seams of the mirror, the barely hanging on sticky notes reminding Eva to be confident and keep dreaming. Little knickknacks went into the box: a worn hand-knotted bracelet in a rainbow of colors, a UV flashlight, a fairy with a broken wing. A plastic ballerina that had probably topped a birthday cake once upon a time. The stack of books varied from romantic adventures to a Hollywood autobiography. Various toiletries lay scattered about the room, soon joining Eva's other belongings.

The worn stuffed rabbit propped up against the pillow reminded Mabel of Keeley's collection. "Hello, Benedict." She held it in her hands, squeezing it as a sad smile curved her lips. This one would have fit right in with its missing eye and torn ear.

She placed the bunny in the box and turned to the closet, spotting a book sticking out from under the bed.

She bent down, picked it up. And noticed a trail of heavy shoe treads in the carpeting.

The hairs on the back of her neck leapt to attention.

The footprints headed *into* the closet.

Mabel set the book aside. She rose slowly and took one, two, three steps forward.

The closet burst open.

Mabel flew back and for an instant was airborne.

Her head and butt hit the floor at the same time, both bouncing a bit. She tried to blink her vision clear, but in the dim light of the bedroom, she could only see the outline of a man looming over her, the bulk of him lowering, hands reaching out as if in slow motion to lock around her throat.

As his fingers wrapped around her, she stared, shocked, at the thick black ski mask that left only slits for his dark eyes. Eyes …

Such strange, dark, dead eyes. Her head spun as she struggled to breathe.

"What did she tell you?" The man leaned down, tightened his hold on her throat. When she didn't answer, he dragged her up, shook her hard enough to bang her head against the carpeted floor once, twice, three times. "Where are they?"

He squeezed his hands. The pressure around her throat grew as the pain increased. Her lungs burned. She couldn't breathe.

Mabel choked, eyes watering as her body tingled in shock. She tried to shake her head. Smacked her hands hard down on top of his as the energy drained from her system. She gasped for air, attempting to speak, to get his attention.

She kicked up her feet, dug her heels into the carpet as she clawed her fingers into his wrists, digging under the edges of his gloves. She turned her head, looking for something, anything to use against him. "C-can't—t," she croaked.

"What?" His hold relaxed just enough for her to break free and shove back. He stood there, looming, eyes dancing as if entertained by her futile scramble for freedom.

He turned his face into the dim light of the lamp and looked to the door.

Those eyes.

She'd seen those eyes before.

At the hospital.

Outside Eva's room.

Panicking, she crab-walked back, attempting to keep his attention, leading him away from the bedroom door.

"Mabel? Is everything all right up there?" Mrs. Lancaster's voice echoed up the staircase seconds before the tapping of her cane could be heard on the wooden stairs. "What's going on?"

Mabel's blood turned to instant ice. The man's hand struck out, caught the box, and sent it and its contents scattering across the floor. He stalked her, looming over her before he reached down and grabbed her ankle.

He tugged her forward. She twisted and turned, clawing at the carpet. Her left cheek scraped against the carpet so hard she expected to see sparks.

She kicked her free foot at his hand and got loose, but before she could scramble out of reach, he had her by the throat again, but this time, he'd left enough space between them to draw her knees in. She tried to shove him off, but she couldn't get past his bulk.

"Mabel?" Mrs. Lancaster knocked on the door.

She had just enough air in her lungs to scream, "Call the police!"

Panting, sweating, raging, she flipped herself over and kicked him hard in the side of the head with her free foot. He stumbled back, tripping over the box's contents as he dived for the window, shoved his elbow through, and smashed the glass.

Shards were still falling as he jumped out, grabbing hold of one of the oak branches and swinging himself out of the room like a demented Spider-Man.

Mabel hurled herself over to the window, gripping the sill as she watched the shadow land, roll, and spring back to his feet before he made a limping run through the front gate.

The beige car she'd seen earlier screeched to a halt in front of him, and he jumped in. In the quiet of the night, she could hear him shout. "I couldn't find them. Go! Go, go, go!"

She shoved back, raced out of the bedroom, and wrenched open the door.

"Mrs. Lancaster?" she yelled breathlessly as she skidded down the stairs, missed the last three, and nearly toppled head over teakettle onto the landing.

Legs feeling like underset Jell-O, she sank back to sit on one of the lower stairs with relief as Mrs. Lancaster rounded the corner, cast iron skillet in one hand, an old cordless phone in the other.

"He's gone," Mabel panted, pressing a hand against her chest. Every inch of her body throbbed, but that was good. It meant she was still alive. "He's gone, Mrs. Lancaster. Are you all right?"

"Course I am." Mrs. Lancaster dismissed her concern. "Yes, operator, I'm still here. No, he's gone now." She held the phone out. "She's asking if you're all right." The old woman didn't wait for an answer. "We need an ambulance. Yes, her name is Mabel Reynolds. Uh-huh."

"I don't need—" Mabel began, only to be silenced with a stern look.

"Yes, you do," Mrs. Lancaster insisted as she set the cast iron pan on the table by the door. "You're bleeding. Yes. I'll leave the front door open."

"I—what?"

Mabel touched her hands to her chest, her waist, her legs. Only when she looked down did she see the smears of blood covering her clothes. Hands trembling, she turned them palms up. A rather large puncture in her palm continued to gush.

"Oh." She looked up and behind her to the bloodstain handprints marring Mrs. Lancaster's banister and wall. "I'm so—" Her head became light, and the room spun. "OH, no. Oh, geez." She squeezed her eyes shut and felt her head get forced down between her shaky knees by a gentle but firm hand.

"After all that, you're not going to let a little bit of blood take you out, are you?" Mrs. Lancaster stroked the back of her head. "Deep breaths, in and out. Land's sake." She laughed. "Haven't seen this much excitement since the Duke got into a scuffle with the stunt coordinator on set. There you go"—Pat, pat, pat— "in and out."

Mabel kept her eyes closed and did what she was told. The adrenaline continued to surge but didn't quite reach her hands, which were beginning to throb even as they trembled. "I need—"

She tried to sit up but ended up having to help Mrs. Lancaster sit beside her on the stairs. Her bright green Crocs acted as a kind of beacon of awareness against the dark wood floor. "I need to call home. My daughter's waiting for help with her homework."

Right now, all she could think about was getting home to Keeley and Barksy. Her entire being ached to see them.

"You can settle down and wait for the ambulance," Mrs. Lancaster insisted as she leaned forward to peer into the living room. "A few minutes more won't hurt anything. Especially if your girl is as strong and stubborn as her mama."

Mabel actually smiled and opened her eyes. "Thank you."

In the distance, she could hear the faint wail of sirens.

"Never had anything like this happen before," Mrs. Lancaster repeated amazedly. "Been living here for forty years and never had so much as a break-in—"

"I don't think he broke in," Mabel said as exhaustion crept over her from behind. The man in the closet had been let in hours ago, as a visitor. Before he'd gone upstairs and waited.

For her.

CHAPTER SEVEN

IT was impossible, Paul thought as he pulled open the heavy door to Formosa Cafe, not to feel history itself land with the force of a century-old motion picture studio the second he stepped inside.

In the years he'd been away from Los Angeles, the iconic Asian-inspired restaurant had gone through its ups and downs and come close to closing more than once.

Somewhat recently, after a serious refurbishment and rededication to its history, Formosa had retaken its place as one of Hollywood's best, shining its revamped spotlight straight onto the past. From its red-tasseled lanterns to the historic old trolley car that sat center stage. The array of Old Hollywood photographs—some he suspected may have been snapped by Riley Temple's grandfather, a renowned studio photographer back in the Golden Age of this city—was rivaled only by the studios themselves and maybe a few additional eateries and museums.

He'd Ubered over—even the promise of one drink had him leaving his car behind—and made it in time to join the early dinner crowd. The noise level was evened out by the high ceilings and a dining room that lay beyond through an oversized doorway. The myriad of tables were filled with some of the best Chinese food in the city.

The sight—not to mention the staggeringly hunger-triggering aroma—made Paul wish he'd suggested dinner rather than a meeting over drinks.

Sitting midway down the bar, a half-filled glass in front of him, Detective Quinn Burton abandoned his conversation with a younger, slightly better-attired man beside him, and got to his feet, extending his hand as Paul approached. "Paul Flynn?"

"Detective." Paul returned the greeting. "Appreciate you meeting me at such short notice."

"If you're buying, I'm meeting." Detective Burton's smile was easy yet guarded, his gaze equally so. They stood nose to nose and shoulder to shoulder, and Burton instantly put him at ease. "And it's Quinn, please."

Paul had told Mabel the truth earlier. He'd build his successful career on his ability to size people up the instant he met them. Everything he'd read in Burton's file confirmed what Jeff Chandler had told Paul over breakfast. Burton was a dying breed of cop. The kind of cop who kept the barest faith in the system alive.

Detective Burton took a step back. "Paul Flynn, my partner Detective Wallace Osterman." Quinn slapped a hand down hard on Wallace's shoulder and had the younger man nearly toppling off his toes. Wallace was shorter than his partner, a bit more compact, and more wide-eyed, although Paul felt confident in thinking that shine would wear off soon enough. "Wallace, it's been grand," Quinn said, "but Paul and I have some things to discuss."

"Uh-huh." Wallace didn't look particularly pleased at being dismissed. "Nice to meet you. I'm sure I'll be seeing you around." Wallace tossed back the last of his drink. "Got myself a semi-date tonight with a certain personal assistant." He waggled his eyebrows. "Might be in late tomorrow morning."

"You'd better not be," Quinn called after him then pointed to the restaurant. "Kid doesn't know it, but Nox'll eat him for dinner." His eyed Paul cautiously. "Have a seat." He motioned to the barstool Wallace had vacated. "Have to tell you," Quinn continued as they sat, "Riley was mad jealous when I told her where we were meeting. She loves this place. That reminds me, I need to bring her home an order of the Dan Dan Mian if I expect to get back in the apartment door."

"Get you something?" The woman behind the bar offered.

"Scotch, two fingers. Neat. Thanks," Paul said.

"And an order of Dan Dan Mian to go, please," Quinn added.

"Given Riley's history," Paul said when they were alone again, "I'd have thought the Temple family would have had their own private booth in a place like this."

"Riley's not one to cash in on the family name. Much," he added with a quick grin. "Moxie, on the other hand, is another story completely. That said, Riley prefers when it's just the two of us in any of these old restaurants. That way she isn't subjected to a Hollywood history lesson and slow saunter down Moxie's memory lane. Don't get me wrong," he added as Paul's drink was delivered. "She loves Moxie to pieces, as do I, but her great aunt is rarely inclined to edit the spicier events of her life. It's a bit like being a teenager hearing your parents discuss their sex lives."

"Some things aren't meant to be heard." Paul would have to take the detective's word for it. His own adolescent auditory memories had nothing to do with fond or even embarrassing reminiscences. "I bet Moxie's stories about the good old days are something, though. Might be nice to hear some myself. I don't exactly have the best memories about this town."

"No," Quinn said slowly. "I don't suppose you do. I restricted my research to public record," he added at Paul's tightening expression. "Like you, I prefer to be prepared for any meeting. And yet …" Quinn sipped, shrugged. "I have no doubt there's a lot more to you than what I've read."

He would have been disappointed if Quinn had come into this meeting without having done his due diligence. "I hear congratulations are in order. Word is you and Riley are an item. Living together now?"

"We are." Quinn eyed him. "Is that a problem?"

"Not for me," Paul assured him. "At some point, I'm probably going to want to talk with Riley about some things. The photos she developed mostly," he added. "I'm sure she's not anxious to relive what happened in the basement of that house."

"She's not." Quinn sipped slowly. "Neither am I. Can I ask you a question?"

"Sure."

"What are you doing here?"

"Having a drink?"

Quinn's gaze didn't flicker. "What's your agenda with this case? Either things have gotten bad enough back east that you jumped at the first opportunity to get away or you enjoy sticking your foot into one big pile of shit."

"Is that what the Tenado case is?"

"You're a smart guy, Flynn. You know it is. It's a Pandora's Box, and once it's open, there's no going back."

"There's a third option," Paul suggested. "Maybe I see this as an —"

"Opportunity?" Quinn suggested and toasted him with a harsh laugh. "Yeah, that right there is what I'm worried about. I'm not a fan of agendas, secret or straightforward. A lot of people end up as collateral damage, not to mention they make for messy resolutions."

"Not always." Ordinarily, a turn like this in the conversation would have Paul backing off or at the very least changing subjects, but there was something under the detective's suspicion that intrigued him. "I know a good asset when I read about them. Call it a gut instinct, but to my eye, it looks as if there are details missing from the reports."

Quinn's brow furrowed slightly. "I'm not one to argue with someone's instincts. Cards on the table? I'm happy to answer any questions you might have. Heck, I'm even willing to lend a hand in whatever investigation you have planned."

Good thing Quinn Burton was on the top of Paul's list for the task force he was secretly building behind the DA's back. "But?"

"Before I get too tangled up in any strings of yours, I'd like to know who's pulling them."

The accusation should have pissed him off. Coming from anyone else, it probably would have. The fact he didn't feel triggered told Paul a lot more about the case in front of him than Quinn Burton probably thought.

"It's funny," Paul mused. "You're the second person today who's accused me of being someone's puppet."

Quinn's brows raised. "Who was the first?"

"Short, blonde, and maybe the first woman I've ever met to actually cause pain with those daggers in her eyes."

"Mabel." He ducked his head but not before Paul caught the flash of a smile. "Did she take my suggestion about the cupcakes?"

"She did. And thus provided me my monthly sugar quota in one serving," Paul said. "Yes, I met Mabel." And he had yet to be able to stop thinking about her.

"What did you think of her?"

"Of Mabel?" Paul did his best to sound nonchalant, but it was obvious from the dubious expression on Quinn's face he hadn't pulled it off. "I think she might just be the human equivalent of an emotional tornado."

"When it comes to the people she cares about?" Quinn suggested. "Absolutely."

"She's ..." Paul trailed off, shocked to find himself at a loss for words when it came to describing her. "I liked her. She's not easily placated or dismissed, which explains why the DA finally gave in and opened a special investigation into the missing women." His hopes of pushing Mabel aside with a simple conversation had been dashed the instant he'd met her. She wasn't going anywhere, and the more he thought about it, the more he was okay with it. "Between you and me? I think it's entirely possible she has bigger balls than the two of us put together."

"She must have given it to you with both barrels." Quinn gave a slow, assessing nod. "What about Sylvie?"

Sensing the not-so subtle shift away from the topic of Mabel Reynolds, Paul played along. "What about her?"

"Do you think she's dead?"

"Yes," Paul said without hesitation. "And so do you."

Quinn's gaze sharpened. "You don't know what I think."

Paul signaled for that second drink he'd told himself he wouldn't order. "You're a cop with more than a decade's worth of experience under your badge. Your instincts are probably the reason Riley's still alive after she was attacked by Beth Tompkins."

"Don't forget her evil twin Skippy," Quinn muttered. "Holden Thompkins," he corrected at Paul's blank look. "Although Riley calls him the Little Fucker. Or LF. Just so you know."

"Noted." From what he'd read, the nickname was accurate. The psychotic siblings had been responsible for serious and targeted violence against Riley after their attack on her friend, Merle. They'd shot and killed another friend of hers just to get her attention. From the security footage he'd seen of the attacks, it was no doubt best for everyone that the siblings were gone. "You know Mabel's sister is dead, Quinn. You know all the women probably are."

"It's one thing to suspect they are." Quinn gave him a hard look. "But it's a whole other thing to throw that thought verbally into the universe by declaring it outright. I won't do that to Mabel," he said carefully. "Mainly because I don't want to kill whatever hope she has left."

"Sometimes, hope causes more damage than the alternative," Paul suggested, but he heard the not-so-subtle warning beneath Quinn's words. The man was protective, and honestly, Paul couldn't blame him. "I don't want to be the cause of any more pain for Mabel," he told Quinn. "That said, chances are, it'll happen anyway." Paul accepted the refill with a quick smile. "The necklace Mabel wears." He touched a finger to his throat. "The half-heart. Sylvie wore the other half, didn't she?"

"Yes. Work this case all you want." Quinn finished his drink, clinking his glass down on the bar. "But the last thing Mabel needs is someone excavating her emotional burial ground."

"Not my intention."

"You never answered my question," Quinn said. "What is your intention?"

"With Mabel?"

Quinn sat up a bit straighter, his eyes sparking with surprise. "Actually, I meant with you taking the case."

"Right." He forced a laugh. He'd walked right into that one, hadn't he? "The case. Yeah, I'm going after those answers she's looking for. The truth. That's honestly all I'm here for, Quinn. Nothing I do out here is going to make my life easier back in New York."

"And if I told you I don't think the truth will be remotely easy to get?" Quinn asked. "There are a hell of a lot of people with a vested interest in keeping a lot of things about this case buried."

"Like your father?"

The steel flashed back in Quinn's eyes as he examined his drink. "Tread carefully."

"I've read his file, Quinn. I know he's a stand-up guy." Paul hesitated, recalling Jeff's suspicions. "It was your father who leaked the photos of Melanie Dennings to the press, wasn't it?"

Quinn simply arched a brow. "If he did, it was because he didn't like the idea of the truth being swept under a carpet big enough to blanket this entire city. You aren't the only one who thinks truth is important. If he did it, it'll eventually become the worst-kept secret in the department, but he'll stand. And he'll survive it. Despite whatever pressure he's put under."

And now Paul had one less question that needed an answer. "Pressure from the same people determined to lay all the blame at Beth and Holden Tompkin's feet?"

"Among others. Arrogant morons." Quinn's eyes hardened. "Let's pin decades of missing women on a pair of tools who weren't even born when this whole thing began." He looked into his empty glass.

"What ... whole thing?"

Once again, Paul couldn't shake the feeling there was a lot more going on than a plethora of missing-women cases.

"Neither Beth nor her brother had the ability or wherewithal to plan what they did," Quinn continued as if he hadn't heard Paul's question. "This entire situation is so much bigger than anyone knows. Those two were guided, instructed. Take your pick of verbs. They did what they were told."

"By whom?"

"That is the million-dollar question," Quinn confirmed.

Paul leaned his arms on the bar and pinned Quinn with his best don't-bullshit-me expression. "What don't I know?"

Quinn's gaze didn't waver.

"You're really just going to send me into this mess blind?" Paul accused.

Quinn inclined his head, remained silent.

"Okay, all this dancing around is exhausting," Paul said, deciding to take a different track. "I find it difficult to believe you'd drop any case that had outstanding questions. Whatever you and Riley stumbled on last year, it isn't over. Not for you. Not for Riley—not by a long shot. You didn't come here because I asked you to tonight. You came here looking for answers of your own."

"Or maybe I was just curious about a new player on the field."

If he wanted Quinn to stop dancing, he needed to do the same. "Would it surprise you to know that I've heard the word sinister associated with this case?"

Quinn's expression didn't shift. "It's good to know Jeff Chandler's paying actual attention to the Dean Samuels conviction investigation. Sinister covers it."

Yeah, the detective was good. Quick "How safe a bet would I be making to say the last thing you did was move on to the next case when Beth Thomkins landed in the morgue?"

"Off the record?" Quinn asked innocently. "Pretty safe."

"So, I ask again. In all seriousness, Quinn. What. Don't. I. Know?"

"Why are you really here?"

Paul met Quinn's steely eyed gaze. "A friend asked me to come."

"Simple as that?" Quinn challenged.

"Yes," Paul said easily, truthfully. "Jeff's one of the few people I've been able to rely on over the years. He asked for help. I'm giving it." He paused as the tension in Quinn's jaw eased. "Did I speak some code word or something? Did I just get into your secret club?"

Quinn's mouth quirked. "If you only knew how funny—" He stopped when his cell phone rang. He pulled it out of his jacket pocket, checked the screen. "Sorry," he said to Paul, as he picked up the call. "Yeah, Burton. Go."

Paul took advantage of the distraction to signal the waitress and hand over his credit card.

"What's the address?" Quinn slid to his feet and grabbed the blazer off the back of his stool, tucking the phone against his ear as he pulled it on. "Yeah. I'm on my way. Let Sergeant Michaels know I'd like to speak with her when I get there." He hung up. "Gotta go." He plucked up the plastic takeout bag. "Riley and I thank you for dinner."

"Was that about Riley?" Paul stood as well, not liking the concern he saw on the other man's face. "The call?"

"No." Quinn paused after straightening his jacket, shot him a look that had Quinn's stomach twisting into an unexpected knot.

"What?"

"It's Mabel." Quinn's uncertainty was enough to send Paul's heart into double time. "Her name came up in regard to a break-in and assault."

"What kind of assault?" The words almost hurt as he pushed them out. He quickly signed the receipt for their server, added a generous tip, and followed Quinn to the door. "Where is she? She was on her way to the hospital when she left my office. How bad is she hurt?"

There was no explaining the sudden spinning sensation in his chest or the fact that the mere mention of her being in trouble shoved everything else in his brain aside.

"I haven't learned anything new in the last five seconds," Quinn said carefully, his cool gaze assessing. "I asked some patrol friends to keep an ear out for her name. They let me know it popped. Beyond that, nothing."

"Why would you put her name out there?" Paul demanded, tight on Quinn's heels as he hoofed it down the sidewalk. "Why would she be a target? Is this about the Thompkins twins? Does it have to do with what happened to Riley? Tell me what's going on."

Quinn swore, stopped, turned, then started walking again. "Wallace's with Nox. Dammit. I can't call him in on this. If I do, everyone at Temple House is going to know what's going on before I even start my car."

"So?"

"So, I don't want Keeley finding out her mother may have been hurt without having any other information to give her." Quinn turned flashing, angry eyes on Paul. "You ever been interrogated by an eight-year-old?"

"No."

"Suffice it to say, I'd rather go ten rounds with a coked-up yeti." Quinn glanced over his shoulder. "You know about Keeley?"

"I do. You're right. She deserves answers if something's happened to her mom." And while he might not have parental instincts or desires, he could appreciate Quinn's perspective. "I'm coming with you."

"I don't think—"

"I'm coming with you." There wasn't any defining this slippery, sick feeling he had coursing through him, but he sure as hell wasn't going to ignore it. Obviously, the only way to get rid of it was to see for himself that Mabel was all right. "Arguing about it is only wasting time."

"Fine." Quinn shoved the paper bag into Paul's chest and strode around the front of the car. "Get in."

"Could someone please get my phone?"

Mabel's plea fell on deaf ears. Well, maybe not so much deaf as otherwise-occupied ears. Her head throbbed like she had a weekend hangover. Her cheek burned, and the pain in her left palm made her glad she could get through life without it.

From her seat on the back bumper of the ambulance, she could see the reflection of the patrol car's spinning lights in her own minivan's windshield. Neighbors up and down the block had emerged to see what was going on. A few had come over to speak with Mrs. Lancaster, and Mabel was relieved to see a few of them take the older woman inside her house where it was warm, insisting they'd stay with her for a while.

"Seriously," she told Buck, the barely-out-of-high-school-looking EMT who was taping the edge of the gauze covering the now butterfly-bandaged puncture in her palm. "I need to call my daughter."

She leaned over in the hopes of locating one of the two officers who had taken her statement. She'd lost track of time, but she knew full well it was way past when she'd expected to be home.

Well past when Keeley had expected her.

Dwelling on that was better than letting her mind focus on the fact some intruder had locked his meat-hook hands around her throat and probably would have been happy to squeeze the life out of her like toothpaste from a tube.

"I'm sure the officers will get it to you as soon as they can," Buck assured her. "Feel better?"

"Yes," she lied as he stood up. Mabel set her jaw. "Thanks. If you're done—"

"I'm not." Buck placed a hand on her shoulder before she could make a break for it and flicked that irritating penlight into her eyes for the third time. "A possible concussion, even a mild one, isn't anything to play at."

"I'm not playing with anything." She gripped the metal bumper with her uninjured hand and ignored how her stomach pitched. "I've had migraines worse than this. If it still hurts tomorrow, I'll get it checked out."

Buck stepped back and peered down at her as if she were a naughty two-year-old who just got caught raiding the cookie jar.

"I promise." Mabel offered the most saccharine smile she could muster. "I just really need to get home."

"Can't let you go just yet." Sergeant Corrine Michaels, first officer on the scene, stepped out from behind the ambulance door, her dark brown hair knotted at the base of her neck. Her Black skin glistened against the glow of the streetlamps.

"Why not?" Mabel couldn't keep the frustration out of her voice. "I've given you my statement, and you and your partner took care of boarding up Mrs. Lancaster's window." She gestured to the now-wood-covered frame on the second floor. "So, tell me why …" Mabel trailed off at the sight of the all-too-familiar black SUV that pulled up to a screeching stop right in front of the ambulance. "You have got to be kidding me."

So much for keeping this low-key.

Quinn wasn't alone. In yet another surprise of the evening, the sight of Paul Flynn slamming out of the passenger side of the vehicle sent her already overwrought emotions into an out-of-control spiral. There was only one way to control that storm of emotions, and that was with forced hostility. "What are *you* doing here?"

"Answering a damsel's call of distress." In the pale glow of the streetlamps, what little humor twinkling in Paul's eyes was muted by concern. It unnerved her that her first reaction upon seeing him was relief, followed quickly by gratitude before annoyance hit dead center of her chest.

Since she'd left his office, he'd earned himself a five o'clock shadow, and damn if that didn't increase his sexiness factor. The man looked like a knight in shining armor or at least a rival for a once-upon-a-time movie hero who would have taken over not only the silver screen but the town that built them.

An uncontrolled bubble of laughter climbed into her throat at the very idea.

Instead of armor, Paul carried a briefcase. Normally. But not now. She wondered if it was bulletproof.

She almost … *almost* let herself sag into him at his cautious touch. That was how long it took for his words to cut through the fog in her mind. Her spine went steel-girder stiff. "Who are you calling a damsel?"

"You," Paul countered with a quick look at Quinn. "Told you that would work." Quinn's grin was quick, and her annoyance grew. When did these two become friends? "How is she?" Paul asked Buck.

"*She* is fine." Mabel looked from Quinn to Paul, back to Quinn. Her eyes ached from glaring so hard. She might be one big walking bruise in the morning, but she could fake it until then.

"She's okay," Buck corrected. "Glass puncture on her hand. Other abrasions and bruises. Bruised larynx, no doubt because of the choking. Possible concussion, which we've discussed at length."

"More like ad nauseam," Mabel muttered, and only now did she hear how raspy her voice sounded. She touched a hand to her throat as if she could ease the roughness. "I guess I don't have to ask how you heard." She narrowed her gaze at Sergeant Michaels who looked far from repentant. "Quinn, it's after seven. I need to call Keeley, and they won't let me back upstairs to get my phone."

As anxious as she was to call her daughter, the idea of going back up and into that room left her nauseated.

Quinn handed over his cell, and Mabel gripped it as if it were a lifeline. "Thanks for the head's up, Corrine."

"Following orders," the officer assured him. "You want a rundown of events, Detective?"

"Yes, thanks." Quinn touched a hand to Mabel's shoulder. "You really okay?"

"Yep." A little freaked out. More than a tad unsettled. And really, really restless to get home and put all this behind her. Most of all, she just wanted to hug her kid. All the rest of it could wait until she was alone and could scream into her pillow.

"I'll be back in a sec." Quinn moved off out of hearing distance, and Mabel looked down at the phone. Only then did she notice her hands were trembling.

"I have to call her." It was as if Mabel had to convince herself, but she looked up at Paul. "I don't know what to tell her. How do I explain this without freaking her out?"

"Maybe you don't just yet. Give us a few minutes?" Paul asked Buck, who snapped his medical kit shut and hoisted himself into the ambulance.

"I don't need coddling," Mabel said when he sat next to her. "You're a stranger," she insisted in an effort to explain these feelings to herself. A stranger who displayed such concern and affection for her, he made her feel as if they'd known each other forever. She didn't want to feel comfortable with him. She didn't want to want or need him. "I don't need …" The warmth of his body surged against hers. When he raised his arm over her shoulders and drew her in, she stiffened. "I said I'm fine." She squeezed her eyes shut as the soft fabric of his shirt caressed her face. Tears she'd been trying to hold onto escaped, and when she fisted her hands to make them stop, an involuntary whimper of pain escaped.

"Humor me." Still holding her close, Paul reached for her bandaged hand and turned it palm up. "How did this happen?"

It felt good, letting go for a moment. Being held. Having someone to lean on. For however short a time, she surrendered to it.

"That was my fault." She felt him tense and quickly clarified, "When the guy broke the window and jumped out, I leaned on the glass." She stared down at the gauze as if trying to figure out what it was. She watched, transfixed, by the way his fingers slipped between hers; she cleared her throat. "What are you doing here, Paul?"

"Riding shotgun and playing detective." The concern on his face heightened as he turned to face her, taking inventory of her injuries. "I was having drinks with Quinn when he got the call—Jesus, Mabel." He lifted his other hand to the rug-burn scrapes on the side of her face and smoothed his thumb across her cheek. "What happened up there?"

"Would you believe me if I said it was just your unfriendly neighborhood creeper?" Her attempt at humor fell flat. Her voice sounded strange, husky, strained. Even swallowing hurt. "Do you mind …?" Dammit, she hadn't been remotely prepared for Paul Flynn or the genuine concern she heard in his voice. The tenderness she felt in his

119

touch. That worry and restrained anger in his eyes …. It was such a counterbalance to the horrific violence she'd seen in her attacker's eyes. She'd long given up hope of finding someone to rely on, a partner. Someone she could care about. She did not need that repressed longing reignited. "I'm sure Quinn's going to have questions for me, so can I just wait to tell you two together?"

"Yeah, sure. Of course." He looked somewhat uncertain.

"What?" she challenged. She knew when someone was figuring out what to say.

"It's been an interesting day. A surprising one," he told her. "And it's now occurring to me that you and I might have a problem."

"Only one?" She wanted so much to laugh, but it just wasn't there. He cupped her face in his palm, looked straight into her eyes. She saw it, felt his barely repressed emotions surging through his fingers. There were so many things she could say to push him away, so many words that would create distance between them, and yet the only thing she could muster the courage to utter was his name. "Paul—"

He kissed her.

It was, she thought, the most tender, affectionate kiss she'd ever received. She could feel his concern, taste his uncertainty, and she all but vibrated in his hold until he lifted his mouth and rested his forehead against hers.

"I was hoping to prove myself wrong." He frowned, shook his head. "I didn't. Dammit. This is the last thing I need."

"Same." Determined to keep up a façade for as long as she could, she kept her tone sharp. Hopefully, whatever transference or emotional dependency she was feeling would subside once they both headed home. Until then, she was stuck feeling like a candle that was in danger of burning itself out. "Just waiting for my defenses to be down, huh? For the record, I always kiss strange men after someone's tried to kill me."

"Happened before, has it?" He lifted his other hand to her face. That wasn't just confusion she saw on his face. There was panic there, as well. Well masked, but there, nonetheless.

"You know what I think?" She challenged, if only because it kept her distracted.

"I couldn't possibly begin to guess."

"I think you lied to me earlier. In your office." She narrowed her eyes as if that would make him seem less puzzling. "When you said you aren't a nice man."

"I'm not."

"Liar." He was nice, which was something solid to hold onto. "Something's happening, isn't it?" Clearly her filter was not operating correctly. "Between us."

"It appears so. But like you said, could be a stress of the moment kind of thing."

"You don't buy that any more than I do," she challenged.

"No." That frown was back. "No, I don't."

"It's not something either of us is looking for." She wanted to give him a way out. Needed to give herself one. The last thing she was capable of dealing with right now was personal entanglement with lasting effects. "If we aren't careful, it's going to get seriously complicated very fast."

"Complicated can be good," he said. "Complicated can be fun."

"I have a daughter," Mabel reminded him. "I have fun limitations."

"I think we both do in that regard."

"Mixing business and pleasure is never a good idea."

Explosive maybe, but not good.

"Right now, I'm inclined to disagree." He brushed his mouth against hers once more.

A throat cleared behind Mabel. She leaned away, but Paul kept her in his embrace.

Quinn's expression was utterly unreadable, and Mabel was grateful for it.

"I got the rundown," he told them. "You couldn't give a description of the guy in the closet?"

"No." Mabel shook her head. "No, I just remember he was wearing a mask." She frowned. "Buck back there said my memory would be fuzzy for a while." Her head throbbed when she tried to focus. "I smelled clove cigarettes. It doesn't strike me as an Eva thing, and I didn't see any hint she smokes. So stupid. That's all I can—"

"Nothing's stupid at this point," Quinn assured her. "Anything else?"

She lifted her hands. "I scratched at him as often as I could. Buck scraped under my nails."

She'd walked the EMT through the procedure, made sure he didn't contaminate the sample by digging beneath her nails too deeply.

"Yeah," Quinn said. "Corrine's got the evidence baggie. She'll get it to the lab and add my name to the report. This Eva Hudson you were here about? Is she one of Soteria's?"

"She will be by the end of the week." Mabel scrubbed a hand across her forehead. "That's who I was going to see in the hospital when I left your office," she told Paul.

"I don't want to go stepping on anyone's toes in another department," Quinn said. "But I'd like to reach out to whomever is handling her case."

Mabel shot off the detective's name. "He didn't exactly inspire confidence when I spoke with him that first night. Eva hasn't given any names of suspects. Before today, she's hardly spoken at all. I was going to look for some paystubs in her room, to find out where she works, then remembered pretty much everyone gets paid automatic deposit. Her friends' names would be in her phone, which she lost when she was dumped." *Names of ....* Recognition flashed. "There was someone, a man earlier today. At the hospital. At first, I thought he followed me out of the parking lot, but ..." Her head seemed to be buzzing, and it was hard to grab hold of a coherent thought. "He grabbed me outside of the hospital. It was fine," she added when Paul's hold on her tightened, and Quinn straightened. "Between the rain and .... I think he was just overwrought. He wanted to see Eva. Or have me tell her it was okay for her to see him."

"He strike you as violent?" Quinn asked. "Did he come across as being responsible for her attack? Do you think it could have been him in that room upstairs?" He indicated the boarded up second-floor window.

Mabel shrugged. "To answer your first question, in my experience, everyone is capable of violence given the right circumstances, but as far as him hurting Eva?" She considered, then shook her head. "No. No, I don't think he's responsible for her assault. He seemed almost—I don't know—scared. And he's way more scrawny than the guy was up there." She touched a shaking hand to her throat.

"How about a name for this parking lot guy?" Quinn asked. "You get one?"

"Leo Capallini. He acted as if he knew her. When I mentioned his name to Eva, she didn't react as if she was scared of him." Hell, Eva had been more apprehensive about the doctor in her room than Leo.

"Okay, we'll give him a look." Quinn nodded as if making a mental note. "Can't hurt at this point. You call Keeley?"

"Not yet." She stared down at his phone, noticed her hands had finally stopped shaking. "I don't know how to explain something like this over the phone." She turned uncertain eyes up at Quinn. "And I won't lie to her."

"So don't." Paul's simple solution almost left her gaping. "Tell her you'll explain when you see her and that you'll be home soon."

"Sounds like a plan," Quinn agreed.

Mabel frowned. "She'll know something's up."

"You aren't home," Quinn reminded her. "She already knows something's up. A quick call will make you both feel better."

"Yeah. I guess you're right." The amount of relief that plan gave her surprised her. "Do I have to go down to the station? Or can I go home?"

"You can come in and sign your statement tomorrow," Quinn told her.

"I still need to get my bag and phone." She cast a wary eye on the second-floor window again. "And all of Eva's things. That's why I was here to begin with."

"I can get them," Paul said. "You want everything in the room?"

"Everything that isn't pinned down. You sure you don't mind?" She certainly didn't want to take advantage, but with the way her mind was spinning around him, some distance would probably do them both some good. Immediate post-trauma reaction. He was easy to rely on. Easy to push away once her initial panic passed. "Most of the stuff's on the floor now. I just didn't get to the closet and her clothes and suitcase."

"I'll take care of it." Paul gave her arm a quick squeeze before he headed up the sidewalk and disappeared into the house, leaving Mabel to stare after him in a bit of a daze.

"So." Quinn leaned against the ambulance door. "I don't know whether to be concerned or impressed." His grin was flash quick. "He's just hit town, and you're staking a claim?"

"Shut up." Mabel half-laughed. "I'm a woman in shock." In more ways than one. She had absolutely no business falling for anyone, let alone a man like Paul Flynn. A kiss and a few moments of comfort did not a relationship or a future make. "No idea what I'm doing."

Then again, maybe she did. She'd never had a fling before. Maybe she deserved one.

"Uh-huh. What else is there? To your statement?" He glanced behind him to check that they were alone.

Mabel tucked a loose strand of hair behind her ear. "Did Mrs. Lancaster mention a guy named Claude Shride?"

"She did." Quinn nodded, his lips quirking. "Now, *him*, we got a description of."

"Weird name."

"It's Los Angeles. What do you expect?"

"Well, whoever this Claude was that Mrs. Lancaster met, I think that's who was in the closet. He was already here when I called to say I was on my way. A few minutes later, he was gone. She thought he left."

"And you think he went upstairs to wait for you? Why?"

"He was looking for something he couldn't find." Something the man had been willing to torture her to get. She touched a hand to her throat, gripped her pendant for focus. What was it she couldn't recall?

"And he thought you'd know where it is?"

"Last-ditch effort, maybe?" Mabel shrugged. "You didn't have to come, you know?"

"Yeah, I kinda did." He looked down the street as neighbors began making their way back indoors for the night. "I asked some friends in the department to keep an ear out for certain names. Yours included."

"I don't even know how to respond to that." She couldn't quite decide how to feel. Protected or … "Why on earth …" She stopped, drew in a deep breath. "Because of the Circle?"

"They're out there, Mabe," Quinn said. "They may have gone dormant since what happened with the Riley and the Blunder Twins, but we didn't make a dent in whatever their endgame is. Someone was at the Tenado house the night Riley was attacked. Multiple someones. I'm not taking chances. With anyone in the know."

"You're right." Although she wasn't entirely sure how much safer she felt knowing her name was in an unofficial police database. "Glad you're looking out for us."

"Gave me some peace of mind. Thanks to Blake's security upgrades around the building," Quinn said. "Temple House is as locked down as it can be. No one's getting in undetected, and no one leaves unnoticed. But we don't live in a bubble, and I can't keep an eye on everyone 24/7. The deeper we go, the more dangerous it's going to get. We can't be too careful, Mabel. They know who we are, and that puts them ahead of us. Speaking of careful …" He leaned over, checked the door. "Before your Prince Charming gets back …"

"Stop. Please." She was never going to live this down. Especially once Quinn got in a room with Riley and spilled everything. She was about to become Temple House gossip in T-minus ten minutes and counting.

Quinn's gaze sharpened. "We shouldn't keep him in the dark."

"About what?"

Quinn's face shifted to his *you know what* look. "Paul's a smart guy, Mabel. He already suspects there's more to what happened at Christmas than he's read in the files. He ran a pretty good interrogation of me, and that's not easy to do. I think we should bring him in and tell him what we know about The Circle of the Red Lily."

"Well, that'll take all of ten minutes," Mabel argued. "Unless you've heard something I haven't. Have you?"

"Heard something? No. But Cass is focused on a few things. Nothing solid enough to risk running with yet."

They probably never would. The existence of a murderous, secret society with supposed connections going back decades in Hollywood sounded like a rejected script from the slush pile. They had supposition, of course, but that was mostly based on the pre-death declarations of two psychopaths who couldn't exactly be considered trustworthy. And they had that strange, blood-dripping image of a lily that popped up every once in a while.

A red lily that had struck terror into a few people of note.

Mabel bit the inside of her cheek. She'd lost two arguments with Riley over Mabel's wanting to talk to Moxie about the odd brand-like tattoo on the back of the older woman's neck.

The second woman they knew of who had one, Joyce DePalma, was in and out of lucidity in her retirement home. Whatever she might tell them couldn't exactly be deemed reliable.

It was going to take something drastic to get Riley to ease up on the protective shield she'd built around her great aunt. She didn't want to push her friend or cause Moxie any distress, but with little to no progress in attempting to get a foothold on whatever this group actually was, they were running out of other options.

"If Cass is onto something, then Nox isn't far behind."

"Yeah, well, they found something that had Cass concerned enough to send Nox on vacation for a while. Exploring the Dark Web isn't something easily done or dealt with," Quinn said. "It's slow going when you need to cover your tracks. Nox knows what they're doing. We have to be patient."

"I know." Mabel sighed.

"The stuff Nox was digging, through," Quinn said. "It's like a slow-acting poison. It got into their system and was affecting their ability to work and think clearly. They're back at it now, and we have to have faith in them."

"Wish I had a boss who would send me on a three-week cruise to Europe to get over my stress." Focusing in on the nebulous, cult-like Circle was one way to get answers about Sylvie, but doing so threatened to open up a whole other can of worms, and if there was one thing Mabel could not tolerate, it was worms. "The reason we haven't expanded our own circle is because we don't know who we can trust." Mabel paused, considering.

"All the more reason to bring someone in with some different connections. And ideas."

She considered him for a long beat. "You really think we can trust him?"

"About this?" Quinn nodded. "Actually, yeah. I do. He doesn't have any love for this city or the people who work here. He doesn't seem to be worried about offending people or speaking truth to power. His reputation, for the most part, is solid. And there's another reason for bringing him in. He's going to start kicking over a lot of rocks in this town. Rocks countless individuals have a vested interest in keeping in place. He doesn't do subtle."

"No," Mabel agreed. "Subtle, he is not."

"Not telling him is tantamount to putting a target on his back. You don't want that, do you?"

"No," Mabel admitted. "No, I don't want that." She'd seen what had happened with Riley when she'd been targeted. Her friend had been stalked, attacked in the basement of Temple House, and nearly drowned in what had been described as a kind of sacrificial pool. She didn't want anyone else going through something like that. She took a deep breath. "Why don't you run this by Laurel and see what she thinks?" she suggested. "She might have another take on him or at least his reputation. If Laurel signs off on bringing him in, I'm sold." Her brow furrowed. "It should come from me, shouldn't it?"

"If it comes from me, he might think it's some conspiracy theory gone wild. From you?" Quinn glanced over his shoulder. "He'd give you the benefit of the doubt since it involves your sister. I'll give you one guess which would go over better. In the meantime, I'll go check on your … Paul and see how he's doing," he said at Mabel's warning glare when she sensed another moniker about to drop. He gestured to her to raise an icepack to her cheek. "Be back in a bit."

The knots of tension that had been tightening inside Mabel suddenly eased, and it felt as if she could breathe easy again. This time when she raised the phone, her hands were steadier and her mind clearer.

"Hey, Kee," she said when her daughter answered.

"Mom?" Keeley's voice went up a few octaves. "How come you're calling me from Quinn's phone? What's wrong with your voice?"

"I'm without my cell right now and, well, I'll explain when I get home." Score one for her. So far, she hadn't lied. "Did you take Barksy for his walk?"

"Uh-huh. I let him run all over the dog park. Mom, where—"

"Great." One thing she wouldn't have to take care of when she got home. "Since it was after seven, I just wanted to call and let you know I was on my way."

"Sutton said you'd call." It was evident in her daughter's voice that she'd been worrying. "It's okay. Laurel's here. We've got leftover pizza in the oven. She fixed a salad, too."

"Laurel's there?" An idea sparked as she got to her feet and caught sight of Paul and Quinn heading out of the house.

"Yeah, you want to talk to her?"

"No, I'll be home soon. Have her hang around until I'm there, okay? Tell her there's an open bottle of wine in the fridge."

"She already found it," Keeley said.

"Of course, she did." Mabel paused, strained to hear. "What's that noise in the background?"

"Oh, um. *The Birds*."

"The horror movie?" Mabel dropped her chin to her chest. "Awesome."

"Laurel's on a Hitchcock kick," Keeley announced. "Next time, we're going to watch *Psycho!*"

"Uh-huh." Fabulous. Now that Mabel probably had a phobia about closets, it only made sense that her daughter might develop one around showers. Leave it to Aunt Laurel to make Keeley's recent reading habits seem tame. "Keeley?"

"Yeah?"

She hated the tears clogging her throat. "I love you, baby."

"I love you too, Mom. Are you sure you're okay? You still sound funny."

"I'm fine," she whispered, clearing her throat that only now was beginning to ache. "Thanks for walking Barksy. I'll see you soon." She clicked off and handed Quinn's phone back to him and flashed a smile at Paul. "How do you feel about leftover homemade pizza?"

"Mildly obsessive," he said, caution in his eyes.

"I was wondering if you'd mind driving me home? I'm not really feeling up to being behind the wheel." She reached into the box and tweaked the stuffed bunny's ears, turning on a bright smile that she suspected didn't come across as remotely happy. She should ask to make a detour and deliver a piece of comfort to Eva on the way, but she could already feel the adrenaline crash taking its toll. Besides, Eva didn't need to see the result of Mabel's visit to Mrs. Lancaster's. Mabel didn't want to add to Eva's already overwhelming burdens. "I could use some help getting all this up to my apartment."

"Okay." Paul's expression appeared to be a combination of surprise and suspicion, but he hefted the box. Only then did they see the small plastic bag clutched in his fingers.

"What's that?" Mabel asked.

"Oh, maybe evidence?" He flicked the bag at Quinn. "You mentioned something about the guy's eyes changing color?"

"I said they seemed to," Mabel frowned.

"It's a contact lens," Paul told Quinn. "Since crime scene wasn't coming out, I used a tissue. Tried not to mess with it too much. Unless Eva wears contacts?"

"Not that I know of," Mabel said.

"This is great." Quinn looked more than mildly impressed and, given the arched brow he shot at Mabel, seemed another point in his argument about brining Paul in on their Circle hunt. "I'll get this to the lab and have it processed with the nail scrapings."

"You want this box in the back seat?" Paul asked Mabel.

"Oh, right. Keys." She pulled them free of the front pocket of her bag, avoiding his gaze. The idea he read her so well as to suspect she had another agenda did not sit well with her at all.

"Laurel's at your place?" Quinn murmured once Paul was out of earshot.

"Yeah," Mabel said. "Maybe you could give her a ring, fill her in so she can do some in-person evaluation?"

"Sneaky, Mabel."

"Motivated Mabel," she corrected. "If you're right, Paul might be the best chance we've had in a while for some answers. Besides, the sooner we solve this case, the faster he'll be on his way back to New York." And far away from Mabel so she could stop thinking about the man. She did not need to add Paul Flynn to her already overflowing, complicated life.

"Sounds like you're anxious to get rid of him," Quinn said.

"I'm anxious to get answers. Thanks, DSP."

"DSP?" Paul walked around the front of her minivan to open her door, a gallant action that made Mabel's stomach flutter and earned a chuckle from Quinn. "What's DSP?"

"Nothing!" Quinn yelled over his shoulder as he walked away.

"Don't worry," Mabel said as she climbed into the car. "I'll fill you in on the way."

CHAPTER EIGHT

"WHICH parking space?" Paul asked after the sliding gate to the Temple House parking lot closed behind them. The historic landmark of an apartment building was located not too far off the exit of the Hollywood Freeway and nestled in an area filled with small businesses, local groceries, and, just across the street, an all-too-familiar yet redesigned park from what he remembered.

"Yeah, no, that sounds good, Theresa," Mabel said into her cell, then focused on Paul. "Space twenty." She pointed ahead and off to the right for Paul while she continued the call. "Last I spoke with Alicia, she said the plan is to discharge Eva on … uh-huh. No, yeah, I can totally do that." She shot Paul a look and mouthed *sorry*. "Does that still … okay, great. I'll check in with you tomorrow."

"Everything okay?" He clicked off the engine as she slipped her cell phone into her purse.

"Didn't think we'd ever get a solid answer on Eva's discharge, but now we can get things moving." She let out a long sigh, one that belied the dark circles forming under her eyes, not to mention the exhaustion she could no longer conceal. She'd had a long day; they both had, which made her invitation to drive her home strangely curious.

He'd have thought she'd be looking for some serious solitude about now. Or, at the very least, an excuse to ditch him. She was not thrilled at the sparks between them. And honestly? Neither was he. He'd already broken one of his self-commandments. He wasn't about to break another. "What's his name?"

"Huh?"

"The rabbit." He pointed to the stuffed animal in her lap, the one she'd reached into the box for halfway through their drive.

"Oh." Her lips curved as she touched a finger to a floppy ear. "Benedict Cumberbunny."

"Benedict Cumber—" He broke off, surprised at how easily this woman made him laugh. "The female mind never fails to both baffle and amuse."

"Please." Mabel rolled her eyes in a way that eased the concern he'd been harboring ever since he'd first caught sight of her in the back of the ambulance. "Straight men like you have your own obsessions. Let me guess." She leaned back against the door, narrowed her eyes in the darkness. "You're an Angelina guy."

"Nope." He grinned at her doubt. "How's your head?"

"Well, it's still attached to my shoulders, so there's that." Her smile was quick. "Like I told the EMT, my migraines are ten times worse."

Worry he wasn't quite familiar with coursed through him. His fingers itched to touch her, to confirm she was all right. Seeing that scrape on her cheek, that bandage on her hand, the bruises darkening around her throat—knowing she was hurting ate at him in a way he couldn't quite explain.

So much of the last day didn't make any sense to him. He'd known her for a little more than a blink of an eye, and yet, the idea of anyone hurting her conjured up such anger and thoughts of violence that it was as if he was sixteen years old again. He needed to get himself under control and his heads out of the clouds.

He felt more like a pre-teen suffering the effects of his first schoolboy crush, and those rarely, if ever, turned out well. "Can I tell you a secret?"

"Why not?"

"I spent most of my childhood wondering what the inside of Temple House looked like."

"Really?" The puzzled expression quickly disappeared. "Oh, that's right. You grew up here."

"Yes, I did." He wondered what kind of power this woman had over him that she had him walking down a pothole-filled memory lane. "Not in this neighborhood, of course. My brother and I used to ride our bikes all over Los Angeles. That park across the street back there?" He pointed behind them. "It looked a lot different back then. Was a lot rougher. There was a whole bunch of us from different schools who would meet up there all the time. This neighborhood was a kind of central meeting place for kids all over the city. I remember one of Alden's friends was a studio brat. His grandfather and father were both the head of one of the studios, and he was next in line. That guy knew everything there was to know about movies, movie stars, and the studio system. Speaking of obsession …" He jerked a thumb toward the white façade. "Temple House was his. He used to sit in that park for hours, staring at it. It rubbed off on us for sure. We actually made a bet that someday, one of us would own the place."

He almost laughed.

He hadn't thought about those days in a long time. It made sense that here, now, he'd recall some of the actual good times he'd had growing up.

"Fat chance of that." Mabel scoffed. "Riley wouldn't let the place go for any price, and believe me, people have tried. I didn't know you had a brother."

"The park's changed quite a bit." He went on as if he hadn't heard her. "If it wasn't for Temple House, I'm not sure I'd have recognized the whole area."

"I've heard tell. About ten years ago, the residents and business owners got together and revamped it as a playground and dog park. Barksy loves it."

"Barksy?"

"My dog." She frowned, glanced over at him. "You okay with dogs?"

"Never had one, but in theory, they're fine."

"That's sad." She sounded as if she meant it. "Every boy should have at least one dog growing up."

She pushed open the door and climbed out.

Paul waited a beat before following. Given his father's violent proclivities, Paul had come to the early conclusion that not having any animals in the house was a good thing.

He climbed out and opened the back door so they could gather up Mabel and Eva's belongings. He grabbed the box while Mabel grabbed Eva's suitcase and her own purse, stuffing the rabbit into it. She locked the van behind her and hit the digital code to pop open the pedestrian gate leading to the street.

"I really appreciate the help," she said as they headed to the corner. "I don't think I have the energy for two trips tonight."

"Not a problem."

"Like I said, we're having pizza for dinner," she said. "Always room for one more at the table."

"Definitely beats hotel room service and the news."

"And it's not just any pizza." She sounded quite serious about the subject. "We're talking Sutton's homemade pizza with her special veggie-enhanced tomato sauce."

"Sutton's one of your neighbors?"

"Sutton O'Hara. Neighbor. Friend. Childcare backup. Carpooler and multitasker extraordinaire." Mabel flashed a smile. "She lives on the first floor with her two kids. She works as a nutritional consultant personal chef. One of the perks of living in Temple House. We're all her culinary test subjects, and she rarely has a failure."

"Sounds like a sweet deal." He waited for her to climb the trio of stone steps and key in a pass code on a surprisingly sophisticated entry system. He glanced up, noticed the state-of-the-art cameras that covered every angle amidst an array of architectural details harkening back to the decades of old.

Paul frowned. He didn't recall this part of Los Angeles as being a high crime area. The surveillance seemed like overkill.

The door buzzed, and Mabel pulled it open. The door made a gentle woosh as if an air seal had been broken. "Well, here we are. Home sweet lobby." Mabel waited until the door closed again before she started down the steps. "Keeley actually knows more about the building's history than I do. She hangs out a lot with Moxie after school."

"Moxie Temple," Paul murmured, trying to take in all the details at once. "I can't believe I'll be this close to *the* Sally Tate. In college, the sorority next door to my frat house used to have Sally Tate night at least once a semester. They'd all dress up in that bandana thing she wore on her head and the overalls, carried toolboxes, and play the movies on a loop."

"You'll win Moxie over for life with stories like that," Mabel warned with a snort. "Tell me, were you a Sally Tate fan, or were you just happy about all those female coeds in short costumes?"

"I'm a lawyer," he said easily. "I know when to plead the fifth."

But the idea of doing so flew out of his mind the second they stepped inside.

It was as if he'd stepped through a time portal. He could all but hear the clink of martini glasses and muted conversations about studio contract deal-making. The wheeling and dealing with constant one-upsmanshipping that built the city of angels—and broken dreams—into the movie Mecca it had become. All that was missing was that distinctive pop of flashbulbs and *oohs* and *ahhs* of the famous and infamous.

"Would you like a few minutes alone?" Mabel teased as he grinned like an absolute fool, shaking his head as he turned in slow circles and wandered the seemingly endless open space.

White marble and gold accents lodged the area into the Art Deco design that had crept in around the original Spanish architectural idea. He knew the basic history of the place, that it had been built originally to house female Hollywood extras and chorus girls back in the heyday of the big movie studios. When the Temple family had taken possession, he wasn't entirely sure, but one of Riley's great-someones had been determined to keep the place going, hence the turning it into the apartment building it had become.

The arched, oversized windows were broken up with meticulously hung framed photographs and shelves displaying various Hollywood iconography and memorabilia. Images he'd never seen before dotted the walls, including Clark Gable and Carole Lombard on their wedding day and Bette Davis laughing at something James Cagney was saying. And a pre "wine before its time" Orson Welles posing with a certain Rosebud sled as if it were his co-star, which, of course, it had been. The candid shots were mesmerizing. This place was better—and more personal—than any Hollywood museum.

He wandered to the extensive bar along the far back wall. A number of mini-fridges sat behind it and above them a selection of high-end alcohol behind locked glass doors. Baskets and bins of fruit and snacks sat atop the glossy white counter, complimented by the upholstered stools he suspected may very well be original to the building.

A gigantic, cushioned center settee broke up the space leading to the sofas, angled toward an enormous floor-to-ceiling fireplace across the lobby. On the mantle, beneath a large oil painting of the Hollywood sign he suspected could be seen from the roof, sat a glass display case. As Paul drew closer, he couldn't believe what he was seeing. He peered at the small plaque beneath it, gaped at Mabel. "That's ... that's Gene Kelly's umbrella from *Singin' in the Rain*."

"Mmm-hmmm." Mabel nodded. "Moxie has quite a collection of memorabilia, and she keeps in touch with a lot of her former contacts in the movie industry. Remember when Debbie Reynolds sold off her collection? She gave Moxie an early look and first op-portunity to buy. Now Moxie rotates movie props in and out of her storage facility all the time. A couple of years ago, she actually came across Jimmy Stewart's camera from *Rear Window* at an estate sale. Telescoping lens and all. I think Riley put it under lock and key in a safety deposit box," she added with a laugh.

"Unbelievable." Paul wasn't often without words, but if there was one thing he did enjoy about his childhood, it was the city's firm and often entertaining grasp on the past.

"There's a screening room just back there." Mabel gestured down the hallway on one side of the fireplace. "It seats about fifty people. Moxie hosts different movie nights, usually a couple times a month. This summer she's going to have a 40's film festival and bring out the residents of the Golden Age Retirement Home as special guests. I haven't made it to a lot of the screenings, but Keeley's gotten a great movie education, and she's always finding new favorites."

"*Wizard of Oz*?" Paul guessed. "*Pollyanna*?"

"Not hardly. *Maltese Falcon*," Mabel corrected. "She's in a Bogie phase, currently. Although I have a feeling that's about to change."

Her mouth twisted as if she'd bit into something sour but shifted into a smile almost immediately. "Blake, hey."

Mabel turned her attention to a man who had emerged from a room down the same hall she'd just referenced. To the man's left sat the staircase that from a different vantage point, all but hid an elevator. "Blake Redford, this is Paul Flynn. Blake's our apartment manager and security expert. Well, he tag teams that with Cass, but—"

"Nice to meet you." Blake nodded to Paul, but his attention immediately turned to Mabel. "Saw you come in." He gestured to Mabel's face in a way that had Paul's attention.

Blake wasn't the kind of man anyone could ignore. He had a clean-cut appearance, trimmed full beard, and laser sharp, dark-eyed gaze that could probably slice someone in two. Paul had no doubt the man didn't miss anything going on in this building. He was also a good two inches taller than Paul and had at least twenty pounds of muscle on him, as displayed by his dark T-shirt and cargo pants.

"You okay?" Blake motioned to the rising bruises around her throat. Bruises that were going to haunt Paul as effectively as his sunrise excursion to the Tenado house.

There was friendly concern in Blake's voice, but that was all. Paul didn't exactly appreciate feeling relieved about that.

"Quinn called you, didn't he?" Mabel accused. "Honestly, I'm fine. It was just unexpected. Those self-defense classes you gave us last month came in handy." Paul recognized a forced laugh when he heard one but refrained from commenting.

"Yeah, well, maybe it's time for a refresher course," Blake said. "I'll schedule one on the calendar." His arm flexed as he reached into his back pocket for his phone. "Maybe we can sub out Mimosa Yoga one Saturday morning once it's warmed up?"

Mabel shrugged. "If you can get that idea past Riley and Laurel, I'm in." She reached up and patted his shoulder with her uninjured hand as she passed. "Need to get up to Keeley before she eats all the pizza."

"Nice to meet you," Paul said, a bit disappointed he didn't have more time to look around.

The only thing he'd taken with him when he'd left LA had been a solitary suitcase and his love of old movies. Being in Temple House felt a bit like a full-circle moment and had him checking off a major item on his bucket list.

"Nice to meet you, too," Blake agreed and watched them until they stepped onto the elevator.

"So, the place comes with a bodyguard," Paul said once the doors had closed. The elevator was small, and he could see Mabel had gone ramrod straight once she was on board. "What's the matter? Spooked?"

"No more than usual. Heights," she added with a sharp laugh. "Small spaces." She tried to shrug it off. "I like to avoid both when I can."

That explained her wanting to take the stairs to his office and yet he never would have guessed. Mabel was not a woman who gave anything away if she could help it. "And yet you live on the fourth floor."

She stared up at the lights as they blinked at each floor. "The higher up in an apartment building you are, the safer you tend to be." She winced at the grinding and whining of the gears overhead.

"Is that true?" In his experience, if someone wanted into your space, they found a way no matter what floor you lived on. But that didn't sound like a keen observation to make in an effort to ingratiate himself. "Keeley was what? Five months when you moved in?"

Mabel shot him a side-eyed look. "Been reading up on us, have you?" She all but darted out of the car when it came to a stop. She dug into the front pocket of her bag for her keys.

"I know you moved out here after Sylvie went missing."

"Someone has to be here when she's found." The tension was back in her voice, tight and taut, like a rubber band about to snap. It made him wonder, moving forward, how to converse with her about her missing sister without setting her off.

"But your parents stayed back in Wisconsin."

Mabel's jaw tensed. "Someone has to be there when she comes home."

Message received. Tonight was not the night to push. "You really lucked out with this place." It was his lame attempt at changing the subject.

"Guardian-angel lucky," Mabel agreed. "I was barely making do at a motel in Hollywood when I read about an open house for this place online. I was working remotely for an online accounting business so my schedule was flexible. The second I stepped inside, it felt like home." Her smile flashed again. "A really expensive home."

"I can only imagine."

"I'd had a really crap week. Computer issues, lousy internet hookup, and the hotel manager was giving me grief about Barksy. Barksy was Sylvie's dog," she added at Paul's quizzical look. "One of her neighbors had taken him in, but it was clear from the start that was temporary. Motels aren't built for puppies. My money was running out faster than I'd planned, plus Keeley had just started teething, and she was not happy about it. She had a major freak-out in the lobby, and I just broke down. Sometimes I swear I can still hear the echoes of her crying when I walk down the halls."

Paul smiled in an attempt at comfort and understanding as Mabel headed to the solitary apartment door on the left, across the hall from another three, which he assumed were smaller, units.

"I was so embarrassed," Mabel continued as she dug out her keys. "But Riley and Moxie could not have been nicer. They wouldn't let me leave. Instead, I got a private tour, lunch, and an unexpected nap while Keeley earned two of the best babysitters around."

She slid her key into the door. "When I woke up, Riley offered me a deal on the rent. They changed their policy on pets and gave me a break on the first and last month's rent if I'd move in the next day and do their taxes every year and offer a discount to any and all tenants interested." Her lips quirked. "I ended up with six clients before I moved the first box in. Now I've got sixteen and triple that around town. I ended up with a great apartment and the best friends I've ever had in my life." She pushed open the door, and music blared out. "Speaking of friends. Hey, Barksy." Mabel dropped her bag on the floor and wheeled Eva's suitcase into the corner by the door. "Hey, boy. You have a good day?"

She crouched down to greet the black-and-gray, short-haired dog that beelined right for her. She gave him a good scrub, buried her face against the top of his head. "Don't turn those eyes on me, big boy. You already got your walk tonight. And I bet you've had plenty of treats."

Woof.

Arms full, Paul stayed in the doorway, caught in a staring match with the animal. "I know you asked if I had dog issues," he said to Mabel when she stood up to hang her coat. "But does Barksy have man issues?" He tilted his chin down as Barksy walked over to stand directly in front of him. "Hey, dog. Barksy," he added at Mabel's amused look.

Hefting the box under one arm, he held out his other hand, wondering if he was going to leave the apartment with all his fingers.

Barksy gave him a good sniff, looked back at Mabel.

"He's okay," Mabel said, and Barksy shoved his head solidly under Paul's hand for a good pet.

"Were you talking to the dog or to me?" Paul asked.

Mabel grinned. "You can just leave that anywhere." She pointed to the box as the sound of laughter echoed toward them into the entryway above the din of Taylor Swift singing over the speaker system. "Come on in, if you can stand it!" She had to raise her voice as they moved farther into the apartment. "You want something to drink?"

"No, actually, thanks." The odd unease growing inside him since he'd followed her through the door lodged like a boulder in his chest. "I'm good." He'd have bet good money he could have anticipated what Mabel Reynolds's apartment looked like, design-wise, at least. Sensible, put-together, little flash, and all practicality.

Oh, how wrong he'd been. Mabel's home was like walking into the mind of the woman herself: a little chaotic, a whole lot of color, and a comfortable, semi-organized mess. Bookcases were filled not only with hardcover and paperback novels, but also board games, video-game consoles, and endless framed photographs. Child artwork hung on the wall, crooked clay statuary, a multitude of ashtrays—why did kids always make ashtrays?—and a collection of listing, languishing vases. Every single thing brought a smile to one's face, especially the pictures of Mabel and Keeley. Of Mabel and a variety of friends. Of Keeley in her school uniform, right down to the navy button-down blazer as well as a few of an older couple Paul assumed were Mabel's parents. And Sylvie.

Paul skimmed the shelves. Lots and lots of pictures of Sylvie.

But not in a shrine or museum dedicated to her memory kind of way. Just in a "there's no way I can ever forget you existed" fashion.

A pair of handmade scrap quilts had been tossed over the back of a worn, brown-suede sofa. The fireplace, filled not with wood but a collection of burned-down pillar candles, balanced the wall on the other side of the room with its brick façade. The furniture was a mishmash of comfortable, cushy styles in varying colors. Some pieces appeared to have been painted recently in gaudy, animation-bright colors. The flat-screen television over the fireplace was currently playing unfamiliar pop music that was no doubt an effort to test someone's age and patience.

Other than the hallway off to his left, the entirety of the apartment was one big open space save for a few brick-stabilizing pillars. The spacious kitchen was accented with a black marble counter and divided from the living room by a large rectangular table, half of which was covered with a combination of school worksheets and textbooks and files with accounting folders and a laptop. Mismatched chairs in a rainbow of hues were piled with bookbags, reusable grocery bags, jackets, and sweaters.

The distinctive aroma of fresh-baked pizza with a garlic edge mingled in the air, and above the din of the music, he heard the clink of glasses being set out.

It was, Paul thought with an odd lump in his throat, the most perfect home he'd ever entered. It felt like a family lived there. *Loved* there.

He abandoned his observations of Mabel's very pleasant and welcoming apartment to join her on the other side of the sofa where she stood enjoying the entertainment in the kitchen, all the while his heart pounded in time to the frenetic music.

Dressed in black shorts and a bright pink Taylor Swift T-shirt, her blonde hair in a bee-bopping ponytail on the top of her head, Keeley Reynolds skidded and skated back and forth in her socks, singing into a wooden spoon, and belting out her very off-key rendition of *I Knew You Were Trouble*. A tall, dark-haired woman was shaking her hips and singing along as she refilled her empty wine glass.

"Dinner and a show," Mabel yelled when there was a break in the song. "Didn't quite expect that."

Keeley yelped. Her feet flew out from under her, and she dropped out of sight. She bounced right back up, grabbing hold of the counter and hauling herself into view, her hair tangling around her grinning face. "Hi, Mom. We're celebrating."

"My coming home?" Mabel teased.

"Me *finally* finishing my math homework," Keeley announced. "Laurel helped me."

"Thanks, Laurel." Mabel glanced at Paul. "Fractions."

"Ah." Paul nodded even as he stopped himself from admitting he loved math. Especially fractions. But he made certain the impulse quickly passed.

Even if Paul hadn't heard Mabel say her friend Laurel was watching over Keeley, he'd have recognized Laurel Fontaine.

She was one of the top five defense lawyers to the stars. Actors, actresses, movie studios, producers, and at least half the members of the Fortune 500 had consulted with her at one point or another. The rich, famous, and infamous had the woman on speed dial, and yet here she stood, in Mabel's kitchen with a large wine glass at hand, wearing white yoga pants and an oversized white sweatshirt that offset her dark hair and eyes like a snow queen holding court.

Eyes that landed on Paul with the power of an asteroid hitting the earth dead center as she clicked the music off with the remote. "We were just keeping busy waiting for you."

Keeley barreled around the counter and dining room table and slid right into Mabel's open arms. Keeley beamed up at her mom in a way that stole the breath from Paul's lungs.

He glanced back to the photographs on the mantle, the one displaying Mabel and Sylvie Reynolds. Something broke apart inside of him as he realized just how much Keeley looked like her aunt. He couldn't imagine how much that must help Mabel at times. And hurt at others.

"I was practicing for my party!" Keeley said, her voice filled with laughter. "Are you ready for … holy schmoley. What happened to your face?" The little girl jumped back up as Mabel released her hold. "And your neck! Wow, Mom. Does that hurt?" Keeley grabbed Mabel's bandaged hand, turned it palm up. "What happened?"

Paul looked beyond them toward Laurel. Even as she drank, her attention—all of it—was firmly on him. A chill raced down his spine as he realized this was how witnesses must feel being questioned by her on the stand. Her reputation for never missing a trick or being surprised preceded her.

"I ran into some issues at a friend's apartment," Mabel said. "I'm fine. Just a bit banged up is all."

Paul could hear it, the steadiness in her voice, and his admiration for her grew. She'd been so worried about how to talk to her daughter, and yet when the time came, she did an effortless job. Whatever reason she'd brought him here, it hadn't been because she'd needed his support. It was more than clear that Mabel Reynolds was capable of handling anything.

"Thanks for hanging out, Laurel," Mabel said.

"Yes, it's been a real hardship." Laurel sighed and walked over to hold out her hand. "Laurel Fontaine. Paul Flynn?"

"Word travels fast."

"Only at the speed of cell phones." Laurel's hold was hard and firm, her dark-eyed gaze slightly intimidating. Barksy padded over and nosed his way into the group. Laurel released Paul's hand to pet the dog. "Hey, kiddo." She angled a look at Keeley. "Why don't you go wash up for dinner?"

Keeley frowned up at her mom, then at Paul, then at Laurel. "You just want me out of earshot, don't you?"

"Yes," Laurel confirmed. Paul had to give the women credit. Mabel's policy of not lying to her daughter about anything appeared to be shared by her friends as well.

"Mom?" Keeley asked.

Paul shoved his hands into his pockets, trying hard to quell the growing anxiety rioting around inside of him. The last thing he expected to feel around Mabel was unsettled. At least in this way. And yet …

It was one thing to know Mabel had a daughter. He hadn't been concerned about being around them. Together. Or even around Keeley herself, and yet …

He could entertain his attraction to Mabel as long as Keeley remained invisible or at the very least an image in a file. But now that he had …. The easy way they had with one another, it was obvious they shared an abject admiration and devotion, one Paul couldn't for the life of him reconcile with any reality.

His reality at least.

This wasn't a troubled house or a sad one or one that balanced on the edge of emotional or physical explosions. This was a loving home with a mother who loved her child without hesitation, reservation, or obligation. He could only imagine what a flourishing young woman Keeley would turn out to be as a result. Personally? He couldn't relate to this life at all. This was not the life he and Alden had known—grown up in.

"We just need a couple of minutes," Mabel insisted to her daughter.

"Is this because you brought a boy home?" Keeley's innocent question had Paul's face flushing for the first time he could remember. "Hi. I'm Keeley."

"Paul Flynn. Nice to meet you, Keeley." Paul found her enthusiastic and easy welcome both entertaining and terrifying.

"Are you staying for dinner? Is he, Mom?"

"Maybe." He ignored Mabel's sudden frown of surprise.

The longer he stood here, the more anxious he felt to leave. He couldn't shake the feeling he was somehow tainting them with his presence. His attraction for Mabel notwithstanding, being here, now, just didn't feel right. "We'll see."

"Cool." Keeley shrugged and sighed. "Come on Barksy. The *adults* want to talk."

Paul swore the dog gave him a warning look before he trotted after his miniature mistress.

"Quinn called," Laurel said to Mabel the second Keeley was gone. "You really okay? He said you got the crap beat out of you."

"Well, Quinn was wrong," Mabel assured her friend as she headed straight for one of the other glasses of wine. "I'm still full of crap."

Paul couldn't help it. "The EMT gave her painkillers," he told Laurel, who spun and, without hesitation, plucked the glass right out of Mabel's hands.

Mabel glared at him. "Really? You good with narc-ing on me?"

He shrugged. "You said you didn't feel right to drive."

"I'm not driving in my apartment," she muttered. "I'm fine." But even as she said it, she rubbed two fingers against her temple.

"She telling the truth about that?" Laurel looked back at Paul.

"They gave her the all clear," he said without elaborating. "Except to say if she still has a headache in the morning she should head to the ER," he added and glared right back at Mabel when she scowled again. "Sorry."

"No, you're not," Mabel grunted.

Laurel stood up straighter, as if his declaration had somehow inflated her confidence. "Okay, then. One trip to the ER in the morning, it is."

"Prophetic, are you?" Mabel challenged. "He said *if* my head still hurt. And you just lost take-home privileges," she told Paul.

"Yeah, about the pizza," Paul said before he changed his mind. "I think I'm actually going to pass." He was already backing up toward the front door. "Laurel, it was nice to meet you." He spun around and double-timed it, shoving the regret over leaving aside and reminded himself it was for the best.

He had his hand on the knob when Mabel grabbed his arm. "Hey." She moved in front of him when he barely turned to face her. "What's going on? You were fine about dinner until you came in here."

"I just wanted to make sure you got up here okay." He didn't want to look at her, didn't want to see the questions in her eyes, but he surrendered and turned, met her confused gaze.

"Is it Keeley? Do you not like kids? Or the dog? Is it Laurel? It's Laurel, isn't it? Cause I can kick her out, no problem."

But she wouldn't. He could see that as clearly as he saw her love for her child. A love he wasn't capable of offering or displaying or, as far as he knew, experiencing. Never before had he felt so completely lost in someone else's world. He needed to keep this professional. Professional and distant. For everyone involved.

"I can't think of a way to say this without sounding like a dick."

"Dick away." She released her hold, stepped back, and folded her arms across her chest. "I'm not a fan of filters anyway."

"I'm not father material."

She blinked. "Exactly what kind of pizza do you think we're having?"

"Dammit, Mabel." He rubbed his hand across his forehead as his mind raced to keep the damage to a minimum. He should have known she'd try to make a joke out of it. "I'm not kidding."

"I can see that. Paul—"

"Just … take my word for it. Me and kids are not a good mix. I thought, maybe …" But then he'd met Keeley, and he could already feel an odd and sudden connection to the girl that he didn't want. Or like. "This was a bad idea. You said so yourself back at …. It's better this way. Ending … whatever this is … before it gets going. I'd only hurt both of you in the end. I'll be in touch"—he pulled open the door and stepped into the hall—"about the case." As he closed the door, he added, "I promise."

"I know you're an overachiever, Mabel," Laurel said as Mabel walked slowly and dazedly back into the kitchen, "but that's got to be a record of some kind. What's it been, like twelve hours since you met him, and you already scared him off?"

"More like ten." Mabel grabbed her wine glass, dared Laurel to stop her with a look, and took a long drink. "That was weird, right? I mean …" She set the glass down with a clink, looked back at the door, then to Laurel. "The way he just left like that? It was weird?"

Please let it have been weird; otherwise, she'd completely misread all the signals he'd been sending. Signals she'd been more than happy to follow.

Laurel shrugged and walked over to the oven, turning it off. "Pizza's ready. You want to do the honors?"

As she had little doubt Laurel would take away her glass, Mabel brought it with her and, after grabbing the oversized cutting board off the back of the counter, quickly slid the half pizza off the baking stone and set it on the counter to rest.

"Didn't even give you time for a solid evaluation," Mabel grumbled to Laurel.

"Yeah, that's what's bothering you." Laurel craned her neck and looked down the hall. "That I didn't get a chance to get a read on him. You're thinking Keeley spooked him."

"He said he's not father material." Mabel planted a hand on one hip and stared at her friend. "Who … who says something like on impulse?" She lowered her voice. "I asked him to dinner, not to

145

march me down the aisle. He hates my kid?" Anger mingled with disappointment. "Do you know how many guys I've let Keeley meet over the years?"

"If it's the same number you've let your friends meet, then I feel safe in saying none. Wow." Laurel blew out a long breath. "Eight years. Has it really been that long since you've …. Hey, Kee."

"Did I take long enough?" Keeley looked around the kitchen and frowned. "Where is he? Did he leave?"

"He did," Mabel said. "You guys must be as hungry as I am, right? Kee, grab the plates, will you? Then clear off a spot on the table."

"How come he left?" Keeley frowned. "I thought he was going to—"

"He just did." Mabel pinched the bridge of her nose and squeezed her eyes shut. "Sorry, Kee. It's been a really long, crappy day. Mr. Flynn had someplace else he needed to be." She rummaged around in the drawer for the pizza cutter. "It doesn't matter," she muttered when Laurel placed a hand on her shoulder. "I mean, so what if he's the first guy who's felt remotely …" Interesting. Appealing. Desirable. Mabel slammed the drawer closed. She was way overreacting to a simple dinner rejection. "It doesn't matter. What the hell?" She looked up at Laurel, who appeared at her side. "Why do I care? What's the matter with me?"

"Nothing." Laurel rubbed her arm. "Men, sadly, are complicated, but they also universally suck. Even ones you haven't known for very long. But that said …"

"What?" Mabel did her best to keep her voice down as Keeley very cautiously set the table, her gaze slipping back to the two of them as if expecting more information to follow. "What could you possibly—"

"I was watching him, Mabe," Laurel said. "From the second he walked in."

"Yeah? So?" Mabel chucked a cheese grater out of the way so she could close the drawer.

"I don't think he was reacting to Keeley. Not only Keeley." Laurel had that think-y expression she wore when she was puzzling things out. "I think it was seeing the two of you together that spooked him."

"What does that even mean?" Mabel gaped. "Why would that be any different?"

Laurel shrugged. "Not everyone has the experience with happy families that you do, Mabel. It might warrant a more extended conversation if you're interested in pursuing something with him. Which it sounds like you might be, given how bitchy you got the second he left." She shrugged again. "But like I said, I'm just thinking out loud."

"You were meant to evaluate him for our investigation, Laurel," Mabel reminded her. "Not my …"

"Bed?" Laurel attempted to help. "Oh, relax. Honestly, you'd think I was talking to a Carmelite nun. For the record, the only reason I know you aren't one is because of that one over there." She inclined her head toward Keeley. "Seems to me there's a story behind Paul Flynn not thinking he's father material. Maybe find out what that story is before you write him off completely?"

Mabel pinched her lips together. She didn't have a response, mainly because either way she went wouldn't particularly make sense. Not to Laurel, and not to Mabel.

"Yeah, okay." Mabel would give that some thought. "Moving on." She turned her attention to the pizza and stabbed the cutter into it. From beside her, Barksy whimpered and nudged his head against her knee. "Let's eat."

CHAPTER NINE

"BAD day?"

Paul barely registered his Uber driver's question. He couldn't help but feel as if he'd somehow crammed a year's worth of emotional upheaval into a solitary day. From the back seat of the Prius, he pulled his attention away from the passing buildings, late-night diners, and over-lit storefronts. "Sorry?"

The middle-aged man glanced over his shoulder after stopping at a red light near the Museum of Contemporary Art on South Grand Avenue. He was a big guy, bulky, with wire-rimmed glasses and a friendly, open face that suited his current job perfectly.

"Sorry, man. Craig, is it?" Paul recalled from the app. "Did you ask me something?"

"I asked if you had a bad day. Vibes," he added at Paul's frown. "I pick up on them sometimes."

The whole town thrived on vibe readings, didn't it?

They made a left turn at the light.

"It's been a long day," he admitted.

Bad? He supposed it had had its moments.

The Westin Bonaventure rose out from behind the skyline like a beacon of loneliness ahead. It was a building so iconic it had been featured in dozens of television shows and movies in the late seventies and eighties and was still used to this day as a "you're definitely in LA" symbol.

Ten-year-old Paul would have thought he'd hit the jackpot staying in such a classy hotel. He'd come a long way from that ripped jeans, worn-out sneakers kid who had more attitude than good sense. Nights like tonight, however, he had to wonder if he wasn't still that bike-riding, foul-mouthed ragamuffin who had found every excuse possible not to go home at night.

"Guess I should stop transmitting so loudly," he said with a strained smile. He caught sight of the photo hanging on the rearview mirror in much the way cab drivers in New York displayed their loved ones. "Big family, huh?"

"Oh, yeah." Craig's smile was almost contagious. "That's Sara there." He pointed to the blonde woman, whose arms were filled with little ones. "She's a public-school teacher. Fourth grade. She has the absolute patience of ten saints. Kevin's six, Bella's four, and that's little Calvin." He flicked an affectionate finger against the image of a miniature version of Sara. "He just turned two last week. He's named after Sara's father, who passed last year. Best part of my day is coming home to them."

"Pretty late homecoming tonight," Paul observed.

"Needs must." Craig shrugged. "Kids have their hearts set on a trip to Disneyland this summer, and I'm gonna give them the best trip I can. Four, five hours of fares a night for a few weeks, and I should be able to make that happen. Best second job around, letting me set my own hours. I get home for dinner, spend a little time with them all, then I head back out. Wife puts them to bed, and sometimes, I even get to listen in during story time. Miss those evenings at home, but my kids are worth the moon." He sounded almost wistful. "How about you? You got a family?"

"No." Paul returned his focus out the window as the car moved forward once more and did his best to squash the image of Mabel floating through his head. "Not in the cards."

Craig chuckled. "Careful you don't say that too loud. Once upon a time, I thought the same thing, then *bam!*" He slammed an open palm on his steering wheel. "When I met Sara, I was done for.

149

Like completely done for—you know what I'm sayin'? I call her my lightning bolt because, man, was it over for me. Now I'm working eighteen-hour days to keep smiles on their faces."

"Lucky man," Paul said as the hotel drew closer, and a low buzzing started in his ears. He scrubbed a hand across his heart that had stumbled a bit after that last turn.

"Don't I know it. You from around here?"

"I grew up here, actually. Other side of town," Paul told him. "Came back for work. Temporarily," he added as if he needed to remind himself of that. "I'll be going back to New York." Hopefully soon. LA was suddenly feeling much too small to be sharing with a certain accountant/victim advocate.

"New York. Man." Craig shook his head. "Los Angeles is crazy enough. Never been back east, myself. Can't imagine being anywhere other than here, you know?"

"No," Paul argued. "I couldn't wait to get out." Speaking of getting out. Paul leaned forward, pointed at the dimly lit entrance gate on the right. "Do me a favor? Pull over just ahead. There's something I need to do."

"Ah, sure, man." Craig zipped the little car to the side of the road. The area wasn't exactly teeming with activity, which wasn't surprising given what was just on the other side of those gates. "This isn't some kind of hidden camera prank, is it?"

Craig leaned over to look out his window, then frowned at Paul.

"No." Paul shoved the door open. "Not a prank. I won't be long."

The night air was cool, swirling around him like a misty blanket. There was no predicting the weather these days, not even in a city like LA. Down the street, a pair of homeless pushed shopping carts piled high with their lives' belongings down and around the corner from the endless beige brick wall.

The rusted iron gates sat crooked and uneven, the chain around them pulled loose, giving him enough space to slip through. "Just like riding a bike."

His chest brushed against the iron.

He caught a glimpse of the rotting wooden letters spelling out Eternal Souls Cemetery, except, with a missing E and S, it read "ternal ouls."

Eternal Souls had never been one of LA's more prestigious afterlife locales. It had, at one time, been one of the city's potter's fields where the unclaimed and forgotten found their rest. It had had its ups and downs over the years, at least the years Paul recalled. He also was all too familiar with the skin-prickling sensation of stepping into a kind of darkness beyond the night as he made his way down the cracked and uneven road.

He pulled out his cell, tapped the flashlight app, and held it at his side as he made his way down and around, instinct rather than memory guiding him. Once lush, overhanging trees now arced naked, gnarled branches up against the moon. The broken-down land— the untended, now dead grass—had wrapped gravestones in thick tendrils of weeds, a reminder that life still attempted to exist. Even in a place of death.

If he looked down, Paul was convinced he'd see the red-and-white sneakers he'd worn as a kid, not the imported leather loafers he now wore. Shoes were an indulgence, especially to a man who had grown up wearing hand-me-downs that almost always came with holes and tears. He felt small among the shadows and memories that crept up his spine like talons of the past that refused to release him.

The trio of tombstones rose up in front of him like a sunken ship pushing out of the frothy sea. He stepped over the broken curb, his feet crunching in the dead grass. His younger self counted the steps, as it had that day. Five, six, seven. Twenty-three, twenty-four …

He stopped, his gaze falling on the small, stone mausoleum decorated with tiny gargoyles along the doorframe. As a child, standing here, he could have sworn he'd heard the stone creatures scream. Now he knew those sounds had been his own silent cries of desperation. Cries he hadn't once let slip through his determined, bruised lips.

His toes scrunched in his shoes as he crouched, one knee hitting the ground as he shined his cell against the weather-worn and obscured marker. He set his phone down, used both hands to scrub away the debris and weeds overgrowing his brother's name. The only proof, other than Paul's memories, that Alden Flynn had even existed.

The dates obscured behind his suddenly blurred vision.

"Been a while, brother," he whispered into the darkness. His voice sounded raw, even to his own ears. The math never failed to shock him even as it sobered him. It didn't seem possible someone could die at eighteen. Or that it had been more than twice that time since his brother was killed.

The anger he'd banked for most of his life spun inside of him, but he didn't set it free. He couldn't. Emotions like despair, anger, frustration, *rage* … they were as dangerous to the Flynn family line as heroin was to a drug addict. Giving in to them—surrendering to any emotion—always, *always* led somewhere impossible to come back from.

Like here. Buried and all but forgotten by the entire world save one.

He finished cleaning off the stone, doing the best he could before telling himself he'd be back. It was a lie, of course. Although he'd promised himself when he'd left New York he wouldn't come anywhere near this place again. Hell, he'd promised himself the last time he'd walked out of those gates he'd never return to the city. It had been a promise he'd intended to keep.

He picked his phone back up, turned his attention to the stone on the left. The rage, subtle and simmering at first, burned low in his belly. It barely deserved his attention, let alone his thoughts. It seemed strange that Paul couldn't feel the actual fires of hell arcing out of the ground, given it was where Orlan Flynn had no doubt been residing the past few decades.

"I did it, old man." He stood, his free hand fisting at his side so tight his fingers went numb. "I'm still here, and you're gone. Dead. And buried."

But not forgotten. Never forgotten. Not so long as blood flowed through Paul's veins. When he was gone, then, finally, his father would be as well.

His father and all the despicable, abusive, violent men of their family who had come before.

"I made it. I made it out, and I made something of myself. Despite you." Or maybe because of him.

No. No.

He instantly scratched that idea away. He wasn't going to give his old man any credit for the success he'd made of his life.

But he could damn well blame him for what he didn't have. What he could never trust himself to have.

It hadn't bothered him so much before today. Not until he'd come face-to-face with a woman who tempted him to ignore the demons that lived inside of him. The demons he'd battled back every day of his life. The demons fathers visited upon their sons.

"You son of a bitch." He wouldn't bring himself to think about Mabel in this place. Not Mabel or her daughter or that quick burst of light he'd felt inside of himself when he'd seen them together. "You're still dragging me down, aren't you? I was going to tell you that I won, but I didn't really, did I?"

Because no matter what else Paul accomplished or what he did with his life, he was still going to be what he'd always been, ever since Alden had died.

Alone.

The air seemed thinner on his walk back to the car. The darkness, a bit less intimidating. The sight of the white Prius sitting on the other side of the cemetery entrance acted as a kind of beacon of moving forward. He'd been dreading the idea of coming here, of what seeing those graves would feel like, and now he knew. He'd exceeded his own expectations. Definitely his father's expectations. Now he only had to keep going to be the man Alden believed he could be.

"Wasn't sure if I was going to have to come looking for you." Craig's greeting when Paul climbed back into the car sounded a bit tense. "Don't think I could have gotten through those gates …" His attempt at a joke fell flat. "You okay, man?"

"Yeah." Paul reached into his pocket for his wallet, pulled out every last bit of cash he had. "Yeah, thanks for stopping. For you. And the family." He handed the money over. "Maybe take a few nights off and enjoy story time."

"Man." Craig balked as he counted the cash. "This is … this is way too—"

He started to hand it back, but Paul held up his hands.

"You take that family of yours on the best trip you can. Enjoy every single second. You're a good dad, Craig," Paul told him. "Believe me, there's nothing better in this world to be than that."

"Knock knock!"

Mabel jerked awake at the sound of Sutton's voice echoing through her apartment.

She groaned, rested her head in her hands, and tried to untwist out of the pretzel she'd made of herself while attempting to work. Barksy whined and shoved his nose under her hand and earned himself a quick pet as she turned in her chair. The headache from the other night had indeed faded over the last few days, but that didn't mean she wasn't waiting for it to come back full throttle. The aches and bruises, on the other hand …

"Hey." She felt herself transported into some kind of culinary heaven at the aroma drifting off the plate that Sutton waved in front of her nose. "What time is it?" She glanced at her watch and felt the panic set in as Sutton grabbed a couple of plates out of one of the kitchen cabinets. "Holy—"

She shot out of her chair, made it halfway down the hall to Keeley's room before Sutton called, "I already took the kids to school. Keeley came down for breakfast. She said you passed out working and didn't want to wake you up but that you have to pick someone up at the hospital later this morning. Which is why I'm here." Sutton leaned around the corner and grinned at her. "Consider me your alarm clock. With pastries."

"Right."

Pastries. Her stomach growled.

Barksy whined, but instead of earning himself one of Sutton's goodies, Mabel grabbed his bowl and filled it with kibble. Barksy's claws tapped on the wood floor as he approached, shot her a look that was clearly meant to convey his displeasure, and began to eat.

Mabel ran her hands down her face. The week was almost over, and she felt like she was stuck on a treadmill, running as fast as she could but getting nowhere. Even Sylvie, it seemed, knew to stay away from her subconscious. She hadn't dreamed about her sister in days.

She rubbed her fingers against her heart and tried to focus on her to-do list.

The only thing she'd managed to do to help Eva, other than arrange to get her to Soteria, was drop off Benedict Cumberbunny the other morning. She was improving, slowly. Enough that the hospital had approved her discharge before the weekend. Seeing the young woman's half-smile of gratitude had been well worth the drive.

"Thanks. Was she okay? Keeley? Dammit!" She picked up her phone, noticed it was completely dead, and blew out a frustrated breath.

"Seemed okay." Sutton glanced up, an uncharacteristic frown on her girl-next-door face as Mabel returned to the table after plugging her phone in on the hall table.

With her straight brown hair, light brown eyes, and killer aptitude in the kitchen, Sutton had always struck Mabel as a cross between Sydney Bristow (Sutton's all-time favorite TV show was *Alias*) and Julia Child, with a healthy dash of sass thrown in. The woman was as responsible and reliable as a Rolex and often, much to Mabel's frustration, stepped in to pick up whatever slack Mabel dropped.

"Fair warning, though," Sutton added. "Keeley thinks you're moping around because of a man."

"What man?" Mabel returned to the kitchen and the counter and breathed in the fresh-baked aroma of apple turnovers, glistening with butter and glittery, crunchy sugar. She kept an arm across her ribs, as if by doing so she could ease the still throbbing ache of loneliness.

"Huh." Sutton set a turnover on a plate and held it out, pulling it just out of reach when Mabel grabbed for it. "And here I thought you'd take offense to the idea of you moping. What's his name?"

"Gimmie." Mabel snatched the plate and returned to the table, sweeping the piles of files, receipts, and her laptop aside. "Other than this guy." She nudged Barksy as he brushed past her on the way to his bed by the fireplace. "The only man in my life is the one coming up to replace my showerhead. Which should be any time, so if you want to make an escape before Blake gets here—"

"I don't make an escape for anyone, especially a man." Sutton shot her a glare before plucking up her own turnover and biting in. "Mmm." She inclined her head from side to side, as she often did when evaluating a new recipe. "This is good, but it needs more cinnamon."

"How do you know that?" Mabel asked, enjoying what was turning out to be her breakfast, even if it did give her sticky fingers. "I'll take your word for it, though."

"You only get cranky like this when you haven't had enough coffee." Sutton refilled the maker and set it to brewing, smoothed a hand down the front of her pale-yellow shirt. "It's after ten, and you've only sucked down one pot. No wonder you're clenched so tight. Keeley might be onto something. You need a man."

"Do not," Mabel grumbled. "Why do you think I need a new showerhead?"

Sutton snorted, grabbed the cream out of the fridge, and brought it over to the table for their coffee. "This man Keeley mentioned wouldn't be Paul Flynn, would it? Quinn might have mentioned him when he and Riley stopped by last night."

Mabel glowered. It had been days since Paul had left her apartment, and despite Mabel's claim that it didn't bother her, it did. And she couldn't, for the life of her, figure out why.

"It's a stupid crush," she admitted. "It'll pass." But it sure hadn't yet.

The man had taken to inserting himself into her dreams, supplanting her sister, hence the sleepless, uncomfortable nights and early morning hours sleeping on her laptop. Now she could feel a migraine pricking behind her eyes. A migraine she should have anticipated, given her whacky schedule and lack of sleep.

"Sure, it will." Sutton shrugged. "Just like you got over the last one. And the one before that. Oh, no, that wasn't you. Ever. Have you even dated anyone seriously since you've lived here?"

"There are more important things in life than relationships."

"Funny how it's always people who aren't in one who say that." The aroma of coffee filled the kitchen. "Laurel said he's hot."

Obviously, the topic was not going to change any time soon. "Laurel thinks every man she meets is hot."

"Not true," Sutton argued. "Remember that doctor she met at that fundraiser last year?"

"Jabba the Butt?"

"Yeah, that was an unfortunate comment I made." Sutton cringed.

"Within earshot," Mabel reminded her all too happily.

"Proof I should not be left alone at the bar."

"Or it's evidence you need to go to them more often," Mabel teased. "You were just out of practice. And for the record, Jabba was a little slimy looking." The front-door buzzer rang. "Speaking of prac-tice." Mabel giggled when Sutton rolled her eyes and made her way back to the coffee. "Hey, Blake." She stepped back to let the building manager and his oversized toolbox in. "Thanks for the assist."

"Not a problem." He sniffed the air, handed over the packaged showerhead for Mabel's approval, which she gave immediately. "Sut-ton's been baking. Apple something."

"Why, yes." Mabel kicked the door shut and trotted after him. "She has. Apple turnovers, as a matter of fact. You want one?"

"Maybe to go," Blake said when Sutton turned, holding two cups of coffee. "Mrs. Yan needs her washing machine checked, and the dishwasher in Carly's apartment's acting up again. Full sched-ule. I'll just be … back there." He pointed down the hall before he disappeared.

Mabel frowned at Sutton. "What was that?"

The man was moving like he had jet packs in his work boots.

"Avoidance." Sutton shrugged, handed off one of the mugs, and walked back around to the table. "I think I make him nervous."

"The man's former military intelligence and still carries a gun," Mabel reminded her. Both those qualities had been part of the rea-son Riley had hired him late last year after their previous manager quit without any warning. "I can't imagine Blake Redford has been nervous a day in his life."

"Given the alternative is he just doesn't like me, I'm sticking with nervous." Sutton shrugged, but it was impossible to miss the confu-sion in her eyes. "I've been nice. I've even baked him things."

"It is your secret weapon, after all." Mabel considered, reached for a second turnover. Being nice was a given; her friend had "nice girl" written all over her in very practical blue ballpoint pen. "He's good with the kids."

"He really is." Sutton nodded. "He tolerates Lucas tagging after him on the weekends. It's lucky he can get any work done. And then there's Addie, who stays as far away from him as possible." She sighed, rested her chin in her palm. "I think maybe he reminds them of their dad."

"It's possible, I suppose." Mabel took a slow sip of coffee. "They weren't that old when your brother and sister-in-law died."

"My brother had a way of making a lasting impression." Sutton's faraway, haunted smile looked all too familiar. "He's a hard person to forget. And like Blake, he was military."

Mabel recognized that grief-tinged longing in her friend's eyes. Their shared loss of a sibling was something they'd bonded over almost immediately when Sutton had been granted custody of her then four-year-old nephew and three-year-old niece. Becoming an instant parent to two young ones who were suddenly without their parents was a tough road to walk alone, but as Mabel had learned, no one in Temple House was ever completely alone.

For Mabel, it was the first time she'd felt as if she could help someone in return for the support she'd received upon moving in. Their common emotional pain was something no one ever got over. Learning how to navigate those now-lonely waters, however, was a particular kind of angst, especially with two little ones in tow. Hers and Sutton's shared single-motherhood load created an additional bond Mabel didn't share with anyone else.

As close as she was to Riley, Laurel, and Cass—not that anyone was particularly close to Cass—Mabel's relationship with Sutton existed on a different, supportive, almost telepathic level.

"You know about Blake's wife and son, right?" Mabel asked, this time lowering her voice, just to be safe. Not that Blake Redford had ever shown any inclination to eavesdropping. If anything, the man seemed to go out of his way to avoid most anything related to conversation.

"That they were killed in a fire while he was stationed overseas? Yeah, Riley told me." Sutton's confusion shifted to sympathy. "I guess that explains a lot of things."

"Hey, Mabel." Blake emerged from her back bedroom down the hall, old showerhead wrapped in a dirty rag. "You're good to go. Let me know if it gives you any problems."

"That was fast."

"Places to be, things to do." He flashed them an uncharacteristically wide smile.

"Take some turnovers. Hang on. Let me get you a bag." Mabel returned to the kitchen, grabbed a plastic baggie, and slipped two of the turnovers inside. "Your reward."

"Thanks." His gaze shifted to Sutton. "I'm sure they're delicious."

"That's always my aim," Sutton said easily. "This weekend, I'm trying out a new cinnamon roll recipe."

"I look forward to the results." He saluted them both before he headed for the door. "And for the record, all of you make me nervous." His light blue eyes sparked when he glanced over his shoulder. "Some of you in different ways than others."

Mabel waited until the door closed behind him before she swung around to look at Sutton, whose cheeks had gone fire-engine red. "Something tells me that comment had absolutely nothing to do with me."

"Shut up." Sutton picked up another turnover. "I need to get upstairs and change. I've got a meeting with the new manager at Golden Age Retirement. Word is they're making some staff changes, and I need to show how indispensable I am."

"Can a nutritionist be indispensable?" Mabel teased as she followed her friend—sans leftover turnovers—to the door.

"I plan to be the first," Sutton smiled. "I'd offer to get Keeley when I pick up Addie and Lucas, but she has science club after school, right?"

"Yeah. She won't be done until around four. Don't worry. I'll get her after I get Eva settled at Soteria." Her best intentions to have Eva's things waiting for her in her new room had fallen by the wayside under the responsibilities of recent days. Helping Eva unpack would have to do as a show of camaraderie. She glanced at her watch. "Which reminds me, I really should get going. Time to test run that showerhead."

"Be kind." Sutton laid a hand on Mabel's shoulder and grinned so wide Mabel could see her back teeth. "Showerheads can only take so much abuse."

"Now you need to shut up." Mabel laughed and pushed her out the door.

The buzzing on Paul's desk sounded like a constipated bee. Not that he knew what one sounded like, but it seemed an apt if not entertaining description.

What little time he hadn't spent attempting to flesh out details of the Tenado case had been focused on playing phone tag with Maya Rivera, a US Marshall he'd met at a law enforcement convention a few years back when he'd been one of the keynote speakers. Her years with the Marshall service and her experience with the penal system in particular were what he was banking on when it came to getting some answers about the whereabouts of Dean Samuels, their missing and potentially wrongfully convicted killer of Melanie Dennings. Finally, this morning, he and Maya had connected, but Paul hadn't heard much optimism in her voice when she told him she'd see what she could find out.

The conversation had not been the ideal way to start his day.

Without pulling his attention away from his computer screen, he reached over and tapped the intercom. "Yeah, Kent?"

"You have a visitor," Kent croaked. "Laurel Fontaine? I'm afraid she doesn't have an appointment."

Paul pulled off his glasses and frowned, then he couldn't help but chuckle at the dismay in his assistant's voice. Paul had only briefly met Laurel once, but he could understand the affect she might have on a malleable male mind. Rather than answering, he got up and opened the door. "Good, ah …" He glanced at the clock. "Yeah, it's still morning."

"I hope I'm not intruding," Laurel said easily. "I was hoping for a couple of minutes?"

"Is Mabel all right?" The question was out before he even thought to censure himself.

"She's fine." Laurel's smile was lazy and all too knowing. "I'll be sure to let her know you asked."

"Great." Awesome. Ugh. "What?" he asked at his assistant's slightly panicked expression. "What's wrong?"

"You need to be downstairs for the press conference with the DA by eleven," Kent reminded him.

"He won't be late," Laurel assured them both before she breezed through the door into his office on the tallest, thinnest heels Paul had ever seen in his life.

He'd seen his share of stilettos and immediately thought these should be labeled as lethal weapons. That said, they didn't hold a candle to a certain someone's scuffed, black, flat-heeled boots he'd developed an affinity for.

Dammit!

He eyed the coffee cup and white paper bag in her hand with curiosity as he closed the door but not before he caught Kent's gaping expression. The lack of a smile on Laurel's face when she looked at him, however, had Paul faltering.

His heart skipped a beat. "I thought you said she was okay?"

"She is." Her eyes narrowed in a particularly unnerving way. "A little ticked at how you left things the other night, but she'll get over it." She set the tray and paper bag on his desk before dropping her own tote onto one of the two empty chairs.

He could not, for the life of him, figure out what Laurel Fontaine would want with him. "May I take your coat?"

"Thank you, yes."

She shimmied out of the white pseudo-wool coat as he lifted it from her shoulders. As she moved, the faintest hint of roses drifted off her skin. Her white slacks were pressed so precisely he could see razor-sharp seams running down the front of her long legs. The matching white waist-length blazer was accented with tiny gold buttons and threading offsetting the rose-red blouse she wore beneath. Her outlined dark eyes were the exact same brown as her hair that caught the dim light of his desk lamp and glistened a bit. She was a woman who took possession of any room the instant she entered it. His office included.

"I have a meeting with a client and Jocelyn Alcina upstairs in a little while," she told him easily. "I thought I'd be a little early and pay you a visit."

Her coffee back in hand, she wandered around his office without giving away an iota of a clue as to what she thought about the meager and uninspired décor. *Blah* was just about the only word adequate enough to describe the mostly empty bookcases, worn leather sofa, and other additions that appeared to have been dragged up from a forgotten storage unit in the basement of the DA's office. But he wouldn't be here long enough to necessitate any changes.

"I'm not interrupting anything, am I?" Laurel asked.

"Not at all." If anything, he'd been spinning his wheels organizing all the nebulous details of the case that had presented nothing but more questions. Questions he intended to start publicly addressing in a little over an hour.

Unfortunately, all his wheel spinning meant his simple plan to walk away from Mabel and not dwell on *what might have beens* had been a miserable failure. That and the universe's propensity for using him as a cosmic emotional punching bag. He should have known nothing about Mabel Reynolds, including any attempt he made to put her firmly in the rearview mirror, would be simple. Or forgettable.

"That's for you," Laurel gestured to the bag as she walked past his desk. "Sutton's in baking mode most mornings these days. Apple turnovers."

"Homemade?" As his breakfast had consisted of a watery kale smoothie from the hotel snack bar, Paul pried open the edges of the bag as his stomach betrayed him and rumbled. "I think this might be what heaven smells like." He met her gaze. "Not that I'm not happy to accept, but dare I ask the reason behind it?" He reached in and pulled out a paper-wrapped turnover that crunched between his fingers.

"Do I need a reason?"

He bit in and happily accepted the surge of sugar into his system. The crisp sugar coating and still-warm chunky apple insides made him practically swoon and swear off smoothies for life. "You strike me as the kind of woman who has a reason for everything she does."

"Perceptive. And straightforward. Definite points in your favor." Her perfectly painted lips curved as she strode over to the whiteboard, coffee cup clasped between her hands as she perused the notes and pictures he'd organized over the past days.

"Hard to believe all these faces belong to people who had lives." Laurel tapped a long red fingernail against the board, right near the image of Sylvie Reynolds. "It seems so out of the realm of possibility that they're gone, and yet no one seems to have been looking for them. What do you see in all this?"

"Other than the fact I need another half dozen boards? Confusion," Paul admitted without hesitation as he took another bite. "Obfuscation. And that's just on that side." He nodded when she reached down to flip the board over. The trail of anyone with a financial stake or tie to the Tenado estate looked like a maniacal spiderweb of misinformation and garbage. None of it seemed to make sense. At least, no sense he'd been able to ascertain. "Tenado's been dead for going on four years."

"Yes. I remember when he died. Drowned, I believe," Laurel said. "In his backyard pool. Tragic, if not a bit strange."

"As a fellow successful attorney—"

"Successful," Laurel chuckled. "You're cute, Paul."

"As a very successful fellow attorney," his lips twitched, "if the DA asked you for your clients' files and information, what would you turn over?"

"Oh. A what-if game. Fun." She glanced over her shoulder. "Honestly? As little as I could get away with." She paused, as if tapping into his thoughts. "You had DA Eichorn approach Holland Young about Tenado's financial records?"

"What makes you think I didn't ask for them myself?"

"Because your request wouldn't mean anything to them," Laurel countered.

"I wouldn't have put it exactly like that," he mused, "but you're right. I also pushed for her to get Tenado's list of clients at the time of his death, along with his will and/or trust."

"The client list might be an overreach," Laurel mused. "But the will, any trusts he might have had, and all his financial records are within your purview. Why do you ask? What did they give you?"

"Everything but the trust."

"Everything?" Her brows arched. "Even the list? After the first request?"

"Yep." He liked how she had the same reaction he'd had. He'd been ready to do battle over any and all records in regard to Anthony Tenado. And yet here they sat, in a half-dozen file boxes piled next to his desk, which he pointed to now. "Right down to his financial statements and a document listing all of his accounts and investments from every institution he did business with. They even sent that list of clients. All of them, right up to the time of his death."

"Really?" Laurel's head tilted, gaze skimming the boxes. "Do you know if they consulted with Tenado's former agency partners before releasing that information?"

"I don't. If they didn't, that's not my problem."

"You know as well as I do that isn't necessarily surprising. Yes, they could have strung it out, but they really don't have standing to refuse the request given the investigation. Not complying with the request gives you ammunition to use against them with the press. Tenado's estate would have been settled ages ago. Not getting his will or trust—"

"Oh, I got the will."

Confusion and surprise mingled in her dark eyes. She walked away from the board and took a seat in the same chair Mabel had occupied earlier in the week. "They sent the will but not the trust. How do you know there is a trust? If his will was in order—"

"Exactly. So, I assumed, given what was missing from that will, that there had to have been a trust."

"I changed my mind." Laurel's eyes narrowed. "This isn't fun anymore. What was missing from the will?"

"The house."

"The house." Laurel paused. "You mean the Tenado estate? The entire property?"

"The itemization of what he left to people went on for thirty-two pages. Cash, investment certificates, other property, his cars, his gold cuff-link collection, for crying out loud, his shares in a private jet he's had at his disposal for more than a decade. Every antique, every piece of art, it was all there. But there's not one mention of the house he lived in for more than twenty years."

"Which led you to believe there's a trust," Laurel reasoned.

"Actually, it led me to think there wasn't one."

"Circling the point." Laurel waved a finger in the air. "Land anytime."

"I went through every file and report connected to the Tenado Estate. I even went back into the Melanie Dennings file to see if there'd been some mention there, but nowhere does it say anyone actually verified who owned the property."

"And did Tenado own the property?"

"Nope." Paul sat back, feeling more than pleased with himself. Surprising a woman like Laurel felt like an ego boost. "Not unless he's going under the name Sumatra, Inc. It's the company that's listed with the county clerk's office as the owner of record." He paused. "And they've owned it since 1939. You ever heard of it?"

"Sumatra?" Laurel frowned. "No, I don't think so. I can have my assistants do some digging, but it's not familiar. It should be, though. If it's that old."

"Agreed, but so far, I've found zilch online. No website for Sumatra. The only things that pop up when I type in Sumatra are coffee, TripAdvisor, and some rare flower that was once only cultivated in specialty greenhouses."

"A flower." Laurel pursed her lips, her gaze narrowing once again. "I don't suppose it's a type of lily?"

"A red one, yes." He inclined his head, kept his eyes on her face. She'd leapt on that even faster than he had. "The stained-glass window over the front door of Tenado's house is a lily. I'm thinking whatever company this was, if it's even still around, is ahead of the curve with branding."

"Do me a favor?" Laurel stood, set her cup on his desk, and circled around. "Pull up the property records again."

"Ah, sure. I took a screenshot, actually." He clicked and scrolled as she braced one hand on the back of his chair, the other on his desk. She leaned over, her long hair spilling over her shoulders. "What are you looking for?"

"That." She poked a lethal nail at the address on file for Sumatra, Inc. "Oh, they're good." She shook her head, and as he tilted his head to the side to look at her, the smile on her face gave him chills. "They underestimated you, Paul. They thought giving you everything you asked for meant you wouldn't go digging in a different direction, and here we are. All the way back to 1939."

"You lost me."

"Young & Fairbanks is a law firm that goes way back. To before the talkies. Do you know how many businesses pre-date movies in this city?" Laurel asked.

"Sometimes, I think we should have stuck to silent films," Paul muttered, recalling a childhood affinity for Chaplin, Keaton, and Valentino. Then he answered her question. "Not many, I suppose."

"Correct. Not only did Young & Fairbanks represent Sheldon G. Powell, but the law firm was one of the first investors in his film studio. They were paid with stock, and they're part-owners even today. And that address there?" She tapped the screen again. "That was their very first office." She paused, frowned. "Damn."

He could almost hear her jaw clench. "What?"

"Powell Studios." She somehow managed to make it sound profane. "I really didn't want to think Riley was right, but suddenly, that movie offer they made Moxie makes a hell of a lot more sense."

"I'm sorry, what mo—"

"Powell Studios might be involved in all of this!"

Paul was finding this new information hard to swallow. "Are you sure about that? Powell Studios *and* Granger Powell?"

"Paul, please." Laurel dismissed the question. "You're forgetting who some of my clients are. I've been privy to some information that would scald your ears off your head. Hollywood biographies? Studio tell-alls? They haven't scratched the surface as to what machinations have gone on in this town. For decades. And the Powell family being involved makes more sense than you can ever imagine." She seemed to have shocked herself, and she stood up, her interest having shifted to caution. "I need to be going."

"Hang on." Paul jumped to his feet as Laurel returned to her chair and retrieved her coat, bag, and coffee. "Should I be looking at who Young & Fairbanks's other clients are?"

"I would," Laurel agreed.

"Yeah, but that's not something I can compel with a court order. Client lists are confidential unless I come at them with something really big."

"Who knows," Laurel said easily. "Maybe you'll do just that."

"If Tenado is considered complicit in regard to the missing women, wouldn't all this mean Young & Fairbanks is as well? We were basing our suspicions about Tenado due to the assumption he owned the property."

"Why are you asking me a question you already know the answer to?" Laurel asked. "But you don't have enough to wiggle around a judge's ethics. Especially not a judge in this town."

"What does that mean?"

"It means you're going to have to find a work-around, which means you're going to need help." Laurel's eyes sparkled, and it felt as if she'd made a decision that would somehow affect him. "You need help well beyond what that young man out there is capable of providing. You know what would help?"

"A sledgehammer over my skull?"

Her smile was quick and understanding. "You need a team."

"You mean a task force? Yeah," Paul let out a harsh laugh, "I'm currently in a holding pattern with that." He hadn't given the DA enough time to come back at her on that front yet. "Why? Do you have an in with the DA? You want to make that suggestion, so I don't have to again?"

"Johanna Eichorn and I have a guardedly professional and cordial relationship," Laurel told him. "Trust me, I'm the last person you want asking her for anything of benefit to you. But I can do this: I've got contacts, and a lot of them feel no love for Powell Studios or the family and law firm behind it. Give me a day, maybe two. Let me see if I can get at least a partial list of their clients."

"Isn't that unethical?"

"You're dealing with Young & Fairbanks. Unethical is the only way they operate, believe me. That said, I'm a lot smarter. And determined." She hesitated, her arm tightening around the coat she was holding. "Have you been up there yet?"

"To the estate?" Paul asked. "Yes. Yes, I have." And he'd been having nightmares about the place ever since.

"I haven't." Her brows pinched. "I'm not a coward by nature. When I see something coming at me, I tend to barrel ahead, full bore, crash right through. But that place …" She shook her head. "It's a horror I prefer to avoid if possible. I prefer my human cruelty to be confined to my television screen. I witnessed what that place did to Riley and Quinn." There was a shadow of fear, a little concern, and more than a flash of anger that sparked in her eyes. "And Mabel shortly after. She came back with … shadows on her heart."

"I hope she didn't go alone," he murmured. "The place is—"

"Haunted," Laurel mused. "Riley's word, not mine. Mabel hasn't talked about it. I think, until Sylvie's photograph was found there, she still had hope, however thin, that her sister was alive."

"There's little worse than losing hope." Paul probably should have kept that thought to himself.

"No," Laurel agreed and eased his mind. "There's not. I've tried to get her to open up, but she's locked that part of herself away, and the door isn't budging. She's different, though. Since she went there. She's …"

"Angrier?"

"I was going to say determined, but angry as well. She's spiraling. She's doing her best to hide it, but we see it. Keeley sees it, even if she doesn't recognize it for what it is. Mabel needs someone in her life who understands those feelings." She looked at him until he felt like a witness squirming in the witness chair. "I think you understand those feelings all too well. Don't you, Paul?"

"Is that why you really stopped by? To spy on me for Mabel?"

"Mabel can take care of herself, but for the record, you hurt her the other night when you left. I've never seen her that way when it comes to a man." Confusion clouded her dark eyes. "You must have reached her in some way. Some way her friends have never been able to."

"It wasn't my intention. To hurt her," he clarified. Whether he'd reached her or not … "The other night at her apartment."

"That's between the two of you," Laurel assured him. "I came here today because I had my own questions."

"About the case?"

"And about you. Funnily enough, you've managed to answer just about all of them."

He took the last bite of turnover and made a mental note to have a salad for lunch. "Don't be offended, but I didn't intend to."

"No offense taken. Mabel has a theory about why you jack-rabbited the other night. I have another." She paused. "It wasn't Keeley that freaked you out, was it?"

"Keeley?" He blinked. "Of course, it wasn't Keeley. Is that what—?" He trailed off, replaying the scene in his head. "Jesus." He frowned. "I guess it would look that way. I'm sorry. I never intended …. My leaving the other night had nothing to do with Mabel or her daughter."

"Of course, it did." Laurel inclined her head in a way that gave Paul an inkling of what it might be like to be cross-examined by this woman. "A man your age, who's never been married, who does the kind of work you do? Who had the childhood you did? You think you're protecting them."

"How could you know that?" Paul demanded.

"I'm a good reader of people. Something I believe you have a talent for yourself." She hesitated, readjusted her hold on her bag. "I know what it's like to want to leave everything about your past behind. Reinvention is a tricky thing. Just when you think you've moved on, *bam!* You get hit in the face with everything you think you don't want. You like her, Paul. You like her a lot. You aren't as clever at hiding your emotions as you'd like people to think. It's okay to take a step into her world. Take it from someone who has. Dip a toe in. You won't be sorry."

He clenched his fists, resisted the urge to drag frustrated hands through his hair. He could not believe he was having this conversation with someone who was, essentially, a total stranger.

"I'll admit I like her, and I'll admit it happened in a flash. Like a …" He recalled what his Uber driver had said the other night, and damn it if he didn't agree. "It was a bolt of lightning. I know this. Kissing her was a mistake, but at the time …" He stopped at Laurel's arched and amused brows. "You didn't know about that part, did you?"

"No." Laurel's smile was slow to emerge. "But it explains an awful lot. Please, continue."

He gritted his back teeth. "What happened the other night shouldn't have." He'd been scared and worried and angry all at the same time, and he'd needed to …. Hell, he'd needed to convince himself she was really okay. Little did he know kissing her would mean he probably never would be okay. Ever again. And yet it was just about the only thing he wanted to do. "I'm not going to be here for very long. Getting involved with anyone while I am—especially someone who has a kid—is a straight-up bad idea. You care about Mabel, Laurel. You probably did your own check on me before you walked into this office. You know I'm not a good guy for her. I just want to do my job and get back to my life."

"That is a very logical, mature, and thought-through argument." Laurel nodded slowly. "You make complete sense. You're protecting them. From getting attached."

"Exactly."

"And from something inside of you that might not actually exist. None of us default into becoming our parents, thank God." Her smile was quick and clearly held more secrets than she was willing to share. "The choices we make, not who we're born to, define who we are, Paul. Just something to consider. Good talk." Laurel reached for the door handle. "Excellent conversation, Mr. Flynn. I feel a lot better now about how things should move forward."

Whatever peace he had in closing the proverbial door on his relationship with Mabel vanished. "What things—?"

"You'd best get over whatever issues you have about keeping Mabel at a distance. You need her on this case with you. Heck, she may as well have her own board over there. But there are more parts, bigger pieces you haven't even begun to see yet on that board of yours." She flicked a finger toward his display. "Stay close to your phone, Paul. We'll be calling."

Following Laurel's train of thought was a bit like running a 5K without any training. But something she'd said … "*We*. First Mabel, then Quinn, now you. Who's this *we* you all keep talking about?"

"All in good time." She tossed him another one of her smiles as she pulled open his office door and walked out. "Lovely to meet you, Kent," she said to Paul's assistant on her way out. He followed, chuckling to himself as she said, "If you're ever interested in the other side of the courtroom, give my office a call. I can always use a sharp and protective intern."

"Should I ask what that was all about?" Kent asked once she was gone.

"You can ask," Paul said with a slow shake of his head. "But I don't think I have anything remotely close to an answer."

CHAPTER TEN

A chill raced down Mabel's spine as she stepped out of the shower.

The odd sensation of being exposed, of being watched, slid through her as she reached for her purple-flowered robe and tugged it on, knotting the belt so tightly her ribs hurt.

She held open the bathroom door and listened. Barksy's low whine and cold nose nudging against her knees had Mabel shaking her head and reaching down to pat the dog firmly on the head.

"Must be imagining things," she murmured. "You'd let me know if something was amiss, wouldn't you, boy?"

Of course, he would. Barksy was nothing if not attentive to their surroundings. Even familiar locked-down ones like the apartment.

She turned to the sink, casually glancing out the fourth-floor window overlooking the parking lot and dog park.

She shuddered.

There it was again.

She clasped a hand over the back of her neck and moved closer, scanning the area with narrowed eyes. The noise from the playground on the other side of the dog park was muted to the point of near silence. Mabel watched a few people walking around, some with their dogs, others with their children. She stepped to the side, made note of the cars passing on the side street and the mostly familiar vehicles parked in the area.

Out of the corner of her eye, something moved. Her head swiveled in time to see someone step out from behind a tree. Her heart thudded heavily as she watched him. Was it him? The man from Eva's bedroom? She couldn't tell. From this distance, there was no judging his height or build accurately.

He moved slowly, deliberately, and yet … he didn't seem particularly familiar or curious about anything other than …

He stopped walking, turned. He lifted his chin and looked directly at her. Through her.

"Shit." She leaped to the side, gripping the edges of her robe against her throat, offered a less-than-calming pat to Barksy who whined in sympathy. "Shit. Tell me I'm imagining things, Barks," she demanded and carefully, slowly, stepped back to the window to look out once more.

The man was gone.

But she did not breathe easier.

She grabbed her phone, dialed before she talked herself out of it.

Blake's strong, comforting voice answered after one ring. "Hey, Mabel? How's the shower—?"

"Can you come back to my apartment?" The words came out in a rush. "I think I …" She considered her next words: that she saw some boogey man lurking in a park in Los Angeles. There were probably a million of them in this city. "Can you just—"

"On my way."

Mabel clicked off, tucked her phone against her chest and paced a few steps before heading to the door. Barksy whined in the way he always did when anxiety struck. She pulled the door open as Blake, sans toolbox, ran up the last two stairs to the landing.

"What's wrong?" he demanded, and she got a flash of how he must have been in the military.

"I saw someone. Outside, in the park." She waved him in, closed the door, and returned to the window. "He was watching me. I'm certain of it." She pointed to the tree.

He didn't question her sanity, even if she did. "Did you get a good look at him?"

"Not enough for a description," Mabel admitted, and as she said it, wondered if she was overreacting. "He looked up at this window, Blake. Right when I was standing here, but from this distance ..."

"Okay." Blake nodded, reached up, and pulled down the blind. Then repeated the motion with the other park-facing windows.

"Well, he's gone now." She tried to laugh. "I don't think—What? What are you doing?" She stepped closer to see what he was typing on his cell.

"There's a product on the market—a security film that prevents anyone from seeing inside without obscuring your view. I didn't think it was necessary, especially this high up, but that might have been wrong. Stupid," he muttered. "Should have listened to my gut. It shouldn't take me more than twenty-four hours to get them installed. As soon as I get my hands on it."

Mabel bit her lip. "You don't think that's overkill?"

"No." Blake said without looking up. "I do not."

"How much—?"

Now he did look up, and for the first time, she thought she saw irritation flashing in his eyes. "I might be a building manager in title, but I'm responsible for the security of both Temple House *and* its residents. This?" He waved his free hand up and down the height of her windows. "You didn't feel safe, did you?"

"No," she admitted with a wince. "I didn't." But she felt safer *now*. Blake tended to have that effect on her.

"Then this is on me. I'll talk to Riley, let her know what I'm doing and why. Added security offsets insurance costs, so she'll be amenable."

"Knowing Riley, she'll want them for herself and Moxie."

"Already planning on it. Full building upgrade," Blake said. "Now, if you'll excuse me. I've got a tree to check out."

"You're ..." She hurried after him. "You're seriously going to look at the tree? For what?"

"No idea," he told her. "He could have left behind a cigarette butt, footprints—something we can analyze. I'm not taking any chances." He paused before making his way to the door, studied her closely. "You okay now?"

"Yeah." She nodded, clutched the collar of her robe in her hand. "Yes, I think so."

"Okay then. I'll check in with you later about the film. In the meantime," he gestured back to the windows, "keep the shades down until they're in place, yeah?"

"I will."

She closed the door after him and, unable to resist temptation, hurried back to the window and peeked out around the corner of the shade.

Moments later, Blake made his way down the street to the park, did a sweep around the tree she'd pointed out, then—just as he was about to walk away—stopped, stooped down, and reached out to touch something. Next thing she knew, he'd pulled out his cell and snapped a few pictures. He looked up at her window, and instinctively, she jumped back again. If he saw her, she couldn't tell before he pocketed his phone and headed back to Temple House.

It wasn't necessarily the promise of protective film that eased her nerves. No doubt just telling Blake what she saw had done that. He'd be even more vigilant from here on, if that was possible, and she'd bet half a year's pay he had plans to install additional cameras aimed right at the park if he could get away with it. But then that was what they had Laurel for, wasn't it? To identify those pesky ordinances they might be violating.

With her heart back at a steady beat, she returned to the bathroom, grabbed a towel off the hook beside the shower, and used it to scrub dry her hair as she made a quick tour of the kitchen to clean up. Doing so burned off the last of the nervous energy.

She closed her laptop and gathered up her paperwork, straightened her workspace, and then focused on Eva's belongings.

Between her accounting work, Keeley's homework, and her daughter's obscenely overactive school-event schedule, Mabel hadn't had time to reorganize the box and suitcase after she and Paul had brought them in from her van.

Paul. There he was again. Just popping into her thoughts like an undefeatable whack-a-mole that couldn't take no for an answer. There was no earthly reason for her to keep dwelling on him, and the idea that Keeley had been unintentionally designated as some kind of man repellent did not sit well.

"Just as well," she told herself. Better to learn this now rather than later on, when she or Keeley had become attached.

Mabel did find his declaration about not being father material a little overreaching. The man clearly had issues if that's where a visit to her apartment had led him. Heartbreaking issues but issues, nonetheless.

"Every person on the planet has issues," she muttered to herself.

She couldn't hold it against him, not when her own issues circled her like a blood-sniffing shark. Everything else she thought about Paul Flynn remained firmly in place, though. Especially when she unzipped Eva's suitcase and sorted through the young woman's belongings.

He'd taken care with them—enough care that half the straightening work was already done. And what had been done included gently draping three—no, make that four—beautiful evening dresses that made Mabel hear cash registers ringing in her ears around the breakables.

"Are these …" She lifted the first one, a navy beaded gown with spaghetti straps and a plunging back, into the air. "It's a Siriano."

And not an off-the-rack number. She wasn't up on a lot of designers, but she recognized that work, as well as the green Ralph Lauren and a ruby red Carolina Herrera. The strappy shoes wedged into the bottom of the suitcase were a practical style and would complement each of the dresses. Dresses she'd been given. Eva had alluded to that fact when she spoke of whomever was responsible for attacking her. Were gowns traceable? She'd have to ask Nox.

She turned her attention to the box after repacking all the clothes and shoes.

The photographs were all stacked together, so she found an envelope to put those in. All the toiletries she put into a large plastic bag and made a mental note to pick up an all-in-one soft-sided bag the next time she shopped. The few collectibles got wrapped in tissue and set inside.

She frowned into the bottom of the box. "Where did you come from?" She hefted out the thin laptop covered in cheeky stickers that belied Eva's pre-attack mindset. Mabel hadn't come across that in Eva's room.

She turned it over. It wasn't Paul's laptop, unless he'd bought a sticker that declared well-behaved women rarely make history. Besides, she hadn't seen him carrying anything when he'd arrived at Mrs. Lancaster's.

Mabel retrieved her cell, which was still charging, and dug in her purse for the card Paul had given her back in his office. She hesitated, debating as her heart started to pound. Should she call and ask about it?

She didn't want it to come across as if she was looking for an excuse to contact him, and she didn't want him to think she was desperate or trying out for stalker of the month. He'd made it pretty evident the other night that he intended to keep things professional between them.

"This would be professional," she argued with herself as she dialed, but she still cringed when the phone rang on the other end. Lord, she hated the idea of sounding or coming across as pathetic.

"Paul Flynn."

"Paul, hi. It's Mabel. Reynolds," she added as if he'd ever met another Mabel in his life. "I'm sorry to bother you—"

"You aren't bothering me, Mabel." His voice sounded as easy and polite as always. "In fact, I was going to call, and—"

She plunged ahead before he could finish that thought. "I just have a quick question, and I know it's going to sound strange."

"Go ahead." He sounded as hesitant as she felt, as if they were somehow tiptoeing around an unfortunate encounter that had left both of them ... unfulfilled.

"I was just getting Eva's things organized—"

"Is she being released?"

"Yes, this afternoon." Even as she said it, she could hear the ticking of lost minutes. "I found a laptop in the bottom of the box."

"Oh, right. Yeah. I meant to tell you about it."

"Was it in her closet?" It had been the only place she hadn't had a chance to look herself.

"Under the bed. Well, more like *in* the bed."

She was only getting more confused. "I don't get it."

"She'd cut an opening in the bottom of the box spring and had it stashed in there with some other things. Papers and stuff. I put them all in the box."

"How ...?" Mabel couldn't for the life of her figure this out. "What made you think to look in the mattress?"

"My college roommate used to keep his pot stash in the box spring."

"Your college roommate?" She didn't mean to sound quite as disbelieving as she did.

"Yes," he laughed. "My college roommate. Frat brother, actually. Drugs weren't my thing. Beer and porn, on the other hand—"

Ah, there was that stereotypical frat boy she'd had an initial image of.

"Okay, thanks." Mabel ran her fingers over the top of the laptop. Her stomach knotted hard at what the man who attacked Mabel had demanded to know when he'd had his hands locked around her throat. *Where is it?* Was this what he'd been looking for? "I appreciate the info."

She was about to hang up when he spoke again.

"It wasn't Keeley."

Mabel blinked. "What?"

"The reason I left the other night. Your little girl is great, Mabel. It's just—"

"You're not father material," she finished for him. "I get it. I just thought …"Thought what? That he'd be a good distraction? That she liked the idea of spending time with him, someone who seemed to understand the complexities of coping with an indescribable loss that only seemed to increase each day? "I just thought we were having a good time together. In between me getting attacked and everything."

"Yeah. I thought the same thing."

Until he didn't. Something had stopped him from pursuing her. She should feel relieved. Instead, she felt … disappointed.

"How's your hand?" Paul asked. "And your head?"

"I'm fine, Paul." She didn't want to appreciate him asking. "Like I said, I'm on my way to the hospital so—"

"Yeah, sure. I'll keep you up to date on the case."

"I know you will. Thanks again." She clicked off before she said anything she might regret. Or let on that him taking off the way he did had hurt more than she was willing to admit. Especially to herself.

She set her phone back down, shifted the laptop on the table, and reached into the box for the thin stack of envelopes that, as she pulled them out and slipped the interior card free, revealed themselves to be invitations of some kind.

The paper was heavy, and very, very smooth. Imported, no doubt. This was fancy paper, not the kind that came in an economy pack at the discount store. The black was so deep it almost shimmered. The wording was brief with only a "Your presence is requested …" written in an elegant gold cursive, the kind of script one might see on a historical document or declaration.

She flipped it open.

Her eyes went wide, and she gasped.

The invitation dropped onto the table, interior exposed. The entirety of the inside was one, gold wax-embossed image.

Barksy padded over, nosed the edge of the invites back onto the table.

"It's a lily." Her heart pounded again as her thoughts spun.

More than *a* lily. It was the same flower icon that was on full display in the stained-glass window above the front door of the Tenado Estate. It was the same image that had been printed on the bottom corner of each of the photographs found in the basement. And it was …

Mabel drew in a trembling breath.

It was the same mark that had been branded onto the back of the neck of at least two women she knew of. One was an elderly resident in the Golden Age nursing home. The other?

"Moxie."

Mabel's eyes burned with tears that instantly evaporated beneath the anger surging through her system. She hadn't seen it for herself, but Riley had. And both Mabel and Riley had witnessed Moxie's reaction to Riley pressing her about it.

Mabel sorted through the stack of invites. Five, six, seven in all, each with different kind of code on the inside; a mishmash of words and numbers that made absolutely no sense. But each one contained the same waxed impression of the flower, the glossy upraised lines smooth against her fingertip.

Her two worlds collided with the force of the Big Bang. Eva and …. The Circle? It was as if someone had suddenly turned on a blinding Hollywood spotlight and aimed it right into her mind.

"What in the hell did you get yourself into, Eva?"

Hands shaking, she gathered up the invitations and stacked them on top of the computer. She whipped the towel off her head and walked back to her bedroom to get dressed. By the time she'd brushed through her wet hair and jumped into her jeans, a bright blue v-neck tee, and grabbed an ankle-swirling lightweight long sleeve sweater, she had at least part of a plan.

She abandoned any plans to off-load Eva's belongings at Soteria on her way to the hospital and hugged the laptop and invitations to her chest as she grabbed her bags, keys, cell, and Barksy's leash. She whistled for the dog and quickly clicked the leash to his collar, and they headed out the door.

Rather racing to the lobby, she stopped on the second floor, knocked twice before hitting the camera doorbell. She'd barely taken a step back when the door swung open.

"Hiya." Nox, Cass's personal—and professional—assistant, stood on the other side, jet-black spiky hair glistening against the glow of the lights behind them. "Hey, Barksy." They bent and rubbed a hand on the top of the dog's head. "Elliot, look. Playdate! Come on in."

Nox waved Mabel inside with an oversized metal tumbler that no doubt had a good thirty minutes worth of coffee in it. Mabel unhooked Barksy's leash and hung it on a hook by the door next to the guest bathroom as her dog scampered down the hardwood floor hallway in search of his canine companion.

"Cass is in the recording booth finishing up the last of her lectures for the week."

Nox was on the short side and possessed no less than twice the energy of the sun on any given day. Their clothing style ran from typical Goth black jumpsuits and studded metal collars to oversized sweatshirts harkening back to the *Flashdance* era of yesteryear. Today's attire consisted of cutoff, multi-pocketed cargo pants and a faded Ramones gray T-shirt.

Stepping inside Dr. Cassia Davis's apartment never ceased to amaze and slightly terrify Mabel. Her friend, a child prodigy turned nationally renowned forensic specialist, had transformed the original three-bedroom apartment into a kind of laboratory that included computers, testing equipment, and at least ten other things Mabel remained clueless about. Work was absolutely her main focus, from writing text manuals, teaching various online criminalist courses, and taking on cases as a special consultant; she'd made a comfortable—if not different kind of—life for herself.

Amidst all the technology and workspace, she'd set aside a surprising amount of area to entertain her limited number of guests. Cass wasn't the most frequent of entertainers, but her beautiful modern kitchen that took up a good third of the apartment spoke of her inclination toward experimentation of the culinary sort. Not to the same extent as Sutton, but their mutual friend had been known to use Cass's kitchen when in need of additional cooking space.

Cass's bedroom suite and a separate guest bath sat in the far west corner of the apartment, and she'd recently added an extra sleeper sofa in Nox's office for those frequent occasions their work went too late into the night.

A notorious insomniac with a brain that was incapable of slowing down, Cassia had created a locked-down apartment that she felt—or at least tried to feel—safe in. Even with all the security measures they'd taken where Temple House was concerned, Mabel couldn't help but suspect Cass still had more than her share of days that were spent, if not in sheer terror, certainly feeling less comfortable than she'd like.

"I'm heading out," Mabel said to Nox as she followed her inside. "I was hoping you'd keep an eye on Barksy for the day?"

"Sure thing."

Nox returned to their L-shaped desk that was covered in three large monitors, at least that many CPUs, and a lighted keyboard that flashed between green and blue. A stack of laptops took up a good portion of desk space in the far corner, while the bookcases that underlined the stretch of windows were piled high with books, notebooks, and various pieces of computer art.

"Elliot could use the company." Nox craned their head to look beyond Mabel where Barksy and Cass's golden retriever Elliot were greeting each other with a good sniff before heading over to nose their way through the open crate filled with toys. "I'll take them for a walk in a bit," Nox went on. "What's that?" Their violet eyes—courtesy of contacts—lit up, and they scrubbed their hands together when they caught sight of the laptop Mabel clasped against her chest. "A present for me?"

"Maybe." Mabel looked down. "I haven't decided yet. It's … tricky." And well beyond an invasion of privacy. Eva'd had enough of her trust shattered. She didn't need additional issues as a result of Mabel's suspicions. However well-intentioned they might be.

"Tricky is my favorite word." Nox grinned and waggled their fingers. "It's also my favorite kind of electronic."

A door down the short hall opened. "Nox, recordings are ready for editing and upload. Do me a favor and …. Oh, hey, Mabel." Cass inclined her head, her brow furrowing. "Everything okay?"

"Yes. Well, with us. Me and Keeley. And … all this." Mabel waved a hand around the spacious room humming with white noise. She always wanted to be careful with anything she said to Cassia, who dealt with severe agoraphobia and rarely, if ever, stepped foot out of this apartment. Even her attendance at Saturday morning Mimosa Yoga—when they'd routinely had it—had become infrequent since the attack on Riley in the basement back in December. Mabel didn't ever want to be the cause of triggering Cass's phobias or bouts of depression. "Have you spoken to Quinn lately? Or have you talked to Wallace, Nox?"

"Haven't been *talking* a lot these days," Nox confirmed with a telling grin. "But I can put it on the agenda for our next date."

"What subject in particular are you curious about?" Cass, dark auburn hair hanging long over her shoulders, pinned Mabel with familiar green-eyed suspicion.

"That." Mabel pointed to the rolling white boards meticulously displaying every single photograph of the women in the Red Lily case.

In the months since evidence had presented itself, every single bit of information Nox had been able to glean from the Dark Web, coupled with Cassia's meticulous research, had been noted and stored. The fact that, at one time, they'd had half a dozen large whiteboards filled with information spoke to their dedication to the case despite Cass's virtual return to the classroom. "Anything new?"

"Since you asked last week?" Cass frowned. "Nothing substantial." She stood shoulder to shoulder with Mabel and approached slowly, her eyes drifting to the computer Mabel tapped restless fingers on. "Laurel just called a little while ago with an interesting new tidbit. We're chasing it down now. That said, we've gone from streams of information to occasional drips. What's going on? You have something?"

Mabel blew out a breath. "I don't know. This is … this is probably skirting some privacy issues with one of my—"

"Eva Hudson?" Nox asked and earned a disapproving glare from Cass. "What? She's hedging and anxious, which means she needs to be fast. Right?" Nox blinked heavily lined eyes at Mabel. "Quinn and Riley might have mentioned her the other day."

"This is a bad idea." That gut feeling Mabel had, that doubt that had started niggling the second she'd picked up the laptop, ignited full force. "I can't do this to her." Not yet. She slipped the laptop back into her bag. She could just leave it behind. No way would Nox be able to resist temptation, and she could claim ignorance if it came to it. Still uncertain, she shook her head. "Sorry."

"No apologies necessary." Cass touched a hand to Mabel's arm and headed into the kitchen. "Hey, Barks." Cass clicked her tongue and had the two dogs trotting over to her as she opened the fridge. She pulled out a tub of homemade dog treats and had them sit before they got one. "Good boys." When she straightened, she caught Mabel staring, thinking. Contemplating. "There's something else." Cass clicked the tub closed. "What is it?"

"These were found in Eva's room." Mabel walked over, handed the invitations over. "She had them hidden with the computer."

Cass's brows arched as Nox joined them.

Cass set the stack down, picked one up, and fiddled with the paper. "High-quality stock." She held it up to the light of the kitchen. "That's writing, not computer or crafting machine work. I can see the pen marks, the ebb and flow of the impression. Fancy. Expensive. The paper and the ink. I think … yeah. I think I can see a faint watermark."

"That would help identify who sent it, right?" Mabel asked.

"It could help find out the supplier of the paper. Who bought it is another question. Especially if it's a popular item." Cass's gaze met hers. "Why?"

"Open it," Mabel told her.

She didn't know what to expect, watching Cass's face for some kind of telltale expression. Her friend was notoriously cool and unreadable. Rarely flappable. Unless she was on the other side of her front door. The wide eyes and surprise that swept across Cass's face both confirmed Mabel's own feelings and triggered a new bout of dread.

"Holy—" Nox literally jumped.

Cass's gaze slid slowly to Mabel's.

"I know." Mabel shook her head. "Or rather, I don't know. Cass—"

"It has to be some kind of message." Nox's voice was filled with something akin to wonder or excitement. Knowing them, probably both. "Aw, man, please let me run with this. I wanna play!"

"Slow down." Cass went through each of the invitations, setting them aside when she was done, each earning their own space on the table. "We'll examine these for prints first. Can you get Eva's if they aren't on file anywhere?" she asked Mabel.

Mabel shrugged. "Might take some convincing, but probably. You'll need mine—"

"I have yours." Cass held the last invite up into the light. At Mabel's frown, added, "I have everyone's who lives in Temple House."

"How—?"

"Probably a long shot." Cass had already moved on. "This Red Lily group hasn't stayed hidden this long by being careless with their prints," Cass murmured. "Or their communications. The wax stamp is probably a custom job, but it could be from anywhere. This is the first we've come across anything close to actual evidence of their existence beyond rumor."

"And the window at the Tenado estate," Mabel reminded her.

"Right," Cass said absently. "She had these hidden, you say?"

Mabel nodded.

"Then you were right to give them to me. Definitely not something to ignore and, hopefully, the break we've been hoping for."

Mabel bit the inside of her cheek. The man in Eva's closet had been looking for something, something he hadn't found. Something he'd been willing to lie in wait in an attempt to recover. The invitations and laptop fit the bill, especially where they'd been hidden. Anxiety and hope flared to life inside of her. They might finally have found something that didn't come across as coincidence, supposition, or, in Mabel's mindset, a desperate attempt to connect dots.

"Did anyone else touch them?" Cass asked.

"Oh. Um. Yes. Paul Flynn." Dammit! Did her face have to heat up whenever she spoke his name?

"The special investigator appointed by the DA." Cass nodded. "Quinn sounded impressed by him. This is really interesting. Nox, get the equipment together, will you? And stop foaming at the mouth. You can play with your ideas once we collect whatever prints are on here."

"Fine." Nox practically stomped their way over to the dedicated lab space that included multiple long tables with expensive testing equipment Mabel couldn't for the life of her begin to identify.

"This is going to take a while." Cass told her.

"Yeah, sure." Mabel nodded. "I'm on my way to take Eva over to Soteria." She dug for her cell. "Damn. Had it on silent. And I forgot to charge it." Only now did she notice the missed calls. And three voice messages. "Do you have a—"

"Chargers are over there." Cass's absent wave told Mabel she was already focusing on whatever those invitations might reveal.

Mabel plugged in, flipped the vibrate switch on her iPhone, and quickly tapped open the call log. She recognized the numbers immediately. And the earlier hour the calls had come. "Shit."

"What's wrong?" Cass asked absently.

"I missed calls from the hospital. Hang on." She tapped to listen to the first voicemail on speaker.

"Um, it's Eva." Mabel's stomach flipped at the sound of the young woman's voice. "I'm sorry, I know it's late, but I was …. You said if I needed to talk, I could call. I guess you're asleep. I can't. Sleep." Her laugh sounded like a half-sob. "I think … I think I'm starting to remember who hurt me. But I don't know who …" Her voice faded and became muffled, as if she were holding it against her chest. There was a rustle, a fumbling sound before the call went dead.

Mabel could barely hear anything over the roaring in her ears. "That was at three this morning." She couldn't bring herself to meet Cassia's concerned gaze. "I missed her call. Oh. God." She pressed a hand against her churning stomach. "She called me for help, and I missed it." Her head spun.

For a blink of an instant, all she could see, could hear, was Sylvie's voice.

"Are there any more calls?" Cass asked.

"Um, yeah." Mabel shook her head to clear it of the past. "One from a few hours ago. My phone was dead," she whispered as if that explained everything. "I can't believe I let it run down. I never let that happen. Never!"

"Mabel." Cass reached across the kitchen counter, grabbed hold of her hand. "Listen to the other voicemails. She might have called back."

"Right." Hope, however small, ballooned inside of her. But as she tapped the next message, she knew it wouldn't be Eva's voice on the other end.

"This is Constance from Consolidated Data, asking if you'd be interested in participating in our online—"

"Telemarketer," Mabel muttered as if the word were a curse and deleted the message before tapping open the last one.

"Hi, Mabel. It's Rita Kumari at St. Marcus Hospital. We have you down as an emergency contact regarding Eva Hudson. If you could, please give us a call back as soon as possible—"

"You didn't listen to the rest of the message," Nox said when Mabel stopped the playback.

"I don't have to." Mabel's hands shook as she hit the call back number. "This can't be happening. Not again." The dread pooling in her stomach felt thick and greasy. It was a feeling she hadn't felt in more than eight years. A feeling she'd never wanted to experience again. "Yes, hello. This is Mabel Reynolds. I'm returning Rita—"

"Mabel, thank goodness." The voice on the other end was the same as the woman who had left the message. "I was just about to give you another call. We have a situation with Eva."

"A situation? Is she all right?"

Rita hesitated before she lowered her voice. "I've been advised by the police not to—"

"What police? The police are there? Why?" She lifted her gaze when Cass squeezed her hand harder. "What's going on?"

"There was an incident overnight."

"She's dead." Mabel could barely squeak out the words.

"No. Or … we don't know." Rita's voice dropped even lower. "We can't locate her."

"Can't locate her." Mabel felt as if she was speaking from outside her body. "What do you mean, you can't locate her? How does that even happen?"

"Her night nurse checked in on her at just after three this morning. Everything seemed fine, but when we switched shifts …" The nurse did sound as if she were completely baffled. "The police are looking at our security footage now, but I don't know how else to put it: She's gone."

"Nice backdrop for a press conference." Paul sidled up beside Jeff Chambers who cast an overwhelmingly relieved look over his shoulder.

"You're late. Again," Jeff muttered, only this time, he didn't sound remotely entertained. "You've been here a week. You aren't running on New York time anymore. You might try to make an effort when it comes to making a good impression on our boss."

"Stop by my office after," Paul told him. "I'll be happy to show you the work this circus is pulling me away from." He scanned the media-laden crowd with what he hoped was a disinterested eye. He'd spent the time after Laurel left scribbling down notes on their conversation.

"Progress?" Jeff's eyebrow arched.

"Officially? No." Paul's gaze fell on the tight group standing to the side of the podium that included the District Attorney and Chief Alexander Burton, dressed to the nines in his full-dress uniform. "Between you and me?" He made certain not to move his mouth too much. He didn't doubt more than a few of those reporters looking for a unique headline were above lipreading. "I'm about to start kicking over some of those rocks we talked about."

"I heard our boss got you the information from Tenado's lawyers you wanted."

"Yes, she did." But now wasn't the time to go into the labyrinth of information they'd revealed. "I'll have to give the firm a call and personally thank them."

"Please don't." Jeff ducked his head, shoved his hands into the tan slacks of his suit. "I get the feeling the request wasn't received well, and it's put DA Eichorn in a mood."

"Oh?" Paul asked, but didn't get a response as DA Eichorn approached, the Chief, her deputies, and a few DA office barnacles on her heels.

The middle-aged woman was clad in a tailored, blue-skirted suit with a trim, waist-length blazer. Her dark hair was highlighted by stylish streaks of silver Paul suspected she kept in place to make certain her youthful face didn't betray her years of legal experience and expertise.

"Paul Flynn," Jeff introduced them. "District Attorney Eichorn."

"Paul." Johanna held out her hand. Her grip was firm and quick. "We meet at last. I apologize for having to cancel our meeting the other day."

"Not a problem, ma'am. Appreciate your help with the documents and records."

"I hope they've been helpful."

Oh, so helpful. Paul simply smiled and nodded.

She tugged at the hem of her blazer. "I hope this will conclude any business we have with Young & Fairbanks."

"I wouldn't count on it, ma'am." He couched his response. "I've been compiling a list of questions I'm hoping they'll be able to answer."

Paul caught a flash of a smile on Chief Burton's face before he hid it behind his hand as he coughed. In that moment, there was no mistaking the similarities between the Chief and his detective son.

"Questions about what?" DA Eichorn's voice carried a hint of irritation.

"I'm still working on them. Actually, you might be able to help me. I've come across a company I'm not familiar with. Sumatra, Inc.? Does that mean anything to you?"

"Sumatra? I think that's what I brew in my coffee maker in the morning," she said with a laugh, but that was as far as she went. Whatever answer there might have been died behind wary eyes.

Johanna Eichorn had worked her way up the rungs of the Los Angeles DA's office for the past twenty-five years with a kind of single-minded and ruthless ambition. She'd done so while maintaining a surprisingly strong marriage to a state judge and overseeing a household of three children, all of whom were currently in college. The fact she'd been appointed as DA after the unexpected resignation of her predecessor and mentor seemed a bit anticlimactic, if not coincidental, as far as Paul was concerned.

Paul's research revealed the previous occupant of the DA's office had been one of the attorneys involved with the Dennings prosecution. He was also a good friend to Anthony Tenado. One coincidence too many for Paul. One reason he had the former District Attorney at the top of his wanted-to-talk-to list. Too bad the man had moved out of town, his forwarding address confidential.

"Chief Burton." Paul shifted his attention to the distinguished man at DA Eichorn's left. "Good to meet you, sir. I had drinks with your son the other evening."

"Quinn did mention." His smile was friendly and easy and more than a little amused. "And before you ask, I'm happy to speak with you at any time. Just call my office for an appointment."

"I'll do that. Thank you, sir."

"Before we start the presser, Todd Blankenship." The man to the DA's right offered his hand to Paul. He stood almost as tall as the Chief, was Black, steel-jawed, and carried that same hint of skepticism in his eyes the DA possessed. "I'm the press liaison for the DA's office. I'd like to stop by your office later, talk about setting up a schedule of media updates as your investigation proceeds."

"I think I can save us some time there," Paul said easily. "I don't speak to the press unless I've got something to say."

Todd cast a knowing look at his boss. "That's not—"

"I find it keeps them on their toes, staying fluid with the information we choose to share," Paul went on. "It also makes our work with them a bit more give-and-take. There's no point of me standing up there in front of cameras when I can't answer their questions."

"Can't or won't?" Todd challenged.

"Either. Both." This wasn't Paul's first go-around with this conversation. Instead of addressing Todd directly, he shifted his gaze to the DA. "If they can expect information at a set time, then we're running on their schedule. I don't work that way. Let's get them on ours.

That way, we can use them when we need them." He glanced at DA Eichorn. "And they can't push back because without our cooperation, they won't keep up with their headlines. Unless you disagree, ma'am?"

It was clear Todd's scheduling suggestion had been hers. He could see the irritation growing in her dark eyes. But she nodded. "All right. We'll do things your way. For now."

Translation, Paul thought, she was going to give him just enough rope to hang himself. Then pull the lever on the trapdoor herself.

It was a good plan. One Paul had used himself on multiple occasions. "I appreciate that. While we still have a moment, I'd like to talk about my request for an investigative task force."

"Yes, Jeff did mention you'd brought that up again," DA Eichorn said.

"I anticipate the amount of information I'm gathering is going to need more than just my eyes on it," Paul said.

Out of the corner of his eye, he saw Jeff shake his head, his mouth quirking in his "you just can't help it, can you?" way he had.

"I think at this point," DA Eichorn held up a hand when one of her deputies was about to interrupt, "we'll see what you do with the information you've already obtained. I'd rather not have too many people involved at this point. The fewer people who know all the details about either yours or Jeff's investigation, the better. So far, interested parties have been cooperating, have they not? I don't think introducing additional detectives will do much good at this point."

"Other than speeding up the investigation, no, I don't suppose it would," Paul said. "But just a thought. Approving a multi-person task force could be seen as a signal to the Los Angeles community at large that you're taking these disappearances seriously enough to throw as much man and woman power as you can at it."

"Which is why Jeff has one. One that you're part of. This early in your assignment, I don't think the people of Los Angeles would appreciate pulling additional detectives and officers off of their established responsibilities. They're stretched thin as it is, and I don't relish making more enemies in the department. If circumstances change, I'll reassess. Until then, you have your assistant. And whatever resources Jeff can spare from his office. Gentlemen? Shall we?"

Jeff's grimace was a silent thanks Paul could have done without. Then again, he'd been warned. It was his own fault for not heeding that warning.

"Jesus, Paul," Jeff grumbled. "Way to make an impression. What's this Sumatra thing you mentioned?"

"Just taking a lesson from a new friend and testing a theory."

He had to admit, Laurel's tactics weren't bad. He'd wanted to see the reaction his mentioning the longtime company would illicit, and he'd gotten one. Enough to know that Sumatra, Inc., wasn't as unknown as it would probably like to be.

The cell in Chief Burton's jacket went off. "Excuse me, won't you? If you want to get started, I'll join you shortly." He frowned down at his phone as he moved away.

"Still living by the 'how to win friends and influence people' mantra, I see," Jeff mumbled out of the corner of his mouth as he and Paul followed the DA and her entourage over to the podium. "You couldn't play nice, just this once?"

"Playing nice works for you, not me."

Jeff grimaced, opening his mouth to say something, then halted.

"What's going on?" Paul kept his voice low as Todd began his spiel at the microphone, giving the reporters the guidelines of the press conference. Not that Paul anticipated any of them following whatever rules were in place. "Look, if I'm overstepping—"

"I brought you in to overstep," Jeff said, his frigid tone leaving no room for doubt. "I think I'm being followed."

"What?" Paul couldn't help but look at his friend. "By whom?"

"No idea, and I said, 'I think.' Probably being paranoid."

But Jeff didn't get paranoid. It was one of the things that made him so damned good at his job. "You say anything to the DA?"

Jeff smirked. "Who do you think told me I'm being paranoid?"

Paul gnashed his back teeth. "The more things change …"

"Were you able to reach out to your contact about Dean Samuels's whereabouts in the prison system?" Jeff deftly changed the subject. "Any idea how a nationally recognizable inmate just up and disappears?"

"Still working on it." Paul made certain to keep his voice low. "I'm hoping to have something on that later today, tomorrow at the latest. I'll call you—"

"No. Don't call," Jeff said as cameras and cell phones were raised in the audience, and the crowd moved in as the DA approached the microphone. "I'm supposed to take Max to Grand Park on Sunday for some father-son playground and food-truck time. And to give Lindsay a break. Why don't you meet us there ... say, about noon?"

"I can do that." It wasn't like Paul's social schedule was overflowing with activity. Of course, if Laurel Fontaine could be believed ... "You sure you want to mix family time with this?"

He needed to put all thoughts of Mabel Reynolds out of his head. Jeff needed his full attention on his case.

"I sure as hell don't want to discuss any of this in the office," Jeff told him. "We'll talk at the park. Maybe we'll both be lucky, and our cases will break before then."

The only bright side Paul could see to the day thus far was the fact that the drizzle and rain had decided to take a break. He'd almost forgotten what the sun looked like and felt like as it beat down and baked into his skin.

Still, he breathed deep. He was grateful not to be cooped up in his office for the time being. If he'd had the chance, he'd have taken a long walk to clear his head of the post-Laurel Fontaine questions and concerns she'd left swimming through his already crowded mind. If he didn't like being psychoanalyzed when he paid for it, he sure as hell didn't appreciate it when it arrived unsolicited.

Focus on the case. Close the case. Get out of town.

He really needed to get back on board with that plan—pronto. Getting caught up in the tidal pool that was Mabel Reynolds needed to be avoided at all costs.

The front steps of the Los Angeles courthouse had clearly been a strategic choice, with the promise of justice looming behind District Attorney Eichorn and her Mabel-nicknamed minions swarming about. The building, like so many others in the city, had become iconic thanks to countless appearances in movies and television. Overhead, the trio of Donal Hord sculptures representing truth, law, and justice stood watch—three values Paul anticipated the DA would be emphasizing in front of the mass of reporters milling about on the other side of the podium that had been situated just outside the front door.

Front and center at damage-control central. Just where he wanted to be.

"Sorry," Chief Burton murmured as he took his place beside Paul.

Paul didn't like the expression on Chief Burton's face. "Everything okay?"

"Not remotely." Chief Burton stood almost at attention beside Paul as DA Eichorn finished her preliminary statement that included details about Paul and Jeff's professional history, lending credence to their appointments to the Tenado and Dennings cases respectively.

Paul's mind wandered, as it often did when his professional lineage was echoed back at him. He wasn't psychic, but he knew full well what one of the first questions was going to be. It would be up to him to put a swift and decisive answer in place that gave the reporters nowhere to go. His past held no bearing on this case. Other than the fact that it had freed him up to come out here and lead the investigation.

"Hey." Jeff elbowed him. "Earth to Paul."

"What?"

"Mr. Flynn?" DA Eichorn stepped back and motioned to the microphone. The steely look in her eyes told him she was well aware he hadn't been paying attention.

He stepped forward, made a conscious effort not to adjust his tie or jacket. He could hear the clicking of cameras and cell phones, the muted conversation amidst the dozens of reporters mere feet away. His job was filled with necessary evils, and none were more necessary—or some would say more evil—than the Los Angeles-based press.

His heart pounded heavier than it had when he'd taken the Bar exam. It had been months since he'd stood before anyone in any official capacity, and all he could hope was that it was like riding a bike. And that he wasn't going to hit a rock and go flying over the handlebars.

"Good afternoon, everyone."

He kept his hands in his pockets, fisted his fingers until they went numb. Projecting a calm demeanor would either trigger the wolves or have them eating out of his hand. But as much attention as he needed to play to those on the other side of the podium, he was

also putting on a performance aimed at the law offices of Young &
Fairbanks. No way were they going to turn a blind eye on him now
that they'd sent him the Tenado documentation. They were watching.
Probably every move he made.

"First, I'd like to thank DA Eichorn and her entire team for in-
viting me into this investigation," Paul began. "I can assure you, just
as I've assured them, that my reasons for being here are simple: to
find out the truth regarding the evidence found at Anthony Tenado's
estate. But more than that, I want these women found. I'm going to
follow whatever trail I need to in order to make that happen."

"You don't think your history with the McFiltry case will work
against you?"

Damn, Paul thought. He really should have put money down on
that being the first question.

He didn't blink, and he didn't even attempt to identify the voice
in the crowd that had shouted it.

"No," he said simply even as his stomach knotted. "Ross McFiltry's death brought an end to the investigation into his associate's
death. He could have made his argument in court. He chose not to.
Next question."

"Does the congressman's suicide—"

"As we are in Los Angeles and not New York," Paul said, even as
the knots in his stomach tightened, "I suggest you address any additional questions about the McFiltry case to the office of the New
York DA or the congressman's mother. My part in that case is resolved.
Next." He pointed at a Latinx woman standing in the back of the
crowd. "Ms. Ramirez, isn't it?" He'd asked Kent to give him a rough
rundown on the usual reporters who showed up at the DA pressers.

"Yes, Lana Ramirez." Her shoulders straightened. "Is Anthony
Tenado a suspect in these supposed disappearances?"

The question wasn't unexpected, but the tone in which it was
offered grated on his exposed nerves. "Given there were missing person's reports filed for most of the women in question, let's say we
officially dispose of any and all speculation these disappearances are
anything other than authentic. Until these women are located, they
are considered missing. Remove 'supposed' from your vernacular
where this case is involved, please. Next?"

He scanned the crowd, ignoring the shouts, and located a young man he recognized from a smaller network's newscast. He looked as if he were about to be swallowed up by the crowd surrounding him.

"Jimmy Pinon." Paul pointed at him. "Question?"

"Yes." Jimmy's voice all but squeaked as he blinked up at Paul. "Is this expected to remain a one-man investigation going forward, or will you have additional assistance for the case?"

Paul almost grinned. God bless Jimmy Pinon. "That's an option being discussed," Paul confirmed and felt the hair on the back of his neck prickle, no doubt as a result of Todd's laser-eyed stare. "Ne—"

"Sorry. A follow-up," Jimmy's voice strengthened. "Do you really believe that you, as a solitary individual, have the wherewithal and necessary resources to investigate and bring to a close a case that, from what we've already learned, goes back decades?"

"I've been assured I'll be given all the necessary resources to bring this case to a swift conclusion," Paul responded.

"What do you consider a conclusion?" another reporter shouted from the back.

"Nothing short of these women being located and returned to their loved ones," Paul said. "Next?"

"You didn't answer the rest of my question," Lana Ramirez's voice cut through the rising tenor of the crowd. "Is Anthony Tenado a suspect?"

Todd, the media liaison, nosed his way to the microphone. "I don't think—"

"Mr. Tenado resided in the house where the photographs of dozens of missing women were on display for more than twenty years." Paul stepped to the side and gently nudged Todd out of the spotlight. "I believe, and let me stress this is my opinion only at this time, that we would be remiss not to consider him a person of interest. Let us not forget," he added in a purposeful calm tone, "Mr. Tenado was Melanie Dennings's agent at the time she disappeared. I believe the fact he was never called to testify at Dean Samuels's trial raises possible concerns about how the case was investigated originally." He glanced over his shoulder at Jeff, hoping his change of direction might shift the conversation over to Jeff and his investigation into the Dennings's conviction. He paused, giving those scribbling down notes time to catch up. "Seeing as Mr. Tenado died a number of years ago, I look forward to meeting with his attorneys at Young & Fairbanks in an effort to clear up any misconceptions about their client, who, even after his demise, they have continued to represent. I've already been in contact with them and hope to maintain our cordial communication. In fact, I'd like to take this opportunity to publicly thank Hollister Young who has personally assured DA Eichorn that his firm will happily comply with any additional requests for information we might make."

Paul almost smirked. *Let the trust lawyers suck on that for a while.*

He continued on, responding to questions he couldn't answer, questions he wouldn't answer, and questions that came so far out of left field he almost suggested the reporter board their flying saucer in an effort to chase down a response.

"Last question," Paul said as the energy of the reporters seemed to be abating finally.

"Mr. Flynn, David Robertson from the *LA Sentinel.*" A Black man with a tie the color of a stormy sky raised his hand. "Do you see any possibility that last night's disappearance from St. Marcus Hospital has any connection to the case?"

Paul's ears began to ring. "I'm unaware of a disappearance." He looked over one shoulder only to find blank stares on the faces of the DA and her backup group. Paul shifted his attention to Chief Burton. "Chief?"

Chief Burton stepped forward, the tension in his body so tight it felt like a tidal wave wafting over Paul as he took Paul's place at the microphone.

"We have a detective and officers on scene at St. Marcus right now, Mr. Robertson," Chief Burton spoke carefully and deliberately. "Connecting Ms. Hudson's disappearance to anything other than its own event is reckless and a bit irresponsible. The last known disappearance connected to the Tenado estate was Jemma Fielding, who disappeared more than—"

"Two years ago—yes, Chief." Mr. Robertson planted his feet as if he'd just entered into a one-on-one interview. "But Ms. Hudson was admitted to the hospital after attending a party in the Hollywood Hills last weekend. The same kind of party Melanie Dennings attended twenty-five years ago. Surely, the similarities are being addressed or, at the very least, paid attention to?"

"We're paying attention to everything," Paul said before the Chief could respond. "Believe me when I say Jeff Chandler and I will be asking questions about anything and everything remotely connected to anything where the Tenado case is concerned. Chief?"

"What Mr. Flynn said," Chief Burton said with a quick nod. "I believe we'll let DA Eichorn take the rest of your questions. Mr. Flynn?" Chief Burton motioned for Paul to follow him away from the podium.

"Eva Hudson," Paul said when they were out of earshot, not only from the reporters, but Jeff and the DA's cavalcade as well. "What do you know?"

"Do you know her?" Surprise jumped into the chief's icy-blue eyes.

"I know Mabel Reynolds," Paul told him. "She's been working with Eva on behalf of Soteria. What can you tell me?"

Chief Burton rubbed a hand across the back of his neck. "Sometime between three and seven this morning, Ms. Hudson disappeared from her room at St. Marcus. When security attempted to access their security tapes from the floor, they found the system was down for the time in question. We're going to have a department tech go and see if they can retrieve it or at least find out if it's a coincidence."

Paul arched a skeptical brow.

"I know," Chief Burton continued. "Normally detectives would assume she left on her own, but her doctor and attending nurses all state she wasn't in any shape to do that. I don't think there's anything normal about it at all."

"Someone took her out." The second he said it, he wanted to take the words back. They sounded so final. So … sinister. Paul glanced at Jeff, who looked more than stressed as he was forced to continue to stand there through the DA's endless acceptance of questions. "Quinn assured me the other night you'd be willing to talk to me, answer any questions I might have. I think, given this new development, my questions are multiplying exponentially."

"As I said before, my door is open for you anytime." Chief Burton reached into his pocket, pulled out a card. "My personal cell. I'd suggest the sooner we talk, the better."

"Agreed." Paul pocketed the card. "Would it be out of line to ask you for a favor?"

"Depends on the favor," Chief Burton said.

"I'd like you to stay on top of the Eva Hudson case. All aspects of it, but especially her disappearance. It would mean a lot," he added. "To me and a friend."

"I can absolutely do that. I think we share a talent for deflecting and distracting. I'd be happy to put that into play if," Chief Burton said with a quick look over his shoulder, "you were inclined to want to make a quick getaway from this circus."

Paul flashed a grateful smile. "I'd definitely owe you one."

"And I'll collect," the chief assured him. "Go." He patted Paul's shoulder. "And tell Mabel Reynolds I'm at her disposal, as well."

CHAPTER ELEVEN

MABEL stood at the window of Eva's second floor hospital room, the faint din of the bedside television speaker echoing the replay of the DA's press conference that had concluded just a little while ago.

"Mabel?" Erin, the nurse who, days before, had been working the station desk when Mabel visited a conscious Eva for the first time, called her name softly from the doorway. "I'm sorry, but we need to get the room cleaned and ready for a new patient."

It struck Mabel that now would be the time to wipe the tears from her cheek, to gently concede defeat and accept that Eva was gone and, most likely, would never be seen again.

It was, unfortunately, the attitude and conclusion Detective Harrison had apparently reached after the solitary crime-scene tech had done a cursory inspection of the room. As far as Detective Harrison was concerned, Eva had done a runner, no doubt in the hopes of putting what had happened behind her.

Anger and Mabel were old, combative friends.

She couldn't, for the life of her, as she stood staring down into the meditation garden, remember a time she hadn't been angry.

Mabel lowered her head, tightened her two-armed hold on the stuffed rabbit she'd found wedged under Eva's bed almost the instant she'd raced into the room.

Mabel's insistence that Eva would never have left the bunny behind had her leaving been voluntary was dismissed as coincidence along with the missing hours of security footage. The doctor and nurses' insistence that Eva had not, in any way, been in a condition to walk out on her own power carried no weight.

It was, for all of Detective Harrison's intents and purposes, case closed.

"Mabel?" Erin stepped into the room. "Did you hear—?"

"I heard you. I'm going." Even if doing so felt as if she, too, was surrendering to Eva's unknown fate.

"I'm so sorry," Erin whispered as Mabel walked past her and out of the room. "It's so horrible. Whoever took her just ripped out her lines. Didn't even bother to take the IVs out of her arms. I wish I had an explanation—"

"So do I."

Mabel walked down the hall, her nerves so far on edge she could feel the other nurses and orderlies' gazes on her. Mabel couldn't quite reconcile the utter vacancy of thought as she punched the button on the elevator and stepped back to wait.

She gasped when the doors opened, not only because she'd been about to step inside without a second thought, but because of who stepped out.

"Paul." Her heart squeezed in her chest, as if he'd reached out and taken it in his hand. Her breath caught in her chest, lodged in her throat as she realized, reluctantly, that she was glad to see him.

"I came as soon as I heard." He dropped his hands on her shoulders, ducked down slightly to meet her dazed gaze. "I—what can I do?"

"Turn back time?" She didn't want to meet those blue eyes of his. She didn't want to see the sympathy shining there. But when she surrendered to temptation, she found comfort, and that, she silently and eagerly embraced. "She called me. My phone …" Her breath shuddered as it left her lips. "I had my phone on vibrate when I fell asleep, and I didn't hear it."

Paul straightened, slipped his arms around her, and drew her in. She suspected it was his attempt to get her to let go, to give up control of the tears, of the screams, of the fury that all battled for first place in how she was possibly going to move forward.

"It's happening again," she whispered as she released one hand free of the rabbit and slid it around his waist. He felt like an anchor, one she couldn't pass up, as she finally felt as if she had stopped floating loose in the ether. "It's just like before. She's gone, Paul. Just like Sylvie. Eva's gone."

"You don't know that."

"Yes." She squeezed her eyes shut, and in the darkness, she could envision those damned noir-inspired invitations Eva had wedged under her bed. "Yes, I do. I should have been there. I should have made sure someone was watching—"

"Stop." He gave her a hard, quick squeeze and set her back. "None of this is your fault. None of it." His insistence did nothing to convince her, something he obviously saw on her face. "Let's get out of here."

It touched her that he didn't recall the elevator that had since left, but instead turned her toward the staircase door. Their footfalls were muted on the cement steps, and when they emerged in the lobby, he steered her straight out the sliding doors into the fresh air.

"Where do you want to go?" he asked her.

"Home." She couldn't manage to separate Eva from Sylvie. Logically, rationally, she knew it was Eva who had gone missing. But deep inside, in those dark corners she'd kept hidden even from herself, she couldn't help but think she was getting a firsthand glimpse into what had happened to her sister. That fear she must have been feeling, the abject hopelessness and dread. It was all just … too much. "I just want to go home and sleep."

The promise of oblivion was, in fact, the only thing that remotely appealed.

"Yeah, I don't think that's a good idea."

"Well, it's a good thing it doesn't matter what you think then, isn't it?"

She started to walk past him, to get to her car so she could lock herself in and then maybe, maybe, she'd let out the scream that had been building inside of her. He caught her arm, his grasp gentle but firm. She stopped, reminded herself to breathe. She didn't want this man's kindness or concern. Not now. Not when she could feel the control she had over her emotions slipping.

"Let me go, Paul."

"No."

He moved closer but didn't release her. Instead, he steered her over to one of the side benches, out of the way of the people moving in and out of the hospital entrance.

She sat because he expected her to, because it was something to do. It took all her effort not to scoot away as he sat beside her.

"I owe you an explanation."

"You don't owe me anything," Mabel said on a sigh. "Flirtation and attraction is a great thing until the responsibilities of the real world rear up and smack you in the face. I'm a risk for anyone, Paul. I come with attachments I will always possess, and while I see Keeley as a bonus, I understand not everyone does."

"Mabel—"

"If anything, I should be grateful. You were upfront with me," she insisted at his dubious expression. "Being with you was nice, but one kiss doesn't a future make. It felt good, and I hadn't felt good like that in a really long time, but you know your limitations." She laughed, scrubbed a hand across her grainy eyes. "I must be more out of it than I thought. Listen to me, confessing all this to you when you have no interest—"

"I have far too much interest," he interrupted. "That's the problem. I've spent the last few days trying to convince myself otherwise. It's clearly been a waste of my time." He reached out, stroked a finger down her cheek. "Tell me what happened with Eva. Are the police still up there? What's being done about the missing security footage?"

"You know about that?"

"I spoke with Chief Burton before I left the press conference."

"Right. The press conference." A shard of light broke through the darkness. "You impressed me up there," she admitted. "You handled yourself perfectly. Not entirely sure you earned much favor with the woman who hired you," she added with a twitch of her lips. "I've never really understood the phrase 'spitting nails' before today. She's pissed."

"You saw?"

"I watched in the nurse's break room," she admitted. "Detective Harrison wouldn't let me in Eva's room until they were done. Not that they did much." She looked down at the rabbit. "He should have taken this for evidence."

"You wouldn't let him?"

"I would have," she said slowly, "if he thought it meant anything. As far as he's concerned, Eva is just another troubled girl trying to get herself out of a bad situation." She reached out, rested her hand on his arm when she felt the frustration and heat of anger wafting off him. "Don't. It's not a surprise. I've been doing this work for so long now, nothing comes as a surprise anymore."

Except for Paul.

He'd surprised her. He surprised her in his office, and then at Mrs. Lancaster's, and he sure as hell had surprised her by turning up now, at the hospital when it turned out she needed someone. "It's like history's repeating itself."

"You said that upstairs. Tell me," Paul urged.

She shook her head. "You've heard enough of my sob stories."

"They aren't sob stories," Paul corrected with more than a bit of edge in his voice. "We are all made up of our experiences, good and bad. It's been obvious to me from the start Eva hasn't just been another name in the books for Soteria. It's more for you. She's more. Why?"

"You know why," she whispered. She couldn't—not yet—tell him the truth. Tell him that Eva's disappearance connected to so much mor than her sister. "Or at least you suspect."

"She reminds you of Sylvie. In a lot of ways, I imagine." He tucked a strand of loose hair behind her ears. "Most of the women you help probably do. It's why you do it, isn't it?"

"Boy, you are good," she managed, laughing weakly.

"Earlier you said history was repeating itself. Tell me."

She pressed her lips into a thin line, felt them go numb before she plunged in. He was asking, and it wasn't as if she was risking alienating him by telling him.

"The last time I talked to my sister, we fought. I mean, we always fought—in a good way. We were just so different. But that last time, about a week before she disappeared, I blew up at her." The guilt of that conversation hadn't abated in the eight years. If anything, it had grown to the point of taking up half her soul. "She wanted me to move out to LA, move in with her so we could raise Keeley together. It was one of her usual pie-in-the-sky dreams, and I reacted … badly." She cringed. "I was so exhausted and getting used to being a new mom. I was determined to make it on my own because I'd made such a horrendous mistake with Keeley's father, a guy my parents and Sylvie had never liked. Shocking, I know," she added when he looked down at her. "In my mind, I had to rebuild their faith in me. I was struggling to figure out my job, what to do as a mother, and Sylvie's solution was to walk away from everything and start over in LA. Do you know what I said to her?"

"What did you say?"

"I told her I didn't have time for her dreams. That I had actual responsibilities now that she couldn't comprehend. I hung up on her, but not before I told her to get her head out of the clouds and grow up. And then I spent the next week avoiding her calls. The night she disappeared, I turned off my phone. I didn't want to spend another night staring at a ringing screen, so I turned it off." More tears burned. "The night she disappeared, she left a message, practically begging me to answer, that she was sorry for being selfish but that things were turning around for her. She said …" she took a deep breath, "she said she'd call me with all the details. I never heard from her again."

"And last night, Eva—"

"She called me when my phone was essentially off. I didn't hear it ring. I missed …" Her breath caught. "Dammit, Paul." She hated, *hated* the tears that blurred her vision, and she blinked them back. "I'm so tired of being someone's last call."

"You don't know that's the case with Eva."

No, she didn't. But she was afraid that was the case. And that fear threatened to completely paralyze her, both physically and emotionally.

"I think maybe Alicia was right the other day." Mabel cast her gaze to the busy street on the other side of the hospital roundabout. "I don't think I can do this anymore. I need a break."

"Sounds like sage advice." Paul covered her hand with his. "When was the last time you took one?"

"A break? I haven't. This would be my first." And probably her last. "When I called Soteria to tell them not to expect Eva, I was all ready to say I'm done, but I chickened out. I can't just … quit."

"I don't think protecting yourself emotionally can be considered quitting," Paul said.

"No, yeah, you're right. But I literally can't just quit. My number is listed on dozens of hospital bulletin boards all over the city."

"Since when?"

"Last year. I was having doubts about how much I was helping, and the answer seemed to be to make myself more easily accessible."

"So, you put yourself on call 24/7."

"I've helped a lot of survivors," she insisted. "And I've lost a few."

More than a few. But it was only times like this that they all came back at her in full force.

"If you want a break, the solution may be as simple as getting another cell phone for a while."

"All those women," she whispered. "They're going to need help, and I don't think I can—"

"You aren't the only person in this city who cares about them, Mabel. Soteria and other facilities like it are evidence of that. You can't be a one-woman salvation service. Believe me, I've tried being the answer for hundreds of people. You'll lose yourself."

"What if I already have?" And that, more than anything, scared her the most. For her daughter's sake, not her own.

"Well, you can stop worrying about that because …. Well, you're wrong," he said firmly.

"Am I now?" He had the oddest way of making her laugh at unexpected times.

"You haven't lost yourself. And don't say I can't say that. I saw you with Keeley the other night. You two are magic together. No woman who's completely lost can be the light you are to your daughter."

"Okay, you need to stop." Her heart wasn't in any condition to come face-to-face with the man she'd let herself start to fall for the other day. And she *had* started to fall. Immediately and completely. Damn it if that didn't complicate every iota of both their lives. "You don't get to say the perfect thing and then swear off any possible dalliance between us."

"Dalliance?" He brightened, the smile on his face lighting the darkest corner of her grieving heart. "I can't remember the last time I heard that word. It sounds … tempting. Are we back to tempting each other, Mabel?"

She closed her eyes, doing her best to steel herself against his charm and appeal. She could feel herself balancing on the very edge of falling for him. "Paul—"

"You know I'm right," he challenged. "Not about the dalliance but about the magic between you and Keeley. And that little girl of yours isn't going to let you go anywhere."

She both liked and didn't like the fact he seemed to read her so well. "I'm so tired." The confession slipped from her lips before she could stop it. "I'm so tired of being angry. It's exhausting. And I can't bring myself to drag down everyone else around me."

"That's something else you're wrong about."

"You really think you're in a position to keep telling me I'm wrong?"

"I can when I think I've identified your fatal flaw."

"My what?"

"Your fatal flaw. You don't trust anyone outside your circle, do you? You'll ask for help when it comes to Keeley—"

"Keeley's important."

"So are you." He sounded frustrated that she didn't see it. "Your friends wouldn't see you asking for help as being dragged down. They'd see your reaching out as a way to keep you afloat. That you trust them. That you need them. Friends like that are rare. Take it from someone who has one, maybe two, of them in total." He scooted just that little bit closer, slipped his arm around her shoulders, and pulled her close. "I've told myself for years that I don't belong here anymore, Mabel. I came back to do a job, a job one of those friends asked me to do, but when it's all over, I'm going back to the life I've built for myself. I'm going back as fast as I can."

"Why does it sound as if there's a big 'but' in there?"

"The only big 'but' is you."

"Thanks a lot." She laughed again. "Does that rule out any dalliance?"

"It should." The fact that it didn't seemed to completely lighten her mood. "But while I'm here," he added with a bit of a chuckle, "I'd like to spend time with you. Beginning right now; I want to take you somewhere." He rested his chin on the top of her head, squeezed her arm tighter. "Somewhere I used to go when the anger got to be too much."

She was intrigued but glanced at her watch. "I have to pick Keeley up at five. She has science club after school."

"I'll get you back in time to pick Keeley up. I promise."

It occurred to her that he was far more in tune with father-behavior than he realized. And because of it, she surrendered.

"All right." What did she have to lose? "I'm officially putting myself in your hands."

Paul had long ago given up on impulsivity because, in his vast experience, doing so more often than not led him straight into trouble.

Fortunately, most of that trouble resulted in instant self-education in regard to discovering efficient ways to evade pursuers of all sorts: cops, bullies, or, in one particular instance, a bodega owner who had the reputation for overcharging kids for their after-school snacks. That same learning curve meant Paul could traverse nearly every neighborhood in Los Angeles, if not blindfolded, certainly in the dark. It made driving through in the middle of the day all the easier. Mostly.

There wasn't any place his bike hadn't taken him. He'd discovered secret, amazing, history-rich places that had yet to be equaled by the metropolis of New York City and sped his way down streets, hiking trails, and roads that took him miles from home.

With the car parked, he and Mabel walked in silence, much as they'd made the drive through the city. Slipping through the welcoming area of the Griffith Observatory felt a bit like walking into the past for him.

This place tended to land on most tourists' must-see list, but few actual residents visited unless, like Paul, said residents possessed an affinity for the silence and wonder the view provided.

The fact Mabel had slipped her hand as easily into his upon exiting his car awakened something inside of him he'd been desperate to avoid. He knew now what it was about her that kept him so off-kilter.

He was different around her. He felt different, acted different, wanted to *be* different. A man he wasn't entirely confident in inhabiting. With her, he could see possibilities that until now, felt like unreachable dreams. In a strange way, he felt as if meeting her had placed him at an unexpected fork in the road. Each possible path skirted the edge of those promises he'd made himself all those years ago.

Selfishly, he wished to snap those promises into shards. But he couldn't. No woman deserved him breaking those promises.

Especially Mabel.

"If you brought me up here to look at the stars, we're going to have quite a wait." She swung their linked hands, twisting and turning her head as if it were on a swivel to get a look at the verdant welcome of the lush, pristine landscaping leading into the building itself.

"The stars are for another time." He'd always considered the stars his last hope.

In the past, it would sometimes take him hours to make his way from his house to the hills leading to the observatory. Hours he didn't mind because it was less time to spend inside the house. The desperation, the fear, the anger, it all faded as he'd pedaled into the night.

This place and its pristine—if not smog-tinted—view of his limited world at that time had become a kind of haven, a place no one other than he was aware existed. Daytime or night, it mattered not. All that did matter was that up here, he was safe. With the Hollywood sign providing a glowing, constant reminder of his place in the universe.

A place where dreams really were possible. Some of the time.

His father certainly never would have thought to look for him here, and, in his more sneaky days, Paul had managed to stay just long enough to be locked inside the gates for the night.

That was before the addition of security systems and cameras, which Paul could now see were perched along various sight lines. The white cement walls gave the feeling of a city on the top of the world, overlooking that which held millions of souls below. There was no escaping the wind or the sound of it battering against his ears, but he heard it as the sound of an old friend welcoming him back.

"It's been a while." He led her around the side of the main building, the windowed dome looming behind them as they walked past other visitors ooh-ing and aah-ing and waiting in line for the telescope that would give a closer-up view of the city this place oversaw. "It seems smaller somehow." He could see his spot as they rounded the corner. A corner area that had been more obscured by trees than it was now. Now, the wedge of space provided a steeper view into the city he remembered staring down into with loathing and hate. "Every single bit of it feels completely the same, and yet ..." he trailed off.

It wasn't this place that was different. *He* was. He wasn't the scared kid who needed the safety of the silence any longer. He'd found his way out, made his new path. Coming back didn't have to be a reminder. It could be a new beginning. Funny he'd never considered that before now.

"I hate it," Mabel whispered. "This place. This city."

Paul's arms tingled with the goosebumps her vehemence triggered.

"When I look out there," she continued, "at all the hope and the promise, all I can see is the city that kill—took my sister."

He knew the feeling.

"My parents have never been able to come out to LA. We argued," Mabel said. "We argued so much when I told them Keeley and I were moving to Los Angeles until Sylvie was found. I think they finally just gave in or gave up because they knew how hard it was to change my mind about anything. I got a three-bedroom apartment so they'd have a place to stay, so they could at least spend time with Kee, but," she shook her head, "they've never been here. Because all they see is the place that killed their daughter." She heaved a heavy sigh. "You want to hear something terrible?"

He nearly said that he already had, but he nodded.

"I'm angry at them for it. So goddamned angry." Her fists pressed hard into the top edge of the wall. "Even while I understand it, I feel like, I don't know, like they somehow abandoned me to do all of this myself. Like I lost them when we lost Sylvie. They don't come here, and I can't go back because, when I return home, everywhere I turn, there she is. There *we* are. Walking to school or hanging out at the mall. Playing basketball in the front yard."

He covered one of her hands with his and just held on.

"They don't want to hear about the case," she continued. "Or about what might be happening, or anything about her. When we talk, it's all about Keeley or my stupid accounting work or Barksy." She swiped at the tears on her cheek as she steeled her jaw. "Every time I talk to them, when I hang up, I just feel so incredibly alone."

There were no words, he realized, that could ever ease the pain she had every right to feel. "I'm sorry seems so incredibly inadequate," he finally managed. "But you aren't alone, Mabel. Surely, you see that. You've surrounded yourself with friends and people who care about you."

He cared about her.

So much more than he should.

More than he had any right to.

"Thanks." Her smile was quick, almost dismissive. "It is what it is, right? You just find a way to deal with whatever hand you get dealt. I coped by coming out here to fight for her, and my parents cope by taking vacation after vacation so they don't have to sit in an empty house and think about everything they've lost."

"For what it's worth, I think you've done an amazing job keeping everything together. Keeping Keeley from feeling anything other than supported and loved. Even though she has the hardest job of everyone." He ducked his head when she frowned at him. "Keeping a smile on your face when you mire yourself down in other people's pain. You've shown her what a fighter is, and she is one. Because of that."

"Well, damn, Mr. Flynn." Mabel shook her head in what he interpreted as befuddled amazement. "There you go, proving yourself a liar once again. Not father material." She snorted. "Please. I don't know if anyone has ever said anything more perfect."

His heart tilted even further into her favor. "You continue to stun me speechless."

"Now *that* is impossible." Her sadness eased. "You know, I think the last time I came here, I was supervising a field trip for Keeley's class." Mabel released his hand and stepped right into the spot he'd last occupied the day he'd left Los Angeles. "It gives you a slightly different perspective, doesn't it?"

"Yes, it does." He moved in beside her, rested his hands on the white wall, pressed his fingers into the solid surface as he was whipped into the past. "Growing up, this was a haven of sorts. There's always someplace to go, a new street to explore, a new alley to follow." Or hide in.

"It's so quiet up here. It wasn't quiet with Keeley's class," Mabel's voice lightened a bit, and Paul's doubts about bringing her up here faded. "Twenty six-year-olds don't do quiet."

"I was about that age when my class came up here for the first time. I thought this, out there, was the whole world." He took a deep breath, closed his eyes as he tried to recall that first day of wonder. "I broke away from the rest of the group. Didn't go inside to see the stars. I just wanted to be out here, where I could see anything and everything and not worry about what was waiting for me at home. I sat here for hours, down here. Like this. They had to come find me." He turned and slid down the wall, crouching in the corner that he was now larger than. He tried to bring that boy back to the surface, but the kid he'd been when he'd lived here had long gone dormant inside of him. "It felt safe. Solid. I felt like I could let everything go in this space. I don't know, maybe send everything I was feeling out into the universe. Because the sky felt so much closer."

She sank down beside him.

"Home wasn't a good place for me," he told her. "It was bad before my mother left. After? It got worse." Until it became intolerable, and then …

"How old were you when she left?"

"Four, I think? I just remember she was here one day and gone the next." Funny that. He could barely picture her anymore. "Alden was seven."

"Alden," Mabel said quietly, gently. "The brother you mentioned the other day."

"Yeah." Paul rubbed his fingers together, much in the way he'd done when he was little. A nervous habit, a tick almost, that, at times, had rubbed his skin raw. "He was killed on his bike in a hit-and-run when I was fifteen." He rolled his head to the side, looked at her while he spoke. "He'd gone out late to the grocery store, after our dad passed out on the couch, because it was safer that way. Alden got a job there as soon as he turned sixteen and saved every penny he made in this old tin box under the floorboards of our room. He never took any out, but that night, he did because I wanted mac-and-cheese. I'd gotten an A on a math test and wanted to celebrate. And celebrating meant that blue box."

"I know it well. Don't tell Sutton," she added and eked a smile out of him as he felt her hand on his arm. Her touch acted as a kind of anchor, keeping him steady as he bobbed into the tumultuous ocean of the past. "She'd never forgive me for loving that stuff."

"The next knock that sounded on the door changed everything," he said. "I can remember racing to open it because I was afraid they were going to wake up Dad and ruin dinner. It was the police. Alden never came home."

"And you were left alone, in that house," Mabel murmured. "With a father who hurt you."

"Every single day, I can remember." He could still, if he let himself, feel the blistering skin on his back from where the belt had whipped against him. Feel the bruises forming on his cheek from where the punches landed. "I got a few months reprieve after Alden died. My father drank himself into a stupor that never seemed to end, but then it did, about a year later. This time, when he came after me, I made sure it was the last time."

"You couldn't have been very old."

"Sixteen. It was the first time I hit back. I scared him. Even now, I can see him so clearly." His hands clenched. "I stood over him, my fists bruised and bloodied as he curled up on the floor and cried. I thought how small a human being he was. How insignificant and small. I pitied him. For about a fraction of a second." He turned his hands over, examined the thin scars on the backs of his fingers. Fingers Mabel reached out and grabbed hold of, and for an instant, he felt healed. "I don't make excuses for him. It doesn't take a lot *not* to become a monster. But he got dealt a bad hand. His father, his grandfather—both abusive. The entire line of Flynn men—it's like our DNA is contaminated with violence. It's been there, in my family, for as long as I can trace back."

211

"Violence isn't a foregone conclusion for everyone," Mabel said. "I'm a counselor, remember? I know what I'm talking about. If anything, you're evidence that the cycle can be broken."

"You don't know that's true anymore than I do," he countered. "And I don't believe enough in nurture over nature that I can let the fear go. I decided when I was very young that I would never put myself in the position of having to find out for certain. Broken or not, that cycle still exists inside of me. Flynns aren't built to be fathers."

She inclined her head, touched her fingers to his face. "And here I didn't think I had a heart left to break."

"Don't go feeling sorry for me, Mabel. There's absolutely nothing unique about my growing up, and I've lived a life that surpassed anything my father could have conceived of." The last thing he ever wanted from this woman was pity. "There are thousands of kids who have the same story, and a lot of them had it—have it—even worse. Alden taught me early on there was only one way to get out. Education. My mind was the main weapon I had. The only one I could always take with me. After Alden died, I did everything I could to pave my path." He refrained from telling her he'd stop at the cemetery to do his homework sitting beside Alden's grave. He spent more time there than he had almost anywhere else those last years of his childhood.

"You and I, we both know what it's like to be left behind," he murmured. "We know what it's like to lose the one person who meant the most, our anchor. One minute, they're there, and the next, they're gone, and we don't know why, and we're adrift in an ocean that will swallow us whole. It's something that's indescribable."

And, at times, insurmountable.

"What happened to your father?" she asked.

"He died just after I graduated from high school. He just didn't wake up one morning. It barely registered at the time. I'd gotten a partial scholarship to college and had the next five to eight years planned down to the minute. I buried him next to my brother then went home and pulled that tin can out from under the floorboards. Alden's money bought me a crappy used car that lasted me all the way through Stanford and, from there, I never looked back." He turned his head, looked down at her. "Not until now."

He stroked a finger down her cheek. "I didn't want to come back here. I resented the hell out of it, despite knowing it was for a good reason. Jeff asked for my help and he's someone I can never refuse anything. Even after all these years, everything he knows about me, and he's always been there."

"He's a good man," Mabel murmured. "He sees you for who you are. Not what you were raised in."

"I'm going to owe him big time for this, though," he said with a heavy sigh. "If it hadn't been for him, I'd have never met you, and that," he offered her his best smile, "I am very, very grateful for."

"Me, too," Mabel whispered and squeezed his hand hard.

"Get those stars out of your eyes," he warned. "I'm not a knight on a white horse."

"I never thought you were." She inclined her head and smiled. "Sylvie was the romantic, Paul, not me. And FYI, I don't need to be rescued. By anyone."

"I can only imagine what you would do to me if I tried," he joked.

"I can assure you it would be swift, painful, and incredibly memorable." She surprised him by leaning forward and pressing her mouth against his. The contact was quick, lasting only long enough for him to want more. "I shouldn't have to tell you this," she murmured against his lips. "You aren't your father, Paul. You aren't anyone else in your family but you. You're not capable of cruelty like he was."

"You don't know that." It hurt more than it should have to say, because he wanted more than anything to believe it.

"Yes, I do. Because you got out. You didn't let grief swallow your future. And you made promises to yourself. Promises you've kept. You've defended those without a voice. You don't have to sacrifice anything more to prove yourself worthy."

"I've kept most of my promises." There was one in particular he was most in danger of abandoning because of her. "And I can't make any to you, Mabel. I don't know how long I'll be here, but I can't stay. It's not my home anymore."

She nodded. "I know."

"I'd like you to be one of the bright spots of my staying." He inhaled deeply. "I'd like to see you while I am here."

"Such a poet." She cupped his cheek in her palm. "I'd like to see you, too."

"I won't take away from your time with Keeley," he said as he shifted his feet under him and stood up, drawing her with him. "I won't intrude. I know my place, and I know what's important."

"I'm not sure you do." She kissed him without pity and without hesitation, and as his hands rested on her hips and he drew her in, she reached her hands around his neck, rose up on her toes, then stopped. "You don't scare me where Keeley's concerned. You trust my judgment on that, don't you? I know she's safe with you."

It was more of a relief than he wanted to admit. "But I scare you in other ways."

"Only one." She touched her fingers to his lips. "It scares me how much I want you."

Desire slammed through him with the force of a Los Angeles summer. Hot and steamy, unrelenting and suffocating. As her lips moved on his and her tongue swept in to taste him, he had the fleeting thought that he'd be perfectly fine never breathing again. His fingers clenched, and he tugged her even harder against him. He wished, as he let her take whatever lead she wanted, they were anywhere other than where they were.

"I could," she murmured against his mouth without fully pulling away, "see if someone is available to pick Keeley up after her science club. Maybe keep this dalliance between us going?"

He thought of the king-sized bed in his hotel room and the copious number of files and notes and scribbling scattered everywhere. The image acted, unfortunately, as an effective cold shower that doused any thoughts of spending the rest of the afternoon with Mabel Reynolds in his bed.

"As tempting an offer as that is," he said, reluctantly, "I think it's best if we get through today without making any rash decisions."

He set her back when he heard the all-too-familiar sound of embarrassed giggles emanating from nearby. Clearly, they were attracting attention. Looking down into her dazed eyes and a sultry smile aimed at him and only him, he also knew it wouldn't take much to change his mind, but he had to stay firm.

"And given how I left things at the press conference, I really should get back to the office."

"Damage control, huh?"

"Something like that." He tugged her beside him, gave one last glance out over the city. He'd thought he'd come here for her, but it had done his own soul just as much good. A reminder of how far he'd come. And the promises he had kept. "Come on. I'll get you back to your car."

"I'm just over there." Mabel pointed to where her van sat around the corner on the first level of the parking structure. "Lucked out for a change." She checked her watch again. "You're good for my schedule," she teased. "I might actually shock Keeley by being early for a change."

"Hang on." He zoomed up the ramp and pulled into one of the other empty spots. "Late afternoon, hospitals tend to empty out," he said as they climbed out of his car.

"I've heard of walking me to my door before, but to my car?" She rolled her eyes. "You sure you aren't trying to earn your white knight status?"

"Not remotely. That would require a horse, and I don't do horses."

"Good to know." She side-eyed him with suspicion. "Look, I had an idea about Eva. That guy Leo, the one who was waiting outside the hospital the other day?"

"The guy who wanted you to get him in to see her?"

"He said something about not knowing what they were going to do to her. I think we should ask him about that."

"It's interesting how often you and your friends use the word *we*."

Mabel cringed. "I might be getting ahead of myself." She trusted Quinn's judgment about bringing Paul in on their secret investigation into the Circle, but she really wanted Laurel's two cents before she pulled the trigger. "You know what?" She quickened her pace, dug into her bag for her keys, and disarmed her minivan alarm. "I'll give you a call about this later." She pulled open the driver's door, then yanked open the back door to stash her purse inside. "I just need to check on a few …"

Mabel froze. Her keys dropped out of her hand, and she stumbled back into the car parked next to her.

"What's wrong?"

Paul moved in, pushing Mabel behind him, but she peered around him. Heart pounding against her ribs, she covered her mouth to stifle the half-scream threatening to escape. Her breath came in short gasps.

The knife had been plunged hilt-deep into the driver's seat, but the blade wasn't what sent the shudders of fear rioting through her system.

"That's a picture of Keeley," she whispered, trying to move closer, but Paul continued to block her way. "That's taken outside of her school." The knife had been stabbed right through Keeley's throat. Below the blade, the word *stop* had been written in dripping, red ink.

And on the seat lay a solitary and perfectly preserved red lily.

CHAPTER TWELVE

"NO, baby. Quinn's going to hang out during your science club meeting, then bring you home." The fear Mabel attempted to keep out of her voice filled her eyes when she looked across the center console at Paul.

He offered a quick smile and glanced at the dashboard clock. In the sixty-three minutes since Mabel had opened her minivan's door, he felt as if he'd lived multiple lifetimes.

Paul reached out, grabbed hold of her hand, and squeezed. If she was surprised by his action, she didn't show it and instead offered a tremulous smile as she clung to him.

Stopped at a red light a few blocks away from the hospital, he was doing his best to get his own bearings. He'd been down-to-the-bone scared a number of times in his life. His father's rages, worrying about getting into college, feeling utterly alone when Alden had been killed. Hell, hoping he was doing enough to bring justice to people who couldn't fight for it themselves was a specialized anxiety few understood.

But none of those things, nothing in his life, could have ever prepared him for the blood-curdling, paralyzing terror that overtook him at the sight of that picture and knife.

"No, I don't know what we're having for dinner." Mabel rolled her eyes. "I'll have to give that some …" She broke off, took a slow deep breath that spoke of both frustration and uncertainty. "No. I haven't had a chance to look into getting a karaoke machine for your birthday. We'll figure it … okay, yeah, you go on back to your meeting. I'll see you when you get … uh-huh. I love you too, Kee." She clicked off, stared down at her phone, and let out a sharp laugh. "I don't know how her mind works on so many different tracks, but for once, I'm grateful. She hasn't started to ask questions." She leaned her head back and closed her eyes, and kept hold of Paul's hand as he continued with the traffic flow back into downtown. "You have questions, don't you?"

"I have questions." But there was only one that mattered right now. "She's okay?"

"Yeah. She's fine."

"And Quinn?" Paul asked. "What did he say?" The detective must have broken the land-speed record making it to Keeley's school minutes after Mabel called him.

"They haven't had any reports of strangers around the school or unfamiliar cars in the area. One of the benefits of private school," Mabel said with a heavy sigh. "They can afford specialized protection. A lot of high-profile people's kids go to Summerset, so it's top-notch. He'll talk to the principal, tell her about the threat, and we'll go from there. In the meantime," her lips twitched a little, "Keeley has an LAPD Detective to show off to her science club."

"Between him and Wallace, things seem under control." He hesitated, trying to decide how best to approach his curiosity. "Care to tell me why you called Quinn before you called 9-1-1?"

"Because Quinn wouldn't immediately think I was an overreacting whack job."

"Because he understood what was left in your car?"

She hesitated. "Ye—yes." She tugged her hand free and made a show of straightening up her purse between her feet, caught the stuffed bunny in her hands, and drew it up against her chest. "Where are we going?"

"Temple House," he told her. "I'm taking you home."

She looked at him, frowned. "Where are *you* going?"

"I need to put in an appearance at the office," he told her. "I haven't been back since the press conference, and I need to check—"

"I'll come with you."

Keeley came by her talent of interrupting naturally, it seemed. "You sure?"

"By now, Quinn's called Riley, which means if I go home, I'll be besieged by questions from everyone who lives there, and right now, the only question I could possibly answer is where my car is, and I can't believe it's being impounded in an evidence lot, which means I have no idea when I'm getting it back. So, no. I'd rather not go home just yet."

Paul waited a few beats before finally giving into the frustration that had grown like a balloon to the point of popping. "Maybe Wallace can answer those questions at this meeting you all are having tonight."

"Maybe," Mabel mused.

He counted to five, forced his voice to remain even. "You do know I can probably help with whatever it is that's going on."

"Yeah," she said quietly. "I know."

"But you don't want my help." He clung tighter when she attempted to pull her hand free.

"I don't think *want* enters into it." There was something, regret maybe, in her voice. "It's not just my decision to make. I'm waiting to hear back from the others …"

As much as he was tempted to bulldoze his way in, he didn't think that would earn him anything remotely close to goodwill. Or trust. "How about this?" It was killing him to play nice. It was also a bit baffling. "How about you take a look at what I've got displayed in my office, and then you can tell me if I've earned an invite to this gathering of yours."

"You don't have to earn your way in, Paul."

"Don't I?"

"No. This isn't about …" She managed to pull free of his grasp and pivoted in her seat, looking at him. "This isn't about trust. Exactly."

"Sure, it is."

"Not in the way you're thinking. It's … complicated."

"Everything's complicated. Do you trust me?"

"Yes." Her automatic reply loosened some of those knots inside of him.

"Okay, then. We'll take it a step at a time." He turned left and zoomed his way down the street toward the DA's office. "One step at a time."

"Do you think it's me or the rabbit getting all the strange looks?" Mabel asked Paul as they made their way up the lobby stairs to his office.

"I'd go with it's probably a combination."

She reached back and touched the bunny's head sticking out of her bag. Just to remind herself it was still there. She could have left both her bag and the rabbit in the car; it was, after all, a basement parking lot with decent security, but then she'd bought that story before. Best to keep Benedict with her for the foreseeable future. She would keep him safe. For when they found Eva.

"Thank you," she said as they reached the second-floor landing.

"For what?" Paul glanced over his shoulder at her.

"I don't know." She shrugged. "Just … everything, I guess. It feels weird," she admitted, even as she wished she'd kept her mouth shut. "Relying on someone."

"Maybe we both need to get used to that."

Kent, Paul's assistant, jumped to his feet so fast that the young man's chair flew back into the wall. She anticipated that poor, plain wall was going to have a crack or hole in it within days.

"I didn't think you'd be back today," Kent said, eyes wide as Mabel followed at Paul's heels. "Ah, the DA's called twice about scheduling a meeting following the press conference. I get the feeling she wasn't too pleased with the way things … went. Ah, sir?" Kent stood just inside the door to Paul's office. "Will Monday suffice?"

"Monday's fine." Paul sounded as if meeting with the DA was nothing more than a teeth cleaning. "Mabel and I are going to be going through some—"

"Paul?" Mabel frowned as she circled the room. The room, was of, course different than the first time she'd been in here. He'd filled up most of the office with whiteboards covered in notes and evidence, but that wasn't what caught her attention. She sniffed the air. Her eyes watered a bit. "Do you smell that?"

"Smell what?" Paul took a deep breath, and his gaze sharpened when his eyes met hers. "Isn't that—?"

"Clove," she confirmed. "I smelled that in Eva's room." She started to say something else, but Paul held up a hand.

"You don't smoke, do you, Kent?" Paul asked the younger man.

"No." Kent shook his head.

"Did anyone come by today? Did you see anyone?"

"No, but I went out around noon." Kent pushed his glasses higher up on his nose. "The assistant DA invited me out to lunch, so that was pretty cool. Well, me and a few of the other office assistants. I locked the door behind me, though. I'm certain of it."

"When did this invite happen?" Paul asked.

"Ah, this morning, right after you left for the press conference." Kent frowned. "Why? Should I not have—?"

"What's wrong?" Mabel stepped forward, but Paul silenced her with a raised hand, sat down, typed into his laptop. Without taking his eyes off the screen, he stood up, ushered them both outside and into the hall beyond Kent's office.

"What's going on?" Kent demanded in a stage whisper.

"Someone's accessed my files," Paul said.

Mabel heart skipped a beat. "Are you sure?"

"Yeah." Paul shoved a hand through his hair. "A hacker friend of mine installs specific programs on all my computers. Gives me access into when my system's last been used. I check it every time I log on. Someone was on my computer at one this afternoon. I was on my way to the hospital to see you." He glanced at Kent. "And you were at lunch. If someone's been in my office, we can't rule out someone's listening in now."

"You mean someone's bugged the office?" Kent practically squeaked.

"Stay with me, kid," Paul ordered. "We're going to have to make another stop on my way to taking you home. Kent. Can you find me a handcart? Something big enough to haul four or five boxes?"

"Someone got in here because I went to lunch. They got in and bugged the place?" Beneath the dismay, Kent's voice carried a hint of anger.

"Can you get me one?"

"Yeah." Kent nodded in dismay. "Yeah, there's one down the hall in the closet."

"Great. Go get it." Kent raced down the hall, around the corner, and out of sight. "Okay, think." Paul knocked a fist against the bridge of his nose. "Nothing looked disturbed. Getting into my computer would have taken some time. They knew Kent would be out of the office." His eyes narrowed. "I'm thinking it was probably a good thing you didn't bring me in on things before now, Mabel. This is why, isn't it?"

She looked at him, pinched her lips tight.

"Right," he muttered and rested a hand on her shoulder. "Okay."

Kent was hurrying back toward them, a heavy-duty handcart rolling ahead of him. "Got it."

"Great. Mabel, once we go back in, use your cell and go take pictures of the white boards. We can't take them with us."

"Okay." She dug into her bag for her phone.

"Kent, did the forwarding system get set up for my cell?"

"Yeah."

"Good. If anyone asks, I'm in and out of the office all the time. No set hours. No set schedule. Anyone wants to talk to me, they go through you, understood?"

"Yes, sir. Yes," Kent said.

"You good with a little cloak-and-dagger?"

"Apparently," Kent said with a strained laugh. "Where should I say—?"

"I'm working. Doesn't matter from where. Make it up."

"Your hotel room?"

"Sure." Paul barely shrugged. "Tell them that. Help me move the boxes from my office into yours, but don't talk about what we're doing while we're in there. In case of bugs."

While the two of them moved all the boxes, Mabel took multiple photos of the mapped-out information and evidence Paul had compiled on his whiteboards.

"Do you want to clear them off?" Mabel asked when Paul closed his office door and they'd left the vicinity of any possible hearing devices.

"No, no. Leave the board. And the coffee machine." He looked more pained at the last mention than the previous. "If I leave that behind, they'll figure I'll be back."

"You know what they say about a man and his coffee machine," Mabel said in an effort to ease the tension. "You don't want to let on you know they've been in here."

"Exactly. They probably already took pictures of what's on the boards anyway, so we have to consider that a loss." He turned to his assistant in the hall. "Kent." Paul lowered his voice. "I want you to start keeping a log of every single person who calls and stops by. I don't care if it's a janitor. I want you to use it to send a daily report of anyone who comes into or contacts my office. You send it at different times, each night, and from a different public networked location—an internet cafe. Send nothing from your apartment. Send me nothing from here. Got it?"

"Yes." Kent turned wide eyes on Mabel. "Are you going to tell me what's going on?"

"It's better for you if you don't know any more. We're going to solve this damned case before they come after anyone else." Paul looked at the stack of six boxes. "I don't want to take two trips. I need to decide what to take."

"Follow the money," Mabel said. "Financial statements first."

"Take those, and leave the rest for me," Kent offered. "I can deliver them somewhere. Your hotel room, maybe?"

"How about getting them to Wallace?" Mabel asked Paul. "He's probably back at the station by now."

"Detective Wallace Osterman?" Kent said. "I know Wallace. We hang out at some of the same bars. Yeah, I can take them there, no problem."

"Thanks," Paul said. "I'll let him know to expect you. Tonight, please. On your way out." He did a quick search of the boxes, divided them into two piles. "I'll take these. You good with the rest?"

"Go," Kent assured him. "Don't worry about these. They're in safe hands."

"What about your laptop?" Mabel asked.

"Can't risk them having installed something on it."

"Bring it anyway," Mabel told him. "I know someone who can clean it for you. I'll bet they even know your hacker friend."

"All right." He didn't look entirely convinced, but he returned to his office and re-emerged with his laptop case and handed it to her. "I'll check in at least once a day," Paul told Kent as they loaded up the cart. "No set time. Leave your phone on from six a.m. through five p.m. If you don't hear from me by five in the afternoon on any given day, I want you to talk to Jeff Chambers, and no one else."

Kent's eyes were wide. "What do I tell him?"

"Just tell him you haven't heard from me. He'll take it from there. Hey," Paul stopped short in the doorway, "I'm trusting you with this, yeah? You're my eyes and my ears in this building. You hear anything about anything connected to Tenado, you put it in that daily report. I don't care how insignificant it might seem. You're my guardian at the gate, Kent."

"Yeah." Kent's chest puffed a bit, and his eyes sparked, as if he'd suddenly been activated. "Yeah, I've got you covered. Don't worry."

"Great. Thanks, Kent. I'll be in touch. Be careful, yeah? You get spooked, you head straight for Wallace or Jeff. No one else."

Kent nodded. "All right."

Mabel followed, her anxiety taking a giant leap when he headed to the elevators. "Ah, Paul?"

"I know. I'm sorry." He punched the down button, kept the hand-cart tilted back. "We'll run into fewer people this way. Takes us straight to the basement parking." Clearly, she didn't look convinced. "I'll get asked questions if I'm seen with this much stuff. Someone will find out." Even now, he was looking over his shoulder as offices began to close for the weekend. "It'll be two minutes max, Mabel. Promise."

So far, he'd kept the promises he'd made to her. "Fine."

She clutched his bag against her chest. Already she could feel her heart skipping multiple beats. When the doors opened and he stepped inside, her knees trembled as she followed.

She walked straight in, spun around, and pressed her back hard into the corner of the car.

He hit the B on the panel, and the doors slid shut.

The air whooshed out of her lungs. Her arms went numb from holding his bag so tight. The car seemed to be dropping in slow motion, which was good, but that also extended the panic struggling to burst free of her chest.

Paul set the cart straight, stood over her. She wanted to tell him to move, that he was only making it worse. But the words wouldn't come. When she lifted her chin and looked at him, her eyes wide with fear, he planted his hands on either side of her. His face moved toward hers, and before another coherent or anxious thought slipped through her mind, he kissed her.

The sob that escaped was caught by his open mouth. A mouth that seemed determined to coax hers into utter and complete submission. The tension in her body melted as his tongue swept in and over hers. He tilted his head, deepened the kiss, and had her almost losing her hold on the bag as the elevator dinged and the car settled.

When the doors opened, he stepped back. "I suspect that was a dick move, but I also think it worked." That charming smile of his revealed a slight dimple she hadn't noticed before. Not that she had much time to process that before he retrieved the box and led her out of the elevator. "Imagine what we could do if we went up to the top of the Empire State Building."

"For future reference, I like your dick moves."

His grin lit the dark corners of her fractured heart.

"Where are we going?" She added his bag to the box in the trunk, and he slammed it shut.

"First? My hotel." They climbed into the car. "Then I'm going to find another one. One no one knows I'm staying in."

"Or." Mabel's mind raced to keep up with her mouth. "Hold off on that for now, and stay with me."

He didn't even blink as he started the car and pulled out. "I don't think that's such a good idea."

"Why not? I've got a spare room, and if you're worried about security, you won't find better than Temple House."

"I need a place to work, Mabel." He zoomed out of the parking lot and headed straight for Santa Monica Boulevard. "And I don't think you want Keeley anywhere near the information I need to keep up and in easy sight."

"If only the spare room had ... what are those things called again?" She snapped her fingers. "Oh, right: doors."

"Ha."

"Keeley isn't a snoop. And for the most part, she does what she's told. If I tell her not to go in when the door is closed, she won't."

"And what kind of message do you think we'll be sending to Keeley with me moving in across the hall?"

"That friends help each other out when we can. Whatever else we're about to become, we're friends first, Paul." She fluttered her lashes at him even though he wasn't looking at her. "Unless we aren't."

He stopped at a red light and finally turned his head. "You sure about this?"

"You wanted to talk to Riley, right? She lives one floor down from me. You wanted to meet Moxie. You want someone to bounce ideas off of? You've got Quinn right there with them. And if you need a bodyguard, there's Blake. We are a full-service apartment building."

Before he could argue, she leaned over and kissed him, and this time, she didn't pull away until she felt some of the tension and doubt melt away. "It's a good solution for all of us, and you can set any doubts you have about being around Keeley aside. I've already told you I trust you with her, Paul. Maybe it's time you start trusting yourself. Now, shut up," she kissed him again, this time quick and hard, "and drive."

"ETA on Keeley: fifteen minutes." Restless, Mabel set her cell down on the dining room table and continued to straighten up the mess she'd already straightened ten minutes before. She'd been spinning so fast since getting home it had taken her a while to remember Barksy was downstairs at Cass's with Nox and Elliot. Even now, pacing around her apartment, she found herself catching glimpses of her pictures of Sylvie. The pictures played tricks with her mind, giving her some comfort as if her sister was actually here. She touched cautious fingers to her pendant, felt it warm slightly. "She'll be home soon."

226

"Mabel, she's fine," Paul reminded her, not for the first time since they'd arrived at her apartment. "Hopped up on ice cream probably, but fine. Quinn's called and said so himself."

"I know, I know, he did."

She couldn't explain the nerves except for her impulsive suggestion he move in with her. It made sense. Maybe *too* much sense. Or maybe it would make more sense once he got an earful from Cass and the others as far as the truth behind the case he was working on. The only thing making her feel remotely better were the telltale signs that Blake had installed the new security film on her windows overlooking the park. The note he'd left behind said he was waiting on another delivery but that he should be done with the rest of the windows in the next few days. She could only assume his career in the military left him with seriously connected suppliers given his immediate acquisition of technology that included not only the window film but the state-of-the-art security system he'd installed around Temple House.

Paul staying in her apartment was a logical development, even if it did come across as the teensiest bit selfish. She liked being around him, and maybe being a part of a family unit for a change might make him see he fit in better than he thought he did. "Is the room okay?"

"The room is perfect." The fact he could write coherently while holding a conversation irritated but impressed her. "Private bath, fabulous kitchen, and entertainment just outside that fabulous door that's included." His smile flashed again, eyes twinkling. "The Bonaventure cannot compete. Oh, wait. Is there a gym in this place?"

"Ah, there's a treadmill on the roof, actually. I'll leave the key out."

"I was teasing," he said easily. "But I'll check it out. Bet there's some great view up there."

"You would not be wrong."

Blake had been in the lobby when they'd gotten back to Temple House. Together he and Paul had made quick work of emptying out his car—not only of the boxes from his office but also a duffel from his hotel room.

She'd waited in the car at the hotel and, when Paul returned with only the one bag, she wondered if he'd changed his mind. But he hadn't. Nor had he checked out of the hotel. While he hadn't found any indication anyone had been in his room, he didn't want anyone knowing he wasn't staying there any longer.

"Might be a little crowded to get a full display going of the case," he went on as his pen scratched across a legal pad, "but I can't beat the ambiance. Or the company."

"Well, that's sweet." She grabbed a stack of coloring books and magazines and moved them for the third time. Where had all this stuff, all this *junk* come from? She felt like a pack rat on speed.

"Did you take anything for your headache?"

"My what?" She stopped, hands locked around a stack of Keeley's books and looked at him. He was sitting there, at her dining room table, top button open, his tie loosened, and those blue eyes pinned on her as if she were the aforementioned evening's entertainment. "How did you—?"

"In the car, you kept rubbing your temple. I dated a woman once who had migraines. Stress brought them on." He closed clicked his pen closed. "Or a lack of sleep." He reached out, caught her hand, and threaded his fingers through hers. "Or stress."

"You said stress already."

"It bore repeating."

"I'm not a slob." Why she felt like defending herself, she couldn't say. Or maybe she could. "Why do I care what you think? Geez." Still caught in his hold, she sank into the chair at the head of the table. "Why did I just say that out loud?"

"Because you've had a crap day, an even crappier week, and no one is giving you any answers you want—*and* you've invited someone into your home for an extended period of time, and you're wondering if it's a mistake."

"No." She shook her head. "No, you've got the last part wrong." Funny, that was the one bit of today's puzzle that did make the most sense. She searched for that ache of loneliness she'd felt for years, but it wasn't there. At least not as strong and commanding as it once had been. "That said, I *am* wondering how long it's going to take for the shine to wear off where me and Keeley are concerned."

More importantly, she was worried about how he was going to react to the avalanche of information that was poised to come tumbling down on him.

"You must have me confused with someone who's familiar with shiny. Mabel."

He squeezed her hand.

"Sorry. I've got all these different things spinning in my head." Seriously, it was like a family of rodents had taken up residence and had all jumped headfirst into the hamster-wheel Olympics. "No one's called about Eva, have they?"

"No." His thumb rubbed against the pulse in her wrist, and while she was certain he was trying to calm her down, the action only wedged another wheel into her head, and this one did not contain hamsters of any sort. "Chief Burton assured me he'd call if there were any developments with Eva's disappearance."

"I should have gone to the bar Eva works at. We need to find Leo." That whole idea had fallen by the wayside the second she'd seen that freaking flower. "He probably knows something."

"No, you shouldn't do anything like that," Paul said far too calmly. "I get that you want to do something. Anything. A woman you care about has gone missing. Someone symbolically stuck a knife in your child's throat," Paul said far too calmly. "You're entitled to be freaked out. But I can assure you there is zero chance of you or Keeley going anywhere alone for a good long while. No matter what investigative bug you've got up your butt." He leaned over, cast his gaze down. "As cute a butt as it is."

"Really?" Mabel glared at him. "Butt talk does not bode well for our future activities."

"Oh, I don't know …" That grin of his was probably the reason he'd lived as long as he had. Talk about a get-out-of-jail-free card.

"I'm going to sleep with you. Just thought I'd make that clear," she added as if she needed to explain her explosive verbiage. "I'm not sure when, but it'll happen."

"Is this something that deserves a warning?" His eyebrow raised, and the corner of his mouth quirked up.

Did his eyes really have to twinkle that much? Or was his playfulness his way of distracting her from the terror that continued to cling to her?

She hesitated, then rambled on. "It's been a while, so I'm trying to get all the awkward conversation bits out of the way now. You know, before—"

"Your daughter walks into the room?" The amusement in his eyes faded. "How long?"

"Huh?"

She knew perfectly well what he was asking.

Maybe she needed a drink.

Yeah, that would probably help.

Mabel started to stand, but he tightened his hold and kept her in place.

"Mabel. How long has it been since you've slept with someone?"

"A while," she said, her smile far too wide considering her back teeth just caught a chill. "I mean, not so long as anything's really changed. It's still done the same way, right? But it's ... well, it's been a Keeley-age, shall we say."

His eyes widened. An added intensity flared in his eyes. "You haven't slept with anyone since Keeley was born?"

"Why does it sound as if I've suddenly sprouted a second head? No—I mean, yes, that's how long it's been. Keeley's father left skid marks on both our hearts, so I've been a bit, well ... cautious since then." She took in a big breath. "You're the first guy I've ever let cross over the threshold, so to speak," she added with a grin of her own. "Don't worry," she insisted, "nothing's grown back or anything. And I'm hoping you'll find stretch marks endearing since .... Man, I got really big with her. Like"—she held her free hand out almost to the edge of the table— "I didn't see my toes for months. I was huge."

"And no doubt beautiful." He inclined his head toward the collection of photographs on the shelves. "How about I try to put your mind at rest regarding a few things. First, I'm more than happy to agree to your declaration of carnal plan-age. Consider me on board for that. Second, I've been trying to figure out a way to action this chemistry between us since you sat across from my desk the other day, so thanks for making it easy for me. Third," he pushed his chair back and stood up, drew her up with him and tugged her around the table and into his arms, "I am more than happy to reintroduce you to whatever activities interest you." He kissed the side of her neck and sent chills racing down her spine. "My goal is to at least reduce the intensity of those skid marks that douche bag of a man might have given you."

"How do you know he's a douche?"

His teeth nipped at the skin under her ear, and her knees nearly buckled.

His answer was simple, to the point. "Because he let you go."

He kissed her then, slow and deep, making her wish the impossible, that her daughter wasn't due to get home at any minute and that there was nothing on her list of things to do this evening other than him.

"It's really irritating how you always say the right thing," she whispered against his lips. "Do you think I have time for a quick shower?"

"Yes."

"Are you saying that so I'll do something to calm down?"

"Yes."

"Careful. You don't want me thinking you're a nice man." She grabbed the back of his neck and pulled him down for another kiss. "You're going to have to decide, in a few hours' time, just how far you plan to venture into my crazy life. However short-term it might be."

There was obviously something about having her child's life threatened that spurred her into reckless behavior. Or maybe she was looking for anything to stop her from dwelling on what truly was lurking over her shoulder.

"Might as well take the full plunge," he said in a tone that sounded half like a warning. "I'm not a forever man, Mabel. I can't be. For both our sakes. You might have faith I'm better than that, but I don't. I've been on the other side of it." He touched her face. "If that's a deal-breaker, so be it. I'll walk out that door right now."

"No." She couldn't, she realized, let him go without knowing what it was to be held by him. To be with him. To be with him long enough to be reminded what it was to be wanted. "I don't want you walking away from me. Not yet. Okay?" She nodded and smiled, neither of which belied the rioting emotions of disappointment and sadness she could feel lurking beneath her jumping heart. "So, I'll take what I can get while I can get it."

And maybe she could show him there was a potential for his life to contain more. *Be* more.

"I will never lie to you, Mabel. That's one promise I can make and one I will keep."

"And what about Keeley?" She wanted to ignore the flash of fear she saw pass across his gaze. But it was only a flash, which gave her a little hope, at least. "You aren't going to avoid her, are you?"

"If she's anything like her mother, I can say with some certainty that would be impossible. No," he added at the doubt she knew shined in her eyes, "I will not avoid Keeley. She may very well get sick of me and solve all our problems."

It was better than have him racing for the door again. "Okay." She touched his face, and when the key rattled in the door, she sighed. "So much for that shower."

"Painkillers it'll be, then."

He dropped a kiss on the tip of her nose just as Keeley burst through the door and raced down the hall. The navy plaid skirt, crisp white Peter Pan collared shirt, and blue blazer were rumpled and well-worn from a week of activity.

"Mom! Oh, my gosh, Mom, this was the most amazing day! You sent Quinn to get me from school!" She grabbed hold of Mabel's suddenly free hands and swung them back and forth. "I got to tell everyone a *detective* was picking me up. *And* he sat in on science club and answered questions about lab tests and evidence and stuff! How cool is that?"

"So cool," Mabel said, glancing up as Quinn joined them. Affection she rarely let herself feel swamped her. Wallace had been right when he'd said Quinn would play it low-key. He'd simply retrieved her child and brought her home without any indication that there was a potential psychopath out there wanting to do Keeley harm. "You remember Mr. Flynn, don't you?"

"Oh, yeah, sure. Hi." Keeley turned her high-beam bright eyes on Paul and hugged her mother. "You came back."

"I did." Paul's smile seemed completely genuine.

"He's going to stay with us in the guest room for a little while." Mabel purposely kept her eyes on her daughter and didn't let her gaze wander anywhere near Quinn's face. "He's going to be working most of the time, but he needed a place. That okay with you?"

"Sure." Excitement and more than a little mischief glowed in Keeley's eyes. "Do you know how to make pancakes, Mr. Flynn?"

"As a matter of fact, I do. And call me Paul, okay?"

"Okay. Can we have pancakes on Sunday morning? Mom always tries, but—"

"My pancakes suck," Mabel confirmed without hesitation.

"Then pancakes on Sunday it is," Paul assured Keeley. "I appreciate you letting me stay here while your mom and I work together."

"You helping her find out what happened to Aunt Sylvie and all those other women?"

"I—" Paul looked first to Mabel, then Quinn, then back to Keeley. "Yes, I am, actually. How did you know about that?"

"You're all over the internet. You were talking to reporters today. I heard some of the teachers talking about it at school." She tilted her head so her pigtails actually aligned. "This means you won't have to be so sad anymore, Mom," Keeley announced as she dumped her backpack on the ground. "And you won't have bad dreams that make you cry. I told you there was someone who could make you happy. It's him, isn't it?" The last question was stage-whispered loud enough to bring a hint of pink to Paul's cheeks, which Mabel reveled in.

"Is that where that goes?" Mabel avoided Paul's concerned expression by pointing at the bag and then her daughter. She earned a quintessential dramatic sigh as Keeley hauled it up and plopped it in the chair Mabel had vacated. "How about we talk about what we're going to have for dinner?"

"I've got plans for tonight." Keeley shook her head and looked at Quinn. "Right?"

"Right," he confirmed. "Go get packed."

"Packed for where?" Mabel asked as Keeley raced out of the room to her bedroom. "What's going on, Quinn?"

"Sutton's arranged for a slumber party downstairs in 1C for Keeley, Addie, and Lucas."

"1C," Mabel mused. "Shirley's?" The tenant was the backup babysitter for the rest of Temple House. She was also a graduate student in elementary education.

"Yep. Worry-free overnight care. As for what's going on?" Quinn walked around into the kitchen and retrieved a bottle of beer from the back of her fridge. "Sorry, I really need this." He popped the cap and took a long pull. "For the record, if I'm ever given the choice between a classroom full of almost nine-year-old science geeks and a prison visit, I will happily take the convicts. Riley and Cass called the meeting tonight. Eight o'clock. Cass's apartment."

"Oh." Mabel swallowed hard. There was no stopping it now. "Okay. Eight o'clock. Right. We'll … ah … we'll be there."

"Any word on Mabel's minivan?" Paul asked.

"Not much of one," Quinn said. "Preliminary results show no prints on the knife, the photo, or the flower. No surprise on the latter, of course. We also have yet to trace the flower to any particular florist in town because guess what? While they were, not so long ago, a specialized species, they're easily grown from bulbs now. That one bloom could be from any greenhouse in the city. I got an unwanted botany rundown from Susie at the lab. Red lilies are commonplace these days. So, zippo there. Your van is currently in evidence being given one hell of a once-over, but not holding out much hope on that front." He stopped long enough to take another drink. "I'm waiting to hear back on the nail scrapings from other night after your closet creeper guy made a play for you. FYI, I got the contact lens to Susie a little late, so that'll take extra time, but hopefully, we'll know something by Sunday? Oh, and my dad called." Quinn faced Paul, grimacing. "After a meeting with his Lieutenant, Detective Harrison has been sidelined on Eva's case, and her file should arrive in my email at any time. Unfortunately, the techs examining the security feed at the hospital can't retrieve something that was never recorded. Someone remotely switched off the system, replaced the feed with a looped tape, and let it run for more than three hours."

"Parking lot cameras?" Paul asked.

"Same. Shorter time frame but nothing there."

"You going to have Nox take a peek?" Mabel asked.

"Am I going to ask a known computer hacker to interfere with an ongoing police investigation and break into a secured system to prove my lab techs right?" Quinn challenged.

"You'll win Nox's undying devotion," Mabel suggested.

"Yeah, I know." Quinn grinned. "It's why I'm going to have Wallace ask them to do it. Speaking of Wallace: Kent dropped off those boxes at the department. Wallace'll bring them tonight. Seems to me there's something … else." Quinn feigned confusion. "Oh, right. And the timing on this is entirely coincidental where your cohabitation shift is concerned. Shirley's expecting Keeley around six thirty for dinner," he added. "All little ones will be out of earshot for this guy's initiation and whatever fallout might take place as a result." He aimed his beer bottle at Paul then grinned at Mabel. "You're welcome."

"I was right," Mabel muttered as she struggled to process. "I do need a drink."

"I have a question,"—Paul held up one hand as if it was his first day at school— "and it's not about the initiation, as delightful as that sounds to be ..."

"Only one?" Mabel asked, amused.

"You have a resident at Temple House named Shirley?"

"You're a funny guy, Flynn." Quinn's smile was quick and cursory. "You ready for what comes next?"

"Yes," Paul said, but looked directly at Mabel. "I most certainly am."

Now it was Mabel's cheeks that went hot.

"Anything I need to do to prepare? For the meeting," Paul added when he realized how that might be interpreted.

"Nope," Quinn said. "Just be secure in the knowledge that we live in one seriously fucked-up world." Quinn headed back to the door, stopped long enough to give Mabel a quick shoulder squeeze. "I don't see any reason to tell Keeley anything about what happened today."

"You're sure?"

It was one of those wheels in Mabel's head that had been spinning out of control.

"For now, yes. Blake's got a couple of ideas he's running with—"

"Blake knows?" Mabel looked for a hint that Quinn had been made aware of her stranger-in-the-park encounter.

"I called him." Quinn nodded. "He was a big help when Riley went missing, and he's got the security around this place locked down tight. He'd dealt with threats like this when he was active duty, and he knows what it takes to protect family." There wasn't an ounce of doubt or hesitation in his voice. "We'll see where we are after the weekend. Until then, we take it a day at a time."

Mabel's throat burned with unshed tears. "I really lucked out when Riley snagged you, didn't I?"

He puffed out his chest playfully. "You all did." He pressed a quick kiss on her forehead. "See you down at Cass's later. I'm going to go try and grab some sleep."

When the door closed behind him, Mabel sagged back into the chair, shoving Keeley's backpack onto the floor right where it wasn't supposed to be. "He's not usually such a whirlwind of information."

"Why don't you go take that shower? And whatever you take for your migraines."

"I didn't say it was a migraine."

"You didn't have to." His smile said it all.

"That girlfriend?"

"Once again, I'm pleading the fifth."

"What about Keeley?"

"What about me?" Keeley, uniform gone, had changed into bright yellow leggings and an oversized K-Pop band T-shirt. Sticking out of the overnight bag hanging on her shoulder was Lord Squidly, the octopus that doubled as a snuggly sleepover pillow, and the new Barbie make-up kit she'd gotten for Christmas. "I'm all ready to go."

"Yes, well, Shirley isn't expecting you just yet," Mabel said. "Why don't you get a start on your weekend homework while you wait and put the bag by the door?"

"Aw, Mom," Keeley whined. "I don't wanna do homework now. You're harshing my buzz."

"Where on earth did you hear that?" And did she even know what that meant?

"I dunno." Keeley's shrug said otherwise.

"Did I see Star Wars Monopoly around here somewhere?" Paul asked far too innocently for it to have not been pre-planned.

"Only the one based on the *original* trilogy," Mabel said firmly.

"Because it's the only one that matters," Keeley sang back as if it were an often-repeated refrain. "That's *Mom's* game," Keeley announced. "I got it for her for Christmas a few years ago. You wanna play?" There was no mistaking the mild disbelief in her child's voice. "Can I be Princess Leia? Mom always chooses her, and I let her. Cause, you know, it's her game and all. Usually, I'm C3P-0."

"Only if I can be Darth Vader." He flashed that winning smile of his. "I have a soft spot for a complicated villain."

"I sense an interesting discussion in our future," Mabel said as Keeley raced to retrieve the game. "You don't have to do this."

"I know I don't." Paul shoved his hands in his pockets. "I want to, and you need to shoo. It'll be fun."

"You sure?"

"You aren't the only one who could use a distraction. Go take a shower. Maybe grab a quick nap. We'll be fine. And I'm keeping my hands in my pocket, so I'm not tempted to do something completely inappropriate in front of your child. Go, Mabel."

His nod of encouragement made her wonder, if only for a flash of a second, if something more than just a fling was possible between them. "I'll be twenty minutes. Half hour tops," she promised.

"Take your time," he said as Keeley dumped the box on the table and flipped open the lid. "Something tells me we'll be playing for a while."

"That's Coruscant Imperial Palace with three cities and a spaceport, which means you owe me ..." Keeley scrunched up her face and tapped her fingers on the table, "three thousand four hundred dollars!" Keeley held out her hand and, rather than looking superior—as she had every right to feel—she had an ego-smashing expression of pity on her face. "Sorry."

"I've lost court cases I feel better about," Paul muttered as he cleaned out his cash and placed the last of his money in her palm. "You know, originally, I planned to 'let' you win."

"Mom always says, that, too." Keeley counted out the money and arranged it onto the nice thick piles she'd been collecting since the first roll of the dice. "She says I have a diabolical mind."

"I'm not in a position to disagree."

"Do you like my mom?"

"I do."

"Like ... *like* like her, or just friends like her?" Keeley pinned him with a look that was all too much like her mother. "'Cause friends like is fine; it's cool and all. But if you maybe wanted to take her out on a date or something, I'd be okay with that."

"You would?" He didn't know why but the idea of having earned Keeley's approval gave him a bit of an unexpected boost.

"Yeah." She shrugged. "You make her smile. Even when she thinks no one's looking. She's been smiling a lot since she met you—well, except for that little time after you left last time."

"Good to know." He couldn't imagine a more uncomfortable conversation to have with anyone, let alone an eight-year-old.

"My dad didn't make her smile. I don't think." She scrunched her nose. "I don't know for sure, actually. He didn't want to be a dad. I've only seen him a few times."

"Being a dad isn't always an easy thing to be." He couldn't imagine a man being more shit out of luck than having lost Keeley Reynolds as a daughter.

"I guess. Sometimes, I miss having a dad, but a lot of my friends don't have one. Maybe it's not that big a deal."

"Sometimes, not having a father is better than having the wrong one."

"Huh." Keeley straightened in her chair. "You think so?"

"I know so, actually." Not that he was going to go into detail about his own familial experiences. "My dad shouldn't have been one."

"But if he wasn't, you wouldn't be here." Clearly this was a puzzle she was determined to solve.

"I don't suppose I can argue with that."

"Is that why you don't like kids?"

"Who said I don't like kids?"

"I heard mom and Aunt Laurel talking. The other night when you left."

"I think they misinterpreted my decision for leaving. I like kids just fine, Keeley. And I like you."

"Oh—good." Her smile was back, and boy did he appreciate it. "Did you have the wrong dad?"

"I did. He wasn't a very nice man."

"He wouldn't have played Monopoly with me, would he?"

"No," Paul assured her and glanced at his watch. "We should probably wrap this up. Your sleepover starts pretty soon."

"Oh. I guess. You still have a couple of properties you can mortgage," she said with a not-so-subtle peer across the game board. She'd had her eye on Endor Forest since he'd landed on it on his fifth roll. "I'll cut you a better deal than the bank would."

"I think I know when to quit."

It was the only pride-preserving way he could think to protect what was left of his ego.

"That's probably a good idea."

Paul glanced up and found Mabel standing with her shoulder braced against the kitchen wall, arms crossed over her bathrobe covered chest. She was barefoot, her hair loose and long around her face. A face that was still a bit rosy from sleep. "Hey—sleep okay?"

"Better than I have in a while, actually. And a lot longer." She walked over to stand behind Keeley. "You cleaned up again, kiddo."

"Uh-huh. And guess what?" She pointed to the notepad she'd been scribbling on. "I own more than three-fourths of the available properties and one-third of the utilities."

Mabel bent down and kissed the top of Keeley's head. "That sounds suspiciously like fractions."

"That's because they are!" She beamed with pride. "Paul taught me to look at them in a different way. Numbers can represent something and when they do, I can kinda see how it works. I need more practice though." Her bright blue eyes landed on him. "Can we play again while you're here?"

"Sure." Paul said. "Maybe your mom can play with us next time."

"Aw, man." Keeley pouted. "Then neither of us is going to win. She's ruthless."

"But imagine all the math you'll get to practice with all the rent I charge," Mabel suggested and earned a little-girl giggle that touched Paul's heart. "Why don't you go brush your teeth? It's time to get down to Shirley's."

"Okay." She uncurled her legs, then stopped when Paul began gathering up all the playing pieces. "This was fun. Thanks for playing with me." Then she turned her impish smile Mabel's way. "Mom, you were wrong. He likes kids."

"I, um …" Mabel's eyes went horrified wide. "I don't recall—"

"I heard you and Aunt Laurel talking the other night. You can relax. He likes me." She nudged her mother with her shoulder. "And he likes you, too. Like, he *like* likes you. And look!" She pointed to Mabel's twitching lips. "See? You're smiling. Which means you're happy."

Mabel laughed, rolling her eyes. "Go brush your teeth, please."

Paul chuckled at the desperation in Mabel's voice as Keeley scampered down the hall to her room. "You *were* wrong, Mabel. I do like kids. Spent a lot of time at a local boys and girls club when I was in college. FYI, none of them played Monopoly like that kid of yours."

Mabel lifted the Princess Leia token. "I suppose the torch has officially been passed then. Thanks—for keeping her entertained. And for letting me sleep."

"You're welcome. I had fun." He was surprised to find that he meant it.

"Well, you earned points in my book."

"Just let me know when and what I can cash those in for." When she didn't respond, he stopped sorting and looked at her. "What's wrong?"

"Nothing. Nothing really," she added. "Just kind of feels like there's this haze that's descended over all the craziness from earlier. Like all of this, you being here with me and Keeley, is somehow normal. And it's not. Nothing is." She sank into the chair at the head of the table. "It's like I'm caught in this huge ball of uncertainty and confusion, and yet …" she waved a hand in his direction, "somehow, you fit and make me feel less … chaotic. And I might need another nap because that sounded all kinds of incoherent."

"No, it doesn't." But he did have to shove the sudden swirl of panic circling inside of him. "I think we're both trying to figure a lot of things out. I kind of like thinking of myself as some kind of anchor for you, but Mabel—"

"I know." She rested her head in her hands. "I know. You're not staying, and we shouldn't get in a position of relying on you too much or getting attached, but," she dropped her hands on the table and sighed, "you played Monopoly with my kid, Paul. That's just not a fair thing to do if your intention is to keep me at an emotional distance."

"You're not staying?" Keeley stood almost in the same spot as her mother had moments before, a frown on her face that had her brows almost touching. "How come?"

"Keeley, that's none of our business," Mabel said.

"But we're friends." Keeley returned to the table, folded her hands together as if presenting herself at court. "He's my friend, Mama, and you said friends like you and Aunt Laurel and Aunt Riley can always ask each other anything."

"Kee—"

"Because I have a life back in New York," Paul said simply before Mabel tried to deflect for him. "I have a job and an apartment and people who rely on me." Even as he said it, he realized he didn't have any of the latter. He might not even have the job anymore, for that matter. The only thing he absolutely did have was an expensive, empty apartment that didn't feel remotely as homey as the one he currently sat in. "I'm sorry, Keeley, but I'm only here for as long as I'm working on this case."

"Oh. Does that mean …?" She turned confused eyes on her mom. "Does that mean we shouldn't be friends?"

"On the contrary," Paul said before Mabel could find the words. "I could use every friend I can get. But I'm going to be going home at some point in the near future, Keeley. I'm glad you want me to stay, though. I'm sorry if you thought there's going to be more between me and your mom. Whatever time we do spend together, it's only going to be temporary, but I will love every minute I spend with you both." It dawned on him he'd never had anyone want him to stay anywhere before, and didn't that just crack the foundational beliefs of his life like the San Andreas Faults? "Understand?"

"I guess." She sounded as deflated by the concept as he felt.

"You ready to go to Shirley's?" Mabel shoved herself to her feet, avoiding, to Paul's eyes, at least, meeting his gaze. "Want me to walk you down?"

"I can go on my own. It's just downstairs." She walked over to her bag that she'd dumped on the sofa behind Paul.

"Kee," Mabel began.

"I'll see you tomorrow morning," Keeley said and gave them both a wave over her shoulder, Lord Squidly peeking out from the top of her bag that she'd slung over her shoulder. "Night."

"Night, baby." Mabel sighed and when the door closed again, Mabel faced Paul. "Well, shit."

"Couldn't have said it better myself. I didn't think this would get complicated until *after* you and I slept together." He finished packing up the game and carried it over to the shelf where Keeley had retrieved it earlier. Still crouched, he skimmed the countless board games and puzzles and tried not to let himself imagine spending future evenings just like the one he'd spent with Keeley. Everything inside of him screamed at the risk it meant taking, just as a teeny, tiny part of him screamed back that some risks were worth it. "You know, we can stop this now. Before she gets more attached to the idea of me being around. You and I can just meet in my office and keep it completely professional and—"

"Paul."

He hadn't heard her come up beside him, but as she rested a hand on his shoulder, he looked up and couldn't for the life of him decipher what was on her face.

"You keep focusing on the damage you might do if you stay," she said softly. "Have you considered you might do even more damage by leaving? To yourself."

"Not fair." He shook his head, fisted his hands. "Seriously, not fair."

"Nothing about life is fair, Paul. We've already established that. We play the hand we're dealt. The entire hand, win or lose. And personally? I'm really tired of losing." She bent down and captured one of his hands, wedged her fingers through his until he had no choice but to ease his hold and let her take possession of him. "Aren't you?"

Mabel could count on one hand the number of times she'd known precisely what to do. The number of times she, without doubt or hesitation, had known that the steps she took next would both change her life and keep her on track for where she was supposed to go. Never once had that certainty ever revolved around a man.

Until now.

She didn't know her soul could ping with need. Need not only to fulfill herself with the comfort and physical closeness of another person but to bring that person some inkling of what they meant to her. What Paul meant to her. She couldn't imagine having lived his life, the abuse, the distrust, the abject determination to change his circumstances and his entire world. He'd done it, though, and he'd done it to near absolute perfection. Save for one thing.

Paul had done it all without being loved.

His brother's faith in him had sustained him. Alden's love, however brief it had burned, had sustained him until this moment. Now he was here with Mabel, and she took that responsibility as deeply into her heart as she could.

She'd slept long enough to rid herself of the headache that had been plaguing her most of the day. Almost long enough to push past the air-choking terror of seeing that picture stabbed onto her seat. Keeley was okay. She had to keep telling herself that. And she had to stop from panicking over the fact that someone out there wanted to pull her focus away from the Red Lily case. The STOP had been clear evidence of that.

All that meant was that they were getting somewhere with their investigation.

I'm going to find you, Sylvie.

Mabel had woken far earlier than Paul had realized. She'd stood in her open doorway, listening to him and her daughter interact, and as she did, she'd felt herself falling—falling into that inescapable, endless spiral of affection, emotion, and devotion she suspected she'd never pull entirely free of.

He wasn't the man he'd convinced himself he was. There was no brutality inside of him. There was compassion and understanding and a willingness to embrace even that which terrified him to his very core. She'd seen an instinctive yearning in his eyes the first time he'd walked into her apartment, in equal measures with his fear; she'd seen a flash of the dual emotions when Keeley had come running into their home with Quinn at her heels. But he'd pushed all his fearful thoughts he carried with him every day aside and turned all that positive attention and focus he possessed on her child to give Keeley a joyful moment. To help Mabel rest.

And so, she'd stood there, in her empty bedroom, listening to them, and fell in love.

It hurt her to think he felt he was undeserving. That he wasn't worth taking a chance on. He'd come all the way out here to the one city he didn't want to be in because a friend had asked him to. That alone told her he was a good man.

Now, as she drew him down the hall, she ached for who he'd been, even as she desired the man he'd become, the man he'd made himself into.

"Wait." He pulled on her hand but didn't release her as he drew her into the guest room. He let go of her as he unzipped his duffel bag, pulled out a box of condoms. "I might have made a quick stop at the hotel gift shop for essentials."

His smile belied a confidence that boosted her own.

"I do appreciate a man who's always prepared."

Still in his room—amidst the double bed, the secondhand dresser she and Keeley had repainted just last year, the folding card table she'd dragged out of the closet for him to use as a makeshift desk—she stepped forward, slipped her hand free of his grasp, and moved into his arms.

This time when she kissed him, she left no doubt what her intentions were. She'd known almost from the moment she'd first seen him that this was where they'd end up. Now? There was nowhere else she wanted to be.

She pressed his lips open, dived in before he had time to think—before he could even consider reacting—and took what she wanted. He met her kiss, demand for demand, stroke for stroke. She could feel his muscles tense as if he were struggling for control. He slipped his hands down her sides, sending shivers of promised pleasure up and down her spine. There wasn't a place on her body she didn't want him to touch, and as she stretched up and pressed herself fully against him, her arms locked around his neck, she drank him in even deeper.

His hands roamed over her back, the thick terrycloth robe a frustrating barrier between them. But as his hands came up to her shoulders and tugged at the band holding her hair up, he pulled it free and set her hair to tumbling down around her shoulders. He plunged his fingers into the length, an almost growl sounding in the back of his throat.

"You wouldn't believe how much I've wanted to do that," he murmured against her mouth.

She breathed him in like oxygen, as if her system would starve instantly without his touch. She could smell the aftershave remaining on his skin, that spicy aroma of citrus and spice that set her head to spinning.

His hands tightened on her, tugged her closer. "*Mabel.*"

The way he said her name made her feel like a long-forgotten goddess with a reawakened devotee. She pried herself off him, inch-by-reluctant-inch, and stepped back, recaptured his hand to lead him out of the guest room and toward her own. She'd taken the time to change the sheets and remake the bed and close the blinds just enough to let the setting sun stream its fading light through the slats.

When she turned to him, she let go of his hand so she could untie the knot of her robe.

He stepped closer, eyes dazed, as if entranced. He slipped his hands beneath the fabric, gently pushing the robe off her shoulders until it pooled on the floor at her feet. The thin T-shirt she'd thrown on after her shower suddenly felt heavy, but in a desire to keep the teasing even, she reached up and slowly nudged his tie aside and flicked open the buttons of his shirt. One by one by one.

"For the record, I deserve a goddamned medal for letting you set the pace." His voice was low, husky, strained, and the sound of him struggling for control tightened every bit of her into anticipation.

He tossed the box on her bed, ripped the tie over his head, and, as she smoothed her hands beneath the edges of his shirt, covered her hands with his.

She took slow, deliberate breaths, wanting—needing—to sear this memory into her mind. His skin was smooth, his nipples hard beneath her palms, and as she tugged his shirt down his arms, she couldn't resist the temptation of lifting her mouth to his.

It was as if she'd released a caged tiger from his prison.

He enveloped her in one fluid movement, had her up and into his arms, his leg slipping between hers. The fabric of his slacks rubbed against the bare skin of her core, the part of her that pulsed with pent-up desire. She panted into his mouth as he held her there for a long, breathy moment. His mouth released her long enough so he could stare down into her heavy-lidded gaze.

"I told you before that I'm fond of foreplay."

His lips curved into that delectable smile before he reclaimed her mouth and walked them the remaining steps to her bed. Hands on her waist, he raised her high enough for her to kneel on the mattress. No sooner had she gained her balance than he leaned down and trailed his mouth between the covered valley between her breasts and drew the hem of her shirt up. His tongue swept across her skin, sending shivers of desire through her very core.

With her hands raised, she almost, once she was free of the fabric, had enough time to regain her hold on him, but he stopped her, hands grasping her wrists as he drew her arms down and followed with his mouth.

He lowered himself until he could draw one hardened peak in between his lips, lave the tip with his tongue, leaving her gasping. When his hold eased, her arms remained limp at her sides as he moved to the other breast before dipping lower, skimming the sensitive skin of her belly, then dipping down to her navel.

She gasped, her head dropping back as his fingers lightly traced over the marks she'd teased him with before.

"Just as I imagined." He kissed each and every stretch mark, smoothed them with his fingers. "Beautiful."

Mabel caught her lower lip between her teeth, focused on pushing out every thought from her mind except for what this man was doing to her. What he was making her feel.

"Paul," she whispered his name when his touch moved lower and brushed against the curls covering her core, "not yet."

She tugged him up, drew him in, and locked him in her arms as she pulled him back for another kiss.

"I'm trying to remember the last time I did this," he whispered almost dazedly. The glow in his eyes made her smile as she identified absolute confusion in the blue depths. "I don't think I can. I think ..." He pressed his lips into a hard line as her fingers worked at his belt, at the button on his slacks. She drew the zipper down. "I think you've made everyone before you irrelevant."

"Good." She nipped at his chin and pushed him back just enough for him to finish undressing. When he returned to her, it was with a determination and focus that had her on her back and opening for him. "I want you inside me," she breathed as he leaned over her, brushed the backs of his fingers down the side of her face.

Drew them lower, over her curves, until he dipped inside and pressed into her.

She moaned, arched her back off the bed, trying to increase the pressure as he moved and teased. The whimper that escaped her earned him a smile of pride. She gripped the sheets in her fists, tugged them up as the pleasure mounted inside of her. She could feel herself beginning to crest on release, but it wasn't enough. She wanted more. She wanted *him*.

"Not yet," she panted, but it was too late.

The orgasm ripped through her, washed over her as she trembled under his touch.

Paul's mouth locked on hers and drank in her cries as her body eased back to earth beneath him.

"That was amazing." He brushed his lips across hers, but as she caught her breath, he lowered his head and pressed his lips against the swell of her breasts.

"You're too good with those hands of yours."

Mabel reached for him, fingers desperate to draw him close, when he pulled back. But when she worried he was abandoning her, she heard the sound of the box being ripped open, the crinkle of foil, and when he returned, she felt his cock pressing against her.

"No more waiting," he said into her neck, voice almost hoarse with desire. "I need you."

"Paul." She reached her hands up to pull him more fully onto her as he pressed in. Stretching her. Filling her.

She gasped, arching again as she felt his teeth on her throat, and she spread herself wide. She was wet and ready for him as he thrust heavily into her. There was no describing the sensations rioting through her body. She had no desire to describe them as she rode a new crest, and, lifting her hips to meet him pulse after pulse, she forced her eyes open. And found him watching her.

Instinct had her drawing her legs in, wrapping him into her so tightly she couldn't imagine where they remained separate. When he pressed out one arm and rolled them over, she laughed, sitting up with his hands clasped with hers. She drove herself down, drawing him even more deeply into her as they rocked together. Their rhythm was immediate, and when she felt herself rising up the peak again, she surrendered to his need, to his frantic desire. This time, they came together, cresting their matching passion as they were locked in what she wished could be a permanent embrace.

It was, Mabel thought, as she let herself ride the seemingly unending wave of ecstasy, a moment of perfection she never believed possible. A sensation of utter completeness she'd given up hope of ever experiencing. The emptiness that had been carved out filled with his caress, his touch, his kiss.

She pushed him back on the bed, marveled at the way his head crushed into her pillow as he drew her down, one arm tight around her waist. "Stay there," he murmured against her throat, his lips gentle yet demanding against hers. "If you move, it just may kill me."

"Wouldn't want that," she murmured back as her hands got restless to explore. And explore they did as she touched his hips, curled her fingers around him, and earned a moan of pleasure. "Exceeded my expectations," she whispered against a smile. "And, believe me, my expectations were stratospherically high."

"There's always room for improvement. I let you take the lead on that one." He rolled her under him again, pressed forward, and she gasped as he hardened inside of her. "We've got time, haven't we? For me to return the favor?"

"Yes." She lifted her hand to his hair as her heart twisted. "We have all time in the world."

CHAPTER THIRTEEN

"YEAH, thanks, Maya." Paul glanced over his shoulder as Mabel scooted past him to the fridge. "I appreciate you looking into it. If anything comes up, you'll let me know? Yeah. Okay. Have a good weekend."

He set his phone down on the kitchen counter.

"Everything okay?" Mabel popped open the fridge and peered inside.

"Everything? No." US Marshall Maya Rivera had nothing to report about Dean Samuels. She sounded just as puzzled about the convicted murderer's disappearance into the penal system and even more frustrated that she couldn't get him any answers. Paul's meeting with Jeff on Sunday was going to be one big walloping pile of nothing. When Mabel began unloading glass containers and setting them on the counter, Paul couldn't help but grin. "Hungry?"

"Starving. And get that self-satisfied smirk off your face," she ordered. "I haven't eaten since Sutton brought me apple turnovers this morning." She stopped, shook her head. "Feels like that was days ago."

"You weren't kidding about her culinary abilities," Paul agreed as he popped the lid off of a container and looked inside. "You know, since I met you less than a week ago, my carb intake has multiplied exponentially." Still, he lifted the container and inhaled the distinctive aroma of oregano, basil, and tomatoes. "Spaghetti?"

"Um …" Mabel leaned over his arm and nodded. "Yep. I've got a mango and quinoas salad in here somewhere." She started sorting through the containers. "Going to have to throw most of this in the compost can if we don't eat it soon."

By the time they'd opened all the containers, he was staring at a virtual feast. She had the quinoas salad, the spaghetti, some leftover pizza, roasted chicken …

Mabel grabbed a couple of plates, shoved one against his bare chest. She was back in her thigh-skimming T-shirt. Forget bank-breaking lingerie. Watching her bounce around the kitchen left him with a new all-time favorite sexy outfit.

He'd grabbed a pair of his jeans out of his duffel on his way to grab his cell phone when Maya had called. His experience with post-coital workouts usually resulted in a record-breaking getaway. His guest-room status aside, he didn't have the urge to leave, either Mabel or her home. That felt … odd.

"Microwave's over there." She pointed to the over-the-stove unit. "I'm sure Sutton's going to bring food to the meeting, but if we arrive starving, everyone's going to know what we've been doing."

"Quinn knew what we were going to do before he left." Paul scooped out a good portion of chicken and set it to reheat. "If this building works the way I think it does—"

"Everybody knows what we've been doing."

Paul chuckled at her embarrassed frustration. Oh, how he loved that pink tint to her cheeks. "On the bright side, we did it very well."

He caught her when she started past him, wrapping an arm around her waist and ducking his mouth to hers. It didn't take long for her to soften in his arms and melt against him.

"If we're late, we'll never hear the end of it." She sighed against his lips. "And, honestly, I need sustenance before we go another round." She patted a hand against his chest and pushed away.

While he chowed down on his chicken and quinoa, she kept her distance across the table with two slices of pizza and a serving of berry cobbler she'd dug out of the freezer. Huh. He hid his grin behind his spoon. Apparently, he was capable of being charmed by a woman's eating habits.

"Can I ask you a personal question?"

"Given where you had your hands a little while ago, I think we're past you needing to ask." Mabel grinned.

"I was wondering about Keeley's father." He winced. "Is that out of bounds?"

"No." She shrugged. "Short story even shorter: Jeremy was my college boyfriend. My first serious one. Nice enough guy. He's a dentist now. He sends Keeley a card on her birthday."

"How generous of him."

"He didn't want to be a dad." Another shrug. "Still doesn't. Keeley was a complete surprise and proof condoms don't always work."

Paul felt the blood drain from his face.

"Don't worry." The amusement in her eyes shined for only an instant. "Wrong time of the month for me on that front, so we're good. I knew from the time I saw that positive test I was going to have her. Jeremy respected that, and I respected the fact he wasn't interested in being part of her life. He was there for me, financially at least. That first year was rough, especially after Sylvie, but he stood up for me— even gave me the money for my first few months of rent out here. He's a good guy who knows his limitations." Her smile didn't quite reach her eyes this time. "Seems I have a type."

Paul didn't particularly like the idea of being lumped in with Jeremy the college boyfriend, but what did he expect? He'd made his own stand on fatherhood well known. "Keeley seems okay with it."

"I hope when she isn't, she lets me know," Mabel said. "She's met him a few times, and I've kept an eye out for behavior changes after she did. It is what it is. You going to tell me what that phone call was about?"

"I'm not sure I can." He should have been grateful for the change of topic. "Seriously, it's something that hasn't been made public, so I don't know what I'm allowed to talk about."

"Okay." She nibbled on a pizza crust. "My turn to ask a question: It's about Congressman Ross McFiltry."

Somehow, that question managed to make quinoas feel like a brick in his stomach. "What about him?" He shoved his plate away.

"Was he guilty?"

"Of murder?" Paul nodded. "Yes."

She inclined her head, brows raised. "No doubt?"

"No doubt." He debated. "As far as the press knew, he didn't leave a note when he killed himself. But he did leave one. His mother found it when she discovered his body." He hadn't known he could feel both equal pity and anger for someone he'd been planning to prosecute. "I read it when I got on scene."

"So, he killed that girl? The intern in his office?"

Paul nodded. "He did. He …" How did he even put this into words? "He'd wanted to know what it was like, to kill someone. He said he'd always wanted to know. She presented an opportunity, and he took it."

"But you already knew that," Mabel said. "Because you investigated the case and indicted him."

"I knew he'd killed her. I wasn't aware of his lifelong proclivity toward torture and violence."

"Did she? His mother?" Mabel asked.

"She said not."

"But you didn't believe her?"

"I'm a bit biased when it comes to living with a monster in the house." His smile was tight. "I don't see how she couldn't have known, or at least suspected, but I took her at her word. And she took me at mine when I said I wouldn't comment publicly further on the case."

"Strange. I think that's what I remember most about the case," Mabel said. "That you went dark and stepped back from your job after he died." He saw the instant she connected the dots. "You did that on purpose. To take the heat off the Senator."

There she went again, painting him as some kind of hero. "Whatever else Ross McFiltry did, whatever his mother did or didn't do to help him, the woman lost her son and in a way that put an end to whatever was left of her career. She didn't need the continuous hounding the press is notorious for."

"Are you kidding me?" Mabel dropped her pizza and glared at him. "You threw yourself under the bus to save that woman? A woman who raised a monster?"

"A woman who has two grandchildren to worry about and a daughter-in-law who discovered she was married to a psychopath." He sat back in his chair. "I didn't find it a particularly difficult decision to make."

"You are, without a doubt, the most ..." She shook her head, knocked her fist on the table. "You've let everyone believe you were incompetent, that you hounded a man to his death. That you *caused* his death."

"It's not my responsibility what other people want to think," Paul countered. "I did what I thought I had to do at the time. I don't regret it, Mabel." He hesitated. "My boss knew the truth. That was enough for me. Like you, he didn't agree with what I did, since it tied his hands as far as the cases he could assign me. Turned out there wasn't one, and I ended up on extended leave." Somehow being a consultant didn't have nearly the appeal he anticipated it might. "Hindsight being what it is, maybe I should have done things differently. But if I hadn't ..." he met her gaze, "I wouldn't be where I am right now. And honestly? It's the best place I've been for a really, really long time."

"So, you just let people think you're a cold son of a bitch."

"I've found it's easier in the long run." It also kept his circle very, very small. Only a handful of people believed him to be anything else. His boss back in New York. And Jeff. "The important people know the truth. You know the truth. I think Laurel suspects." Thinking back on his conversation with Mabel's attorney friend, he was fairly sure she'd done more digging into his past than she'd let on. "What happened with Ross McFiltry put me in the perfect position to look into these cases now. To be here for Sylvie and the others. I'm not going to regret that, Mabel."

"I wouldn't be so sure about that."

"Is this where you tell me what all this cloak-and-dagger crap is about?"

"Oh, how I wish it were crap." She picked up their plates and carried them over to the sink. She stood there, hands gripping the edge of the counter, and dropped her head forward. "I can't believe how much I'm wishing you really were the bastard the New York press made you out to be."

Sorry to disappoint?

He almost said it. Instead, he got to his feet and walked over to her, rested gentle hands on her shoulders.

"Tell me, Mabel. Whatever it is I'm walking into, I'd prefer not to do so completely unprepared."

"I don't know that there is any preparing for this."

"Tell me what you can."

She shook her head, but when she drew in a breath, he could feel her tremble.

"Mabel." He slipped his arms around her, drew her back against him, and nuzzled the side of her neck. "I'm not going anywhere until this is finished. Until you have answers about Sylvie. I'm not going to stop until we find who's responsible for her disappearance. Or who left that brutal threat against Keeley in your car."

"That's just it." Mabel grabbed hold of his arms and squeezed. "We already know who's behind it."

All in all, Mabel thought, Paul took the revelation about a Hollywood-based secret society relatively well. He hadn't laughed or teased her or asked if it was some kind of joke, so that was good news she supposed. That said, she couldn't help but feel he didn't entirely believe her.

That part hurt. It shouldn't have. She understood his reaction, but she probably shouldn't have dropped a bomb of conspiracy-laden non-information on him at that particular moment.

He'd gone quiet and a bit standoffish. That had been new for her as she hadn't known Paul could go more than a few minutes without filling a void of silence. It had put some distance between them as they each withdrew to their respective rooms to shower and change.

Suddenly, she was walking on eggshells, uncertain if she'd damaged whatever fragile bond had been established between them.

She'd done the right thing. He'd said he didn't want to walk into this gathering unprepared. He needed to know. Maybe it would have been better to let him hear it all from Cass or Quinn or even Riley. They spoke evidentiary language far better than she did. But it was done now, and all that was left was pulling him in the rest of the way.

"I did the right thing, didn't I?" She glanced at the picture of Sylvie perched on a nearby shelf. "Keeping it from him?" Blindsiding him with it. But all she got in response from her sister was a brilliant, carefree smile that reminded Mabel of what was truly at stake.

The nerves surging through her system fired at a spectacular rate, and as she paced the living room, the doubt continued to circle like a cautious shark.

"I didn't think we should tell you," Mabel blurted when Paul emerged from his room, his laptop bag in one hand. "Quinn wanted to bring you in all of it as soon as he met you, but I …" She shrugged. "I'm sorry. I didn't know if we could trust you. We don't know all who is involved with this group except that there have to be members who are high up, either in law enforcement or the DA's office—maybe both. And yes, I know how important the case is as a whole, but there's a part of me that only cares about Sylvie, and I didn't want to do anything that might stop me from finally finding out the truth."

She tried desperately to get a read on him. He looked different to her now. Sleeping with someone changed things. Changed perspective. Changed perception. She didn't see the elegant-suited man in front of her now but a casual facsimile in jeans and a dark shirt that made him look like a completely different person.

She didn't know why alienating him affected her so much. He'd said countless times he wasn't here to stay, that he was only here for the case. But she'd let herself believe the fantasy, even as she held the pin that could puncture that balloon of hope. That somehow having him here, with her, in her home, would somehow change his mind and turn him into something—someone—he wasn't.

His face remained blank as he set his bag on the sofa, circled around to where she'd been pacing around the coffee table, biting her thumbnails as if she were waiting for a bomb to go off. He stepped in front of her, stopped her cold, took hold of her face between his hands.

"Trust is earned," he said in a quiet, controlled tone. "No one understands that better than me. Trust takes time, and I've been here less than a week. You have nothing to apologize for, Mabel." He pressed his mouth to hers. "Absolutely nothing."

Relief punched through her. She grabbed hold of his wrists, wanting to keep him standing right where he was for as long as she could. "These people, whoever they are, they're evil, Paul. Pure, unadulterated evil."

"Yes," he murmured as he drew her into his arms. "I got that much from the message they left in your car. For that alone, I'm going to find out who they are and make them pay. I'm not going to let them hurt you or Keeley. That's a promise, Mabel. As I've told you before, I don't make promises I can't keep."

Mabel squeezed her eyes shut and held on. And she'd keep holding on. For as long as he'd let her.

"We should head downstairs," Paul said.

"Yeah." She sighed. "Before we do, there are a few more things you should know."

"You mean that secret society reveal wasn't the biggie?" He let out a slow breath. "Okay, then. Let's have it."

She loved him for trying to make her laugh. Loved him …

She stepped away from him, turned her back so he wouldn't see the shock on her face. Or the fear in her eyes. It was a terrible thing, to think her love for him might drive him away, but it very well might. And she needed him. At least for now.

"It's mostly about Cass. Cassia. Dr. Cassia Davis." She wrapped her arms around her torso and faced him again.

Paul's face filled with recognition. "Dr. Cassia Davis? The forensic specialist?"

She nodded. "Given your prosecutorial record and years with the DA's office back east, I had a feeling you'd be familiar with the name."

"Yeah, of course I am. She used to give special seminars at Quantico. The NYPD brought her in on a few cases—the FBI, too. I've never worked with her personally. Damn." His eyes went wonder-wide. "She all but disappeared a few years ago after some big case she was working on went seriously off the rails." He shook his head. "So, this is where she ended up? In Los Angeles?"

"She moved into Temple House shortly after Keeley's fifth birthday," Mabel confirmed. "Obviously, it's not common knowledge that she's here."

"Yeah, of course." Paul nodded. "Don't worry. I won't tell anyone."

"I just thought you should know before we head down there so you were, well, prepared."

"To meet her?"

"That," Mabel hedged, "and so that you aren't surprised by her … situation. Her apartment is her sanctuary. Fortress, actually."

"Not surprising. The woman knows her technology and—"

"She hasn't left Temple House since she moved in." Once again, Mabel found herself blurting out the truth. "If we're lucky, we can get her up to the roof for some fresh air, but for all intents and purposes, she's a shut-in, Paul."

"Oh." He frowned. "Well, that's sad. And a real loss to law enforcement."

"She still teaches and consults," Mabel said. "She just works from her apartment. She's never told me what happened to her. I don't know if the others know, but I don't. And I don't push."

"Neither will I," Paul assured her. "I'll tread carefully; don't worry."

"Thanks." Relief swept through her. "That trust you talked about taking time to build? It's taken years for her, Paul. Sometimes, I'm still not convinced she trusts everyone in this place. Bringing you into this is a big step for her to agree to take."

"You don't want me going in there, reawakening whatever ghosts she's put to sleep." He nodded. "I get it."

"I don't think she's put anything to sleep." If anyone could understand that, it was Mabel. "She's also a kind of a secret weapon we don't want to lose." Mabel pressed her lips together until they went numb. "I already lost one sister, Paul. I don't want to lose another one. That's what she is. Cass and Riley and Laurel and Sutton. They're my family. Mine and Kee's."

"You say that as if it was some kind of secret." The sad understanding in his eyes broke her recently filled heart. "Is there anything else?"

"Her assistant, Nox?"

"Nox, the magical technician who's dating Detective Wallace?" Paul asked.

"That would be them." Mabel waited for the recognition to shine in his eyes. He'd gotten the message.

"Anything else?"

"I think I've hit you with enough for one day. We can go now." She held out her hand, and he stood up, reached out. And took it.

"Hey, Barksy. Were you a good boy today?"

Between her dog's jumping and licking and scrambling around Mabel, Paul couldn't help but interpret the dog's sour expression aimed in his direction as an accusation. Was it wrong he felt the need to defend himself? It wasn't his fault Mabel had dropped Barksy off for a playdate that ended up lasting all day. In part because of Paul.

"Okay, boy?" he offered a hand and at least earned a good sniff. "I think I need a peace offering. Can I get him a—"

"Don't say it," Mabel said.

Paul frowned. "Actually, I was going to spell—"

"Don't do that either." Mabel stood up and gestured to the dark-haired, round-faced individual who resembled a Gothic pixie with attitude and a unique fashion sense heading down the short entrance hall. The skull-accented flipflops on their feet seemed an appropriate choice. "Nox has been teaching Barksy to spell. Nox, Paul. Paul—"

"Ah, you're the magical Nox I've heard so much about." He held his laptop case with both hands. "I also hear you enjoy a challenge."

"It's my raison d'être." Nox's purple contacted eyes went almost as wide as their smile. "Whatcha got for me?"

"Can we at least wait until they're inside before you grab his briefcase?" Laurel's dry drawl emanated from farther down the hall. She pinned Paul with a quick look before her gaze flickered to Mabel. "You're late."

"Two minutes," Mabel countered as Laurel sauntered away.

"What's up with this?" Nox asked as she accepted Paul's case.

"I don't know that anything is," Paul said. "Someone was in my office when I was out, and they logged in. Definitely on site. Not remote. I want to know if they planted something or if they found what they were looking for."

"Wicked." Nox nodded. "Challenging. How do you know—?"

"Foxtail's a friend," Paul said. "Of sorts." He didn't think now was the time to admit he was responsible for arresting the one-time black hat and turning him toward the light of law enforcement. "He's my East Coast contact for all things technical. He maintains all my computers."

"Right on. I know his coding as well as my own," Nox confirmed. "I'll have an answer pretty quick. Come on in. Elliot, Paul. Paul, Elliot." They motioned to the golden retriever sitting at the end of the hall. "You need his approval to pass."

"Right." He approached the dog with caution, held out a hand. "I come in peace." Elliot lifted his nose, got a good sniff, then pushed forward to earn himself a pet. "I guess I know where Barksy learned that move," he said to Mabel, but any other comment he might have made faded at the sight of the apartment he'd stepped into. "Holy crap."

"Now that's nice to see." A soft-spoken voice responded almost immediately. "An open mind, a love for advancement, and perhaps a cautious penchant for AI."

When Paul pulled his attention away from the large flat screens displayed along the entire left side of the apartment, he found himself face-to-face with Cassia Davis, the legend herself. He hadn't been exaggerating earlier. Her reputation in the law enforcement community was legend, her tenacious attention to detail renowned. He'd seen videos of her testimony at various trials, listened to a number of her online talks. No one broke down forensics into understandable language better than Dr. Davis.

She was on the shorter and curvier side. Her black long-sleeve shirt matched the black ends of her burgundy hair. She stood just out of arms' reach, which was a subtle hint not to hold out his hand.

"I'm curious ..." Politeness be damned, he couldn't help but return all his attention to the apartment. Very little was devoted to what he'd consider normal living space, with a large circular sofa recessed in the middle of the room. But surrounding it? Screens and tables filled with lab, computer, and testing equipment that made the CDC look anemic. "Does Tony Stark know you robbed him?" He glanced back at her and was pleased to see her lips curve. "Nice to meet you, Dr. Davis."

"Cass, please." Cass stepped back and waved them in the rest of the way. "No wonder Quinn speaks so highly of you. You practically share the same brain given that look in your eye."

Speaking of Quinn, the detective abandoned his post at the long black-marble kitchen counter and approached. "You two get some rest?" The taller brunette beside him elbowed Quinn in the side. "What?"

"Hi, Paul. Riley Temple." She offered her hand. "Good to finally meet you."

"You, too." The other people in the room seemed to suddenly be at attention. "I'm a big fan of your Aunt Moxie. I was hoping she might be here tonight."

"So was I," Mabel added. "Riley, shouldn't we at least try—"

"I don't want Moxie involved with all this," Riley said sharply, then, when Quinn touched her shoulder, sighed. "Not yet. She's not …. *I'm not* ready to ask her to dig all that up. Not yet."

Paul glanced at Mabel, then at Riley, then Quinn. "Is this something else I should know about?"

"Like I said," Riley said quietly, eyes pinned on Mabel. "Not yet."

Mabel shook her head, but Quinn cleared his throat as a clear indicator for Mabel to drop the subject. "Is there any word on Eva?" she asked Quinn.

"The second I know anything, you'll know." He squeezed her shoulder as he passed. "Promise. I haven't even gotten copies of Harrison's file yet."

"It's good to meet all of you, finally," Paul scanned the group with a smile. "As you're the only unfamiliar face, you must be Sutton."

"Saved the best for last." The woman in jeans and a simple button-down yellow sweater offered a quick wave. "Good to meet you."

"How's Keeley?" Riley asked Mabel, her smile faltering.

"Oblivious to what happened in the parking lot," Mabel assured her friend. "No doubt having a blast at Shirley's after trouncing Paul in Monopoly this afternoon."

"It was a gentle trouncing," Paul felt the need to defend himself. "Okay, she completely cleaned me out." The good-natured laughter he received in response to his confession made him feel a bit less embarrassed. "What's the word from Wallace?"

"He's on his way," Quinn said. "Blake, too."

"Do you want to wait for them before we jump in?" Paul's curiosity was beginning to take on a life of its own. It was one thing to know something, in Jeff's word, sinister was going on in this town, but it was quite another to have heard they believed some secret society was responsible. Of all the things he ever anticipated hearing during his stay in Los Angeles, that wouldn't have even made the top 100. "Mabel gave me a brief rundown on this Circle of the Red Lily group. I'm anxious to get a full, detailed report about it." And why any of them thought this so-called organization was responsible for so much violence and mayhem.

"You don't want to grab something to eat first?" Cass asked. "We've got sandwiches and all kinds of munchies." She motioned to both the coffee table and the kitchen itself.

His stomach was jumping all over the place. "Actually, I'd be good with just a beer."

"I've got it," Quinn said as the others stepped down into the recessed center of the living room. "Cass, why don't you get started?"

Paul touched a hand to Mabel's back when she stepped down. Barksy toddled beside her before curling up at her feet. He could feel everyone's eyes on them as he joined Mabel, but rather than playing coy, he slipped his arm behind her along the back of the sofa and scooted closer.

Mabel did the same, even as she tucked an imaginary strand of hair behind her ear.

"Who had Friday afternoon in the pool?" Laurel asked the group as she slipped onto a section of the sofa, half-filled wine glass in hand. "Oh, that's right. I did." She held her arm up over her head, palm up. "Where's my money? Gimmie."

"What pool?" Mabel asked as everyone dug into pockets or purses. "What the—"

"I think they had a bet on when we'd have sex," Paul said easily and eyed Laurel. "For the record, someone might have hedged her bet with a visit to my office this morning. Would that be considered legal?"

"We didn't set strict parameters." Laurel's sickly-sweet smile only increased Paul's enjoyment of the situation. It had been a long time since he'd been a participant in banter of this kind. He hadn't realized how much he'd missed it.

"You went to Paul's office?" Riley yanked her hand back, cash crumbled in hand. "Why?"

"I wanted to know how he was coming along with the case," Laurel said. "Other topics might have been discussed. And I gave him some of Sutton's turnovers."

"So, you used my turnovers for bet hedging?" Sutton challenged.

"What other topics did you discuss?" Mabel asked as she leaned back to look at Paul. "Me?"

"Yep," Paul said, without looking away from Laurel as he held out his hand for the beer Quinn brought him. "Give us fifty percent, and we'll call it even."

"Fifty? Pfffth." Laurel gave him a look. "Twenty-five. Maybe."

"Fifty. Definitely," Mabel countered. "And stop watching horror movies with my kid."

"Keeley loves them," Laurel argued.

"She loves you," Mabel returned fire, but the smiles they exchanged told Paul there was no animosity between them.

"Nox?" Cass walked to the east bank of windows where Nox was huddled behind their own collection of computer screens. "Remote?"

"Oh, right. Here." They handed it over without looking away from Paul's laptop screen. "Cursory look tells me they didn't install anything. No malware or—"

"I was wondering if they put a keystroke program on there," Paul suggested.

"If they did, it would be showing right … oh. Huh. Give the other lawyer in the room a prize. Got it in one. I can get it off pretty eas—?"

"No." Paul earned surprised looks from everyone. "No, leave it there. I don't want them to know I know. Need every advantage we can get, right? Speaking of which …" He had to concentrate on remaining seated, still, and casual. "Are you going to read me in on all this, or—"

The screens in front of him blinked to life. Forget whiteboards with pinned photographs and scribbled notes made with flat-tipped markers. Every single photograph from the files he'd memorized popped up.

"We needed a more efficient way to keep all the information in one place." Cass took on a professional, instructional tone Paul suspected was her comfort zone. "The boards stopped working when we hit forty missing women. If I click on an image … let's start with

262

Clarissa McHugh." Cass clicked one of the grainy, black-and-white scanned photos found at the Tenado estate.

The other photos pushed into the background while the singled out one dropped to the bottom of the screen. A different picture, one clearly taken from Clarissa's 1963 high school yearbook, took its place as the central image.

Bullet points of information rose onto the screen, one by one. Name, birth date, family members, both living and deceased, education information, work record, arrest record, social security record … information it would have taken Paul and his solitary assistant ages to track down. It was all there.

"Clarissa was reported missing in November of 1964, six months after she came to Los Angeles. We used Clarissa as our test subject when putting this program together as she was the one we found a lot of information on."

"You've done this for all of them?" Paul sat forward in his seat. It took a lot to shock him, and right now, shock was so far down his emotion meter he could barely think straight. "All sixty-seven?"

"Yes." Cass clicked the remote again, then again, and again, filling each of the six screens with countless photographs. "And we think more."

"More." Paul rose to his feet. "How many more?" When he didn't get an answer, he looked back at Cass. He saw the sad truth shining in her eyes. He felt slightly ill. "You don't know because you're still finding them."

"We've narrowed the parameters of our search," Cass said with that analytical detachment she was renowned for. "We've tightened it, given commonalities we've found with more recent disappearances. We thought it would slow our findings, maybe even stop them completely, so we could start to move on. We haven't been able to do that just yet."

"How do you know the extra missing cases are connected?" Paul asked.

"A couple of things. Mainly this." Cass toggled over to the third screen, pulled up a photo of a small bungalow house that, given the style and design, had to have been from the mid-40s. "After what happened with Riley at the Tenado estate, Nox and I added a new keyword to our online search. Tell me when you see it." She clicked another button, zoomed in. Zoomed again, then once more.

"Fuck me," Paul breathed as stepped over the back of the seating in front of him to stand in front of the screen. There, on the center of the welcome mat at the front door … "That's the same flower someone left in Mabel's van."

"Certainly looks like it."

Paul caught the edge in Mabel's voice. "All the photographs in the basement shared the same logo in the bottom corner," she said.

Cass clicked again and brought up a close-up of one of the images.

"First time we saw that image was on the film I got from Merle at Buried Treasures," Riley said. "That's what started this whole thing."

"The Melanie Dennings photos." Paul's mind raced. The pictures that had also called Dean Samuels's conviction into question.

"You can't put something like that on a negative," Riley pointed to the logo. "But you can, if you're patient and talented enough, create a kind of burn on the lens. Normally, it happens with wear and tear. Something this intricate? It's absolutely deliberate. And it's in the same spot on every picture. Not to mention the stained-glass window above the front door of the Tenado estate."

"Going back over all the reports," Cass said. "We found at least a quarter of the missing persons files mention having found a red lily when looking for the women at their last known whereabouts. Left behind. Probably deliberately."

"Why only some?" Paul challenged.

Cass shrugged. "Incomplete reports? Lack of attention to details? Who knows."

"We might have to start calling the estate by another name," Paul told them. "It was never Anthony Tenado's. Legally, at least."

"What does that mean?" Quinn asked. "When I looked into the property, I was told it was sale pending." He cringed. "Guess I should have dug deeper."

"Tenado never owned it," Paul explained. "Name's not anywhere on the deed, and the property was not in his will, nor did he have a separate trust. I went through every file Young & Fairbanks sent over. No mention of it anywhere in Tenado's financial or personal records."

"They could have taken it out," Sutton said. "Couldn't they?"

"Maybe." But Paul didn't think so. That would have been seriously tedious work. "It makes more sense that it was never there in the first place."

"Okay, so if Tenado didn't own it, who does?" Quinn asked as the intercom buzzed by the door. "I've got it." He left long enough to buzz someone in. "Wallace's on his way up, and he has the rest of your boxes."

"Great." One less thing for Paul to have to worry about. "I've got the others up in Mabel's apartment."

"Cozy," Cass commented.

"So, who owns the house?" Quinn asked again after he left the door open.

"An LLC called Sumatra," Paul said. "Laurel helped me piece it together earlier. Sumatra appears to be a shell company, one of many, owned or at least run by the law firm of Young & Fairbanks."

"Awesome," Cass muttered. "Largest law firm in the city with one of the longest histories and biggest client lists. That's one big fish to start our list of suspects with."

"That's a fish that can sink our entire boat," Quinn agreed.

"We need more," Cass said. "A lot more. A lot of this can be explained away, especially the ownership of the house. Hell, they could just claim it was an oversight and reissue new documents."

"Agreed," Laurel said. "It's certainly not enough to go public with, or to apply for a subpoena with. Nothing official can hang on it." Laurel glanced at Paul. "But that's why you build cases piece by piece. It's the little things, right, Paul?"

"It's always the little things," he agreed. "Beginning with the name Sumatra."

"It's a breed of lily," Laurel said. "A red lily."

"Well that just seems … blatant," Quinn said.

"Or arrogant," Riley muttered.

"No doubt both." Laurel sipped her wine. "Turns out there are a whole lot of red lily breeds. Nox …?"

"Already on it. Paul, I've got a new program installing on your laptop. I'll run you through what it does and how to work it when you're done Danny Ocean-ing things."

"Danny …" Paul frowned at Mabel, who waved off his confusion with a roll of her eyes.

"I told Paul I'd see if I could siphon together a list of Young & Fairbanks' clients," Laurel said. "Past and present. Not surprisingly, they've got their site locked down regarding anyone who's not show-cased on their front page. I figure we can tweak Cass's new search engine to make some more names pop. That said." She motioned to Cass who clicked again. "One name is of particular note."

The image that filled the screen surprised even Paul and had him chewing on the inside of his cheek.

"You've got to be kidding me," Riley muttered. "Seriously?"

"Granger Powell is one of their clients?" Mabel asked. "The same Granger Powell who wants to remake the Sally Tate movies with Moxie?"

"The head of Powell Films," Laurel confirmed. "That doesn't nec-essarily make him part of this. Like I told Paul, the firm of Young & Fairbanks was one of the first investors in the studio. It makes complete sense they'd still represent the family."

"A creepy sense," Sutton commented. "Granger Powell has a pret-ty good reputation in this town. One might say stellar. He brought the studio back from the grave, rebuilt it from the ground up over the past five years. He went back to basics, hires at a seriously com-petitive rate, and gives away boatloads of money. His great-grandfa-ther was responsible for building the Golden Age Retirement Home among other businesses in town."

"Oh, my God. I totally forgot," Mabel gasped. "Sorry, detour. How did your interview go, Sutton?"

"Well, up until a few minutes ago, I was thinking it went really well." Sutton flashed a not-so-sincere smile. "You're looking at the new head dietician and nutritionist for Golden Age Retirement. If I want the job."

"That's great news." Riley reached over and gripped her hand. "Why wouldn't you want the job?"

"Gee, I don't know." Sutton's mouth twisted. "Hearing all this kind of reminds me that they previously hired a psychopathic nutjob who tried to drown one of my best friends in an underground torture chamber. And their flower delivery system seems a bit whackadoodle."

"Context, please?" Paul asked Mabel.

"Someone delivered a bouquet of red lilies to one of the residents we were visiting," Riley told him. "Sent her into a serious panic attack. Sorry. That didn't make it into any official reports."

"We didn't want to bring Joyce DePalma's name into it publicly," Quinn explained. "That stays here. With us. For now, at least," he warned Paul, who nodded in agreement.

"All I know I was kind of excited about the whole thing before all this information about the real owners." Sutton sighed. "I know the guy who hired me is new to the place himself, but the more I think about this, the more I get the wiggies about the facility."

"Doesn't give me the wiggies at all," Cass said. "Gives me ideas."

"Yeah," Riley murmured. "Me, too."

"Are either of you going to fill the rest of us in, or are we going to glean these ideas telepathically?" Laurel asked.

"That new business venture I've been putting together," Riley said. "Photographing people who worked in Hollywood in the past, the forgotten ones like Joyce DePalma? I've been collecting names and ideas. What if I were to approach this new manager for help with arranging to meet with some of the residents?" She looked at Sutton. "We could make it so I'd be there at the same time you are, Sutton. It's only going to be a few days a week, right? A lot of your job will be off-site?"

"Yeah," Sutton nodded. "I'd feel better knowing there was actually someone around I could trust." She went suddenly silent when she caught sight of the two men standing in the hallway.

"I'm thinking of buying stock in handcarts," Wallace said as he let the front of the stacked cart down with a thump. "Where do you want these?"

"Just by the door for now. Thanks, Wallace," Paul said.

"Beer's in the fridge," Cass told Blake who, near as Paul could tell, owned only one type of clothing: black.

"Thanks," Blake said. "Keeley okay?"

"She's fine," Mabel said with a grateful smile. "Thanks."

"I've got something for her. Just waiting on a delivery to finish it up. I'll get it to her tomorrow."

"Great." Mabel's brow knitted. "It's not some kind of stealth weapon, is it?"

"It is not." Blake's mouth twitched. "Didn't mean to interrupt. Congratulations on the new job," he said as he passed by Sutton.

Paul might not have been looking directly at the man, but he caught a hint of concern on Blake's face.

"I have a question," Paul said. "More than one, actually, but let's start here. None of you strike me as conspiracy theorists. Near as I can tell, you all have good control over your faculties."

"I *think* that was a compliment?" Riley said.

Paul went on as if she hadn't spoken. "Am I right in thinking you think this Red Lily group is responsible for systematically going after young women? Isn't it more realistic to think it's some kind of play cult for people with too much time on their hands or, to use Sutton's word, whackadoodles?"

"Awww. He was listening." Sutton tapped her hand against her heart.

"Seriously," Paul said when the chuckles stopped. "If they were that impactful and responsible for all this"—he gestured to the screens— "how is it no one has ever heard anything before now? There would have been something, yeah? A headline or story or a website, for crying out loud."

"Depends," Quinn countered.

"On what?"

"On whether the secrecy is responsible for whatever power they wield." Riley tucked her legs under her.

"How many people can we be talking about?" Paul asked. "Three or four? You know what people say about keeping a secret. One can. More than that? Forget about it."

"Unless properly motivated. If they're killing people," Laurel said, "that's a pretty good reason to keep your mouth shut. Especially if you're up to your neck in their activities. Makes everyone complicit, doesn't it?"

"There's more." Riley's voice was devoid of the humor she'd projected earlier. "It's not three or four. It's a lot more. Has to be. Too many wheels to keep spinning for a select few to be responsible for all of these disappearances."

Paul frowned. "You really think—"

Riley grimaced. "When I was in that room with Thing 2—sorry, Beth Thompkins—there was this, I don't know, this haze in her eyes. Like she'd been programmed. She recited statements as if they were commands. Her brother did the same thing when he attacked me here at Temple House. Beth spoke of the Chosen in reference to Melanie Dennings. They were organized. Efficient, mostly."

"They went off script when they killed Dudley," Quinn said. "That's when things started going wrong."

"The homeless man who lived behind Buried Treasures," Paul recalled from reading the case file.

"They killed him to get me back to the scene," Riley said. "Didn't work, though. They just ended up bringing more attention to themselves." She paused. "Not to mention pissing me off. Dudley was harmless. And innocent."

Quinn rubbed her arm.

"At one point," Riley stopped, squeezed her eyes shut. Only when Quinn took hold of her hand did she continue. "At one point, Beth said, *one less sacrifice to make. We will earn forgiveness. I will earn it for both of us.*"

"Her twin brother?" Paul asked. "Holden?"

"Yeah." Riley forced a smile. "She said there were others waiting to take their place."

"The guy in Eva's closet," Mabel said. "He has to have been one of them."

As much as Paul appreciated Mabel's interjection, there wasn't any evidence she was right. "We can't throw everyone we've encountered—"

"He was looking for something, and when he couldn't find it, he waited for me. He thought I had it. I didn't. Not at that time." Mabel flicked her gaze to Paul. "You found it."

"Found what?" Paul asked.

"There are many," Riley recited. " 'We are everywhere. The Circle demands a sacrifice to set things right.' Sorry." Her eyes flashed with apology. "I hear that in my dreams sometimes."

"You don't think what Beth said was just part of her psychosis?" Paul pushed back. "That this was all some built-up make-believe world she was living in?" He stopped, looked back at Mabel. "What did I find?"

"The invitations."

"The cards you called me about?" Paul asked. "The cards I found in her mattress?"

"Yes," Mabel said. "Are you done with the prints?" she asked Cass.

"Yes." Cass strode around the living area, past Paul to the line of examination and evidence tables beyond the screens. Picking up a small stack of black envelops, she handed them over. "I found what I expected. Your prints, Mabel. And Eva's. Hers were in the system back in Ohio."

"Ohio isn't California," Paul said as he flipped the edge of an envelope open.

"He just dazzles you with his smarts, doesn't he?" Laurel teased.

"Your prints were on them, as well," Cass said without missing a beat. "Yours were on file with the state bar."

"Am I the only one wondering what made you look under this girl's mattress?" Riley asked.

"College pot stash?" Quinn asked before he took a drink to hide his grin.

"Something like that," Paul admitted.

"Porn," Quinn corrected himself with a snap of his fingers. "My second guess." He earned another elbow in the ribs with that comment. "Ow."

"Go ahead," Mabel told Paul. "Read one."

Paul did as she suggested and pulled out the folded card. Flipped it open and blew out a long breath.

"What's this?" Laurel shoved to her feet and walked around to Paul, took the invitation from him, flipped it around to the group. "Why is this the first I'm hearing about these invitations?"

"You aren't the only one. What's it to? A holiday mixer?" Riley asked. "Oh, I know, a spring formal. Summer sacrifice?"

"Riley." Quinn's attempt to soothe her only made her eyes flare. He shot her an apologetic look when his cell phone chimed. "Sorry. Need to check … this." He frowned down at his screen.

"We found a QR code under the seal," Nox said. "It peels up. I scanned it—"

"You did what?" Quinn demanded.

"I scanned it with a phone no one can trace," Nox said. Their tone didn't sound pleased to be thought of as careless. "Took me to a secured website that you need specific information to access. Hang on, I'll throw it onto the center screen ..."

Paul stepped back and looked up. "Scheherazade. The men's club? And before you ask, that place was around when I was growing up. Exclusive, isn't it?"

"It was," Cass told him. "Now it's ultra-exclusive." The video of women—and men—dressed in various masked costumes danced, twirled, and seduced their night away in glass cubicles on display for the entirety of the clientele to see. "It'll cost you about a hundred bucks just to walk in the door."

"Check out the font," Nox told them. "See the flower design?"

Paul did, between the z and a. "It's a lily."

"That's not the only thing we found," Cass said.

"Did you get in?" Paul asked.

"I did," Nox confirmed.

"Our scans of the invitation revealed a six-digit code, in invisible ink on the bottom right of the invitation," Cass said.

"Invisible ink?" Sutton asked. "That's comic book stuff, isn't it?"

"Actually, it isn't that hard to make," Cass said. "Baking soda and water, write what you want; the reader just needs a UV light to read it." She glanced at Mabel. "Did you find a black light in her room?"

"She had a UV flashlight on her dresser." Mabel shrugged. "I didn't think anything of it since I travel with one myself. Good way to check for bedbugs."

"That code, along with Eva's name, got us in," Cass said.

"In to where?" Mabel asked. "I don't see a log-in box."

"Because there isn't one," Nox said, "now. But there probably is closer to an event. Or there was one before last Friday. Isn't that when Eva was attacked?"

"Yes," Mabel said. "And she'd been at a party. So, this website is where they come to find out what?"

"Location, theme, time, who knows." Cass glanced back at Nox. "We'll monitor the site through a protected server. If and when that log-in portal goes live again, we'll know about it."

"With that code in invisible ink, chances are, the log-in information changes with each event, hence all the invitations. But it's worth a shot," Nox said. "In the meantime, since I got this far, I found my way into their server—"

"If we could refrain from mentioning any illegalities that might have taken place, that would be great." If only Paul felt as amused as he sounded.

"Sure thing," Nox said. "How about *miraculously,* I was able to obtain their employee records. I found that guy Leo's information, by the way."

"I've got him on the top of my list to track down," Quinn said.

"Mabel," Nox said, "according to their records, Eva's worked there almost from the time she arrived in Los Angeles. In fact, she was put on the payroll two weeks *before* she left Ohio."

"Shit." Mabel blew out a breath. "That's the dream she followed. The dream they dangled in front of her. What was she hired as? Please tell me she was only serving drinks?"

"Doesn't say," Nox said. "But if that was her job, she's the best cocktail waitress on the planet. She was pulling in at least five grand a week."

"Awesome." Mabel locked her arms across her chest and frowned. "Countdown to the media insinuating she'd been asking to be beaten and raped."

"Countdown to you leading the charge to argue them down," Riley countered. "We boring you, DSP?"

"No." Quinn's frown only got deeper.

"What's wrong?" Riley asked.

"Is it about Eva?" Mabel leaned over to read. "Did her file come through?"

"Yeah. Nox, do something with this. Get it up on the screen." He held his cell phone over his head, and Nox crossed from their desk to retrieve it. "Fifth image. Blow it up, center screen."

"Okay. It's gonna take me a sec …"

Paul pushed away the muted conversations and turned his attention back to the screens. The amount of work, the level of detail and the ease with which the information had been presented, there was no arguing that Dr. Cassia Davis—no matter her psychological or emotional state—was still a master of evidence. And these friends of Mabel's …

"What do you see?" Mabel's voice was soft behind him, her touch gentle on his arm as she shifted to his side.

"So much." He shook his head, a bit in disbelief, a bit in amazement. "I couldn't have ever come up with all this. Not in weeks or months. And not without a team, which I will keep being denied until they dismiss this investigation due to lack of findings." That realization fed the monstrous suspicion that his approval in getting this job had been due to the belief that he *wouldn't* come close to exposing the truths he was determined to find. Especially with his "history" in New York implying he was incompetent at his job. "They knew it. Those sons of bitches brought me out here to fail."

"Who? Jeff?"

"Not Jeff." If anything, Jeff was as much a pawn in this game as he was. "Earlier you told me you hadn't brought me in on this yet because you didn't know who could be trusted." He paused, mind racing. "Someone was in my office. They either work in the building, or they were let in by someone *working for the DA*. You were right."

Mabel sighed. "I didn't want to be."

"Neither did I," Paul said. "We could be looking at the DA, someone she's spoken with. Former cops. Cops, lawyers, higher-ups involved with the Dennings case …. When I mentioned Sumatra to DA Eichorn at the press conference, she said she'd never heard of it."

"You didn't believe her."

"No," Paul said slowly. "I didn't."

Right now, other than Jeff, he wasn't sure he believed anyone outside this room.

"Okay, I've got it!" Nox cried as the center screen exploded into color.

"What are we looking at?" Mabel asked as she tilted her head to the side.

"One of the photos the ER staff took of Eva's injuries when she was brought into the emergency room," Quinn said.

"I'm not making it out," Mabel said.

"You see it," Quinn observed. "Don't you, Paul?"

"Yes." Maybe because he didn't want to. Maybe because he was used to horrific, mind-scorching evidence photos that could never be forgotten. That spinning spiral of dread that had been threatening to take hold of his insides kicked up in speed. "Yeah, I see it." He reached up, pointed to Eva's hairline. "That's the back of her neck, isn't it? She's blonde. Pale skin. And that raw skin: the circle, the curving lines. That's not a tattoo."

"No, it's not." The disgust in Blake's voice was all too evident. "That's a brand."

"Jesus," Riley whispered, and as Paul glanced back, he saw her slowly rising to her feet. "Moxie."

"That's the same mark on the back of her neck," Mabel said. "The same one that Joyce DePalma has. They branded her," Mabel whispered. "Branded *them*. But why?"

"Why does anyone brand anything?" Laurel said in a tight voice. "To claim ownership."

"I think history's calling," Sutton said.

"I've got another message," Quinn said. "From Susie at the lab."

"What's it about?" Paul asked when the detective's jaw turned to granite.

"The nail scrapings the EMT took from Mabel the other night at Mrs. Lancasters? They're gone."

"Gone as in they never made it to the lab?" Paul pushed.

"No. They were logged in. Susie signed for it herself. She remembers doing so. She put the sample in to run earlier this week, and now it's gone." Quinn looked up. "Along with any record of it having been there."

"That's not possible," Wallace said, a half-eaten sandwich in his hand. "Everyone who goes into the lab scans in with their ID card. No one can get in the system doesn't recognize. And they can't access it from outside the lab itself because it's on a separate server."

"There are ways around scanners like that," Nox said in a *I-can't-believe-you-didn't-think-of-this* tone. "The key card, not the server room. Depending on the system, it's easy enough to know what information a key card scans for. I could whip up a copy of either of your IDs in about ten minutes if I know what's needed." Nox looked around as if perhaps they'd said too much. "Or maybe someone's card was stolen."

"That risks it being reported and traced," Quinn said with a steely-eyed look at Paul. "We could go with option number three, but no one's going to like it."

Mabel bit the bait. "Option number three?"

"Someone in the department got in and took what they wanted." It was Blake who said it, with a finality that felt like a coffin closing.

"Who all has access to the lab?" Paul asked.

"You mean whose cards could get them in without any questions being asked? Anyone with an LAPD ID, from rookies all the way up the Chief. I think we can rule my father out," Quinn added. "There's also the sheriff's department, some federal agents who act as liaison to the department and the DA's office, of course. I can think of at least a couple dozen people off the top of my head who have access."

"We can assume that the evidence of whomever is responsible is gone," Mabel said. "What about the contact lens Paul found on the carpet? They didn't take that?"

"I turned that in myself," Quinn said. "And I handed it directly to Susie, pretty much told her this was on the Q.T.. She's head of the lab. She can make things disappear when she wants to. Which means we've still got a chance at DNA. Wallace?"

"You want me to go down to the lab and wait for the results?" Wallace said even as he heaved a sigh. "I'm taking extra sandwiches with me. I'll let you know when we've got something."

"It's still like we've got fragmented pieces of a puzzle I can't see the picture of," Paul said after Wallace had left. "It's one thing to play with the idea of some nefarious cult-like organization creeping around LA and Hollywood abducting women."

"Abducting and *killing* women," Mabel said. "They're dead. We all know it. Even if we don't want to accept it." Her voice cracked ever so lightly.

"Mabel," Laurel said sympathetically.

Mabel shook her head as if refusing to hear her. "We've reached out to dozens of the families. They've never heard from their loved ones. Never. Some might be understandable, but *all* of them?"

"Okay, but that brings up a whole other point." The one that had been bothering Paul from the beginning. "You can't just bury sixty-seven—or more—women and not be noticed."

"There's more than one way to dispose of a body." Sutton asked. "Sorry, just came into my head."

"No, you're right, Sutton," Paul said. "Nox, can you start another search? Any business that's applied for permits for crematoriums in the past …" He tried to do the math. "What? Fifty years?"

"Nineteen thirty-two is the first year we've got a woman who falls into the parameters," Cass said. "Mayelle Rappaport, nineteen, blonde—a chorus girl working part time as a secretary to make ends meet. Her brother reported her missing after two days. Nothing since."

Something cold and clammy slithered up Paul's spine. "Nineteen thirty-two." He couldn't bring himself to accept that. "That's almost a hundred years ago."

"That can't be right," Mabel whispered.

"Yes, it can." Sutton shoved to her feet, joined Mabel and Paul at the screens. "Nox, where's the website again? I thought I saw something flicker … yeah." She pointed up at the website address. "It flashed there again. Before the domain name clicked into place. What's the IP address?"

"One sec." Nox clicked a few keys.

"One nine three two dot five nine dot oh three dot seven nine six. That means something." Paul just about had it … almost. "The nineteen thirty-two's there. Coincidence, maybe."

"I don't believe in those anymore," Mabel muttered.

"Don't get the five nine …. Oh," Paul exclaimed, "but the three seven nine six? That's—"

"That's the street number of the Tenado house," Blake said, surprising everyone. "Good catch, Sutton."

"Thanks." Her smile was fleeting. "So, that would make the nineteen thirty-two not a coincidence?"

"The start date of this whole thing?" Mabel answered. "Whatever this whole thing is."

"We need to do more digging. They call themselves the Red Lily for a reason. Let's start there. And," Cass said, "we need to go back to nineteen thirty-two and take it a step at a time. We'll dissect the entirety of Hollywood history if we have to, studio by studio, with Powell Films front and center."

"Granger won't like that." Paul looked behind him when the room went silent. "What?"

"You said Granger as if you know him," Laurel observed.

"I did know him. Years ago." He looked at Mabel and repressed a wince. "The guy I told you about, the one I knew when I was a teen? The one with the obsession about Temple House?"

"The one whose grandfather and father ran a movie studio? You were talking about Granger Powell?" Mabel's eyes went saucer wide. "And you're just mentioning that now?"

"I didn't realize his name would matter, and he was my brother's friend, not necessarily mine," Paul said. "I doubt he'd even remember me."

"Granger Powell didn't get to where he is by forgetting anything," Quinn observed. "We know now, so let's move on."

"Move on?" Mabel gaped. "But—"

"Pocket it for when it's useful. Down the line," Blake said. "Like when you want to talk to him. Would he remember your brother?" He asked Paul.

"Yeah." Paul nodded solemnly. "Yeah, no one could forget Alden."

Blake nodded. "Then we've got an in whether Powell remembers you or not."

"Okay, then." Cass retook control. "Nox and I can put together search parameters and give each of you dedicated laptops, ones that can't be traced or hacked if you get to the wrong place. I'll need a few days to get that worked out." She noticed the expression on Paul's face. "What?" She asked him.

"I'm pretty sure that's his thinking face," Mabel said after one glance. "Paul?" She circled around in front of him as he looked back at the screens, then at the rest of people gathered around him. "What is it? What do you see?"

"A team. My team." DA be damned, he didn't need her approval for a task force, not when he already had one. One where every single member had their own reasons for wanting answers. "The DA's pushed back twice on me wanting a task force. But I've got myself one anyway."

"Not just a team," Mabel said as he drew her close. "A family."

CHAPTER FOURTEEN

"YOU let me sleep again." Eyes still blurry, head still foggy, Mabel couldn't remember the last time she'd slept beyond six. Thanks to Paul, she had no memory of any other man having been in her bed. The man did have creative—and enthusiastic—ways of clearing her memory banks.

She hadn't had the dream last night. She hadn't dreamed about Sylvie since the night Barksy had woken her up and nudged her back to reality. The day she'd met Paul.

Coincidence? She didn't think so. She'd meant what she'd said last night at Cass's. She didn't believe in them anymore.

Her slog down the hall came up short before she reached the kitchen table. She blinked, rubbed her eyes, and looked at the clock. Ten thirty? Panic might have set in if she hadn't just seen Keeley, fresh-faced, dressed, and doing her homework no less, sitting across the table from a rather intense-looking Paul. It was, she thought dazedly, one of the most heartwarming sights she'd ever seen.

He closed his Nox-ified laptop as she approached. "Morning." He flashed that smile that made her stomach pitch like a Tilt-a-Whirl. "Blueberry crumble muffins on the counter. Sutton dropped them off earlier. You want one?"

"Um, sure." Mabel walked over to Keeley, ran a hand down her loose hair. "How was the sleepover?"

She shrugged. "Okay."

"Only okay?" Shirley was renowned for her sleepovers that always consisted of a theme that carried through from the games to the food to whatever they might watch on TV. "Did you thank her for hosting you?"

"Yes." Keeley rolled her eyes. "I did all the things I was supposed to. I just wanted to be here." She lifted her head and aimed a wide, toothy smile at Mabel. "With you and Paul."

Her heart warmed. "Well, that's nice." Mabel turned to head to the coffee machine, only to find Paul standing directly behind her, handing over a mug of steaming coffee. "You were wrong again," she accused as she accepted, cradled, and sipped its contents. "You might just be a knight in shining armor after all."

"Perish the thought." He pulled out the chair at the head of the table. "I hope you don't mind, but I went for an early morning run, stopped at the grocery store down the way, and picked up a few things."

"Healthy things," Keeley mumbled. "He bought celery. And kale. Blech." She shuddered.

"I bought less blechy things as well," Paul countered easily. "You wanted pancakes tomorrow morning, didn't you?"

That brightened Keeley's expression considerably.

Curious, Mabel walked over to the fridge. Inside she found more fruits and vegetables that she'd probably bought in the last month. "I hope you know what to do with all this," she told him, "because I sure as heck don't."

"Worry not."

Mabel wasn't sure what worried her more: her soon-to-be increased fiber intake or Paul's somewhat jovial and solicitous mood. "Been up long?"

"Just since five." He retrieved one of the muffins and put it on a napkin for her. "My normal time. I had some ideas after last night's meeting I wanted to work on."

He angled a look at Keeley that let Mabel know he didn't want to get into details with little ears around.

"Looks like you're working, too, Kee." Mabel broke her muffin apart and stuck her face into the thin thread of steam that wafted from inside. "Homework?"

"Yes." Her daughter didn't sound particularly pleased about it. "I'm getting it out of the way so it isn't looming over my head."

That sounded like a Paul idea. "How much more do you have to do?"

"Just read two chapters of my history book. I already did my English, science, and math."

All that already? And Mabel hadn't even had to fight with her about any of it. "What time did you come home?"

"Seven. Addie and Lucas were still sleeping. Shirley said it was okay to leave." Keeley slid out of her chair. "I'm going to go take Barksy for a walk in the park."

"Um …" That fear Mabel had been able to sideline surged afresh. "I don't think—"

"We'll *all* take him," Paul countered. "We could use some fresh air. Or I can, at least."

"Right, sure. Okay. All of us. Together." Mabel nodded. "I'll get dressed, and we can go." Keeley dragged the thick textbook off the table and went to her room, Barksy trailing behind her. "You think she's okay?"

"Kids are sponges. I think she's picking up on the tension in this building." Paul returned to his seat. "I'm also guessing the idea of me as a houseguest is a bit different than the reality."

Mabel's lips curved. "You made her do her homework. That means your time as the fun adult in the house is officially over."

"That wasn't out of line, was it? Honestly, I have to admit it was self-serving. I just wanted to be able to finish—"

Mabel rose up out of her seat and planted a sugary kiss on his lips. "You were not out of line at all. I'd have thought you'd be a bit more uneasy about the fact you've acted in quite the paternal way with her. Not that that means anything," she added and took another bite of muffin. Somehow, she was going to break down that door of paternal reluctance. Or at least show him there was more to parenting than lording one's will over a child. "What does Sutton put in these muffins that makes them so addictive?" Mabel demanded of the universe.

"It's probably the nutmeg."

"Nutmeg?" Mabel considered, not only the muffin, but the man sitting beside her at the table. "So, you cook, huh?"

"That way, I know what I'm eating." He got up to refill his coffee but stopped to drop another kiss onto her pursed lips. "Go get dressed. The fresh air will do you some good."

Mabel sighed and grabbed a second muffin before she hurried into her bedroom.

When she returned, feeling a bit bloated from having eaten two muffins, Paul handed her one of her metal travel coffee tumblers. "All set?"

"Yeah." She still had a bit of the morning grumps. "Kee!"

"I'm here, Mom." Keeley jumped into sight from where she'd been standing by the door, Barksy clicked into his leash, his tail wagging enthusiastically at the unexpected treat of a walk. "Can we go, please?" Keeley whined.

"Yeah, sure, go on." Mabel sipped her coffee and tried, in vain, to figure out the man she'd fallen for. Despite all his protestations regarding fatherhood and family life, the man fit as easily into their lives as the last piece of a puzzle. It wasn't that he completed the picture so much as …. Mabel sighed. Well, he just fit. "Dammit," she muttered and ignored his curious look as they locked up and headed downstairs.

"Kee!" Mabel yelled once they stepped out of Temple House and her daughter and dog raced ahead. "Stay in sight, please!"

"We will!" Keeley ran ahead anyway. "Come on, Barks!"

Beautiful days in Los Angeles were a dime a dozen, but today in particular felt a bit more sunshiny and bright. It was clear the temperature wasn't done climbing. She could feel the warmth of the sun already beating down on her. But the heaviness Mabel had come to expect with each sunrise didn't drag her down as deeply. She didn't feel as if she were trudging through the seconds but enjoying every minute she had.

"Quinn called while you were in the shower." Paul slipped his hand down her arm and gently clasped her hand.

"Oh?" The coffee caught in her throat, and she coughed. "I take it there isn't any word on Eva since there's no voicemail on my phone."

"No," Paul said gently, "there's not. I'm sorry."

Mabel refused to give in to the tears. The idea that a traumatized, heartbroken woman was out there trapped by The Circle curdled her appetite. "I keep hoping she got away somehow, again. But the odds of that ..." His silence had her glancing over at him. "What?"

"Nox pushed their way into the hospital security system," Paul said as they rounded the corner toward the dog park. "The system was hacked. There's also a thirty-minute gap in the cameras on the second floor, beginning at three yesterday morning."

Her stomach dropped. "Three was when Eva called me."

"Yeah. Whatever override code was used, they found the same one on the parking lot system. Seven-minute lapse this time. Whoever left the flower and the other ... things in your car, they did it without being seen."

"Awesome," she grumbled. "So, we're nowhere."

"We have a general plan of action," Paul countered. "I'm going back up to the estate this afternoon."

"The Tenado house?" A shiver ran down her spine. "Why?"

"I can't shake the feeling we missed something."

"Missed what?"

"Don't know." He shook his head. "But it's bugging me, and that means I need to address it. Quinn's going with me. We'll head out after lunch."

The idea of lunch made her feel slightly sick. She looked ahead to where Keeley and Barksy were playing it up. "Thank you for watching her this morning."

"You don't have to thank me," Paul said. "She's a great kid. Stubborn. And cute." He tugged her closer. "A lot like her mother."

"Ha ha." She didn't let herself dwell on the contentment she heard in his voice. Not for long, anyway. "It's all I can do not to lock her away in the apartment until this whole thing is over."

"Yeah, well, one Cass is enough for Temple House," he countered. "Keeley needs as much normal as you can give her. You start changing her schedule and all the things she can do—she's going to know something else is up."

Mabel was almost afraid to ask. "Something else?"

"Quinn picked her up from school yesterday, she was sent to an unexpected sleepover, and I've moved into the apartment. She's eight, Mabel—"

"Almost nine," Mabel corrected automatically.

"She knows when she's not being left alone."

"Which means I'll probably get interrogated if I leave her with Sutton when I go with you up to the Tenado estate."

"Hang on." He tugged her to a stop when he did. "I never said *we*—"

"You didn't?" Mabel fake gasped. "And here little old me thought I'd been given this thing called a brain that operates all on its own." She glared at him. "I haven't been up there since that time at Christmas." Since she'd first seen Sylvie's photo hanging on that wall. "I want to go back. I *need* to, especially if that internal radar of yours is pinging. I have to do *something*, Paul. I can't just hole up in this house and wait for everything out there to resolve itself. They've already targeted me and Keeley. Don't expect me to stop now."

"I didn't think for a second you were stopping anything."

"I'll be with you and Quinn. Keeley will be here at Temple House. If Sutton can't watch her, Riley can. I think."

"This might be a good time to tell me why you and she are fighting over Moxie."

Mabel shrugged, sipped her coffee as they started walking again. "I want to ask Moxie point-blank about the brand on her neck."

"Ah." Paul nodded, and Mabel rolled her eyes at his tone.

"She knows something, Paul."

"No doubt," Paul said. "But coming at her like a battering ram isn't going to get you the information you need. And there is her age to consider. Whatever happened to Moxie happened a *long* time ago. The mind puts protective barriers in place. They don't come down just because you want them to."

"But if it can help—"

"Riley will come around," he said. "You've planted the seed, and from what I saw last night, Quinn is helping it grow. She'll get there eventually. Right now, we've got plenty of other avenues to pursue where this Red Lily group is concerned. When we run all those to the ground, then we'll go back to Riley and come up with a plan about Moxie."

"I need to know what she knows," Mabel whispered. "I know she was scared the first time we mentioned it to her—"

"She's eighty years old," Paul said softly. "She's lived a lot of life between then and now, and she's found a way to protect herself. Are those answers worth risking your friendship with Riley over?"

Mabel scrunched her mouth. Did he have to make so much damned sense?

"Riley knows there's no avoiding it forever. Let her come around, okay? A few days, a couple of weeks, she'll know when it's time, and then we can work together to make it as easy on Riley and Moxie as possible."

"Is this why they call you the witness whisperer?" Mabel asked, still feeling a bit sour.

"I will neither confirm nor deny," he teased.

She grabbed hold of his hand and squeezed. "Okay. I'll leave it alone. For now." She dug into her purse when her cell phone rang. "Maybe this is about Eva."

"Or it's about Soteria," Paul said. "We need to get you that second phone."

"Until that happens …" She shrugged and answered. "Hi, this is Mabel."

"It's Leo."

"Well, hello." Mabel swallowed hard, managed a shaky smile at Paul as she held up a finger.

"I need to talk to you. Alone." Leo's voice shook. "I can't trust anyone else. I need to talk to you. *Now*."

"I don't think that's going to be possible."

"Is it about Eva?" Paul asked quietly.

She cupped a hand around her cell and opened her mouth.

"If you tell him, I'll hang up." Desperation shifted Leo from suspect to victim in her mind. There was no mistaking the fear she heard in his voice. Fear she'd heard from countless victims, including Eva. "And I won't call back."

A chill raced down Mabel's spine. He could see her.

It was all she could do not to turn around, to search for him, but she'd been around enough skittish victims and witnesses to know if she let on, he'd run. And she'd never get any answers.

The internal debate took less than a second. "This is going to take a few minutes," she told Paul and inclined her head toward Keeley. "Can you keep an eye on them? I'm just going to …" She indicated the ramp leading out of the dog park and back to the sidewalk.

"Yeah, sure." He nodded, but there was caution in his gaze. "Stay in sight, yeah?"

"Of course." Her lips trembled as she smiled. She waited until he was out of earshot, until he'd reached Keeley, who had let Barksy off his leash and was racing around with him and two other dogs in the thick, ankle-deep grass.

Now she searched, turning slowly, eyes scanning the area around the park. Her gaze gravitated toward the tree from the other day, but she only saw a pair of kids pushing at each other as they made their way to the corner market.

"Okay," she told Leo as she looked across the street in one direction, then the other. She saw him, standing in the doorway of a dry cleaners, arms wrapped tight around his torso, hood flipped over his head, phone up to his ear. From a distance, he looked like a junkie tweaking for a fix. "I'm alone." She hurried down the ramp toward the street, around the far end of the dog park as he moved out of the protection of the awning. "How did you get my number?" She was stalling. She already knew. Her number was plastered all over emergency rooms in the city.

"They got her." His voice was flat. Accusatory. "I *told* you they would. I *warned* you! They'll come after me next."

"Why?" Mabel demanded as she walked. The air thickened around her, heated up as if she'd stepped into some kind of pressure vortex. Her mind spun. "Is it the Circle? Is that who you're afraid of?"

The silence lasted so long she was worried she'd lost him.

When he finally answered, his voice was shocked. "How do you know about them?"

"Because I think they took my sister." Now wasn't the time for platitudes or lies. Only the truth was going to get her closer to finding Eva. And Sylvie.

Sylvie …

Tell me what you know, Leo. I have friends who can protect you."

She studied him, now standing behind a parked car. Even from a distance, she could see the trauma, the all-too-familiar grief, on his face.

Mabel stopped at the curb, heard Paul call her name. She glanced back, gave an absent wave, and hoped it was enough to ease his mind.

"Let me help you, Leo," Mabel pleaded urgently as she stepped down between two cars to head in his direction. She tried to take a deep breath, but her lungs had stopped working. The air felt thick, as if a weight or pressure were bearing down on her. The more she tried to move, the more it felt as if she were trudging through water. "Leo, I promise; my friends and I can help. Just tell me what you know." With the road between them, she kept her eyes pinned on his, afraid that if she broke contact, he'd disappear.

"Mabel!" Paul shouted from a closer distance.

"You called me, Leo," Mabel tried again, inched her foot forward. "Let me help you."

He stared at her in wide-eyed terror. "I don't know what to do." Arms hugged around himself, he looked and sounded like a scared kid.

Mabel's heart twisted. Like Keeley sounded whenever she had a nightmare.

"It's okay." Mabel stepped into the street, stretched out her hand, urging him forward. "Come on, Leo."

The pendant at her throat burned against her skin.

She yelped, jumped back, and dropped her phone. It clattered under the closest car. "Dammit! I'm still here!" she yelled and ducked down. She shifted and had to practically lie flat on the ground, twisting and stretching her arm beneath the car. "I'm still here!"

Don't hang up. Don't hang up.

Her fingers skimmed the case, but instead of staying put, it shot out of her hold once more.

Out of the corner of her eye, she saw Leo stretch up on his toes, searching for her. Then he moved between the cars and stepped off the curb.

"Mabel!" Paul dropped down on the other side of the car, locked angry eyes on hers. "What the hell are you doing?"

"My phone!" It was closer to him than to her. "Get my—"

An engine revved. Tires screeched.

Dazed, Mabel got to her feet but stumbled back, the pressure rebuilding around her to the point it stole her breath. Leo headed toward her, phone still at his ear. The screech of wheels filled the air.

Time slowed even as her mind spun faster than the wheels on the white van barreling straight toward him.

Leo didn't have time to freeze. Mabel watched, horrified, as the van plowed right over him.

Mabel screamed as Paul's arms locked around her and catapulted them both out of the way of the swerving van. They landed on a heap on the sidewalk as the van swerved, scraped, and sparked, taking off the side mirror of the car that only moments before she'd been under. The van never slowed as it screeched around the corner and disappeared from sight.

The heat of her pendant died instantly, as did that feeling of pressure that had held her back. Her ears were filled with the frantic cries and screams as witnesses barreled toward them. Paul was back on his feet first. He reached down and hauled her up. Hands locked around her arms, he pulled her close enough she could see panic in his eyes, feel the terror in his touch.

"What in the hell were you thinking?!"

"I—I don't—" She couldn't get anything else out as her wide eyes filled with tears the sight of the broken young man who she'd been speaking with seconds ago. "It was Leo," was all she could think to whisper. Try as she might, she couldn't get her thoughts into cohesive order. "I just wanted to convince him we could help ..." A sob caught in her throat. "Jesus, Paul. They never even stopped." She grabbed at him, and only when she had a hold of him did she feel some semblance of sanity return. His hold on her eased to the point he rubbed her arms in a comforting motion. If Paul was here, where was ... "Keeley?"

"Playing with some friends," Paul said as he pushed her cell phone into her shaking hands. "If you're steady enough, you get back to her."

"But—" She heard the sirens wailing. "I have to give a statement." She turned tear-filled eyes to Leo.

"You'll give one. I'll send them to you. Go see to Keeley, Mabel."

Still, she hesitated. "I don't want to leave him alone," she whispered. He'd been so young. Not much more than a teen. Someone who needed help. He'd come to her, called her, and now ... "Paul—?"

"It's okay." The anger faded from his eyes. "I'll stay with him, Mabel. Go to Keeley."

All around them, people began to gather. Paul kept a hand on her arm as he pulled out his phone, then he gave her a gentle nudge.

Legs weak, her knees numb, she stumbled down the sidewalk back to the park. It wasn't until she saw Keeley, still occupied with Barksy and a half-dozen other dogs, that she breathed easy. Keeley had seen some ruckus had occurred but had been too far away to see anything of note.

"Hey, Mom!" Keeley yelled before she raced over as Mabel re-entered the dog park. "Wait until you see what Barksy ..." She skidded to a halt in front of Mabel, the joy in her eyes fading in an instant. "What happened?"

"There was an, um, a car accident," Mabel managed. "I dropped my phone, and ..."

She lifted the cell, stared in shock at the cracked screen. Her sister's face blinked for a fraction of a second before the screen went dark once more. Hesitantly, she reached up for her pendant, but the heat she'd felt was indeed gone.

"Sylvie," Mabel whispered. She caught Keeley against her as she searched frantically for the face in the crowd she knew wasn't there. She thought .... Her breath caught. She'd *felt* her. She was certain of it. It was hindsight, but she knew. She *knew.*

Sylvie had been there—when she had been talking to Leo. She'd helped her.

"Are they okay, Mom?" Keeley asked. Barksy whimpered and pushed his nose against Mabel's arm. "The person in the accident: Are they okay, Mom?"

"No," Mabel whispered back as she struggled for calm and hugged her kid. "No, he isn't."

"Guess we can mark Leo Capallini off our list of people to talk to." Quinn walked away from the tarp-covered body and joined Paul on the sidewalk. "Mabel doing all right?"

"Yeah." Paul hadn't been so sure at first. "She's fine." Close didn't describe how close she'd come—how close *he'd* come to losing her.

One second, he was being entertained by Keeley and Barksy, and the next, he'd had the overwhelming compulsion to find Mabel. He couldn't see her at first, then she'd popped up in the street, cell phone in hand.

He'd spend sleepless nights flashing on the horrific alternate ending to the accident. Ultimately, it had been Leo who had paid the price, but if she hadn't dropped her phone, Mabel would have, as well.

"I should get back to her," Paul said. "She didn't want me to leave him alone."

"Shit," Quinn muttered with a shake of his head. "Of course, she didn't."

"Did you read her statement?" Paul asked.

"I did. They've got others giving them, too. You can get her back to Temple House." Quinn sighed. "Did you see anything? Make, model? Plate numbers?"

"Nothing." Paul shook his head. "It was like they just appeared out of nowhere and disappeared the same way."

He fisted his hands in his pockets to stop them from shaking.

Seeing the kid get hit had brought back all the memories of Alden's death—of the helpless, sickening feeling he'd felt that night when the only person who had ever mattered to him was suddenly gone. How many years had he imagined what had happened, and now he'd seen something similar happen right in front of him.

Bile rose in the back of his throat as he tried in vain to stop the spiral of grief from dragging him under. "They're getting closer." Closer and more brazen.

"Putting this out as a hit-and-run might get us something," Quinn said.

"No, it won't," Paul countered and earned a disappointed glance from Quinn. "You know it won't."

"Doesn't mean it isn't worth trying," he said firmly. "You said Leo called her."

They glanced back to where Mabel sat on a bench while Keeley and Barksy continued to play. Mabel's attempt at trying to keep the horror away from her child—staying as close to normal as possible.

"What a fucking mess." Quinn planted his hands on his hips. "So, here's a question. Were they following Leo?" He eyed Paul with clear suspicion. "Or Mabel?"

Paul shook his head. He honestly didn't want to consider the answer to that right now.

"Wallace called right after you did," Quinn said. "The lab results on that contact lens you found came in. We've got an ID. I need Mabel to look and see if he's at all familiar."

"Seems a fitting end to the morning." Paul found himself hoping she didn't recognize the guy.

Paul turned at the sound of a laughing, squealing Keeley, who was wrestling on the grass with an enthusiastic Barksy. The sight acted as an instant balm for his pessimistic heart. "She's coming with us. To Tenado's."

"Keeley?" Quinn asked.

"Ha. No—Mabel."

"Just trying to find some humor somewhere," Quinn admitted. "I'll meet you back at Temple House after they shut down the scene."

He walked back to the park and stood there, continuing to watch Keeley ease the grief and anger reflected in her mother's eyes.

Paul had brief moments of peace in his life, mostly with Alden. The times when they'd been away from home, riding their bikes through the city that, for the most part, had felt like a prison to him. The accident should have had him packing his bags and running back to New York faster than a discontinued Concord could fly.

But as that little-girl laughter echoed into the sky and the dogs barked and raced and nudged and leapt, the long-ago wound that had left Paul feeling completely isolated and alone took one big leap toward healing.

Just as he took a step toward Mabel.

"Do you recognize him?"

Back in Mabel's apartment, Quinn flipped his phone screen around so Mabel could look at the face of the man whose DNA had been found on the contact lens. It felt odd, being home, knowing that only a little while before, Leo Capallini had lost his life only a few blocks away.

Mabel shook her head, tried to clear it of the trauma she knew would soon descend. A trauma that was quite possibly being kept at bay by another saving force she couldn't quite come to terms with. *Sylvie ...*

Her sister had been there when she'd needed her. Watching over her. Guarding her.

Mabel took a shuddering breath.

On one hand, that thought gave her comfort ... but that mean accepting the one thing she'd been trying not to for eight years.

Instead, she focused on the image. It was a mug shot, an old one, near as she could tell, which had her wanting to believe it was the man from the closet.

Round head, super-close-cropped hair, thick nose. But it was those eyes .... Recognition jolted through her like an electrical shock. "Hang on."

She nudged past Paul, who had been standing so close she could feel the heat of his body against hers. Mabel grabbed a piece of paper, folded it in half, and held it up to cover the bottom half of the man's face. Then covered the top of his head. "I know where I've seen him."

"It's the guy from the closet?"

"Well, yeah—there, too. But I saw him before that." How had she not connected it before? "At the hospital. Outside Eva's room when I visited after we met." She touched Paul's arm. "I'm certain this guy was coming out of her room. He was dressed like a doctor, so I assumed he was."

"He's definitely not a doctor," Quinn said. "According to his record, which is more than twenty years old, his name is Orson Berwick. Nox is doing a deep dive on him now."

"What about the cloves?" Paul asked. "Did you smell the cloves at the hospital?"

Mabel started to shake her head, then changed her mind. "I smelled something odd. Could have been cloves." The more she looked at the picture, the more certain she became. "Yeah, that's the man from the closet. If we find him, he should have gouges in his wrist. Not that we have anything to compare them to."

"One step at a time. I'll let Wallace know we're on the right track," Quinn said. "He can follow up with Nox, get what information we can. I don't want to put this through a search in the department. Given what happened with the evidence at the lab, I'm not feeling particularly trustful these days."

Mabel just nodded.

"I'm going to talk to my dad later," Quinn went on. "Riley and I are having dinner at my parents'. I'll bring him up to speed. You want me to tell him you'll be in touch?" he asked Paul.

"Monday, if possible," Paul confirmed.

"I'll set it up," Quinn said. "You guys ready to go?"

"Yeah, I just need to drop Keeley off at Sutton's on the way," Mabel said. "Meet you downstairs?"

"Sure." Quinn glanced between them before he left.

"You okay? I'm sorry if I scared you out there." Paul rubbed her arm.

She shook her head. "It's fine. You didn't really," she added at his doubtful expression. "You were scared, too, but calm and relatively rational. But you didn't scare me, Paul."

He didn't look convinced. "Then what's going on in your head?"

"I couldn't begin to sort through everything." She looked up at him, the debate that had been raging inside of her surging to the surface. She wanted, more than anything, to tell him what she was feeling—how she felt about him, in particular—but she couldn't bring herself to get past the idea that hearing her confession, her admission that she loved him, would send him running. She already knew he was going to leave. Why do or say anything that would drive him off sooner than necessary? "It's stupid. I was going to ask if you had a good time at the park. Well, until …"

"That's not a stupid question. Yes, I did." He frowned as if something were on his mind, as well, but he quickly covered it, which left Mabel thinking she wasn't the only one keeping secrets. "I'll see you downstairs."

Mabel stood where she was until the door closed behind him, then headed down the hall to Keeley's room. "Hey, kiddo." Forced bravado was one of her many talents. "You ready to go to Sutton's?" Mabel stepped inside the cacophonous décor of an eight-year-old's mind on display in a mishmash of colors, fabrics, and styles.

From the still-played-with dollhouse in the corner of the room, to the costume tea party Barbie and her friends were having on the top of Keeley's dresser, to the growing stack of Stephen King books on the stand beside her bed, everything within these walls was exquisitely and uniquely Keeley. Except for the stuffed rabbit sitting on her lap. Eva's rabbit.

Knots twisted hard inside her chest. "Where'd you find that?"

"In your room. Sorry." Keeley sighed. "I know I'm not supposed to take things out of your bag."

"That's okay." Sensing something was wrong, Mabel sat beside her on the bed and tweaked Benedict Cumberbunny's ear. "I think he could use a friend."

"Who does he belong to?"

"A young woman I've been helping." Angst tugged at her, threatened to push her over the edge, but she drew Keeley close and stroked her hair. "We can't find her, and I'm keeping this safe until we do. Maybe you can help me with that?"

Keeley nodded against her chest. "Something bad's going on. That's why Paul's here, isn't it?"

"That's kind of right." When had telling her daughter the truth become so difficult? "Something bad is going on, but Paul's here because I asked him to be. And because he wants to be." For now, at least. "Someone's trying to scare me. Scare us," she corrected. "So, it's making everyone extra careful."

"Why does someone want to scare us?"

"Because we're trying to stop people from hurting anyone else. It's all going to be okay, though, Kee. Promise."

Keeley shrugged. "I know."

"You do?" Mabel sat back and looked down at her. "How do you know?"

"Because Aunt Sylvie told me so." Keeley's mumble sounded almost reluctant.

"Aunt …" Mabel's heart constricted. "When did she tell you this, Kee?"

"Couple of times." Her daughter shrugged. "It was supposed to be a secret, I think. And …" Keeley sighed. "I didn't want to tell you because I know talking about Aunt Sylvie makes you sad."

"Can you tell me now?"

"I see her in my dreams. We talk. And laugh. But," Keeley frowned, "I always feel like she comes when she's scared, too. And sad. But then we talk about you and Riley and Quinn and Aunt Laurel, and she feels better. That you and me aren't alone. I told her you are all like the Justice League, only without the costumes."

"I think Paul would prefer you think of us as the Avengers." She needed to joke, to try to find something to laugh about. Mabel talking to Sylvie was one thing, but knowing Sylvie was around Keeley as well offered a kind of hope she hadn't felt in a very long time. "Can you do me a favor?"

"You need my help?"

"I need to know you're safe. Just … if we ask you to go somewhere or do something, at least for the next while, I need you to go along, okay?" Mabel said. "And understand we're asking because it's important and we think it's the best thing."

"Okay." Keeley sighed. "Mom?"

"Mmm-hmmm?"

"I really like Paul. I mean, I didn't so much this morning when he made me do my homework, but I do like him."

"Yeah, I like him, too, baby." Mabel pressed her lips to the top of Keeley's head. "That's not a bad thing."

"He's really going to go away, isn't he?"

"Yes. At some point, he is. When all this is done." It was the first time she felt a shimmer of regret at getting the answers she'd been waiting for for eight years. After all this time, she could feel her life finally falling back into place, falling into something she'd never expected with Paul. Yet she was going to lose him when her past was finally settled. "I know that's going to be hard. Maybe I shouldn't have asked him to stay with us. Is that what you're thinking?"

"Not really. It kind of feels like I have a dad-type person here. I mean, I kinda did with Quinn, but that's different, you know? I think Paul would be a good dad. But he doesn't."

"No," Mabel said sadly. "He doesn't."

"Because his dad wasn't a good dad?"

"Sometimes, our parents leave scars on our hearts, Keeley. And Paul has a lot of scars." She'd seen them. On his back, on his shoulders, the burn marks on his arms. But most of all, she'd felt them on his soul. "I think, maybe, for as long as he's with us, we should prove those scars don't matter, yeah?"

"Do you think maybe he'll change his mind?"

"And stay?" Mabel asked. "I think it's too early for either of us to answer that question." Mabel smiled. "We've only known each other less than a week." She squeezed her eyes shut. "That's really fast to be thinking of anything remotely close to forever."

"Not if it's the right person. That's what Aunt Riley told me about Quinn. She knew right away he was the one."

"I think your Aunt Riley needs to stop reading Moxie's romance novels." If only so Mabel could pretend happy endings like that didn't really exist. Except they did. Riley and Quinn were proving that with each passing day. "How about you leave Benedict up here for today? Paul and I have some things we need to take care of." She kissed Keeley's head again. "We'll pick you up when we get home."

"Can we have hamburgers for dinner?"

"I think we can make that happen."

"IN & OUT?" Keeley's eyes brightened. It was one of their special treat places to eat. "With a strawberry milkshake?"

"Sure." What was she going to say after the past week? No? "Thank you for doing your part in all this, Kee. It means a lot."

"It's my job, right? To do what I'm supposed to do? To help when I can?"

"Absolutely. Because that's what family does."

"And Paul's family now, isn't he? Even if he doesn't want to be?"

"Yes, baby." Mabel drew in a deep breath. "Yes, he is. Now, let's go."

It took a few more minutes to get Keeley's belongings collected for a day at Sutton's with Lucas and Addie.

Thank goodness, Mabel thought for the millionth time, the kids got along as well as they did.

By the time they were headed downstairs, and Mabel slung her bag over her shoulder, Blake was headed up.

"Oh, good. I caught you before you left." Blake's flash of a smile told Mabel he was in work mode. "I have a present for you, Keeley. And for Lucas and Addie, too." He handed her a little box wrapped with a crooked, rather pathetic, purple bow. "It's a good luck charm."

"It is?" Keeley dumped her backpack on the ground and plucked it out of his hand. "Thank you!" She got it open and pulled out a small, plastic, purple, cartoony octopus with an oversized sailor's cap on his head. "He's cute!" She held it up by the keychain. "Cute, huh, Mom?"

"Very cute," Mabel agreed.

"He reminded me of Lord Squidly," Blake said. "But it's only good luck if you always carry him with you. Here." He crouched down, took the chain, and clipped it to one of the belt loops on her jeans. "Whatever you wear, I want you to keep him clipped somewhere, okay? You good with that?"

Keeley frowned, held the octopus in her fingers, and looked at Blake, then Mabel. "This is one of those things I do, right, Mom? Because Blake asked me to?"

"I think maybe it is," Mabel agreed.

"I have some other work to do," Blake said. "Would you mind giving these to Addie and Lucas? I'd like them to have them. Addie's is the yellow one."

"Okay." Keeley picked up her bag and dropped the boxes inside. "I'll make sure they wear them. Thank you."

"You're very welcome."

"Go on," Mabel said and nodded her toward Sutton's door. "They're waiting for you." The second she said it, the door popped open, and a giggling, blonde-haired Addie raced out to grab her friend.

"We're playing Twister! Lucas fell on his butt! Come see! Hi, Mabel!"

"Hey, Addie." Mabel smiled as Keeley (Barksy, as usual, following behind) disappeared inside. "You going to tell me what that really is?"

"Tracking device," Blake said as he pushed himself to his feet and they headed down to the lobby via the stairs, side by side. "Separate GPS signals for each of the kids. Program's installed in both my and Nox's system. I was waiting for a special chip, one that can't be blocked or jammed."

"And where do you get something like that?" Mabel asked, both touched and terrified their building manager was thinking along these lines. "Same place you got the window screens? Or shouldn't I ask?"

"I've got a lot of friends who do a lot of different things," Blake said. "If it's on Keeley, we'll always know where she is. No question. Not that she's going anywhere," he added. "Because she isn't." The full beard did nothing to hide the determination she saw on his face. "Not if I have anything to say about it."

At the landing, Mabel grabbed his arm, stopped him before he walked on. "Thank you."

"It's like you told Paul last night, right?" Blake said with a strained smile. "It's a family thing. We have to protect whatever one we've got."

She released him and let him go, her heart breaking a little at the thought of the family he'd lost. The family he clearly still grieved. No doubt, he always would.

"You coming?" Paul called up the stairs.

"Yeah," Mabel called back and swiped the tear that had escaped down her cheek. What strength it must take for Blake to embrace the children who lived here, when he'd lost his own not so long ago. "Yeah, I'm coming."

CHAPTER FIFTEEN

"WHAT is it you expect to find at the Tenado estate that four de-tectives, a dozen uniformed officers, and at least six crime scene an-alysts didn't?"

Paul mentally filtered out Quinn's irritation as they climbed out of the detective's SUV. "No idea. Probably nothing." Seeing this place in the full light of day, without the early morning rays playing fast and loose with his senses, shifted things a bit. At least for him. "Mabel? You okay?"

"Ask me that one more time," she warned.

It would take some effort to do as she asked. He'd been some-what distracted since the hit-and-run and couldn't quite process his reaction to it. Or Mabel's close proximity to a near tragedy. He want-ed this case solved. Put to bed. Written off and closed off. He wanted Mabel and Keeley safe. End of story.

But that would mean he'd be leaving …. He tried not to think about that right now, pushing it out of his mind.

Stay on task.

Quinn hadn't parked outside the gates like Paul had. Instead, the detective had gotten out of the SUV, unlatched the chain, and driven

298

all of them inside. He parked, presumably, where Riley had the night she'd been lured here. Held here. Almost killed here.

The gravel sounded the same grinding under his shoes as they walked toward the house, the weather far warmer than it had been when he'd explored the other morning. He carried his cell in his pocket, but other than that, he'd brought nothing. No notes or pictures or anything to cloud his judgment or his perception.

"Show me exactly where the tire tracks and footprints were?" he asked Quinn who, after a glance back at a shrugging Mabel, led them around the side of the house toward the pool.

"We got cast prints of five different tire treads," Quinn said. "They were all from high-end vehicles: Mercedes, Teslas, a BMW, if I remember correctly. In this city, that makes them needles in a haystack. Footprints were pointed in various directions in and around the tire marks."

"Meaning someone or multiple someones ran through the tracks *after* the cars left." Paul stood in the center of what Quinn pointed to. Hands on his hips, he turned in a very slow, deliberate circle. There was nothing along the side of the house to hide in or escape through. The only exit in and out of the basement was through the house. So, no joy there. "And none of you heard anything engine-wise when you were out here that night?"

"No." Quinn shook his head. "It's always bugged me that the only cars we saw when we got here were Riley's and Beth Tompkins's. But this area would have been out of our line of sight when we got here, and it was pitch-dark that night. I've come back at night a few times, just to test that theory. From where you're standing, you can't see this spot from the front of the house, and the fog was thick. We all went in the front door. Didn't go around the side until Tompkins was dead and Riley was safe."

Behind him, where Mabel stood, led back to the iron entry gates. Another quarter turn offered nothing but thick-trunked trees grown so tight together light barely squeaked through. That went on for …

He continued turning, ended up back where he started.

"It rained some before the techs got out to take casts of the footprints," Quinn said. "We figured tires were more important. We had to make a call on which to preserve."

"No judgment from me," Paul assured him. "I get it. Hindsight's a merciless bitch." He could easily imagine this place at night. This estate was creepy even now, in full sunlight. He didn't really want to think about how bad it got. "That iron fence—where does it start?"

"The first section crosses right in front of that line of trees." Quinn crossed in front of him, slapped his hand through the bars. "Fence line circles the entirety of the property behind the house. No gaps. No breaks."

"All the way around?"

"Yeah. To the other side of the house."

Paul tilted his head. "Any idea when it was installed?"

"No." Quinn frowned. "Important?"

"Maybe." Everything was important at this point. "Tenado moved in what? About a year before Melanie Dennings was murdered?" That put it at over twenty-five years ago. "I wonder if the fence was here then."

"We can find out. It's good work. Solid craftsmanship." Quinn grabbed one of the rungs, gave it a good shake. "Whenever installed, it was a high-end contractor. Crime scene measured it at eight and a half feet high with, obviously, slanting spear tips alternating sides. Slats are too narrow to get through." He stuck his arm through, got caught at his shoulder. "Going up isn't an option, not without causing serious injury. Property is locked down tight."

"Yeah." Paul turned in a circle again. Tall palm trees outlined the front of the property, almost like a natural frame. But back here, beyond the fence, it was more like a forest? Oak trees mostly. Thick, old, gnarly oaks. "The tire treads led back to the pool, not out the gates, right?"

"There were a mix of tracks in all directions," Quinn said. "The ones headed over there"—he pointed to the back part of the property—"we figured they were distractions. Trying to muddy the evidence, so to speak. Probably backtracked over themselves."

Paul looked at Mabel, who, rather than paying attention to them, made her way to the front of the house. "Mabel?"

"I'm fine." As long as that attitude shone through, he felt better about her being here. Truth be told, he didn't want her out of his sight. This was the last place he thought she should be, but he wasn't about to test the limits of their still-burgeoning relationship by challenging her decision. "Go on," she called. "Do what you need to. I'm not going inside."

Paul glanced at Quinn, who headed back in Paul's direction. "Let me just walk the perimeter. I won't be long."

"I'll keep an eye on her."

Already doubting his decision to explore the property again, Paul started where Quinn had just stood, examined the thicker bars separating the welded sections of fencing together. The bolts had been welded in place, as well—black, hexagonal, about the size of a quarter. He stooped down, ran his fingers over the top then bottom rung bolts. The same bolts held each of the spikes in place, top and bottom welded into horizontal stabilizers. Not even an eight-point quake on the Richter scale was going to budge this fence.

He shook his head. Quinn was right. What did Paul expect to find? But he wasn't going to leave without checking everything. And everything included …

Paul frowned, noticing the multiple Private Property signs on open display. He counted, his confusion increasing when he reached more than a dozen. Something flashed in the corner of his eye. Small. Red. There it was again.

The back of his neck prickled. That steady red blinking light had a pattern. And it was coming from multiple angles within the thick upper branches of one of the oaks.

He stopped looking, forced himself to shift his attention away from the surveillance camera.

Considering the Tenado property had been vacant for almost four years, exactly who was the neighbor attempting to keep out? Or watching? Trespassers looking for a true crime fix? Cold case junkies hoping for what Paul was angling for—an answer to unanswered questions?

He tapped open his notes app and typed a self-reminder to have Nox research all the property in the area: owners, timelines, disputes, or complaints. It wasn't going to be enough to dig through the victims' lives. They needed to find out everything about … everything.

He said he was going to walk the line, so that's what he'd do. Then he'd get Mabel the hell out of here, and hopefully, she'd never have a reason to come back.

The sections of fencing were wide, a good six to eight feet between the main posts. Paul trailed his hand along the spikes, noting the signage on the other side, the way the iron glistened against the sun. There were plenty of trees, not nearly as thick as the ones closer to the front of the Tenado property line, but a significant number of them. Thick, spaced relatively evenly, their overhanging branches so old it created a kind of sun-blocked canopy, keeping the ground below in constant shadow.

He walked steadily, slowly, noting every detail of the fence as he did so. With the pool coming up behind him, he expected the path to narrow, but it didn't. Not for another twenty or thirty feet. The path remained at the same width as it had at the beginning. Bolt, bolt, spike, spike, spike …. It became a kind of mantra, as did checking for the trees looming overhead. Bolt, bolt, spike, spi—

Paul stopped, his hand resting on one of the posts. He stepped back, stood between the sections. As he stared directly out the back of the fence, for the first time, he saw a complete clearing. The trees were even more far apart here. And the posts …

"You find something?" Quinn called from the back porch.

Paul didn't answer. He didn't have an answer—not yet. A car could easily get back here, down this path behind the pool. And if a car could, then multiple vehicles could. So could people.

He crouched, touched the hexagonal bolt that looked nearly identical to the rest.

He ran his thumb along the thin seam that seemed to connect two bars. Except …

He leaned back, looked at the previous sections, then to the ones ahead. This was the only place that particular bar seemed almost double in width.

Quinn's feet crunched in the gravel as he approached. "What is it?"

"Not sure." Paul stood, running his hands up either side of the post. "This one's different. And there, on the other side? That's three, maybe four, times as wide as any other distance between trees."

"Okay." Quinn stepped back. "And that means a possible driveway?"

"Working on it." The bolt at the top of the double black iron post was round. Not hexagonal. And it was at least double the size.

He peered closer, saw the faintest hint of silver beneath the black around the edge of the bolt.

He placed his thumb against the center of the bolt and pushed.

The fence popped open—just the merest of cracks—before Paul instantly tugged it closed.

"You've got to be kidding me." Quinn's disbelieving tone was only rivaled by Paul's own dismay. "Dude, you so missed your calling as a detective. Let's check it out."

"No." Paul clicked the gate shut. "Not yet. I think there's a camera. Don't look," he said quickly when Quinn straightened, as Paul methodically kept moving down the fence, continuing to shake or analyze bars as if he hadn't found anything. "Second tree on your right. I saw a blinking red light."

"Someone's watching this place."

"Can't take the chance they aren't." He pointed to another stretch of the fence, farther down. "Go rattle some railings for me, like you're looking for an opening."

"Paul, look at that ground, that open ground beyond the trees." He sounded excited, frustrated, and horrified in equal measure. "We were looking for large areas where bodies could be buried. That could be it." Quinn moved away to study the section of fence Paul had indicated.

Paul shuddered. "I know." The pressure built inside of him, almost to the point of pushing reason completely out of his grasp. "If we're really chasing after a group that's been around for almost a century, we can't just go barreling in. We need to be sure. We need to be ready."

If there were women buried on the neighboring property, they weren't going anywhere. The bodies couldn't be moved without being seen. The Circle wouldn't risk any attention being drawn to the neighboring property. Best to behave like they couldn't find anything.

"I want to go, too," he said at Quinn's huff of frustration. "Believe me. But we're only going to get one shot at this, or the evidence will be buried, or vanish—it has to be perfect. We need to compile the property records first, do a search on the owners. We scrape up every detail we can so they can't surprise us. Besides, those signs say Private Property. We go in without a warrant, and we're done."

"And if they *are* watching?" Quinn asked. "If they see that you discovered that secret opening?"

"It only opened an inch before I dragged it closed. Let's just go along another few feet or so of the fence, inch-by-inch, and find nothing. It will be painstakingly annoying, but it would imply I didn't find anything yet." Paul shook his head for dramatic effect. "Bang the fence now and walk past me—angry, if you don't mind. Like you're ticked at me for being so particular about the fence, where there is obviously nothing interesting about it."

"Won't be a challenge." Quinn mumbled as he advanced on Paul with enough attitude that Paul took one step back. "We need to work on your fear reactions moving forward."

He swung around and stalked off, smacking his hand against one of the posts for added effect.

By the time Paul checked the next stretch of fence, letting his frustration show, and then caught up with Quinn, they moved into the protection of the tree line, well away from the suspected camera.

"I'll call Cass on the way back," Paul said. "Get her and Nox started on neighboring property research."

"That gate thing you found is big," Quinn said as they resumed their walk to the car and Mabel. "Feels like a huge leap forward after being stuck. You might end up closing this case sooner than you expected."

"Yeah." Paul watched Mabel step off the front porch and head toward them. "Yeah, faster than I thought." He couldn't imagine, at this moment, at least, not seeing her. Not talking to her, laughing with her. Drinking coffee with her in the morning or …

Ridiculous. Feelings like this were nothing more than infatuation. The *new* of it all. Mabel was shiny and exciting and … he couldn't have genuine feelings for her after less than a week. Could he?

No, he couldn't. But when he held out his hand and she took it, his heart all but leaped out of his chest. And straight into her hand.

"You look like you're getting one of my migraines." Mabel leaned over the back of the sofa, sinking her hand into his hair as she brushed her cheek against Paul's. "My turn to ask. What's bothering you?"

"Time." He shook his head, shifted the notebook he'd been scribbling aside. He pinched the bridge of his nose and dropped his head back to rest on her shoulder. "And other stuff."

"I can see that."

"Can you?" He smiled, turned his head, and met her gaze. "What else do you see?"

Responsibility. Pain. Doubt. Determination. "Your eyes spin a bit like a slot machine when you're thinking too much. Every once in a while, I see something drop into place. Not sure it particularly pays off or not. Time will tell."

"Yeah." He touched her face. "Time will tell."

"What will happen to Leo's body?"

"We shouldn't talk about that in front of Keeley."

"That's sweet," she said. "But about that?" Mabel turned smiling eyes on her soundly sleeping daughter. "She's out. Trust me, when she's asleep, it takes a bomb to wake her up."

"Or the promise of pancakes."

Mabel couldn't help but wonder, as she watched Paul stroke a hand over Keeley's hair, if he knew how good he was with her. How patient and encouraging. So completely the opposite of what she knew he believed himself to be. This wasn't something she could tell him. It was something he needed to see for himself. She could only hope and pray that he would.

Once they got home, Mabel held it together to spend a good few hours helping Cass, Nox, and Quinn dig down into the information they needed not only on the property behind the Tenado estate but on other significant-stature properties in Los Angeles as a whole.

It would take a systematic investigation to dig into the roots of Young & Fairbanks—their tangled connections to various businesses, entities, properties, and individuals in the city and Hollywood, in particular. They needed to be precise on the information they were looking to connect. They couldn't make a wrong step. Not from here.

Not if they were going to expose this group and their ongoing crimes against the city. Against dozens of unsuspecting women.

But precision took time. The second they were headed back to Temple House, Mabel had felt his frustration—it had mirrored her own. It had hurt, suspecting Paul was already counting the days until he could go back to New York, but she'd remained quiet even as she'd wished she hadn't driven out to the estate with them.

She'd rather not know that Paul had made a significant discovery that had Mabel desperate to dive onto that property and start digging into the ground with her bare hands in the hopes of finding her twin.

They'd wondered where the victims could be buried. This place made the most sense. Right now, it made the *only* sense, but she gave Paul the two things she didn't think she had any more of to give: faith and time.

"Time to perform your first offspring extraction." Mabel nudged him to the side, gently slipping her hands under Keeley's head as he slid himself free. Keeley sighed and shifted, clutching her new octopus keychain tight in her hand as Mabel laid her out on the sofa. She pulled up the blanket she'd draped over her when she'd brought Paul the copy of *Carrie* to read to her. To his credit and Mabel's heartbreak, his look of horror at the title of the almost-bedtime story took Mabel over that last hurdle to complete acceptance she'd fallen in love.

Terrifying. Exhilarating. Sobering.

She'd gone and done the impossible.

No doubt she'd be adding to her list of adjectives before and after he left. She'd have plenty to unload about when Saturday morning Mimosa Yoga started up again.

"You're going to leave her there?" Paul asked as she led him down the hall.

"She's fine," Mabel assured him. "It's time for the adults to play." She turned around and kissed him, something she'd been wanting to do ever since he'd capitulated over dinner and gone out for the burgers and milkshakes Keeley had asked for. Of course, he'd only agreed to do so if they also ate a salad, so she supposed it was a win for everyone.

"Ah." Paul pulled back ever so slightly when Mabel's hands slid under the hem of his shirt. "I don't think—" He gestured toward the loungeroom, and the slumbering Keeley.

"Okay, you're starting to get on my nerves," she teased. "Either you're a concerned father figure, or you're not. Pick one." She saw the shock and wondered, for an instant, if she'd made a mistake.

"Keeley's easy to care about." He frowned as he spoke, slipped his fingers through hers as she sought his bare skin once more. "You both are. That doesn't make me a fa—"

"There are countless levels to parenting," she told him. "There's countless right ways and only a few wrong ways. I know you aren't scared of her. Or me. You're scared of yourself." She stroked his hair away from his face, looked into his confused gaze. "I told you before: You are *not* your father. You've already broken your family's cycle of pain and neglect. Because you couldn't have had the last week you did and be anything like him." Her lips brushed his. She took another step toward her bedroom. Then another until they got to the door. "We won't wake her—if we just wait until we're in my room and—"

"Mom?" Keeley's sleepy voice echoed through the apartment.

Mabel dropped her head onto Paul's chest as he laughed. "She's got masterful timing. I'll just be a few minutes."

"Okay." He tilted her chin up and kissed her, so completely and fully that her knees nearly buckled. "I'll be waiting." He stepped back and pulled his shirt off as she closed the door.

"I like him."

Sylvie's voice echoed in Mabel's ear before she pried open her eyes. Her heart stuttered, the breath in her lungs freezing. She sat up in bed, shoved her hair out of her face and stared, dumbfounded, at Sylvie, her sister sitting beside her on the edge of the bed.

"He's a little uptight," Sylvie went on, "but he's got a seriously great ass. And a good heart. Even if he doesn't believe it."

Mabel reached out, fingers shaking, but jerked her hand back before she touched Sylvie and made her disappear. "You're here."

"Yep. Always am, actually." Sylvie gave her that saucy wink that usually meant she'd been up to no good.

Certainty settled as loss and gratitude pinged. "That was you, wasn't it?" Mabel asked before her sister faded away again. "With the van. My necklace. You were trying to keep me away."

Sylvie shrugged. "You've got too much going on in life to get yourself killed now. You weren't thinking things through. You were too worried about that Leo kid to pay attention to your surroundings. And you called *me* reckless and impulsive."

"Are you actually lecturing me?" Mabel asked.

"First time for everything," Sylvie teased.

"I haven't seen you for days." Mabel's voice cracked. "Here—in my dreams. Where have you been?"

"You had other things on your mind." Sylvie reached out for the blanket and tried to smooth it. "Not to mention the things you've had on your—"

"Okay, okay." Mabel laughed, then, throwing caution to the wind, dropped her hand on Sylvie's. Eight years of pent-up grief surged, and she sobbed. "You're here. You're really here, aren't you?" Clasping Sylvie's hand between hers, she held it against her chest, on top of her necklace, wishing, *praying* to feel Sylvie's pulse against hers. "Hey, look who's here, too. Barksy."

Barksy wiggled across the bed and nudged his cold nose against their joined hands.

"Hey, boy," Sylvie whispered, tears glistening like diamonds against her ghostly white cheek. "Oh, I have missed you. Had it pretty good, haven't you, with these two?" She bent down, pressed her lips against his head. "It's nice to be with you anywhere but in that car." Her eyes darkened. "In that place."

"Yes." Mabel couldn't help but agree. "I was there again today. With him." She looked at Paul, sleeping soundly on his back, one hand stretched out and touching her thigh. "I'm going to lose him, aren't I?"

"I'm dead, not psychic," Sylvie told her. "But as your sister, I can say you'll only lose him if you let him go. Don't do that, Mabe. Don't let him go. What you have—"

"It's not real. It can't be," Mabel whispered desperately. "It's too fast. A week?"

"Who are you kidding?" Sylvie snorted. "You fell for him the second you stood up from that chair and saw that man holding one of your cupcakes. Deadly combination for the likes of you. You two were locked then and there." Sympathy and the faintest hint of envy glistened in her ghostly eyes. "The only thing that can break you apart now is stubbornness. Or stupidity."

308

Mabel shook her head. "That's your hopeless romantic side shining."

"Doesn't mean I'm wrong." Sylvie drew her hand free, touched Mabel's cheek. Mabel gasped, tears blurring her eyes. She could feel her. It had been so long, so very long ...

"I have to go," Sylvie whispered. "Being here, it takes energy. It takes effort to take form in a tangible way—and I've lingered too long. Tell Paul ..." She sat up straight, sucked in a breath. "Tell Paul he's close, but he's wrong. I'm not ..." Sylvie form wavered—became insubstantial. "I'm not there, Mabel. He's close, so close to the touchstone."

"Sylvie!" Mabel cried out her name, both hands reaching for her sister as her twin evaporated in a haze of mist. "Sylvie." The sob erupted from deep in her diaphragm, surging out of her as if she were drowning in grief.

"Mabel." The arms that came around her were warm and soft, the embrace comforting and firm. "Hey, Mabel. I'm here. It's okay."

"No, it's not," Mabel cried. "She's gone. It's not okay. It never will be."

How did it feel as if her heart had been ripped out of her chest yet again?

He held on tighter. "We're going to find her, I promise. I'm right here. Barksy, too. Aren't you, fella?"

Barksy whined and nuzzled his way closer between them.

"S-sorry." Mabel's voice trembled. "I'm still half-asleep. She's never, she's never been here like this. In this room." She was cold. So cold she could see her own breath as she spoke. "I've only ever seen her in my car or ..." Or at the estate.

"Okay." Paul rocked her slowly, back and forth. "You want to talk about it?"

She burrowed into him, closed her eyes, and inhaled the scent of him, even as she clung to him.

"Mom?" Keeley knocked on the door before she opened it. She stood there, silhouetted in the moonlight streaming in through the bedside window. "Can I come in?"

"Oh." Uncertainty tangled with embarrassment as Mabel tried to push away from Paul, but he held on. And held out his hand.

"She had a bad dream," he told Keeley. "Come on. I think she could use all of us right now."

"Damn you," Mabel whispered as the tears flowed. "Can you please, for once, not do or say the right thing?"

"I'll work on that." He kissed her forehead as Keeley jumped onto the bed.

"It was actually a *good* dream—but, also sad," Mabel said, quietly.

"Good thing we put pajamas on before we went to sleep," Paul whispered before he sat back to make room for Keeley.

"It was Aunt Sylvie, wasn't it?" Keeley said. "I saw her, too. She was sitting on my bed when I woke up. She told me to come in and check on you." Keeley, in the dim light, seemed to glow in the room. "Did you see her, Mama?"

"Yeah." Mabel nodded and swiped away the tears. "Yeah, I saw her." She looked over Keeley's head at Paul. "She thinks you have a nice ass."

"Oh." Was it possible to see a man blush in the dark? "Well, thanks, Sylvie. I guess."

Mabel could tell he wasn't quite sure what to think about their almost-casual declaration their dead relative speaks to them—but now was not the time to explain her thoughts to him about it. She was still trying to wrap her mind around the concept herself.

Keeley snuggled into Mabel, wrapping herself around her as she always did and closed her eyes.

"I'll just go out to the sofa—" Paul flipped back the blankets, but Mabel caught his arm, drew him back and shook her head.

"You're getting the full parental dose today, Paul Flynn. And you haven't had that until you wake up with a hand or foot in your face. I'm okay," Mabel insisted at his look of concern. "I will be, anyway. After I sleep. And I need you, need *both* of you, to do that."

"We'll talk in the morning?" he insisted. "About your ... dream?"

"Yes."

"Don't forget," Keeley murmured sleepily, "you promised to make pancakes for breakfast."

Paul smiled, tucked her hair behind her ear. "Don't worry. I never break a promise."

CHAPTER SIXTEEN

SOMETHING woke Paul up.

He lay there, in Mabel's bed, warm beneath the covers, and stared at the bedside clock. He blinked, shoved up, looked around. It was almost eight in the morning?

"Must be this room," he muttered as he scrubbed a hand through his hair. The last time he'd slept in, he'd been a teenager, and boy, had he paid for that before breakfast.

There it was again. That rattling sound. He strained to hear.

"Keeley wants breakfast." Mabel's hand touched his back. "She's got pancakes on the brain. Your fault." She tugged her hand back under the blankets and pulled them over her head. "You get the early shift."

The comment didn't trigger his fight-or-flight response. But he didn't linger on the thought for long, either. Instead, he found himself leaning over Mabel's snuggled form and nuzzling what he assumed was her neck. "I could get up and lock the door."

"We're not far enough into our relationship for you to know what I look like first thing in the morning." Her voice was muffled, still sleepy, and had a husky, sexy quality he couldn't quite resist.

He took hold of the edge of the blankets and tugged them down, earning a squeal and giggle as he wiggled his way beneath the blankets with her. When he had his arms around her and his body pressed against her, her arched brow had her catching her lip in her teeth and teasingly looking at him.

"Good morning, Mr. Flynn."

"Good morning, Ms. Reynolds." He kissed her and, had the door not been wide open, would have instigated more. If they hadn't both sat straight up at the sound of a crash from the kitchen.

"Boarding school," Mabel said, shoving her hair out of her face. "I think maybe boarding school might be … Keeley?" Mabel called when silence descended.

"Yes?" Keeley's suspicious squeak had Paul shifting to attention.

"You okay?" Mabel asked.

"Um … yeah." Small feet pattered their way down the hall. An echo of doggie paws sounded as well. "I, um, we might need more flour."

"Why?" Mabel started to jump out of bed, but Paul held her back as Keeley slinked into view. She was covered, head to toe, in flour that had clearly dumped on her from above. Barksy had not escaped the fallout and was sneezing his face free of the stuff. "Ah, geez, Kee." Mabel covered her mouth but not before a giggle escaped.

"I was trying to get things ready for breakfast." Keeley's eyes glistened beneath the white powder. On the top of her head sat a little pile of flour that resembled an elf's cap.

"Why don't you keep the flour on a container on the counter?" Paul asked.

"Because I don't bake … and, really?" Mabel shot him a look. "*That's* your question?"

"That is my question. Stay there!" Paul ordered when Keeley lifted a bare foot. "We'll get you cleaned up. This is why you need a patio or balcony with this apartment."

"Yes, that would certainly solve all my problems." She shook her head. "You are such a man."

"I'm sorry." Keeley's lower lip wobbled. "I was only trying to help."

"No harm done," Paul said quickly and extricated himself from the bed. "Messes are easily cleaned. So are you."

312

"So glad to hear you say that." Mabel grabbed the blankets and covered herself back up in bed. "Call me when breakfast is ready."

Paul grabbed his T-shirt and pulled it on over his pajama bottoms. When he turned and saw the shame and fear in Keeley's eyes, he froze. He'd been this child. He'd stood where she stood now, after having done something utterly and completely ridiculous because that was what kids did. But there was nothing other than affection and amusement that washed over him as he approached.

"Hey. What's with the tears?"

"I ruined our breakfast." She swiped the back of her hand across her damp cheeks and smeared the flour with a bit of style. "I'm sorry. Don't be mad and go away yet. I'll be better; I promise. I don't want you to leave us yet."

Paul heard Mabel scramble out of bed. "Hey, Keeley, I'm still here, aren't I? I haven't gone anywhere." Because she seemed to need it, because he needed it, he reached out and pulled her into his arms. She folded into him. Clung to him. "I'm not mad, I promise. Okay?"

"Kee." Mabel knelt beside them, resting her hand on the back of her daughter's head. "What's all this about? You spilled flour. It's not the end of the world."

"I told you; I don't want him to go." Keeley's eyes filled when she stepped back. "I thought maybe if I was good, if I didn't make any mistakes, he'd stay because he makes you smile, and you're happy with him here. I want you to be happy, Mama. Aunt Sylvie wants that, too."

"Baby." Mabel tilted her head. "We can only take things a day at a time, yeah? No one's making promises to anyone right now. Paul and I—we're still figuring a lot of things out."

"But you like each other. You're sleeping in the same room," she accused. "That means something, doesn't it?"

"Yes," Paul said. "It means I care about your mother a great deal. And I care about you, too. And you know what you are to me right now, with that flour all over your face and head?"

"What?" Keeley sniffled and sneezed, sending up a plume of powder.

"You're perfect."

Her eyes brightened. "I am?"

"Let's get you into the shower," Mabel said. "Clean you up, and then …"

"And then you can come out and help me with the pancakes. I'm going to teach you my secret recipe," Paul said. "But only if you promise not to share it with your mom. Cause, you know—"

"She can't cook?" Keeley giggled.

"I must have woken up with a Kick Me sign on my back," Mabel muttered as she stood up, picked Keeley up into her arms, and carried her through the room to the bath, leaving a snowfall of flour all over the floor.

Paul was in the hall, Barksy whining at his side, when he heard the laughter on the other side of the door. Bracing his hand against the wall, he waited for the panic to hit. For the dread. For the abject horror that he'd somehow lost his heart when he'd walked into this apartment that first time. He should be terrified, and yet …

For the first time, perhaps in his entire life, he had everything he'd ever dreamed of having. Which meant he had far more to lose than ever before.

And that, he realized, might just scare him most of all.

"You going to tell me what the dream with Sylvie was about?"

Paul's question brought Mabel out of her pancake haze. A haze she wasn't entirely sure she wanted to leave behind. There hadn't been a lot of emotional upheaval in Keeley's life up until now. The fact her daughter had chosen to display her insecurities about a potential father figure—Mabel's thoughts, not Paul's—was concerning.

Mabel's lack of a dating life certainly hadn't come close to preparing Keeley for the possibility of having someone serious in their life, let alone the actuality.

"Sorry." Mabel blinked herself out of her haze. "What? Oh, Sylvie." Her mind was so full right now, but the fact she'd finally, after all these years, held her sister's hand nearly overwhelmed her. "Yeah. It was strange. Different than usual."

She carried her plate over to the sink where he was washing the mountain of dishes it apparently took to make a batch of what turned out to be spectacular pancakes.

Mabel looked back at Keeley, who was sitting on the sofa reading, her emotional upheaval at feeling the need to be perfect behind her.

"Sylvie said something odd."

"Your ghost dream of a sister said something odd?" Paul arched a brow at her. "Do tell."

"She said you were wrong."

His hands stilled in the soapy water. "Wrong about what?"

Maybe it was time to trust him with the truth. That Sylvie, despite being missing, was still very much here. "She said you were close but that she wasn't where you were looking. There was something about a touchstone? I don't even know …" She shook her head. "You think maybe she meant that property behind the Tenado estate?"

"It's the only place I'm focused on." He frowned. Set her plate into the water. "It's the only one we've got any lead on."

"Do you think it was just my mind playing tricks? It felt like I was awake this time—not dreaming."

He hesitated for a second, then spoke. "There's only one thing I'm certain about where Sylvie is concerned," Paul told her. "And that is I have no doubt of the bond you and your twin had in life. Who says it would be completely severed in death? I'm not about to discount anything. Consider Sylvie's advice accepted and filed away for future reference."

She smiled, oddly relieved. "You have plans for today?"

"Yeah, actually." He glanced over her head to the kitchen clock. "I'm meeting Jeff and his son at Grand Park downtown."

"To talk about the case?"

"He didn't want to talk in the office."

"You two think alike then," Mabel said. "Want some company? Or some cover?" she added with a grin. "That new children's playground is supposed to be pretty awesome. Keeley might enjoy it, and if you and Jeff need to talk, she can keep his son company. How old is he?"

"Six." He hesitated, frowning. "Max is my godson."

"Really?" Mabel's eyebrows raised before she thought to stop it. "That's … interesting."

"I've only seen him a handful of times since he's been born. I doubt he'll even recognize me."

"Well, I think you're in a good frame of mind to meet him now. I talked to Keeley before breakfast," she told him, rested a hand on the back of his shoulder. "I told her we shouldn't be pressuring you into anything you don't want to do. Or can't do." How did she tell him she was willing to let him go if that was what he needed? It might have been easier to admit out loud if Sylvie—or the projected image of her—hadn't filled her head with doubts. Told her not to ever let him go.

"I appreciate that," Paul said, nodding. "We'll work through it. All of us. Like you said, a day at a time, right?"

"Mmm-hmm." Mabel sighed. "Right. What time did you say? Noon for Jeff?"

"Yeah. I guess there's some food trucks in the area on the weekends."

"I hope some of them have vegetables, otherwise you're going to starve." She kissed his cheek. "I'll go get dressed. Kee? You up for going to a playground later?"

Keeley spun around on her knees and looked at them over the back of the sofa. "I'll go change."

"What you have on is … fine," Mabel called after her, but Keeley had already slammed the door to her room. She considered something, biting her lip.

"Spit it out," Paul said teasingly.

She hesitated, then dove in. "Would it make a difference to you," she said impulsively to Paul, "if I didn't want more children?"

He released the plug, let the water out, and grabbed a towel to wipe his hands. "Do you? Want more?"

"I've thought about it." She shrugged. "Honestly, given my dry spell, I figured I was done. That she was it."

"But now?"

"I don't *need* to have another baby, Paul." She touched his face. "So, if that's what you're basing our future on, stop. I hit the jackpot with Kee. It would be almost greedy to want to hit it again."

Paul's phone rang from its place next to his laptop on the dining table. "That's the ringtone for my boss in New York."

That statement felt like an icy bucket of water poured straight over her head. "Okay." She stepped back to let him pass, taking the towel from his hands so she could dry the dishes in the drainer.

He grabbed hold of her hand and squeezed. "We aren't done with this conversation."

"We aren't?"

"No," he assured her. "We aren't."

She tried not to listen in on his side of the conversation when he answered his call, but his surprise at hearing from his boss seemed genuine, even as his tone turned serious.

"Yeah, thanks. I appreciate the update and the head's up. I'll need some time to … yeah. Absolutely. I'll be in touch. Thanks." He hung up and stood there, staring straight ahead.

"Good news?" Even as she asked, her stomach pitched.

"Somehow, I don't think so. My boss back in New York thinks it's time for me to come back to work."

"Now?" Mabel felt the blood drain from her face. "But you've only been here—what? A week?"

"He said the sooner the better. All of a sudden, he's got a bunch of cases lined up that require my expertise."

"Oh." An ache settled between her breasts. "Well, that's one of the reasons you came out here, wasn't it? To get back to work at home."

"I came out here because Jeff asked me to and because I had the time off." He tossed his phone onto the table.

"When do you have to let them know?"

"In the next few days." Despite his protest about coincidences, he didn't look entirely convinced in his statement. "The timing's suspicious."

"Or maybe they really need you back." She could play devil's advocate when she needed to.

"They've gotten along perfectly fine without me for four months, Mabel. That request has nothing to do with my abilities as a prosecutor."

"Someone wants you gone."

"Someone wants me gone." He looked at her. "You know what that means."

"That you have a decision to make." It hurt, despite knowing it was coming. It still hurt knowing she was probably going to be on the losing end of this choice.

He walked around the counter, caught her shoulders, and turned her to face him. "It means someone in this town got to my boss in New York. I told him before I left that I wouldn't be back until the job was done. We've hit a nerve. We've made someone nervous, which means we're on the right track." He drew her forward, pressed his lips to her forehead. "We're close, Mabel. We're going to find her. We're going to find all of them."

"Jeff, you've met Mabel before." Paul couldn't remember the last time he'd introduced anyone—let alone someone he cared about—to one of his friends. "And this is her daughter, Keeley."

"Hi," Keeley said and gave a quick wave.

"Good to see you again, Ms. Reynolds." Jeff offered his hand to Mabel, smiled at Kee. "Hello, Keeley. This is my wife, Lindsay, and our son, Max." He rested a hand on the little boy's shoulder standing between his parents.

For an instant, Paul was transported back to second grade, shortly after he'd met Jeff. Max looked exactly like his father with his round face, dark brown hair, and wide, excited eyes. His superhero T-shirt carried stains from what must have been their early lunch tour of the half-dozen food trucks lined up down North Broadway.

All around them, people, families, children, enjoyed the mild warmth and sunshine, filling the red metal tables beneath an iron awning. Squeals of happiness echoed from the other side of the park where the fountain spewed cold water onto cartwheel-turning kids as they raced around.

"Paul." Lindsay, her brown hair tied up in a messy knot, grabbed both Paul's hands and drew him in for a warm hug. "It's been too long." She patted his back before releasing him and turning those high-beam eyes of happiness on him. "Hope you don't mind me tagging along. You look good! Hi!" She offered her hand to Mabel. "It's very nice to meet you." She side-eyed Paul, a twinkle in her eye. "Very, very nice indeed."

Paul could feel his face heating up.

"Good to see you again, Max," Paul said in an effort to distract everyone. "I bet you don't really remember me, do you?"

Max looked up at his father. "We Zoomed at Christmas," he said finally and gave Paul a wary smile. "You're Dad's friend."

"Your dad is my best friend," Paul confirmed. "We met when we were about your age."

"Wow, really?" Max's eyes nearly popped out of his head. "That's a long time ago."

"Ouch," Jeff laughed, but Paul could hear the tension. Apparently, Lindsay could as well because she rested a hand on her husband's arm and squeezed. Paul glanced back at Mabel, hoping she could read the plea in his eyes.

"Hey, Max?" Mabel reached down and took hold of Keeley's hand. "We were about to go over to the new playground just over there." She pointed behind them, to where a mishmash of colorful hills and bumps surrounded a lime-green tree house-like structure, along with a giant lime-green tunnel slide. "You and your mom want to come with us?"

"Can I, Dad?"

"Go on. Just no more ice cream, okay?" Jeff said quickly. "You have a one-puke-a-day limit."

"He says that as if he had to do the cleaning up," Lindsay teased. There was something unfamiliar in her eyes …. A warning maybe? Or was that … fear?

"Cool octopus," Max said, pointing at Keeley's keychain hanging from the belt loop of her jeans.

"Thanks. My friend Blake gave it to me. It's special. Come on." Keeley held out her hand and let go of Mabel's. "I'll race you!"

"Aw, man. I'm gonna puke again," Max grumbled, but took off, nonetheless.

"You guys talk," Mabel called over her shoulder as she and Lindsay followed the kids. "We'll keep an eye on them."

"So." Jeff shoved his hands into the front pockets of his slacks and rocked back on his heels as they watched the women and kids walk away. "I didn't see this coming at all."

"Didn't see what coming?" Paul feigned ignorance.

"If I didn't know better, I'd think Mabel Reynolds put a spell on you. Happy to be sitting in the front row of this one." Jeff inclined his head toward the path circling the expansive block's long park. "Let's walk."

"I was hoping you'd be less stressed than you were at the press conference," Paul said. "You don't seem to be."

"I was right about being followed." Jeff's voice cut through the cool breeze like a knife. "I caught two different cars behind me while driving, and then one showed up and parked across the street from the house."

"Is that why Lindsay's with you?"

Jeff nodded. "Didn't want to leave her at home alone. I've convinced her to take Max out of school for another week—head back to her parents. I don't want them here. Not now." He reached into his back pocket, pulled out folded piece of paper, and handed it over. "Found this in my car Friday after work."

Paul flipped it open and saw an eerily similar photo to the one Mabel had found in her car at the hospital. Only this one was of Lindsay and Max. The words *Leave It Alone* had been written in the same dark red ink.

The nausea churning in his stomach was tempered only by the rage. "Knife in the driver's seat?"

Jeff balked. "How did you—?"

"Mabel got one, too, of Keeley." He couldn't have hidden the rage in his voice even if he'd tried. "They stabbed a knife through her throat."

Jeff swore, wiped a nervous hand across his forehead. "I'm not a coward, Paul."

"I know you aren't," Paul responded immediately.

"This has me scared. Tell me you heard back from your contact at the Marshall's office about where Dean Samuels is?"

"I did, but she's got nothing." Paul hated to tell him. "I'm sorry. She can't figure out how he got removed from the system or why

320

they can't find him. And when she tried to press for answers, she got waved off by one of her superiors. Looks like we're on our own."

"Shit." Jeff dropped his head back and sighed. "I was afraid you were going to say that. I don't know how far I can take this, Paul. I think someone broke into my office. Can't prove it, of course. It's just a feeling and there was this odd … smell. Spicy. Strange."

"Cloves," Paul suggested, and Jeff's eyes widened when he nodded. "Security footage?"

"System blipped out." He paused. "And by 'broke in,' I mean they got in. With a key."

"Same thing happened to me." Paul wanted Jeff to know he wasn't alone. The only difference was, Paul had fallen into a support system that gave him a feeling of protection. And more than a boost of invincibility. "I've got some help running a name down. We think we have an idea as to who's responsible."

"The DA authorized a task force?" Jeff sounded shocked.

"No," Paul said slowly. "I found one on my own." It was on the tip of his tongue to offer their help to Jeff's case, but he didn't want to get ahead of himself. Or presume that Mabel's friends would be willing to stick their necks out even further than they already had.

"If this was just me, I'd keep the faith," Jeff said. "But whoever these guys are, they're coming after my family, Paul. What the hell did we step into?"

"I don't think you'd believe me if I told you."

Jeff stopped walking and grabbed Paul's arm. "You getting somewhere?"

"You really want to know?"

"I have to know. I have to know something good's going to come out of these sleepless nights." The stress was showing on his friend. "Tell me what you can."

Paul broke it down into the simplest of statements, from the discovery of the meaning of the symbols found on the photographs, to the possible involvement of Young & Fairbanks, right down to the secret latch on the gate at the Tenado estate. "You ever heard of something called The Circle of the Red Lily?"

"No." Exhaustion crept into Jeff's voice. "What is it?"

"Short version? Some secret society kind of thing that has their hands in these disappearances. Including Eva Hudson."

"The girl from the hospital?"

"Yeah. There are ... similarities, ones that connect right back to Melanie Dennings." Probably beyond. Paul paused. "You going to be okay?"

"I'll be better once Lindsay and Max are out of the line of fire. I need to know they're safe. I'll move into a hotel. Stay away from the house." His eyes sharpened. "Sons of bitches stopped us from getting Max a dog for his birthday. Now isn't the time to have a new animal around the house."

Sons of bitches, indeed, Paul thought.

Paul wanted to tell Jeff what he suspected, that the Circle's reach extended far beyond LA, possibly all the way to New York, but what good would that do? It would only add to Jeff's increasing stress. "We should consider working together under the table," he suggested. "I know you wanted to keep this separate—"

"I'm not the one who wanted that, and you know what? I think I'm done kowtowing to the DA. She knows we should be working together. It's time for me to push it. If she wants to fire me because of it, so be it. I'll be free to do what I want then."

Now *that* sounded like the Jeff he remembered. "Whatever you want to do, I've got your back. Always have, always will." He grabbed his friend's hand and squeezed. "You're my family. I wouldn't be here without you. I don't think I've ever told you that before." He turned, looked across the park, and his gaze immediately landed on Mabel, standing beside Lindsay, as they watched their kids race up and down the orange-and-green hills of the playground. "We're in this together."

"I didn't realize just how lucky I've been," Jeff said as they made their way over to the women. "I've lived long enough to see you take the fall. Congratulations."

"I don't know that's what this thing with Mabel is," he admitted.

"That's okay. I do." Jeff's phone rang as they rounded the corner. "Crap. I need to take this." He turned and headed toward the steps to the sidewalk and street. "Might be a lead on Dean Samuels. I'll catch up to you, yeah?"

"Yeah." The crowds had thinned and had flanked out around the food trucks. As Paul walked over to Mabel and Lindsay, he turned and looked back. Jeff gave him a wave and smile.

The explosion blew them both off their feet.

Mabel's gasp was silenced by the ferocity of the explosion. She ducked for an instant, covered her head, then immediately launched herself forward, desperately searching for Keeley. A balloon of smoke and flame pushed up into the air like a mushroom cloud. Black. Thick. Rumbling. The smell of sulfur filled the air, permeating her nose, and she coughed, choked, and shoved herself up.

Screams erupted. Footsteps echoed all around, dull against her ears.

"Mom! Mama! Mom!"

Mabel spun in an incoherent circle, unable to focus as the world around her blurred.

"Keeley!" Mabel tried to scream, but it didn't come out any louder than a choked whisper. "Kee?" She tried again, turning and searching. "Keeley?!"

She shoved her hair out of her face and saw Lindsay Chandler pushing herself up off the ground. Mabel raced over, crouched, grabbed her arms. "Are you okay?"

"Yeah." Lindsay's voice sounded as if she was speaking under water, but when she nodded, Mabel helped her sit up. "What was that? What happened? Where's Max?"

People swarmed around them, racing in various directions, calling and shouting while others screamed. It took Mabel a moment to identify the other smell beneath the noxious aroma. The metallic smell of blood.

She *had* to find Keeley. And where was Paul? Her heart constricted.

"I need to find Max," Lindsay insisted. "Jeff can help. Where's Jeff?" She stumbled to her feet beside Mabel and clung to her. "Jeff?"

Mabel's heart tripped over itself as she looked back to where Jeff and Paul had been standing. A place that was now engulfed in flames and chaos.

"God," she whispered brokenly as she caught the sob behind her hand. "Paul." She spun again. "Keeley!" Mabel's heart began to beat again as she spotted Keeley, there, in the distance, clutching little Max against her as she stood in the middle of the chaos.

Children were screaming and sobbing as parents rushed toward them.

"Max?" Lindsay's broken whisper scraped against Mabel's heart. "I can't see him. Do you see him?"

"I do. I see him." Mabel grabbed her hand. "He's with Kee. I think they're okay. Kee!" She didn't wait for an answer before ripping herself free and running full steam toward her daughter and Max.

"Mama." Keeley grabbed for her, her hands frantic. "Mama, what's happening?" Her little girl eyes were wide and spinning with shock. "I'm scared."

"You're okay!" Mabel did a quick assessment, didn't see any injuries, only the fear shining in her eyes. "Max?" Mabel crouched down, checked him as well. "You okay?"

"I want my Mom and Dad." Tears streamed down his face, but he had his hands locked tight around Keeley's.

"Your mom's right over there, see?" Mabel pointed back to where Lindsay remained, the shock setting in as she began to sag. Mabel pulled her phone out of her bag, dialed the only number she could think of. "Quinn."

"Mabel?" His voice raised. "What's that noise? Where the hell are you? What's going on?"

"Grand Park. There's been some kind of explosion." She held Keeley close and turned one way, then another. There were so many faces, so many people, nothing made sense. In the distance, sirens blared. "Quinn, I don't know where Paul is."

"What about Keeley?" He demanded. "Are you two okay?"

"We're okay. Paul was meeting a friend, Jeff Chandler. He's here with his wife and son." Tears burned her throat and eyes. "Quinn." She lowered her voice and hoped he could still hear her. "They were close to the explosion. I can't find them. Either of them. Can you—"

"We're on our way. Stay where you are. As soon as police are on scene, you find them and stay with them. You and Keeley both, okay? I'm hanging up. We'll be there soon."

Mabel's hand shook as she shoved her phone back in her bag.

"Paul," she whispered as her vision finally began to clear. She steeled herself to look back to the fire and saw him, finally, moving, struggling to push to his feet.

"I have to check on Jeff," he yelled her way, his gaze raking over her and Keeley to ensure they were safe. She could barely hear him over the frantic noise. "Stay there! Wait for me."

Her knees folded and she sank to the ground, holding Keeley and Max close, relief overwhelming her. "He's okay."

"I want my Dad," Max wailed. "I want my Mom and Dad!"

"Max? Maxy, baby, I'm here." Lindsay stumbled over to them, hauled Max into her arms as she reached out a hand for Keeley. "Thank you," she whispered to a confused, dazed little girl.

"Where's Daddy? Daddy!" Max screamed as Lindsay picked him up and carried him away in search of Jeff.

"I want to go home, Mom." Keeley wrapped her arms around Mabel's waist and squeezed. "I want to go home."

"Me, too, baby." Mabel scanned the still spinning crowd. Food truck workers spilled out of their vehicles, checking on people, handing out bottles of water and damp cloths. On the other side of the flames, Mabel saw the spinning lights of the fire trucks, their sirens dimmed by the continuous shrieking of the park's visitors.

"Quinn's on his way, Kee," Mabel insisted. "He's coming, okay?"

"Okay," she mumbled. "Where's Paul?"

"He'll be here in a minute, Kee." She'd seen the fear—the fierce love—in his eyes the minute he knew they were safe. She feared for Jeff, knowing how close he'd been to the explosion.

She looked down at her daughter. When she lifted her head and looked into the smoke, she froze.

It wasn't Paul standing there, a small distance from them. Paul didn't wear heavy boots or black clothing. He didn't have a shaved head, a round face, or cold, empty, calculating eyes.

Those familiar, empty eyes.

Eyes that were looking only at her, not her daughter.

Mabel clutched at Keeley, spun around, and saw one, two—no, three—other men, moving in on them.

She crouched, dropped her bag on the ground, and drew Keeley into a tight hug. "I need you to be brave, okay, Kee? You remember what Blake taught you? What he told you?"

Keeley blinked, and tears plopped onto her round cheeks. "You mean about running until I'm safe?"

"Yes. And you promised to do whatever I say." Mabel caught her face between her hands and fought back the tears. "Can you see Paul? You see where he is?"

Keeley looked over her shoulder. Paul was leaning over Jeff, watching as medics arrived on the scene. Mabel knew he wouldn't be able to hear them over the sirens, even if they cried out.

She turned Keeley back to face her. "I love you, baby." She pressed her lips to her child's forehead, and when Keeley tried to catch hold, Mabel slipped her hand down and unclipped the octopus keychain from Keeley's belt loop and shoved it in her pocket. "Whatever happens, you remember that I love you more than anything. You go to Paul. You run to him right now as fast as you can, do you hear me?" It was the hardest thing she'd ever done when she pushed Keeley away.

"Go!" she yelled at a terrified Keeley. "Go right now! Go!" she continued yelling at Keeley's back as the first hand locked around her upper arm.

Looking up, she saw the red welts scraping his wrist and knew she'd been the one to put them there. She could feel the bruises forming already, beneath his tight grip.

"You were warned."

She recognized his voice. It was the man from Eva's room.

"You can't have her," Mabel said firmly in a shaking voice as the man dragged her to her feet, as she watched her daughter race into a throng of people. Into safety.

A strange calm settled upon her. And then she felt it: her twin's essence wrapping around her, holding her.

"We'll settle for you." The man yanked her around, dragged her beside him as she struggled, but then something pricked in the back of her neck. Something sharp and cold and … her knees buckled. She sagged forward but was held up and dragged into the smoke.

She fought to stay awake, to get one more look at Keeley, to see her daughter one last time. To see Paul.

Paul.

Mabel's sob was lost to the darkness.

She'd never told him …

He'd never know how much he was loved.

"Kee?" Paul didn't understand what was happening when he saw Mabel's daughter racing toward him as he held his bunched-up jacket against Jeff's head to stem the blood flow.

He felt as if he'd stepped into an inferno. Flames billowed behind him, had singed his side, and his friend lay flat on his back, splayed out and unmoving, Lindsay on his other side, holding his hand. Max was huddled beside her, rocking back and forth as he sobbed and asked his dad to wake up.

Paul yelled and waved his arms for a paramedic to take over from him, as emergency services spilled into the park.

"Hold this here!" he told Lindsay as he had her take over applying pressure to Jeff's head wound.

"Paul!" Keeley's cries had him turning toward her as she ran to him. He saw her tears first, heard the sobs next, as he caught the girl in his arms and swung her up.

"Mama said you're safe. She sent me to you to be safe."

"Where is she?"

He'd been so bloody torn when he'd first seen Mabel and Keeley, had assured himself that they were unhurt. He'd wanted to go to them immediately, but if he'd had've left Jeff, his best friend would have bled out. Now with the paramedics taking over from Lindsay, they kept the pressure. Jeff's wife was shoved back and out of the way, grabbing for her son as they watched, wrapped around one another as the emergency unit tried to save Jeff's life.

With Keeley's arms locked around his neck, he cradled the back of her head in his hand, spinning, looking, searching … "Did you see where your mom went?"

She shook her head. "She told me to run."

Her hiccupping explanation did nothing to calm the panic rising in Paul. He headed toward the last place he'd last seen her, but there was nothing but damp grass, Mabel's bag, and …

327

Footprints. He'd seen those same prints outside Eva Hudson's closet when he'd retrieved her belongings for Keeley.

Dread reached up a clawed hand and cut off the air in his lungs.

Additional fire engines and EMT vehicles skidded to a halt amidst the patrol cars screeching, their sirens still wailing.

"Here!" He held up a hand to the additional EMTs. "Here, over here!" He raced back to Jeff, balanced Keeley on his knee when he knelt down. "Jeff? Jeff, I'm here, man." He hadn't prayed since he was fifteen years old, but he was praying now. "Jeff, do you hear me?"

Jeff moaned. It was slight, faint, barely audible, but Lindsay and Max both cried out in relief. His fingers twitched.

"Over here!" Paul shouted and stood up to move back so the paramedics could get to his friend.

"Where's Mom?" Keeley whimpered. "I want Mom."

"So do I, baby." He held her tighter, every cell in his body screaming in agony and frustration. He turned to Lindsay and squeezed her hand as she watched the paramedic bandage Jeff's head and get him onto a spinal board. "I've got to go. Tell him …"

Lindsay spared him a glance—squeezed his hand in return. "Go. He'll understand. Go get your family."

Keeley's arms tightened around his neck, sobs escaping.

Paul held her close, fierce but tender. "We'll find her, I promise, okay? And you know what I've always told you about my promises?"

She nodded, her hot tears damp against his skin.

"What have I told you?"

"That you always keep them."

"That's right." He pressed a kiss to her temple, carried her over to the familiar SUV that skidded to a stop on the other side of the patrol cars. "I'm going to find your mom. And I'm going to bring her home."

"I don't give a damn what the DA has scheduled for today," Paul said to the first assistant Kent was finally able to get on the phone. He stood at the back of Quinn's SUV, one hand on Keeley's shoulder. Riley held the little girl in her arms and rocked her like an infant. "You tell the DA I'll be in her office within the hour. If she's not there, inform her I'm going to rain holy hell on her administration with whatever media contacts I have. You understand me?"

"Paul," Riley's warning tone had him lowering his voice but not his inflection.

"One hour. Tell her." Paul hung up. "Where are we on the property searches?" He asked Riley.

"I don't know." She shook her head, glanced over his shoulder as a car door slammed behind him. "I'm sorry. Quinn got Mabel's call, and we got here as fast as we could."

"I'm here." Laurel dashed up behind Paul. "What's happened? What's going on?" She surged around him and grabbed hold of Keeley, pulling her free of Riley's hold to get her own arms around the girl. "Sorry. I just needed this." She held out her hand to Riley who took it eagerly. "I need to hold her. Oh, my God, Kee."

"I want my mom." Each and every time she said it, she broke off another piece of Paul's heart.

"We'll find her, Kee." Laurel glared at Paul. "Won't we?"

"Paul will," Keeley sniffed and nodded. "He promised."

"We can get her home to Sutton," Laurel said. "Then we'll come back."

"I don't want any of you here," Paul said in a tone that made Keeley jump. "I want you all back in Temple House where it's safe. No arguments."

"Paul," Quinn called him over. Paul blocked out Keeley's cry for him when he walked away. "What the actual hell happened?" the detective demanded.

Wallace, coming at them from a different direction, stopped to talk to the EMTs who loaded Jeff onto a stretcher and wheeled him to one of the nearby ambulances.

"Lindsay needs to be with him," Paul told Wallace the second he arrived and pointed to where Lindsay and Max were huddled together. "Please, get her to the hospital? And don't leave her and Max alone." They'd taken Mabel, probably because they thought she knew something. He wasn't going to take the chance they thought Lindsay did, as well. "Get approval for a police guard. Two officers, minimum. You get any pushback from your lieutenant, you tell them the DA ordered it."

"No pushback, Paul," Quinn said. "My father's en route right now. He'll be here in a few. He'll secure the order."

"Good, yeah, okay." Paul forced himself to watch as Jeff was wheeled past him. His face was covered in blood beneath the oxygen mask. They'd put his neck in a brace and tied him down to a board. "Is he—?"

"He's stable," Wallace assured him. "They're calling it a miracle, but they've got him stable. They don't diagnose, Paul, but they're pretty sure there's spinal damage and burns. Really bad burns. If he'd been any closer to that garbage can—"

"Is that what it was?" Paul demanded.

"Wallace, go take care of Lindsay and Max," Quinn ordered his partner. "You need to take a breath and tell me what the fuck happened, Paul." Quinn's voice was as sharp as glass. "What did you see?"

"Not a damned thing." Paul ran his face down his hands. "I was walking away to meet Mabel and Keeley. Jeff had taken a call, moved toward the stairs to take it. I turned around and—" He made an explosion sigh with his hands. "It went straight up and out. Blew me off my feet. I hit my head. Must have. I was out for a minute or so." He touched fingers against the back of his head. The tacky substance on his fingers glistened red. "That answers that."

"Holy hell, Paul. Medic!" Quinn yelled so loud Paul felt it reverberate through his skull. "Probably got yourself a concussion."

"Too damned bad. I need to get back to Keeley."

"Riley and Laurel are taking her home now. Look." Quinn pointed behind them. Sure enough, Laurel was leading them to her car.

"They need to be followed," Paul said. "I need you to trust me, Quinn. Give them a patrol car, please."

"I don't know—"

"That explosion wasn't just meant for me and Jeff. It was also a distraction. They came for Mabel and Kee."

"You sure?"

"I'm sure. We need that property information now, Quinn. We need to find her, and fast, because if we don't—"

"She'll have vanished. Just like the rest of them."

"Mr. Flynn." DA Eichorn's irritated tone didn't come close to breaking through the rage surging through Paul's system. He stalked into her office without waiting to be announced, Quinn and Chief Burton right behind him. "I think you're under the misguided perception that you're in charge. Summoning me into my office on a Sunday borders on insubordination."

"Oh, summoning you is going to be the least of my offenses." Paul looked over his shoulder as the Chief closed the door. Paul swung on the DA, tempted to tell her it was a good thing the desk stood between them. "You called my boss in New York, didn't you?"

"I—" DA Eichorn's eyes shifted. It was the tell he'd picked up on when he'd asked her about Sumatra. "I thought it best that you be given the option of returning to your own cases."

Paul was poised to pounce, but Quinn stepped in, placing a steadying hand on Paul's chest. "Losing it and getting arrested isn't going to get Mabel back."

"Mabel Reynolds?" The DA looked flummoxed. "Get her back from where? What does she have to do with anything?"

Everything, Paul thought desperately. "We'll get back to Mabel in a minute." Paul had to remember that Quinn was right. He needed to stay calm and focused. For Mabel and Keeley. "You heard about the bomb in the park?"

"Yes, of course. What do we know?" She tugged nervously on the hem of her jacket. "Chief?"

"Multiple pipe bombs in various garbage cans. They went off at the same time to create one large explosion. Evidence is being collected," Chief Burton continued. "It'll get to the lab soon, but we suspect they was set off by a remote detonator."

"They waited until Jeff was just close enough," Paul seethed. "They nearly blew him straight into the afterlife."

"Jeff Chandler?" DA Eichorn paled. "He's been injured?"

"Have you not been briefed on this situation, Madame District Attorney?" Quinn asked. "The bomb went off *in* Jeff Chandler's face. He's currently listed in critical condition and waiting on spinal surgery. There were at least twenty-three other injuries. No fatalities so far." He looked to Paul. "And one kidnapping."

"Kidnapping?"

"The bomb was a distraction," Paul said slowly, deliberately. "They came for Mabel."

"They?" the DA spat. "They *who*?"

"The Circle," Paul said simply.

Her reaction—the way her face drained of color, the sudden glassy look in her eyes, the fact she stumbled back into her chair and sat like a stone—was precisely why Paul and insisted Quinn and Chief Burton accompany him to this meeting. He'd wanted witnesses to what he'd suspected.

"What do you know?" Quinn demanded of her.

Eichorn shook her head, lifted a trembling hand to her throat. "Nothing. N-nothing. I just … get calls. I'd heard rumors, rumblings, all these years I thought The Circle was an urban legend, a myth—"

"That *myth* kidnapped Mabel Reynolds from Grand Park a little more than an hour ago." Paul made certain to accentuate each syllable. "You're going to tell us—"

"Surely, she doesn't know anything," Chief Burton said. "If she did, she'd also know we could bring her up on instant charges and have her removed from office."

The DA visibly swallowed. "You wouldn't."

"Try me, Johanna," Chief Burton said. "You're not going anywhere unless we can get some progress on this case—an olive branch, if you will. Evidence that you're helping us. That you're on our side."

"But—"

The chief was not in the placating mood. "You're. Not. Going. Anywhere. Not for a good long while. You're going to stay here, where you're useful, and then we'll discuss your future." He turned away from her. "Paul?"

"Sir?" Paul's feet were getting antsy to kick something.

"Tell her what you want."

"An official task force," he spat out and watched her eyes narrow. "Of my choosing. Paid for by the city. Top dollar because we're going to be working pretty much around the clock until this Circle of yours is eradicated. You will *not* oppose any of my appointments, and you will *not* install anyone I don't approve of. Detectives Quinn and Osterman will be the first on board."

"Is that all?" The DA had gotten her voice back. She glared at the three of them.

"No," Paul ground out between clenched teeth. "As of now, I'm taking over the Dean Samuels investigation. The wrongful conviction, the search for him—all of it. It's mine now, as I have no remaining doubt it's tied to this Circle crap you're a part of. I want all of this in writing, within the hour, certified, witnessed, and filed with the LA superior court as backup." He stepped forward, leaned his hands on the desk. "They won't like it, will they? The Circle?" He lowered his voice. "A puppet can't serve two masters, and rest assured, where these cases are concerned, you're now mine."

"You have no idea what you're dealing with," she whispered desperately. "*Who* you're dealing with. You think I'm the only one they've got locked in? They're everywhere. *Everywhere.* And you won't see them coming. Not until it's too late."

"You'd better hope you're wrong," Quinn said. "Otherwise, they'll be coming for you, too."

Paul felt some satisfaction at how hard the DA swallowed. "Don't answer your phone," he told her. "Don't open your door. Not until that order is in the Chief's hands. Then you can try to convince them you're still on their side if you want. Now," he leaned closer and felt the chief and Quinn move in behind her, "tell me where she is."

"Mabel Reynolds?" She shook her head. "I don't know. I don't!" she cried when his eyes darkened. "They exist in a spider's web. Everything's tied to everything else. You can pull one thread, and the rest stays in place. Wherever she is, wherever they've taken her, there's nothing you can do. It's going to be up to her to get out."

CHAPTER SEVENTEEN

MABEL awoke with the worst hangover of her life. Everything around her spun and tilted and pitched. Her stomach rolled before she opened her eyes. She was cold. So cold she shivered hard enough that her bones threatened to snap.

Shoving herself over and onto her back, she tried to take deep breaths. Her chest hurt. Her lungs burned. Everything ached. Lying still, she forced herself to relax, to flex her muscles, moving from her feet up to her legs, to her hips, her chest, her arms … her hands.

She needed to be ready to flee.

She heard the trickle of water—faint, just loud enough to make her have to pee. She shifted and squirmed, testing out her limbs. Only when she was completely relaxed, her head throbbing, did she force open her eyes.

It was odd, she thought, as her mind took in the dark ceiling overhead, and she waited for her other senses to kick in, one after another. The cold remained, but there was a smell, a stench she couldn't quite identify. Sour. Decaying. Stomach-churning.

She shoved her hands under her, started to sit up, then froze.

Her hands were free. They hadn't tied her up!

Fear surged through her.

Why hadn't they tied her up? That seemed a risky thing to do unless …

A squeak erupted somewhere behind her, and she scrambled to her knees. A sliver of light arced through the narrow slats of the window halfway up the wall. A wall that stretched up and up and up and proved with one glance there was no way out. That way, at least.

Her fingers dug into damp stone and dirt.

Something skittered over her hand. She yelped and jumped back as a rat made its own desperate attempt to escape. She snatched her hands to her chest but knocked against something soft and heavy as she did.

The fear that crawled into her throat lodged like a stone as she turned her head.

She stared into dead, white eyes.

"*Eva.*" Her sob echoed against the walls of the room, bouncing back on her like an endless drum pounding against her ears.

She touched a hand to the bare, almost-frozen leg. The hospital gown Eva wore was grimy and torn, a depressing shroud of death. Bits of tubing hung from her immobile arms, the bandage around her head a stark against the tiny bite marks marring her once beautiful face.

Mabel let the tears stream free. She'd known, she'd always known, deep down, that Eva was dead the second she'd been taken from the hospital. But seeing her now …

Seeing her now filled Mabel with a rage that felt like a fire stoking in the depths of hell.

Mabel.

"Sylvie?" Mabel shoved to her feet, ignored the intense wave of sickness that came over her as she struggled to catch her breath. She planted her hands on her thighs, forced herself to take measured breaths again. "Goddamn it, Sylvie. Don't play games with me. If you're here, be here!"

Please, she silently sobbed, even as the reality of her sister's eerie presence and warmth sank in on her.

In that moment, a moment that was eight years in the making, she finally accepted the truth.

Sylvie was gone.

Protect yourself. Quick. Sylvie's voice sounded anxious.

With what? Mabel thought frantically, her eyes filled with the sight of Eva sprawled on the damp ground. With …. She gasped, her mind flying back to being in Eva's hospital room, standing there with Eva's rabbit. Something the nurse had said …. What was it?

Mabel dived forward, forced every swirling emotion down where she could get it. She shoved Eva over, ran her hand into the crook of Eva's arm. Her hand wrapped around the IV needle that was still lodged in the dead woman's arm. She yanked it free and palmed it just as laughter echoed from the other side of the hall.

A door with a small, square, barred window snapped open. Just wide enough to poke her fingers through.

"Takes a real big man to taunt a woman from the other side of a locked door." Mabel's head continued to spin. Whatever drug they'd given her, it hadn't worn off completely yet. She couldn't let that matter. She needed to get home. To Keeley. To … to Paul.

To hell with his fears. She should have taken the chance and told him she loved him. She should have screamed it from the top of Temple House. She would do just that. Just as soon as she was home.

She moved her hand to her pocket, felt Keeley's keychain brush against her fingers.

Hope surged.

That's the spirit.

Hope surged around the anger—anger she'd bottled up for eight years. Anger that her twin, her other half, had left her behind.

The hope soon overwhelmed all the anger. She wasn't alone. Sylvie was here. And so, she thought as she touched the plastic octopus pressed into her hand, was her family.

Mabel stepped back as the lock on the door clanged. She would not, would *not*, look at Eva. Doing so felt like a surrender of fate, and she would not lie down beside this girl and die herself. She had too much to live for. Too much she wanted to …

She'd stopped living eight years ago when her sister had disappeared. But she was ready to live now. Just when it all might be coming to an end.

When the door opened all the way, and the man stepped through, she planted her feet. "What do you want?"

"Where is it?" Orson Berwick's voice sounded like his throat had been scraped raw by sandpaper.

"Where's what?" The desperation in her voice couldn't have been faked, could it? "The invitations? Her computer? They're with the authorities."

"No, they're not."

Her lips twitched in humor she didn't feel. "I didn't say *which* authorities."

His smile was slow and menacing, as if he was taking extraordinary pleasure in drawing out her terror. "You're lying."

"Am I?" She spoke as if from outside her own body. She had no desire to taunt him, to challenge him, but each word kept her breathing. At least for another few minutes.

He yelled over his shoulder, something in another language, and she heard skittering footsteps, a slamming door. And then silence.

"We're alone now."

He stepped further inside, shoved his booted foot against Eva like she was a sack of discarded garbage.

Mabel's lungs burned with rage.

Get past him. Put those defense classes to use, and get past him!

Mabel gasped as a flickering of white light vibrated behind her would-be attacker. For an instant, she swore she saw …

"Are you going to sacrifice me to the Circle?" She tightened her hold on the small, thin needle pressing into her palm.

"You're not worthy of sacrifice," Orson breathed. His biceps bulged as he flexed his arms. "Just like she wasn't. So many aren't. Only the few are Chosen."

"Was my sister Chosen?" Mabel demanded.

His blank face told her what she couldn't bear to know: He wasn't going to tell her.

"Even if you get out," Orson told her, "there's nowhere for you to go. Except down. In the end, that's where you all end up."

She could smell death on him. Putrid, rotting death and the cloves.

Her stomach churned.

Bile rose in her throat.

Her foot caught on the rat, sent it scurrying as she backed up against the wall. He came closer yet. Mabel's breath came in fast, panicked pants as he stood over her.

And smiled.

***

"Paul!"

He'd no sooner walked through the lobby doors of Temple House than he found himself locked in Keeley's tiny arms.

"Hey there." He crouched down, wiped at her tears. "I'm back. It's okay."

"Where is she?" Keeley demanded. "Did you find her? Where's Mom?"

"I haven't found her. Not yet. But I will." If it was the last thing he did. He picked her up, astonished at how easily she fit in his arms. "What are you doing down here?"

"She didn't want to stay upstairs," Sutton said. "Riley and Laurel are at Cass's. I told Kee we'd wait in the lobby until you got back, then go back up. Right, Kee?"

"But I want to stay with Paul," Keeley said. "I want to help find Mom."

Paul looked over Sutton's shoulder to where Blake was standing by the stairs. He was as still as stone, hands fisted at his side, the granite look in his eyes chilling. "Tell me what I can do?"

"Meet me in Cass's apartment," Paul told him. "I'm hoping she'll have a place for us to start." He set Keeley back on her feet. "Kee, I need you to go with Sutton. I promise, if I leave again, I will come see you first, okay? I will let you know what's going on."

She held out her hand, pinky out. "Pinky swear?"

He linked his finger with hers. "Pinky swear. That's even more important than a promise."

Keeley's chin trembled as she let Sutton lead her away. Blake started up ahead of them, then stopped, spun around, caught Keeley's shoulders. "Where's your keychain?"

"My ... oh." She patted her chest, checked her pockets. "I lost it. Oh, no. I'm sorry!"

"It's okay." Blake sat down on the stair above her. "When did you last have it?"

"Max spotted it at the park," she said. "Remember?" she asked Paul. "He said it was cool."

"Yeah," Paul said. "I remember."

Blake touched a hand to Keeley's cheek. "You might just have given us what we need." He raced up the stairs as Paul followed.

"What?" Paul demanded while Blake pounded on Cass's door.

When it swung open, Laurel scowled at them. "I know we're in panic mode, but—"

"Those keychains I gave the kids," Blake said. "They're tracking devices."

Paul felt a bubble of relief form within the dread. "You think Mabel has it?"

"Keeley doesn't," Blake countered. "That's good enough for me."

"Mabel sent Keeley to you," Laurel closed the door behind them. "Keeley told us on the drive home. She said not to stop until she reached you because you were safe. She trusted you with her."

"And Mabel's trusting all of us to find her," Paul announced as Cass left Nox typing furiously at their computer terminal. "Okay. Cass, hey. Where are we on the property searches?"

"Question first," Cass asked. "Did you really threaten to expose the DA to The Circle and the media?"

"Yes."

"Good. I hate that bitch." Cass stepped forward and hugged him, shocking everyone, including Paul, into silence. "You just moved up the list of my favorite people. What do you want to know?"

"I need a terminal," Blake said.

"Nox?" Cass called over her shoulder.

"Got one," Nox called and waved him over.

"How many of Young & Fairbanks' clients own property in and around Los Angeles?" Paul asked. "Specifically around the Tenado estate?"

"Bring up what we've got, Nox," Cass ordered.

"Here." Laurel pushed a bottle into his hand. "It's water. Drink. And take these." She dropped a pair of aspirins into his palm. "You think Quinn didn't call? You knocked your head."

"Thanks." He swallowed the pills with one shot. "Cass? What am I looking at?"

"A mess. We're looking at close to twenty thousand properties to start with." She shook her head. "We're trying to narrow it down—"

"Behind Tenado's house," Paul said. "Who owns that?"

"A Brighton Cervantes."

"Cervantes," Laurel snorted. "Like *The Count of Monte Cristo* Cervantes?"

"Gotta be an alias," Riley said from where she was sitting silently on the sofa, nursing a beer. "There's no Cervantes lily by any chance, is there?"

Paul froze.

He looked at Laurel.

Her eyes went wide, and together, they spun to face Cass.

"Shit." Cass shook her head. "I should have thought of that. Nox. New search parameter. How many red lily species did we say there were?"

"Seventeen, including Sumatra," Riley said.

"I want a list of all properties with any of those species used in a company or property holder's name. Now, Nox." She clicked through screens as information shot in.

"Blake?" Paul called. "Is the tracking device pinging?"

"It should be." Blake pounded a fist against the table before he started typing again. "That chip's supposed to work against most jammers. And it's not showing anywhere."

Fear lodged solidly in Paul's throat. He was *not* going to fail. Not in any way.

"Okay, we're down to a hundred and seventeen properties within Los Angeles with a connection to a species of lilies," Nox yelled. "How do you want them?"

"By acreage," Paul said. "They need land to bury bodies."

"We're looking for Mabel, not her body," Laurel reminded him.

"I know what I'm looking for," Paul said almost dismissively. "Nox? Largest lot to smallest, please."

"Yeah, working on it!"

"Dammit!" Blake muttered. "There's nothing. Not a blip."

Paul looked out the window.

The sun was going down. It would be dark soon. She'd be out there. Alone.

"Stop focusing on what you can't change," Laurel said quietly from behind him. "Look at the screens. Think about what you're seeing. Is there anything that makes any kind of sense to you?"

He shook his head as the property listings came up.

Sure enough, the one behind the Tenado estate was on the top of the list.

"Owner?" He pointed to it.

"Red Carpet, Inc.," Nox told him.

"Is that it?" Riley said. "Did we find it?"

"I don't … know." Mabel's words to him this morning came surging back. Something Sylvie had said in the dream. "She said I was wrong and that she wasn't there." He shook his head, tapping his open hand against his temple. "What did she mean? What else did she say …?"

"What 'who' are you talking about? Mabel?" Laurel asked.

"Something about a stone. Touching a stone …. Touchstone! Nox, is there a Touchstone listed anywhere?"

"Um …" Typing commenced. "Yeah. It's a smaller property, on the other side of the Hollywood Hills. 5609 Mulholland. It's about a three-mile expanse."

"Only in LA would three miles be considered small," Paul muttered. "Where is it? On the map?"

"On the left screen," Nox said.

"What do you think?" Laurel said.

Paul shook his head. "I don't know." His gut wasn't talking to him. His instincts were clouded by fear and uncertainty. If he guessed wrong …

"Quinn's standing by at the station," Riley said. "He just needs a location."

"Blake?" Paul asked. "Anything?"

"No." And he sounded seriously ticked about it.

"What are you reading for?" Nox asked Blake.

"It's a multi-channel chip. It should be able to get through any interference or jamming signals."

"Did you scan for signals rather than looking for the physical device location?" Nox asked.

Blake stood up straight. "I can do that?"

"I can." Nox shrugged. "Give me a second."

They all abandoned the screens and circled around Nox.

"So, instead of looking for the signal of the tracker ..." Blake mused as he stood over their shoulder. "You're looking for areas with a large jammer frequency."

"Exactly." Nox's fingers flew over the keys. "Can't let all those satellites up there go to waste. Okay, we've got one there by the Griffith Observatory. And another there—no, that's not it." They sat back, stared blankly at the screen. "Holy shit. I think I got it." They tapped a finger against a location. "Jamming signal's coming from the same area as that last property we found."

"Mulholland?" Paul was already headed to the door.

"Yes!"

"Should I call Quinn?" Riley shouted.

"Yes! Tell him I'm on my way." He stopped at the door, and Blake nearly crashed into him. "I have to make a stop."

"Keeley?"

"I promised," he explained.

"Go," Blake ordered. "I'll get the car."

The day would come, Mabel thought as she squeezed her eyes shut and prayed, that she wouldn't remember the vomit-inducing stench of him.

"You'll be fun." Berwick trailed a sausage-like finger up her arm, over her shoulder. "More fun than she was. She didn't have any more fight." The way he continued to smile, as if he held the upper hand, sent a surge of power coursing through her. The overwhelming odor of sweat and clove wafted off of him in vaporous waves. "You all fight, but you all lose in the end." His hand gripped her throat and squeezed. "You *all* lose."

That light was back, shimmering, tempting, sharp shards of luminescence radiating against Orson Berwick's back.

"We're all alone." His breath was hot against her face. "All alone. No one will hear you scream."

No, she was not alone. She had Sylvie.

She took shallow breaths, refusing to give him the upper hand, even as she felt her head go light. She needed to wait until just the right time.

She moved her right hand until the needle slipped into her fingers. With her left hand, she grabbed his wrist, dug her fingers in, tried to pull him off, but her strength was fading.

He laughed and loosened his hold. And let her slip, just a bit.

Just enough.

She slammed her right arm up and down, plunged the IV needle into the side of his neck. At the same time, she threw her knee up and out, slammed it hard into his groin. His hands dropped away from her neck as he clutched at his own, groaning and doubling over.

She didn't stop.

She kneed him again as he lunged for her, and, as he bent over, she grabbed his shoulders, brought her leg back, and smashed her knee up into his chin.

Something hard and metal clattered to the ground and skidded away. She dived for it, bent down, and snatched it up when she saw it was a gun. She shoved it into the back of her jeans and ripped open the door.

She heard him groaning as she slammed it shut behind her. No key.

She sobbed, imagining him plunging into the darkness after her.

Panting, panicked, she turned and tried to get her bearings as she ran, trying to remember the sound of the footsteps leaving only moments before. It was dark. *So dark.* And her eyes didn't seem to want to adjust.

The walls closed in. Before, she hadn't had time to worry about the close space. There had been other concerns, other terrors to focus on, but now, that claustrophobic sensation grabbed hold even as she struggled against it.

Keep going! This way.

Mabel skidded to a halt, listening for the voice but only seeing a tiny flicker of light in the distance. Down a long, dark passage that led *away* from where her instincts were telling her to go. The light danced, jumping up and down as if demanding her attention.

Hurry! There's not much time. He's coming. He's almost here!

Mabel stopped thinking. She turned toward the light and ran. She'd trust her twin with her life.

She felt like a pinball, caught and bouncing down a never-ending corridor of stone. Thin, narrow walls were shrinking down on her as she scraped her hands against the stone. She tried so hard to keep the light in sight, to keep moving in a straight line, but she was losing strength. And behind her ...

Behind her, she could hear her captor's roar of rage.

Something caught against her face, thready, filmy. She clawed at it, didn't want to think about what she'd run into—run *through*.

She stopped to catch her breath, but the footsteps behind her began to pound.

There's no way out. She'd let her imagination run wild. She'd let herself abandon whatever sense she possessed and ran down the wrong way.

A breeze caught against her face—a breeze that shouldn't have been there, even as the light returned. As if in a trance, Mabel regained her strength, rebuilt her courage, and made one last push toward the light. Just as the path that had been straight and flat suddenly surged up.

"I can't believe I'm doing this again," Blake muttered as he screeched down the curving, winding Mulholland Highway. "Isn't this the definition of insanity? Doing the same thing over and over?"

"You all got to Riley in time at the Tenado estate," Paul said. "I'm counting on the same result now."

Police lights spun in the distance, lighting the darkness in a way he hoped, he *prayed*, Mabel could see.

"Cass?" Paul had the cell phone up to his ear. "How large is the house on this property?"

"It's not a house; it's an old production building." Cass's voice snapped through the night. "I can pull up schematics, but I don't know how much good they'll be with them here and you there."

"Send them to Quinn," Paul shouted as Blake screeched his SUV to a stop about two inches behind a patrol car. The uniformed officers who approached had their hands on their holsters.

"They're with me!" Quinn darted around them as Paul and Blake jumped out. "You bring your gun?" he asked Blake.

"You know it."

"Okay, we've got the property cordoned off," Quinn announced. "No one's getting out—at least, not this way."

"Snakes have their holes," Paul said. "Anyone gone in yet?"

"No. I'm still waiting on at least three cars to help with the search." At Paul's huff of frustration, Quinn added, "It's three miles to search, Paul. And the building is huge with multiple floors. It's going to take time."

"Mabel doesn't have time."

"Property's abandoned, right?" Quinn said. "Wallace's waiting on the judge to sign off on the warrant that's imminent. Do we wait to go in?"

"Yes." It was Blake who answered. "You know we have to wait," he said to Paul. "Depending on what we find. We go in there and find bodies, whoever we deem responsible could slide out of charges. You don't want that. Mabel wouldn't want that."

"Mabel would want to be alive either way. Five minutes." It was all he was going to be able to do. "We wait five minutes, and if the warrant hasn't been signed, we go in anyway. Agreed?" he asked the two members of his new task force.

"Agreed." Quinn nodded. "Setting my timer now."

She was in hell. Somehow, she'd just found her way here without dying first.

She'd slammed face first into a solid wall of dirt. Pounding her fists hadn't done anything but made her hands hurt. She turned, pressed her back against the immovable wall and dropped her head back, eyes squeezed shut so tightly that she sobbed in pain. It was only a matter of time before he found her. Before he circled back. Even as she thought it, she could hear the distant rumbling of footsteps. Of shouts and cries and pounding echoing through the tunnels.

She looked up, tried not to imagine the ground closing in on her. There it was again, that breeze. That and … the light was back, jumping and shimmying its way around her until it shot into the wall beside her. And lit up, just for a moment, metal rungs shoved into the soil.

"*Sylvie.*" Her twin's name came out as a sob, even as she grabbed hold and hauled herself up. "Thank you, Sis."

There was no window at the top. It was dark and small, and the passageway grew tighter the higher up she went. Claustrophobia closed in around her, paralyzing her. The sudden stomach cramps, the dry mouth. Perspiration broke out on her face as her breathing went shallow. Now was not the time for a panic attack!

She felt a soothing pressure on her cheek, spectral hands wiping away tears.

Don't think. Don't think. Just move!

Mabel sobbed, love surging for her twin. "If I died, I'd be with you again."

But Keeley wouldn't, her twin told her, voice tender. *Neither would Paul. You need to fight for the life you've earned.*

Sylvie was right.

She pushed back her fear and reached for the next run, and then the next. When she could climb no farther, when her head hit the moist soil, Mabel threw all the faith she possessed into one final push and shoved her arms up.

She caught something solid, something wood. A door!

Mabel dragged her foot up another rung, pushed harder, and shoved.

Frigid air enveloped her. Thickening fog misted around her as she climbed out of the hole to find herself in some kind of forest.

Teeth chattering, she pivoted, dropped down, and slammed the door shut once more before she scrambled away.

She dove into the darkness, feeling the numbness in her feet and legs. She darted around trees that seemed to be erupting out of the ground fully grown. She couldn't stop. Not until she found safety. Not until she broke free of the man behind her, once and for all.

Through the thick branches of a tree, the moon provided a ray of hope, some semblance of light. Just enough to guide her.

Her chest burned. Her entire body ached. Her head throbbed as if reminding her it had been mere hours since someone had jabbed a needle in her neck. Sweat coated her body, even as she ridiculously wished for a jacket.

She had no idea how long she ran. She didn't want to stop, but she had to. She was exhausted. Panting, screaming for breath, she ducked behind a thick trunk and crouched. She waited to a full count of thirty before she quietly, slowly, peered around the tree. She saw nothing but darkness and gloom.

"Keep going. Keep …" She let go of the tree and turned, ready to pick up the pace and nearly toppled forward.

She caught her footing just as she realized she was standing over a very large, very recently dug trench.

No. Not a trench.

Mabel waited for the horror to descend.

She looked behind her, heard the rustling in the trees in the windless night.

"I'm not dead yet." It seemed appropriate to issue the warning, not only to herself but to the hollowed-out earth at her feet. She dropped to the ground. "This is either brilliant or bone ass stupid."

She crept closer to the edge, looked down into the dark dirt before she bent down, turned around, and, clawing her hands onto the ground, lowered herself into her own grave.

"Any sign of her?" Paul asked as two officers emerged from the building. Their hands were empty, their expressions blank. But at least the search was commencing.

"No." Quinn yanked open one of the patrol car's doors. "But we found Eva Hudson. She's dead."

Paul took the prepared hit, punched it down deep to where he couldn't get at it. To where it wouldn't rob him of hope.

"The pipe bombs were made here," Quinn said. "We found a workshop and explosives. Shouldn't take much to confirm they match the ones used at the park."

"I want a flashlight." He held out his hand, waited for Quinn to give the okay to one of the officers. "We need to start searching the grounds. If she's not in the building—"

"Paul—" Blake started.

"We search the grounds. She's not dead. She's still out there, alone in the dark. I know it." Something inside of him, something that felt like a light of hope, burned against reason. "We search. Until we find her."

"Okay." Blake nodded, accepted another flashlight as Quinn called out more officers. "Let's go."

Damp earth surrounded her, attempted to suffocate her with its tempting promise of new growth and old death. It was darker down here. She hadn't thought that was possible.

Every cell in her body screamed. She didn't want to think about how small the space was. Or how easily the walls of dirt could collapse and bury her alive. The moon appeared to have given up and lost the capacity or strength to light the night. Once again, she felt her way around, to the corner of the hole, then to the back.

She crouched, tucked her knees in, and, before she wedged herself into the corner as deep as she could, she reached back and pulled out the gun.

Clasping it, she rested her hands on her knees, aiming the gun up to the edge of the opening. Sitting in the darkness, waiting, she took a deep breath, let it out slowly. As calm settled over her, she lowered one hand, fingers curling into the earth.

And felt the bones.

Paul didn't stay back with the police line. He wasn't going to walk, not when he could run. Let Quinn and Blake stay back with the officers as they moved slowly across the expanse of the property. She was in here, somewhere. He knew it.

348

His feet barely touched the ground as he ran, dodging and jumping over branches, and debris crunching beneath his weight, the light in his hand flickering.

He could see someone, a shimmering someone, just ahead, darting in and out of the trees like a specter. It was a beacon he let himself surrender to.

When the darkness descended once more, when the moonlight faded against the branches and the silence erupted against his ears, he slowed. Far behind him he could see the waving lights of the officers and his friends.

Paul stopped, strained to hear, waiting for a sign, waiting for anything to show him the way.

Nothing.

Desperate, he spun around and saw that spectral light again. It flickered sporadically, as if begging him to notice it.

Instinct flooded him. *Sylvie.*

A distinct click echoed in front of him. From the same direction as the light. He knew that sound.

"Shit." No choice. He clicked on his flashlight, aimed it into the trees, and ran it back and forth in a frantic search pattern. Holding the flashlight in tandem with his weapon, he began to move forward, slightly crouched, head on a swivel in case whoever he'd been following came flying out at him.

Another minute of inching forward, and then a twig snapped beneath his foot. He froze, waiting, listening.

There!

Movement darted out to the right and let out a cry that, for a split second, sounded like a call for help.

He went to move forward again, but his feet wouldn't move, no matter how hard he tried to make them.

His flashlight flickered, not unlike the spectral light had, the bulb dimming before it blazed at full wattage once more. Something caught his eye, and he aimed the light down to see a great big hole in the ground. Something moved in the corner.

He flashed over, saw Mabel lift her hand up to shield her eyes from the glare. He breathed for the first time in hours.

"Mabel!"

She sobbed, then laughed, then sobbed again as she covered her mouth. "I thought you were him. I thought he'd found me." The gun wavered in her hand.

"I've got you, Mabel. He's not going to hurt you. Not anymore."

Doubt flickered across her filthy face.

"Put the gun down, Mabel." It was the softest his voice had ever been.

"What? Oh." She set it down and shrank away from it. "Final option," she said in a squeak of a voice.

Paul waved his flashlight in an arc, shouted out to the police that he'd found her, and then jumped in beside her. "You okay?" Crouched in front of her, he grabbed her arms and hauled her forward. "Jesus, God, Mabel, are you okay?"

"Keeley? Is Keeley all right?" She shivered in his arms, grabbing hold of him, clinging to him.

"Keeley's fine." He smoothed her hair, kissed her temple. "She's with Sutton. She told us you took her octopus."

"The octopus." He knew hysteria when he heard it. "I think it's my good luck charm, not Kee's. Paul?"

"Yeah?" He pressed his lips to the top of her head. "What?"

"Paul?" Quinn's voice broke through the darkness. "Where are you? Shine a … light!"

"Here!" Paul waved the light again.

"We got Berwik!" Quinn called out, as his voice moved closer. "Or should I say, *Blake* got him. It was not pretty—he was not gentle."

Relief flooded Paul. He returned his attention to Mabel.

"Paul, you need to listen to me," Mabel said and clung to him.

He opened his mouth to speak when he heard Quinn again.

"Here! Over here!" the detective yelled, and within seconds, half a dozen flashlights shone down on them. "You found her. Thank God." He bent forward, threw a relieved smile at Mabel. "Hey, Mabe."

She sobbed and laughed. "Hey."

"You two want to come out of there?" Quinn extended a hand.

"Not yet." Mabel pushed Paul back and shifted onto her heels.

"What are you—" The question faded from his mind as he watched her brush away layers of dirt. She gasped, jerked back, and would have lost her balance if he hadn't caught her. "Mabel?"

350

She turned her face to him, eyes wide with grief, relief, and sadness.

Paul looked down, his heart forgetting to beat for what felt like a lifetime. "Oh, my God."

"I know," Mabel whispered. "We found them."

CHAPTER EIGHTEEN

"MOM!"

Mabel caught her daughter in the tightest hug of her life and lifted her off the ground. "My hero," she murmured against Keeley's neck—a surge of love filling her heart, warming her still-chilled limbs.

Blake and Quinn moved around her to where her Temple House family had gathered in her apartment and went straight for the coffee machine. Riley and Laurel had taken up residence on one of her sofas and obviously kept the coffee going as they each had a mug in their hand.

Stepping back into her apartment had never felt so good to Mabel before. It had taken hours, endless hours, before they'd been given the all-clear to leave. Just in time to watch the sun come up.

Barksy yelped and barked and jumped up to earn his own ear scratches and scrubs.

"I heard you helped find me," she said to Keeley after setting her down.

"Kinda!" Keeley beamed at her. "But Paul did the most. He kept his promise."

"Yes, he did." Laurel, along with Sutton and Riley, kept their distance, but she could see the relief in their expressions. "You really all right?"

"I will be." She wasn't about to lie. She could feel the stress and terror of the past hours threatening to rain down on her. "You all didn't have to wait up for me."

"Yes," Riley said, "we did. *I* did." She winced uncertainly. "You were right."

"About what?" Mabel asked and sat across from her on the second sofa, Keeley still in her arms.

"Moxie." Riley looked down at the mug in her hand. "We need to ask her about the mark. Maybe if we had earlier—"

"We aren't doing that," Mabel ordered. "What happened, happened, Riley. You know that better than anyone. And to be honest, I don't think I was right. At least not in the right frame of mind when I pushed you about Moxie. We'll find a way to do it gently. We'll consult some professionals if we have to, but I don't want her hurt if she had to relive anything remotely close to what I went through last night. What *you* went through a few months ago." What so many other women had gone through. "I finally understand. Let's do this together, okay?"

"Okay, yeah. Together." Riley nodded. "Sutton said she'd see you later this morning. She didn't want to leave the kids alone."

Mabel nodded. "Good. That's good."

"Did Paul leave?" Keeley asked.

"No, baby." Mabel hugged her close. "No, he needed to go to the hospital to check on Max's dad. He'll be back here in a little bit."

"Any word on Jeff?" Quinn called from the kitchen.

Mabel shook her head. "Not that I've heard." Worry of an entirely different sort climbed into her chest. Barksy whined and rested his chin on her knee, looked up at her with those pitiful, dark doggie eyes. "We'll just have to keep a good thought."

"Well, we're going to head out," Laurel announced as she got to her feet. "Looks like you can use some rest."

"That's code for 'you look like crap,'" Riley said in a way that confirmed all was forgiven.

"Yes, I'm sure I do," Mabel murmured.

She felt like it, too, not only because there wasn't a part of her body that wasn't battered or bruised.

She touched a hand to her sore throat and neck.

She knew, just as the rest of them did, that what had happened tonight was only the start of their dealings with The Circle. They were still out there. Lurking. Biding their time. Hunting.

She couldn't wait to take a shower and scrub off the grime and fear that continued to cling to her. "Should we all meet at Cass's later for a kind of debriefing?"

"Ah." Laurel cringed. "We might want to give her a few days to decompress from the last few hours."

"She okay?" Mabel asked.

"Stressed," Riley said. "She had an anxiety attack once we knew you were okay. Nox is taking care of her, but yeah—let's give it a few days before we bring it all up again."

"We'll bring back the coffee mugs," Blake said as he and Quinn followed the women out. "You know where I am, if you need anything."

"Yeah." Mabel nodded and smiled, grateful for his help and friendship. "Thanks, Blake. For everything." For the tracking device. For smashing her kidnapper's face in. For caring. "I appreciate it."

"It was my pleasure."

When the door closed, Mabel turned Keeley around and looked her daughter directly in the eyes. "Tell me what you're thinking, Kee. What you're feeling."

She stroked a finger down her child's face.

A face she'd feared she might never see again.

Keeley shrugged. "Scared. And happy you're home. And worried."

"What are you worried about?"

"That it'll happen again." Keeley ducked her chin, her eyes filling with tears. "I was really, really scared, Mom. But then I wasn't."

"Because of what Paul promised."

"Yeah." She shrugged. "And because Aunt Sylvie said you'd come home. I saw her again, only I wasn't dreaming this time." Her frown returned. "At least, I don't think I was. She was like this light that fit in my hand. It bounced around like a firefly. And then it was gone. And then Quinn called and said you'd be home."

Mabel pulled Keeley close. "I think Aunt Sylvie was looking out for both of us tonight." She kissed Keeley's forehead and set her back. "I need to go take a shower and change. How about you meet me back here on the sofa, and we'll sip hot chocolate until Paul gets back."

"He's really coming back?" Keeley asked.

"He promised he would," Mabel assured her. "And you know—"

Keeley beamed. "He never breaks a promise."

"I feel comfortable saying he has a good prognosis." Dr. Canfield, the surgeon who had spent most of the afternoon and half the night repairing Jeff's internal and spinal injuries told Lindsay and Paul in the surgical waiting room of the hospital. "He'll have a long recovery, and he'll require physical therapy. I anticipate it'll be a few months before he's up and moving around at his previous speed." Her smile was quick and encouraging. "It'll still be a while before he's out of the anesthesia, so if you want—"

"I'm not going anywhere," Lindsay insisted, her arms wrapped tight around her torso. "I'll stay right here if I have to, but—"

"That won't be necessary." Chief Alexander Burton appeared in the doorway. It took Paul a moment to recognize him, given he was wearing dark slacks and a dark long-sleeve sweater, not the uniform Paul was familiar with. "We'll take care of you, Lindsay. You and Max."

"My parents picked him up a few hours ago," she said as she rubbed the tears from her cheek. "Thank you, Chief. For the officers. And the family liaison officer you had stay with me."

"I'm sorry I wasn't here," Paul said.

It felt almost insignificant, knowing Berwick was in custody, locked down under a fake name, with a twenty-four-hour guard. Given The Circle's growing tendency for tying up loose ends, they weren't going to take any chances of something happening to Orson Berwick.

"You were here," Lindsay whispered as she leaned against him. "In spirit. You found Mabel and the man who set off the bomb. That's what Jeff would have wanted you to be doing."

Paul met the Chief's gaze over Lindsay's head. "Anything you need, all you have to do is ask."

She nodded. "I think I'm going to go get some coffee and then go sit with him. If that's all right?" she asked Dr. Canfield.

"It's fine." The surgeon nodded. "I'll have them bring a foldout chair in so you can get try to get some sleep."

The chief motioned for one of the officers to stay with Lindsay before he stepped into the room and closed the door. "What else should we be aware of?"

Dr. Canfield hesitated. "Like I said, I'm cautiously optimistic. But I'm interested to see how long it takes him to come out of the anesthesia. He had a pretty severe head injury. We won't know the extent of it for a while yet. Talk to him," she encouraged Paul. "Tell him stories, jokes, read to him. Keep his brain active for as long as he's out of work. It's the best thing any of you can do right now."

"We will," Paul said. "Thanks, doctor."

She offered them both a smile and left them alone.

"Hell of a day," Chief Burton commented once the door was closed again. "Mabel all right?"

"She's fine. She's home with Keeley." Paul couldn't stop his nerves from jumping now that the adrenaline was beginning to siphon out of his system.

"You should be with them," Chief Burton said. "But before you go, I'd like to talk to you about a few things."

Paul cringed. "If this is about my insubordinate behavior with DA Eichorn—"

"It is but not in the way you think. I have an official request to make of you, Paul. And I hope you'll take some time to think about it before you decline."

Paul's eyebrows went up. "You have my attention."

"Good." Chief Burton motioned to one of the chairs. "Have a seat. This might take a while."

"Well, you sure know how to keep a dead woman entertained."

Mabel's heart swelled at the sight of her sister standing in front of her. Sylvie looked different now; she looked at peace with her white gown swirling around her like an aura. Her face glowed with vibrancy instead of the deathly pallor of before.

"You saved me." Tears clogged Mabel's throat as she stretched out her hand.

Sylvie rolled her eyes but reached forward and touched her twin's hand in a gentle caress. "You saved yourself." She shrugged. "I just reminded you that you could." She crouched and held out her arms to a whimpering Barksy. "I'm going to miss you guys." She pressed a ghost kiss to the top of his head. "I've done what I can."

"You can't leave me again," Mabel ordered. "Not now that—"

"Mabel, my heart." Sylvie tilted her head in that forgotten, sympathetic way she'd had when she was alive. "You don't need me anymore. You've begun to let go. And that's as it should be." She gave Barksy one last pat and stood up. "You have someone else to hold onto now." She looked down at a still-sleeping Keeley, tucked into the sofa. "*Two* someones. Don't worry—I'll still be around from time to time. Give your heart some attention."

"This isn't over yet," Mabel said, thinking of the graveyard she'd discovered. The work that lay ahead. "What if—"

"If you need me, I'll be here. But"—she floated closer, touched a finger under Mabel's chin, and lifted her face—"you've got everything you need. That's all that ever mattered to me. I love you, Sis."

"I love you. I'm sorry we fought. Before ..." Mabel blinked back tears.

"We argued," Sylvie said with an understanding smile. "We never fought. We're halves of one heart, Mabel. I could never be angry with you. Well, unless you mess things up with you know who," she chided playfully. "*Then* we're going to have something to fight about." She swayed back, started fading. "Be happy, Mabel. Live. For both of us."

Mabel's eyes snapped open.

She had to focus on breathing slowly, on pulling herself back to reality. She was home. In her apartment, on her sofa. Keeley was tucked up against her side, sound asleep. The sun streamed in through the kitchen windows, bathing everything in a warm, perfect light.

She heard the key before the lock snapped and the door opened and closed. Her heart filled as she watched Paul step back into her world.

"Hey," she said softly.

"Hey." He blinked in surprise. "I thought for sure you'd be asleep." He surprised her by leaving his keys and cell on the table in the hall and walking over to her. "How are you feeling?"

"Terrible." Sleeping on the sofa hadn't been conducive to easing the aches and pains, but she felt better now that she saw him. "How's Jeff?"

"Better than expected." The relief in his eyes eased the guilt in her heart. "Surgery went well. It'll be a long recovery, and if the head injury isn't too bad, he'll be out of the woods in a few days."

"Thank God." She stroked Keeley's hair. "How are you?"

"I'm not entirely sure." He shook his head, held out his hand, and seemed to breathe easier when she grabbed hold.

"Well, then, I should probably get this out of the way," Mabel told him. "I don't want you to think I'm trying to manipulate you or trap you into something because I get that you've got a life you need to live, and we might not fit into it, but—"

"Mabel," he began.

"I love you." Just saying the words left her breathing easier. As if it were the final weight on her that had finally lifted. "I don't know how it happened so fast, or what we can do about it, but I love you, and I just thought you should know I'm okay with whatever you decide. Even if …" She paused, determined to push out all the words. "Even if it means you go back to New York."

"Yeah, about that." His hand tightened around hers. "I'm not going back."

"You're not? Why not?" Was she hearing this right?

"A few reasons, actually." He scrubbed a hand across his forehead. "I planned to drink a gallon of coffee before I got into this, but what the hell. I'm not going back because A, I promised Jeff I'd stay and finish the job he asked me to do. B, Chief Burton has asked me to stay on as a department special investigator, even after The Circle case is closed."

"You think it will be? Closed?" Mabel asked. "Honestly? Because, right now, it feels more than a little impossible—"

"Not without the right people working on it, it won't be," he assured her. "We're going to get them, Mabel. Every last one of them. However long it takes. And then when we're done, we'll see where we are with things. But there's an even more important reason for me to stay."

"Oh?"

He shook his head, his lips tilting up as he met her gaze. "Because you, Mabel Reynolds, did the impossible. I love you. All this time, I didn't believe myself capable of feeling anything close to what I feel for you and Keeley. Turns out I can feel even more. So, if you're good with me sticking around—"

She launched herself into his arms, dislodging a sleeping Keeley. Mabel kissed him, hard and fast, before he talked himself out of it. "You're going to stay? Really?"

He nodded. "I'm going to stay."

"Do you promise?" Keeley's sleepy voice entered the conversation. She sat up, looking a bit cranky at having been woken up. "Cause you never break your promises. And if you promise, you can never go away."

"I know," Paul said seriously. "I promise."

Mabel sat back as he held out his arms to Keeley. He hugged the girl close, then reached out his arm for Mabel.

"Hey, Mom?" Keeley mumbled as they snuggled together. "I changed my mind about a birthday party. I don't need one anymore."

"You don't?" Mabel couldn't help but feel relieved. She hadn't exactly moved forward with any of those plans. "Why not?"

"Because I got what I really wanted." Keeley turned her face up to Paul and smiled. "I got a dad."

Mabel blinked back the tears as she touched a finger to her heart charm, felt it warm beneath her touch. She smiled and rested her head on Paul's shoulder. And for the first time in eight years ...

Found herself at peace.

EPILOGUE

DR. Cassia Davis stood at her apartment door, the knob cool against her trembling fingers. The hallway thumped as if it had its own pulse. Her heart thudded like a jackhammer. Cold sweat bathed her face as she struggled to draw in breath.

Self-loathing and paralyzing frustration battled for control as she snatched her hand back.

"Dammit!"

She spun around and stalked back down the hall, Elliot padding silently beside her. It wasn't until she was in the kitchen, a glass of cold water in her hand, that she stopped shaking. She sipped, slowly, deliberately, and did her best to recall the meditation exercises Sutton and Laurel had literally bent over backwards to teach her.

"It's getting worse," she whispered brokenly to her dog, the only companion that didn't make her heart hurt. "How is it getting worse?"

It didn't seem possible. Locking herself away should have given her some peace of mind, some semblance of control. It always had before. But whatever safety she'd let herself believe she'd found here in Temple House was just a façade, wasn't it? After what had happened to first Riley and now Mabel .... None of them were safe.

Her friends had come through their traumas relatively unscathed and with a new lease in life. Yet here she was, nearly four years after her trauma, more petrified and panicked than she'd been in the days following …

"Stop it!"

It did no good to dwell. It hadn't done any good to close herself off. In the weeks since Mabel's abduction, she'd struggled to keep herself under control, but instead, she'd only buried herself in solitude, evicting even Nox from the apartment. She needed time to think, to re-evaluate.

Instead, she found herself skimming the edge of the familiar depression that once again threatened to derail her entire life.

She jumped when the doorbell rang. The small screens around her apartment lit up with the camera image from her front door. Elliot whimpered, hurried to the door, planted his butt, and waited.

There was nothing but friendly faces inside of Temple House. Logically, she knew this, but seeing Paul Flynn standing outside her apartment churned up a whole lot of anxiety she didn't have the patience to deal with.

She didn't give herself the time to think and reached the door in record time, pulling it open before she changed her mind. "Hey, Paul." She stepped back even as her pulse raced. "Come on in."

"You sure?" He didn't look convinced. "Mabel said you've been having a rough go lately."

She shrugged, not wanting to confirm nor deny. "I've been expecting you to come by ever since Laurel told me about your new job." She'd endured endless errors in judgement where the DA's office was concerned, but given Paul's new status and power, she was willing to rebuild her faith in the system.

"Yeah." Paul stepped past her and headed into the kitchen, Elliot nipping at his heels. "Where's Nox?"

"They're keeping an eye on my camera equipment at the grave site."

Some people considered the Kardashians their guilty pleasure. Cass preferred the excavation-site of murder victims. The live-feed cameras Blake and Nox had set up at the scene were giving her a 24/7 feed, one she was recording, just to be safe.

"Yeah," Paul said slowly. "That's actually what I need to talk to you about."

"Well, that doesn't sound good. You want a beer?" She made her way back to the fridge.

"No, thanks. I'm good." He stood on the other side of the center island, hands in his pockets. "They've found three more bodies."

"That makes thirty-seven so far, by my count," Cass said.

"They also found this." He reached into his pocket, pulled out a plastic evidence bag.

Cass accepted it, held it up to the light, and felt her throat tighten at the sight of the gold necklace and half-heart pendant. If she still had a whole heart, it would have broken then and there. "They found Sylvie."

"Yeah." Paul's voice sounded thick. "Yeah, I have to come up with some way to—"

"No, you don't." Cass cut him off. "Mabel's known Sylvie was dead for a long time, Paul. You don't have to soften the blow."

"Maybe." He didn't look convinced. "Look, I need to be straight with you, Cass. Now that I'm in charge of this investigation, I need the absolute best working it. I need you working it."

"I *am* working it."

He flinched. "No, Cass. You're not. I need you on the ground. At that site. I need you examining the remains we're finding. Testing the evidence. I need you overseeing all the things I can't."

She swallowed hard. "And you don't think I can do that from here."

He looked back at the necklace. "They found that yesterday." He paused. "You didn't know."

She set the bag down and turned her back on him, punching back on the grief and guilt. "I must have missed that episode."

"This is my point. I trust you, Cass. I trust you with this case. We all do. But …"

"But my limitations aren't working in anyone's favor." She wanted, more than anything, to take a step out of that door, to be on that scene and building an ironclad case against the people responsible, and yet … "You're bringing in someone else."

"I've been advised to," he admitted. "But I haven't. Not yet."

"Looking for recommendations?" she challenged. Fuck, fuck, fuck! Work was literally all she had left in her life. If she didn't have that … "I can get you a list."

Even as she said it, she felt the bitterness rise. This was the case she'd been born to solve. Everything she'd learned, everything she knew, it was all leading to this. And now … "There are some good pathologists or criminalists who can—"

"I'd like to propose a work around. It was Laurel's idea, actually. Hers and Keeley's. They're always watching horror movies together." He rested his hands on the counter. "You ever see *The Bone Collector*? Denzel Washington, Angelina Jolie. He's a paralyzed brainiac investigator, and she's his eyes-and-ears cop."

"I read the book." It took her a minute to catch on. "You're thinking I could Denzel this thing?"

He shrugged. "It's an option. With all the technology you and Nox have at your disposal, it's a good one."

"Technology, I have. What I don't have is trust." In a perfect world Nox would be an ideal choice, but their expertise bent more to the technology aspect of Cass's work rather than delicacy and procedure. Nevertheless …. Cass nibbled on her lower lip. The idea intrigued her.

"Which is why you should do the choosing."

Her eyes widened. "Seriously?"

"Seriously," he agreed. "I don't know what you need, what you'd look for. And I don't know who we can trust. We need someone with impeccable credentials so as not to cause a ruckus but someone you can work with. We need someone who understands forensics, pathology, psychology, criminalistics …" He sighed. "Hell, Cass. We need another you. But there's a catch."

"Of course, there is."

Whatever hope had been building inside of her fizzled.

"It has to be a Fed," he rushed on. "Believe me, I don't necessarily like the idea of the FBI circling around this, but they're going to come in at some point. The missing women are from all over the country. They want an 'in,' and that could give it to them. I'd rather it be on our terms. You bring someone in, we kill two birds with one stone, so to speak."

"So, to be clear," Cass said slowly as her head spun. "If I want to stay on the biggest case of my career," and preserve her sanity, "I have to bring in a federal agent I trust and who will work well with you and your task force and *not* sell us out to the Feds or DOJ."

"Yes." He hesitated. "I don't suppose anyone comes to mind?"

"Unfortunately …" The anxiety roller coaster she'd been riding for the past few months took one steep dip straight into a triple loop. This wasn't an option she wanted to entertain, but there wasn't anyone else who fit the bill. "I … there *is* someone. He retired from the bureau a few years ago, but I hear he does consulting work."

Every cell in her body surged into protective overdrive.

"Can you call them?"

Cass's feet felt frozen to the floor. A move in any direction meant her life was about to change, and probably not for the better.

She couldn't let this case go. No one could play catch up to the work she'd already done, the work she was *still* doing. And as much as she hated to admit it, whatever else had transpired between them, she knew he was the perfect person for the job.

"Cass?" Paul pressed. "Will they take your call?"

She turned and picked up her phone, scanned through her list of contacts, wishing she'd surrendered to the past temptation to delete the number from her records.

She took a deep, stealing breath and dialed. "Let's find out."

It was ringing before she lifted the phone to her ear.

"Yeah, Mitch Keaton."

His voice had every bit of her screaming in both fear and regret. "It's Cass." By some miracle, her voice didn't break. Looking to Paul, she drew on every ounce of courage she possessed and let out a slow, steadying breath. "I need your help."

ACKNOWLEDGEMENTS

EVERY book I write reminds me that I can't traverse this career in publishing alone. *Vanished* is no exception and, in truth, presented numerous challenges only a stellar support system can overcome.

Since the release of *Exposed*, I lost two childhood friends who helped shape who I am today. Not a day goes by when I don't think of Kristen or Victoria. Of the dance classes and slumber parties, of the laughter and the tears. Not a day goes by when I don't feel their absence and my heart aches for their families. I only wish I'd had the chance to tell you how much I loved you both.

To Melinda Curtis and Cari Lynn Webb, never more than a text or email away. I'm so grateful the universe put us in one another's orbits.

Huge shout out to Alicia Florendo Ashley, RN extraordinaire, who answered my questions with speed and kindness. Thank you! I hope I did you justice on the page (I'm sure "she" will be back in a future book).

Thank you to Hannah Gunsallus for once again being an early reader and commenter. You have such a kind, straightforward heart. The world is lucky to have you.

Being part of a writing group, in my mind, is tantamount to success. Only other writers "get it" and the Northern California Romance Writers is my heart's home.

Mary, you must be so sick of hearing me complain about a job I actually love. Sister of the heart doesn't come close to describing you. Thirty years of friendship and you've never once let me down. Everyone needs a Mary.

To all the volunteer organizations, medical professionals (especially nurses), law enforcement officers, and judicial representatives who see all who are suffering and aim to give them a voice.

To the families, friends, and loved ones of every missing person, I hope there's a day of peace for you in the future.

Once again, shoutout to Mickey Mickkelson of Creative Edge Publicity, our hard-working, optimistic publicist who approaches each opportunity with an open and eager heart.

To Shahid Mahmud, publisher and now friend. Thank you for giving The Circle of the Red Lily books a home.

To my editor Lezli Robyn. You inspire me with your undaunted spirit and unnerving attention to detail (the pictures of Bindi the Wonder Dog also help). These books are just as much yours as they are mine. I'm so happy we're on this journey together.

Last, and certainly not least, thank you to my mom, Marjorie McLetchie Stewart. There are no words. Only unending gratitude and love.

Milton Keynes UK
Ingram Content Group UK Ltd.
UKHW012136131223
434291UK00001B/172

9 781647 100803